GOLD MOUNTAIN

GOLD MOUNTAIN

Charlotte Paul

PEOPLES BOOK CLUB
CHICAGO

To my sons, Hiram and John,
because they've always wanted
to be in a book

author's note

This is not a history book. It is a love story. But as anyone who has ever been in the Snoqualmie Valley could see with half an eye, this mountain-enclosed area of big trees and cold rivers has been very much in my mind and heart while I was writing it.

I came to the Snoqualmie Valley four years ago and hadn't been here two weeks when I attended a club meeting where the main address was delivered by a little white-haired lady with a long memory and a twinkle in her eye. She was the third white child to be born in the valley, and the stories she told that afternoon were the first I put down in a notebook which in the next two years grew to weigh three pounds and measure four inches cover to cover.

When the old-timers of the valley came to realize that their memories really interested me they were coöperative to the extreme. I've talked to people who were born here seventy-five years ago, and to others who came here as little children when the whites were outnumbered by the Indians. Two of my informants have died since I began my research, and most of the others are in their eighties, though a couple of them won't admit it. I could write a history book, but I haven't. This book is fiction; the people in it are not "real." But in spirit, in setting, in every detail, from the way people made a living to the way they felt about it, I think it is far more real than a history book would have been.

"You're going to get into hot water," the wife of an old settler warned me when I began this book. "Either you're going to change things around, and people hereabouts will say, 'Why, he didn't do that and I didn't do that.' Or else you'll write just what they did do, and then they *will* be mad!"

But I think she underestimated her neighbors, for two of the "young men" who gave me material read this book before publication, and their only complaint was that they might not be around to receive their autographed copies.

I'd like to express heartfelt gratitude to those who helped me most in the writing of this book: Mrs. Olive Quigley, Grandma Pickering, Tom Bird, Mrs. Charles Carpenter, Chief of the Snoqualmie Tribe, Jerry Kanim; George Foster Kelley, W. W. Stephenson, Albert Prenatt, Otto and Deo Reinig and Elva Polley. I am indebted also to the late Mrs. Alice Rachor and to Herbert Knowles, who has also passed away.

Charlotte Paul

Snoqualmie, Washington
1953

GOLD MOUNTAIN

CHAPTER

1

i

The steam whistle on the riverboat *Viking* shrilled a warning. Two Indians in blue jeans, black hair to their shoulders, feet bare, were stuffing the boiler with lengths of wood. The engine belched mightily. In a moment the paddle wheel would turn and the round-nosed little scow with the crackerbox cabin would begin the struggle upstream. Time to go, the whistle wheezed, like a fat woman calling in her children.

Captain White and his son Carl stood among the crates, boxes, sacks, bedrolls and livestock that crowded the *Viking's* deck, and looked back toward town, checking the progress of the last stragglers. Carl was tall and slender, with a polish to him, a fineness of feature, so different from his father that people often wished they could have seen his mother. The riverboat captain, like the men who were waiting on deck and those approaching along the rutted wagon road, was as solid and as rough as a log cabin; built for weather but no extra trimmings.

"Here they come," Carl said.

"The whistle always brings 'em."

Tall, short, fat and lean, the group of men moved toward the boat like a wave rolling slowly but inevitably toward shore. They were dressed as the captain and his son and every other man, white, red or tan, was dressed in this tree-shadowed valley: rough work clothes, heavy boots, dark felt hats pulled down to the eyebrows. At the gangplank they fell silently into a single file. They were aboard, Carl took hold of the plank, the captain headed for the wheel, when one of them burst out, "Say, who's that pretty little gal?"

To a man, they turned to look. It was a girl, all right, a young girl for all the fact that her red hair was piled in an old-maidish bun on top of her head and a handful of straw and ribbon and artificial flowers had been impaled on top of that by a pair of grown-up hat pins. It was mid-September and hot enough for July, but she was wearing a blue serge traveling dress, the kind a little girl might borrow from her mother for a game of dress-up. Her hands were covered with bright pink gloves, one of them holding a shiny wicker suitcase. Dress, hat, gloves, suitcase—it was clear she was figuring on making the trip on the *Viking*.

Captain White called to Carl, "It might be her. I had a notion she might be coming in this trip."

"Her?" a toothless logger squeaked to the man next to him. "Her who?"

The next man shrugged. "Somebody's wife."

"I ain't heard of nobody sending for his wife."

"Kinfolk."

"Ain't heard of nobody expecting kinfolk."

"You don't have to hear everything."

The man laughed delightedly. "What've we got in this whole crazy valley? Besides Indians and wild animals? Fifty white families and a couple dozen loggers and shingle-weavers? I don't miss nothing, neither do you."

"Might be the new schoolteacher. They're waiting on one at Gold Mountain."

The toothless mouth gaped as the man turned to look more directly at the girl. "That scaredy-looking little thing?" he whispered hoarsely. "You forgot what happened to the last one?"

They stared, but they didn't move. The girl seemed to be taking two steps backward for every one forward. She was in trouble—they sensed it, wanted to know all about it, were so eaten by a desire to see her close up that they pretended not to care whether they ever saw her at all. In the whole crowd of men on the *Viking,* only Carl White thought of walking back up the gangplank toward the strange little girl with the red hair and the dress that was too old and too big for her.

"Now," the toothless man breathed, cracking his friend's ribs with his elbow. "Now young White's on the job. *He* knows how to talk to girls. He learnt how in Seattle."

ii

She was afraid. A dozen steps would take her to the gang-plank. Twelve steps, more or less, and the trip was begun. For a moment shorter than the tick of a clock she felt she could do it. Walk! Her mind commanded and her small body bent forward, tensed with awareness of the movement it was about to make. The hand on the suitcase tightened, one foot lifted. But the impulse died. She stepped backward, timidly set the suitcase down. With a sense of shame she saw her hands were shaking.

It was clearly time to go. The other passengers had all walked across the gangplank and were looking back at her now. "Come aboard if you've a mind to," they seemed to challenge her. "This here tub's good enough for us." And worst of all, one of them, a tall young man with dark hair and a serious face, was coming straight toward her.

How wrong I was, she thought, to believe I could do this without being afraid. It was an old, bitterly familiar feeling. It had come on her the moment she began to walk down the road to the riverboat. As always it began with a tightness in her throat, settled into a knot in her stomach, spread through her body as if it were a disease the blood could carry. Fear—sickening, paralyzing fear. It had crippled her at every important moment of her life, ever since she was a little girl.

The young man was near. The men on deck had fallen silent, watching them. They're all laughing at me, she thought. "Run!" the inner voice shrieked. In senseless panic, her hand groped for the handle of the suitcase. But he was right beside her. It was too late.

She looked up at him. He wasn't a logger—she saw that in her first frightened glance. He was wearing calked boots and rough work clothes but there was a gentlemanliness to him. And he wasn't laughing at her.

"I beg your pardon," he said, inclining his head in a gesture that somehow made her feel he had bowed. "But are you Miss Katherine Duncan?"

The last of her strength went into a gigantic effort to face him calmly. Voiceless, she nodded.

"I'm Carl White, the captain's son. He sent me out to see if I could help you aboard."

But I'm not going . . . The words were loud in her own ears, but looking into the thin, serious face of the captain's son she didn't say them. He made her feel proud. She thought, it isn't as shameful to be afraid if you keep other people from knowing it, and instantly the fear lessened. "Thank you."

He looked down at her thoughtfully. "You *are* the new schoolteacher?"

She answered with a lift of the chin and a quick squaring of her shoulders.

He smiled. "Excuse me." His voice was so gentle that she blushed. "But I wouldn't have been sure, if there had been anyone else on the pier."

She was still too much afraid to be angry. Besides, his words could be taken in many ways. Only a girl without confidence in herself would imagine they were anything but a compliment. And he was bowing, a real bow this time. I am a gentleman, his manner said, and you are a lady.

Katherine Duncan's hand flew to her hat. A pat or two reassured her that it was in place. Quite suddenly her fear wasn't as pressing as the necessity of acting the kind of person he took her to be. The new schoolteacher . . . Men on deck were watching. The young captain's son, so close she could see the shadow of tomorrow's beard on his cheek, was waiting. Her mouth straightened primly and one pink-gloved hand settled protectingly over the other. Thank God I bought the pink ones, she thought. Black gloves tell the world you're poor.

"I didn't know where to buy a ticket," she said. He nodded solemnly. The lie had been accepted. Her confidence grew immeasurably.

"They do things differently in the valley," he said, "than in Seattle."

There was the faintest emphasis on "They." Katherine

caught it, wondered why, and yet admired him for disclaiming a place she already hated. There was a hint of an apology in his voice as well. She could not be asked to push past Indians and step over a crate of chickens in order to buy a steamboat ticket. He took her for a lady from Seattle.

She smiled happily. "I'll follow you," she said, and he picked up the wicker suitcase so quickly that she was saved the mistake of reaching for it herself.

"If you'll excuse me," he murmured, turning towards the *Viking*. Katherine followed, with just the slow and careful step she knew he would think proper. The new schoolteacher, she chanted silently, the new schoolteacher . . . Head high, she walked past the watchful men and sat down carefully on the bench nailed to the outside of the cabin. She felt as if she could see herself just as they did, from the store-boughten hat to the dress that was warm but dignified. I was right, she thought, to pin my hair up on top of my head. The new schoolteacher . . .

She sighed. Carl White did not know how close the new schoolteacher had come to running away. Nor could he know her other, deeper secrets. That the new schoolteacher had never been in school herself for longer than a month or two at a time. That she had lied mightily about that, as well as about her age, in order to get the teaching job in Gold Mountain. That she was alone, utterly and irrevocably alone, as only a seventeen-year-old girl who has run away from home can be.

iii

It hadn't been easy to find a teaching job. The city of Seattle wasn't much more than thirty years old, but teaching certificates were already required, and she had to admit that she could not qualify. "Previous experience?" they inquired next, and she could only explain that she had never taught before. "Almost eighteen" was still seventeen years old to the people who hired teachers. They were impatient, or sympathetic, but never impressed when she said she had had "about eight years" of schooling. A few months in Kansas, a year or so in Nebraska, a few weeks in Montana and Nevada and California and Oregon—it couldn't be made to sound like an education, no matter how earnestly she added, "But my mother taught me, too." Squeezing her conscience, she had lied desperately but not well. Twice she had ended up pouring out the truth to the very person who might have hired her if he hadn't known it.

One of them told her to go back home. Katherine listened to him sermonize on what her duty was to her father and wondered where his own sense of duty lay, that he could exhort her to go back without asking what she had fled from. But the second man was elderly, with a bright and penetrating glance. Like everyone else he turned her down. But he added, "I got an idea you're still determined to go out on your own and teach school."

"I can't go back. The reasons—"

"Are your own business," the man broke in, waving one hand impatiently. "Sooner or later you'll know whether or not they were good ones and that'll be your own affair, too." He studied her for a moment, eyes narrowed. "You know, a female is a deceiving thing. You look like the kind that would cry if someone frowned at you. I'd say you'd never stick with anything. But here you are, asking me for a job, and you've been turned down six, seven times already." He chuckled. "You know, don't you, that you're no more of a schoolteacher than I am a wet nurse."

Katherine's mouth set stubbornly. "I think I *can* be a teacher, because I want to so much."

"Ahh . . ." The white head nodded slowly. "Ever thought of teaching out in the country?"

The country. Log cabins, sod houses, snakes, and doing your washing in the river. If she tried, she couldn't tell him what "the country" meant to her. The mud hut in Nebraska in which she had been born, the first child of a dreamy Scot named Peter Duncan and his Boston wife, Naomi Fairfield. That home had been a hole in the side of a hill. A roof of cottonwood poles stuck into the dirt and covered with matted slough grass. Furniture made from wooden boxes begged from the general store and the only heat from a fire of grass and dung. It had been the children's job and as eldest, hers especially, to bring that fuel in from the prairie. There had been a new "home" every year, always different, seldom better. In every one of them Katherine had learned to hate "the country" and her father, who talked dreams and promises but sent his children out to collect cow chips. She shook her head. "I've lived in the country all my life."

He smiled. "A long, long time," he said gently. "Then you're just the one to be a country schoolteacher."

"No!" she said. There was a shameful catch in her voice. She swallowed hard and added more steadily, "I want to better myself."

He patted his stomach serenely. "Well, my dear, as I said, your reasons are your own. I don't even care to hear them. But if you want to get started in teaching, you may have to come down a little. I began teaching in backwoods Missouri. Whatever you don't like about the country, we had it there in doubles. Never had a schoolhouse, never got paid in money. Got my first knife wound from one of my fourth grade pupils. By the time I had a school in town, I was a good teacher. You could be too, if you've got the gumption."

He pulled a sheet of lined letter paper from the pile on his desk. "Now here's a job," he said, "out in the Snoqualmie Valley. School at Gold Mountain needs a teacher, the letter says." He squinted at the signature. " 'Julian Sparks.' If I was a youngster and dead set on teaching, I'd write to him."

"Where—where is the Snoqualmie Valley?"

The old man gestured vaguely. "Due east, toward the mountains. Gold Mountain's the first prairie town below the pass. Wagon trains from the east stop there to mend their wagons, oftentimes to bury their dead." He smiled. "*They* won't ask how old you are or whether you graduated."

Katherine whispered, "I don't even know how to get there."

"How are you going to teach children to think," the old man retorted, "if you are afraid to think for yourself?"

So she had written to the man named Julian Sparks. The reply came quickly.

"Dear Miss," it began. "If you are determined to begin your teaching career in the Snoqualmie Valley—your reasons for which are mysterious to me—Mr. Bengston says to come ahead. There are always children here to be taught. Until now our children have been more than a match for their teachers but trust your experience will have prepared you for same.

"Gold Mountain is about thirty miles east of Seattle by wagon trail, but most whites find it more comfortable to come in by boat. You will travel from Seattle to Snohomish City by the *Nellie,* which I trust still leaves Seattle every three days. The riverboat *Viking* is the comfortable way to continue upriver to Black River, the end of the line by reason of the gigantic waterfall above it. Someone there

will loan you a horse, if you get that far, and direct you to
the hop ranch, where you will be expected by

Yours truly,

Julian Sparks."
P.S. Bring an umbrella, if you have one."

Katherine read the letter until her fingers smudged the
penciled words.

What was the use of wondering who was this "Mr.
Bengston" who had decreed that she come? In a moment
of rebellion she had sworn to be all that was respectable
and respected. In hate and misery she had recalled the
envious conviction of her childhood, that schoolteachers
wear clean clothes, live in houses with glass windows and
never need gather cow chips to start a fire. "You can't
stop me from being a teacher," she had cried, "and I won't
go back to the country, no matter what you say!" She had
stunned her father, but the facts were not as easily defied.

In the city she would be a housemaid or a store clerk for
two or three dollars a week. Or she could teach school—in
an unknown wilderness called Gold Mountain and at the
command of a mysterious "Mr. Bengston." Once a
teacher, she had reasoned, I can get away from the country
forever. Once a menial, I could never better myself. . . .
Katherine was already dreaming of leaving Gold Mountain
when she wrote Julian Sparks that she would come.

But she did not buy an umbrella. More important, she
decided, were the hat and gloves, and a suitcase so that she
would not have to carry her belongings in a paper parcel.
She would be a schoolteacher and a lady. Whoever, whatever, this Mr. Bengston was, she must impress him from the
first minute he saw her. Her success—her escape—de-
pended on it.

iv

The Valley was wide at first, the gray-black river flowing deep and slow. As the flat little *Viking* groaned her way upstream, the heavily timbered hills pressed closer on one side, and fell away at the other. Vine maples tangled with nettles that were shoulder high, hiding whatever might be on the slopes above.

"It ain't wild, like it used to be," the captain had assured her. "Nowadays there's a settler nearly every quarter section." But as the hours passed Katherine saw little that proved him right. A few homestead cabins were visible in clearings above the river, their doors and windows opening onto the waterway that was their only road. Here and there cedar canoes were moored to a log piling or an overhanging alder. The farther upstream the *Viking* pushed, the darker the wilderness. Teklatuak, Tolapus, Kalakwahtie—these were settlements whose existence was proved only by a muddy landing, a log cabin trading post, three or four bearded men and a shrieking handful of children waiting for the mail.

Katherine sat quietly on the bench, back straight and hands resting in her lap. There was comfort in being sedate, as long as no one guessed the panic beneath. The men kept a respectful distance, staring at her only when they thought she didn't see it. They were going home. She was going into exile. Every thwack and gurgle of the paddle-wheel pulled her farther away from the neat, secure little world she had dreamed of finding in the city. She hated the Valley without seeing it. "I'll go back," she promised herself, "the very first chance I get."

The captain's son spoke to her from time to time. "Are you comfortable, Miss Duncan?" or "Would you like to rest in the cabin, Miss Duncan?" The very ordinariness of it was soothing. Every time he appeared at her side, bending toward her in his solemn half bow, she felt grateful to him for giving her something to live up to. She wanted to ask, "Do you live in the Valley?" and dared not for fear that was too intimate a question. Above all, she longed to inquire about this Mr. Bengston, but if he were truly the man who had sent for her, wouldn't that show childish ignorance? At length she planned a fitting question. "Have you worked on the *Viking* long?"

It had sounded proper enough when she recited it to herself, but Katherine watched his face anxiously for reassurance.

"Only occasionally." For the first time he smiled, and Katherine found herself smiling back. "I don't intend to shove freight on a riverboat for the rest of my life."

"Then you're not in this"—she gestured toward the squat, horseshoe-shaped cabin—"with your father?"

"I'm studying law in Seattle."

Katherine looked at him in open admiration. An attorney. He would live in the city, in a home his children wouldn't be ashamed of. She knew the answer she wanted to hear when she asked, "Then you don't plan to be an attorney out—out here in the Valley?"

He frowned. "I intend to live in town. I don't like Gold Mountain and I never will." Katherine saw that he had spoken more vehemently than he intended to. He smiled apologetically. "Before long," he added quietly, "I'll be practicing law in Seattle."

With this, spoken like a confession, he seemed to ask her to understand him. She responded impulsively, "In two years I'll be in Seattle, too!"

Even as she said it she blushed. But he was nodding matter-of-factly, showing her the courtesy of believing just what she said, hearing nothing more. His dark eyes were solemn, his posture a little stiff. Unexpectedly her mind

raced back through memories of the men she had known
—the admirable, the despicable, the exciting or the dull—
and whispered silently that no one she had ever known had
been as fine as he.

He bowed and excused himself. A few minutes later,
when her pulse had quieted and she had patted hat, skirt,
bodice to make sure the watchful men on deck would see
nothing amiss, she realized that she still knew nothing
about Mr. Bengston.

V

Shadows were lengthening before the afternoon sun when
Carl White stopped at her side to say, "Black River is just
around the bend."

The end of the run—Katherine suppressed a little gasp
of fear. When she stepped off the *Viking,* the last link would
dissolve between herself and the world she had sworn
never to leave. The men on deck were stirring sleepily.
They stretched, scratched themselves, pulled their hats
down hard. Katherine stood up, letting one hand hold the
other steady. "Thank you."

"They expect you to come to the hop ranch?"

"They"—yes, of course it was "they," Julian Sparks and
"Mr. Bengston." But it struck Katherine as strange that
the captain's son should seem to know. "Mr. Sparks wrote
that someone would loan me a horse."

Carl nodded. "I'll get one for you. Wait for me at the
hotel. I'll borrow two horses and ride up to the hop ranch
with you."

"Oh . . ." It was pure relief, but Carl stiffened instantly.
"If you'll allow me. The country is strange to you."

Katherine said quickly, "Please—please do."

Once Carl had left her Katherine peered anxiously toward the settlement they were approaching. A muddy bank, crowded with several dozen people. Behind and above them a clearing so wide it could only be man-made. At first she could see nothing more. As the *Viking* chugged closer, she made out faces and figures of the waiting people. There were children of all sizes, all of them barefoot, even the boys with hair so long it had to be pulled behind their ears to be kept out of their eyes. She saw men in denim work pants rolled high over thick-soled boots, a dark shirt open at the throat and a broad-brimmed hat jammed squarely down to the eyebrows. Young and old, they were bearded, though she could not tell whether they were recognized beards or just the usual growth between shaves. The women were dressed in calico and wore dark shawls.

There were Indians, too. If you counted them, Katherine thought, they might outnumber the whites. Old men, dressed only in breech clouts and blankets of gray and red, their hair long and hanging loose about their faces; younger men in the trousers and shirts and boots of the white man. The women stood with feet planted wide, arms crossed under their blankets, while the children ran around them like a pack of noisy dogs. Most of the Indians were on the north side of the river opposite the village, as if they neither wanted, or were wanted by, the *cheechacos* who were resisting the wilderness on the south side. The whites shouted, guffawed, bellowed greetings across the strip of water between themselves and the boat. The Indians watched, silent and motionless.

Slowly the *Viking* sidled up to the crude wooden landing, and the town of Black River came into view. Katherine's heart jerked in fear and disappointment. Of course she could have guessed there wouldn't be more than this. How many crude settlements had she lived in—and hated—already? Here there were three—no—four, rain-darkened structures. One a store perhaps, another some kind of warehouse. The third a hotel, with a weatherbeaten sign bearing just that one word. And the fourth, a doctor's house. "Dr. Martin Meade, Operative Surgery and Surgical Diseases a Specialty."

The *Viking* settled, her motor gasped to a stop. The men were elbowing forward to the gangplank. Carl walked past, a gray canvas mailbag thrown over his shoulder. "At the hotel," he said quickly. "Ask for Hilke Orvaag." Then he was gone.

Katherine waited as long as she dared. The crowd on the bank had studied the boat, the cargo, and now they were studying her. Slowly, trying not to look right or left, she walked down the plank to the landing and up the muddy slope.

She dared not walk too slowly, and therefore have no excuse for not taking time to look at them. But she would not walk fast, and show how much she wanted to get away from them. The new schoolteacher . . . Their voices hushed as she walked by. Or became louder, as the speaker turned his head to look at her but kept on talking to prove that he wasn't really looking at all. Far behind her at the river's edge she heard a man shout, "Where's that load of stuff for Nils Bengston?" and Carl White's reply, "I'll get to it when the rest of the freight is out of the way."

"Nils is sure in a hurry."

"Tell him to send his own crew down to unload it if he can't wait his turn."

The man swore loudly. Someone laughed. Her heart hammering, Katherine walked down the rutted wagon road to the hotel.

vi

Hilke Orvaag was a round little man with bright blue eyes, tremendous blond eyebrows and almost no hair above that. He fed Katherine and Carl an early supper of cold venison and apple pie, produced a black horse for Carl and a big bay for Katherine, and threatened to clip Carl's ears if he didn't have the horses back by morning.

"I gave my word to my wife, we ride over to Squak tomorrow," he said with a heavy accent. "So tonight I tell people I loaned you the horses. Starting eight o'clock in the morning I tell that you steal them." And he gestured dramatically with two fingers of each hand—snip, snip, snip at the ear lobes.

The trail from Black River to the hop ranch and Gold Mountain went east along a narrow strip of prairie between the woods and the river. To their left the Snoqualmie ran swift and shallow over a series of riffles, sparkling under the late afternoon sun. Ahead, so directly their goal they could sight it off the end of the trail, was a great dome-shaped mountain.

"Old Hi," Carl called over his shoulder. "Bengston's ranch is on the prairie right at the foot of it."

"The hop ranch?" Katherine tried to make it sound like a statement instead of a question.

"Biggest in the world." Carl was ahead and she could not see his face, but his voice was cold. It made her uneasy. Whoever this "Mr. Bengston" was whose wish had brought her to Gold Mountain, Carl did not like him.

Below two Indians were standing knee-deep in the river, fishing with spears. On the opposite bank a raft of logs rode the surface at the mouth of a creek, and a sawmill was visible in a little clearing beyond. Carl pointed toward it.

"Smith's mill," he said curtly, "but I hear Nils Bengston just bought him out."

Bengston again . . . She began to speak and stopped. She would find out soon enough.

The trail bent toward the woods, plunging them from sunshine into darkness. The trees were so tall and the foliage so interlaced that the sky disappeared except for the thin crack of light directly overhead. "It's like falling into a hole," Katherine thought, her teeth chattering, "and never getting out." It had been warm in the sun. Here among the timber it was damp, and the smell of cedar was a cold smell. The forest seemed to press in on the road. Wherever a log had fallen across the trail, it had been hacked away to the width of a box wagon.

The horses lowered their heads and breathed heavily as the way grew steadily steeper. It was a sharp climb. Muffled by distance and the heavy timber came the steady, thundering roar of a waterfall.

They reached a clearing and Carl motioned to rein in. Below them the river crashed over a precipice for three hundred feet to pound into a rocky basin below. Its force beat the water white, raised billows of foam which blew upward into a soft mist. Rocks, derelict logs, tangled in the frothy white water below.

Carl pulled his horse close to Katherine. "Snoqualmie Falls," he shouted. "Hop ranch is about two miles ahead."

Katherine nodded. Two miles, only two miles, before "Mr. Bengston" and "Yours truly Julian Sparks" would see and judge the new schoolteacher. For a time the presence of Carl White had made her forget how much she dreaded that meeting. Panic shot through her. "Two miles," she repeated stupidly.

Between Black River and the Falls the Valley had been narrow and crooked and lost in timber. It widened now.

The ridges on the south, of which Old Hi was a part, were four or five miles from the craggy chain of hills which defined the Valley to the north. Straight ahead to the east, blue and gray and misty in the gathering shadow, were the mountains through which Snoqualmie Pass led to the dry piney land of the eastern territory.

Here in the upper valley of the Snoqualmie the forest crept down off the hills but ended abruptly in open, grassy prairie. Katherine thought, how different it is from the sunburned prairie of Kansas or Nebraska. It was drought time in the Middle West, but here the grass was green as new leaves, darkened by deeper green patches of sallal and Oregon grape.

As they rode, Carl called over his shoulder to name the landmarks. There to the left, the little village of Three Forks. A cluster of grayed shacks, hugging the riverbank. Closer now was Old Hi, dark green with timber, pink-gray with bare rock. Katherine listened half-heartedly. Fear was coming back full force; Carl's voice became a wordless monotone. She took a deep breath, fighting the rising sickness.

For the hundredth time she looked down at her dress. For the hundredth time she was sorry it wasn't alpaca or delaine. Gingham, calico, petticoats of bleached muslin and everything that went under that cut from boiled flour sacks—that was the contents of the wicker suitcase. She looked at her pink gloves, seeking some relief in the fact that they were still clean. The hat—her hand touched it anxiously. It isn't much, she thought, but at least it isn't a sunbonnet. Sunbonnets, shawls, black gloves—the sure signs of a person who's had very little meat with her corn-meal.

"The ranch is right up ahead," Carl called, and Katherine felt her heart pound like a frightened child's. Unconsciously her hands adjusted themselves over the saddle horn like those of a lady at a tea party. How will I look to them, she wondered, how will I look? A seventeen-year-old who doesn't stand five feet three with her shoes on. Freckles from ear to ear and hair so miserably close to red she'd had the same nickname wherever she went. A tip-tilted nose and green eyes. "You were bound to favor your mother," her father's sister had said, but not as if it were something to be proud of. It wasn't her aunt who would look through and through her now. It was the people of the Valley whose children she would teach. It was everyone who might be idling at the hop ranch. It was Julian Sparks, whose letter had brought her, and Nils Bengston, whose word had the power to send for the new schoolteacher.

New schoolteacher, new schoolteacher . . . the words beat in her head. They were coming in sight of some buildings now. Farm buildings, cabins, lean-tos, even tents. And in back, a strange kind of shed that seemed to stretch endlessly into the field. There were people, too. Grouped in the barnyard, watching the riders approach. Indians—there were hundreds of them. Some whites, with hands in pockets. In her panic their figures blurred together before her eyes.

She straightened her back until it ached. She lifted her chin. Carl smiled reassuringly, but her return smile felt like a grimace. Her hands were icy, and the pulse was beating wildly in her throat. Is my hat right, she thought desperately, or has it tipped a little too much over one ear? My skirt, is it covering my ankles properly? The new schoolteacher, the new schoolteacher . . . Nausea rose in her throat, receded. She gulped hard, forcing herself to look straight ahead. Her dress, her gloves, her skirt, her hat, her chin. The new schoolteacher, the new schoolteacher . . .

A boy detached himself from the crowd, ran down the road toward them. He was carrying—dear Lord, Katherine whispered in despair. Yet, it was a slingshot. Carl didn't seem to notice. I'm the new schoolteacher, Katherine thought numbly. She watched with icy fascination, her mind screaming that she was lost but her face frozen into an expression of pleasant dignity. No, no, he wouldn't . . . But he did.

She heard the whing of the stone, felt the horse jerk back, gather his strength, then wildly plunge forward. She was out of the saddle, grabbing for the horn, missing it. The big bay, crazy with shock, bucked again. Too stricken to cry out, Katherine went over the side.

But her foot, one foot, caught in the stirrup. The horse pounded ahead, free, or almost free. Katherine followed, bouncing like an Indian travois through the dirt. She didn't think for a moment about the hooves. "My skirt!" she sobbed out loud, fighting to hold down her petticoats.

Someone grabbed the reins and the horse stopped abruptly. Carl's frightened voice said, "Katherine, Katherine, are you all right?"

There were other voices, too, mingling in excited whispers. She had to look up. She couldn't bury herself in the dirt. Slowly, with an impulsive wish that she had been killed after all, she raised her head.

A hundred people were standing in a circle around her. One of them, an old Indian in a logger's shirt and nothing else, was holding her hat and grinning appreciatively. The hat was mashed and torn. Carl was beside her, lifting her to her feet, supporting her with a strong arm.

"I'm all right," she said stiffly. It was obvious that they all knew who she was. "Really, I'm perfectly all right!" she repeated, a little irritably because it was so clearly untrue. Frantically her hands worked at straightening her skirts. No use trying to arrange her hair. Every pin that had held it in a grown-up knot at the top of her head was gone; the hair hung loosely down her back.

A man laughed. It was a deep, confident, amused sort of laugh. A man wouldn't laugh like that if he were the kind to wonder what he'd do should the same thing happen to him. A laugh with power, with . . . conceit behind it. Katherine wheeled around angrily.

He was standing only a few feet away, thumbs hooked easily in the edges of his trouser pockets. He was big, very big. His blond head, held erect with such easy pride, was inches above those of the tallest. Sun had burned the hair to straw color, made the skin as dark as an Indian's. His eyes were blue—and amused.

He had stopped laughing. Or at least he stopped laughing out loud. But there was mockery in the very way he looked at her. Down his nose, his head a little to one side, his eyes so bright they seemed to be winking at her. He was measuring her, but not seriously. More like a rich farmer who has ordered a draft horse and got a burro. At the corners of his eyes the laugh wrinkles were deep. He was used to laughing. Being bigger than everyone else, Katherine thought angrily, he can whenever he wants to.

She lifted her chin. It had seemed like the end of the world to be dragged into camp at the end of a stirrup, but anger was healing the wounds of embarrassment. She would like to have ignored him. But his bodily presence was too overwhelming. He compelled her, by his very bigness, to look at him.

The memory of a day in the fourth grade in Montana shot crazily across her mind. The moment when shaking with rage she had faced the school bully, crying, "Oh, I'd beat you up if I were bigger!" He had laughed, but instead of slapping her he had kissed her. How she had hated him, then!

"One of the Greene boys," the big man said good-humoredly, pointing to the boy who had hit her horse. But he talked to Carl, not to her. Katherine thought, he sees no reason to explain anything to a woman. "Those Greenes'll have hell filled up by the time the rest of us are ready to go in." He laughed. He was looking at Carl. But his eyes pulled her into the area of his glance, held her there.

Carl's polite voice seemed to break across a heavy current. "Miss Duncan, may I present . . ."

The big man stopped him with a wave of the hand. "I know who she is."

"Hasn't it occurred to you, Nils," Carl said coldly, "that the lady might not know you?"

Katherine felt the antagonism curling behind Carl's words. It was there, too, in the brown face of the man named Nils. But again, the strength belonged to the man who didn't care. Nils laughed. What a silly idea, the laugh said, everyone here knows who I am, and who cares about a skinny little schoolteacher?

Despite his name, it didn't occur to her for a moment that this man who had so little use for her was the one who had sent for her. I'll show you, Katherine thought, and her mouth set stubbornly. "I'm not at all interested in knowing you," she said clearly, "unless you're Mr. Julian Sparks, whom I was to meet here."

"Uncle Julian?" Nils looked at Carl, silently asking, what sort of nonsense is this freckled-faced friend of yours talking? "That addleheaded old man?" he asked out loud. "This time of day, he's usually in his rocking chair, sleeping off his supper."

Carefully, Carl took Katherine's arm. "We'll find him."

Katherine hesitated. What silly notion held her here, aching to say more to this blond giant? "Would you have laughed if that horse had killed me?"

For the first time he looked straight down into her face. He shook his head. "No," he said deliberately, "I would have buried you."

Katherine was trembling all over. "Still laughing, I suppose?"

He grinned. "No, I would have felt real sad." He chuckled. "If you'd been pretty."

The pressure of Carl's hand grew stronger. "Please come," he was saying, and she obeyed blindly. She turned her back to Nils, clutching hard Carl's guiding arm.

"Uncle, come here!" Nils' voice bellowed suddenly behind her. "New schoolteacher wants to see you."

Still holding Carl's arm, Katherine looked back. An old man was shuffling across the barnyard towards Nils and the crowd. Long white hair hung in strings around his wrinkled face. His mouth moved as if he were talking to himself. Katherine turned to Carl. "Is it possible," she whispered, "that the big man is Mr. Bengston, and that is Julian Sparks who wrote me a letter?"

Carl nodded. "Uncle Julian is bright enough, but he's old and he's been saying yes to Nils Bengston for the past nine years. In his clear spells he writes a beautiful hand."

The old man had reached Nils' side and was squinting toward Katherine. "She going to stay here?"

Nils replied brusquely, "Not in my house." With an imperious wave of the arm, he called her back. "Back up," he commanded, "and let Uncle Julian take a look at you."

Katherine felt the anger begin in her throat, spread with a hot flush to the roots of her hair, rush painfully to the very ends of her fingers.

"The riverboat goes back toward Seattle in the morning," Carl was saying. "You don't have to stay . . ."

"No!"

"Don't worry about breaking your word. If Nils decides he doesn't like you, he'll send you back anyway."

"I'll stay!"

"Katherine, there have been six different teachers in Gold Mountain in the past two years. No one stays."

Her voice shook but it had never been stronger. "Is there a hotel in Gold Mountain?"

"Yes, but that's three miles farther on."

She faced him. "Carl, will you ride along with me?"

He nodded. "But you needn't ride. That was a bad fall. I'll borrow a team and wagon from Nils."

"No!" she said, almost crying. Head high she turned and walked back, through the crowd and to her horse. Skirts and petticoats were torn and dusty. Her hair hung below her shoulders, blowing and tangling with the rising wind. The pink gloves, the beautiful, silly pink gloves, were caked with mud. "I'll ride," she announced. The old Indian with the logger's shirt and naked thighs held out the remnant of her hat. She shook her head. Carl at her heels, she walked past old Uncle Julian, past Nils Bengston, and did not look at either of them.

"I'll help you mount," Carl was saying, and she heard herself reply in a loud, clear voice, "No, thank you, Mr. White." Her teeth were chattering. She took a good grip on the saddle horn and with the strength of anger and desperation, flung herself up onto the giant horse without a hand from anyone.

"You'd better let me lead," Carl was calling, but she paid no attention. Leaning forward in the saddle she lifted the reins and kicked the bay into a gallop. The new schoolteacher, she thought, the new schoolteacher . . . Following her, enveloping her in a cloud of sound, was the rumbling laughter of the man who would have been sad, if she'd been pretty.

2

i

Nils Bengston laughed until the schoolteacher and the captain's son were out of sight. Then the laughter faded into a wide yawn, and he lifted both arms to stretch. "I hate schoolteachers," he said matter-of-factly.

Old Uncle Julian looked at him wearily. "You sent for her."

Suddenly the picture of the little teacher bouncing in the dust and grabbing for her petticoats came back to him, and Nils grinned. "I'd send for a dozen more, if they'd all be delivered upside down."

The old man was looking down the trail to Gold Mountain, as if he could still see her if he squinted hard enough. "What did you think of her?"

Nils shrugged. "What's the difference?" He looked out toward the hop fields stretching east and south across the Valley. "Go to bed, Uncle. I'm going to take a look around while there's still light enough."

The old man's voice took on a persistent whine. "It *does* make a difference. Your own daughter goes to school now. School is important. When I was a boy in Pennsylvania . . ."

Nils broke in irritably, "Maybe it is, to old men and weak-minded women. I got a hop ranch to think about." He took a long, deep breath, expanding his tremendous chest and thumping his hands together happily. "By golly," he said, smiling to himself, "and it's the biggest hop ranch in the world."

"Big talk," Uncle Julian said tartly. "Ain't yet picked the first crop. You're land poor. I never saw anyone with more brass and less hard money."

"I'll end up the richest man in the territory."

"Or the poorest," the old man snapped, but he was smiling.

"Go to bed," Nils repeated, walking away.

"You should have asked her to stay here just the same."

Nils turned back. "Who?"

"That scared little schoolteacher."

Nils wheeled around and headed for the field. Uncle Julian watched him. Such a big man, he thought, and getting bigger. When I was twenty-nine I was still waiting for a good idea. Such a strong-minded man. The teacher should have been invited to bunk in at the ranch. Any other settler would have shown that much courtesy, whether he admired schoolteachers or despised them—Nils knew it himself. But Uncle Julian was wiser than to ask Nils why he hadn't. He knew, and knew he dared not say,

why Nils didn't warm up to having whites in the house.
The old man shook his head, talking softly to himself. Nils
was ashamed of his Indian wife, when she was there; still
more ashamed, since he had deliberately made her his wife,
if she were not at home to act a wife's proper part. He's
mixed up in his own mind, the old man mused, and sometime I'll tell him what ails him. Sometime, when I'm good
and ready to die.

ii

Nils held the hop cone as gently as a mother whose new
baby has just been given to her for the first time. The
touch of it went through him to his boots. It lay across his
palm, perhaps six or seven inches long, its overlapping
bracts feeling rough even against his calloused skin. The
green it had been was now ripening to yellow. Carefully,
very carefully, he pressed down on it, conscious of holding
back his strength. He watched it unblinkingly, as if he
could feel and smell it with his eyes as well. It rustled.
The sound was faint, but he knew he couldn't be mistaken.
He pressed harder. A drop of transparent liquid oozed out
onto his hand. And the smell of it—he knew the smell was
right. Sharp, aromatic. Something to stab right up through
the nostrils into the back of the head. Nils crushed the cat-
kin to a sticky wood pulp and triumphantly threw it over
his shoulder.

He had figured it out right. He had won. He *was win-
ning*.

It was a wonderful feeling to stand alone like this in the
hop field, with the last of the sunset dropping off at the
edge of the prairie. Alone he could taste his triumph more
sharply. No Indians to threaten. No foremen to take down.
No quarreling children or wide-eyed, docile Indian

women. He'd built up this little empire by being a good deal more daring or far-sighted than the next fellow, and if anyone had got stepped on in the process, it was a natural process and who could prove God hadn't intended it that way? Nils grinned to himself, wiping the sticky hop liquor off on his pant leg. It was all his, and standing right in the middle you couldn't see the end of it in any direction.

The biggest hop ranch in the world—a broker in Seattle had told him that. Maybe it was true and maybe it wasn't. Nils wanted to believe it but he knew the world and himself well enough to be skeptical for that very reason. Whether it was or not, he muttered with a clenched jaw, it's big all right. And it's going to make me a very rich man.

The vine rows stretched for two miles, clear across the Valley from east to west. Their perfect pattern—seven feet from pole to pole, either way—anticipated the harvest season when the wagons would have to go through for loading. The poles, split from fresh cedar, stood eighteen feet high. And yet the vines had grown to the top of them, crawled out along the connecting strings and spilled over, heavy with the hops that would make him a rich man. Nils felt his pulse quicken, as it always did when he had a chance to view his property alone.

His foremen would trail him from kiln to shed to hop field, supposedly inspecting the ranch but in reality studying him. There were so many ways to fail. The hop louse or bad prices or unseasonable weather or not enough pickers at the right time. Their deliberately expressionless faces, their quick sideways glances, said, "This time Nils Bengston has outreached himself, and he's scared." Or else they said as loud as words that Nils Bengston was lucky again, and how they envied him.

Either way, Nils despised them. He paid them twice what they asked, used them and needed them, and despised them. Or tried to. Looking over the laden vine rows extending in all directions to fade in the gathering shadow, Nils could smile at the idea of disdaining anyone. The crop was good, the crop was ripe, the pickers were ready, the sky was clear, hop prices were high and by the end of the month they'd be talking about Nils Bengston from here to San Francisco. Nils laughed out loud. No one would ever know how scared he'd been.

In the distance the Indian pickers were shouting over one of their gambling games. Those might be the Yakimas. Hundreds of them had ridden through the Pass, leading a thousand or more cayuses they would sell to the Indians who had come down from Canada. They had camped on a stretch of prairie along the river bank toward Three Forks—men, women, children, ponies and dogs. Every night the sound from it and all other Indian camps had been the same. The rhythmic chants rose to the night sky with the smoke of many fires. Horses, wagons, saddles, blankets, jewelry, rifles, bed quilts, shawls, clothing, cash —they were all lost or won as the big wood chips clattered dully to the ground. During the next three or four weeks each Indian hop picker—and there were a thousand two hundred of them—would receive a stack of silver dollars. How many of them, Nils mused, will go home penniless?

He smiled, feeling a little envious. They had no ambition. They would willingly paddle five hundred miles or more in their long canoes, or make the hard ride over the mountains, just for three weeks' work. What could that bring, at a dollar a box and two boxes a day about the best a man could do? Fifty dollars perhaps. There wasn't an Indian on the place who would accept it in paper money either. Only silver dollars were "real." Silver dollars that might buy a pony from the Yakimas, whiskey from the whites if they could find some stupid enough to sell it to them, or else be gambled away in a night. Was it wrong for Nate Tarpee to sell them bluing when they came to the

Gold Mountain trading post begging for whiskey? "New kind of fire water," Nate had said, "but don't drink it here." Nate hadn't cheated them. You can't cheat people of money they care so little for themselves.

"Money is nothing," Nils thought, "unless you use it to get more." The thought hit him suddenly, rippling pleasurably through his body. He burst out laughing. "I don't want much," he told himself, "just to be about ten miles and five thousand dollars ahead of the next fellow."

It was almost dark now. Old Hi bulged upward against the pale gray sky, a black mass that seemed to lean over the fields below. Looking down toward the buildings grouped together near the river, Nils could just make out the outlines of the long sheds in which most of the Indians slept, and across the field from them the farmhouse and barns and kilns. He pushed his hands deep into his pockets and let his shoulders drop forward easily. Slowly he walked down the row towards the farm.

He felt too good to go inside. A white woman would be full of questions if her husband came in at midnight. Not Mary. She hadn't questioned him in nine years. That much could be said for an Indian woman.

Nils checked himself uneasily. He had labeled her, setting her somewhere below the whites, in thinking of her not simply as Mary but as his Indian wife. And he'd been doing it more and more, as if time were pulling them in opposite directions. He was being careful, now, not to call her an Indian. So very careful, and so irritated by a sense of guilt when he did. For she was still Mary, the mother of his daughter Julie, and not even the change in her could alter that fact. Years ago, Nils thought, nothing I said about her could have sounded disloyal, because there wasn't any disloyalty in me. Nor "loyalty," exactly, for you don't start being loyal to the person you love until you discover that sometime you might not be. He shrugged impatiently. Mary had been gone so much during the past year, to stay with her own people for weeks at a time. The Indian camp below the Falls was only three or four miles away. Once it had been near; now it seemed like a distant, separate place. Nils was uneasy during Mary's lengthening absences, but he didn't blame her. He blamed himself, because he had done nothing about it. He should resent her leaving but didn't. He should miss her . . . He swore softly. It was a fine night, the hops were ripe, such thoughts spoiled his mood. He walked faster.

In the barnyard a short square figure pulled itself free of the shadows. Indian Doc, so proud to be wearing one of Nils' old wool shirts, so unconscious of having nothing under or below it. Doc's age couldn't be figured, Nils knew, but only estimated from the wrinkled face and sagging eyes, the scrawniness of his little bent-over body. Poor Doc was a perennial refugee from his own people. For should one of his patients pass to the great beyond—and Nils knew better than most whites how often one did—the doctor was legally obliged to go along. Nils had tucked old Doc behind, over, and even under his own house so many times he had almost run out of hiding places. A lucky thing for Doc and maybe for me, Nils thought with a grin, that Indians have short memories on this particular subject. Even the kinfolk of the departed forgot their intentions after a time and eventually would even bring him another patient.

"What is it, Doc?" Nils asked. He liked the old man. He had done so much for Doc he couldn't help liking him.

Doc's eyes were weakened by age, but they peered up earnestly. His brown face had shriveled into a mask of a thousand wrinkles, with little clumps of scraggling white whiskers bursting out unexpectedly along the cheeks, under the chin, above his mouth. His long hair was white and hung in uneven lengths around his face, so thin that the ears stuck through. Looking at him Nils always wanted to laugh but he had frequently punched the nose of some-one who did.

Silently, Doc extended a hand. There was just enough half light to see what it was. The new teacher's hat.

Nils burst out laughing. She had been so prim, sitting up there on Hilke Orvaag's big bay. The new schoolteacher, eh, and yet the biggest part of her were those green eyes. She hadn't looked so prissy after the horse threw her and she was grabbing at her petticoats like a hen trying to right herself when you carry her by the feet. A schoolteacher . . . Nils snorted out loud. "What you going to do with it?" he asked in Chinook, gesturing toward the little hat in In-dian Doc's hand.

Grinning, the old man explained he would make it a present to Julie.

An unreasonable anger flashed through Nils. Any Indian woman would wear the wreck of a hat proudly, but Julie was his daughter. He snatched the hat from Doc's hands, walked to the horsebarn where a long nail protruded from an outside wall, and with one mighty gesture impaled it on the nail. Instantly he felt better.

He stepped back. The hat was a silly little blot against the wall. Nils grinned. Carl White wouldn't like to see it stuck to the barn wall. Old Carl had certainly been wearing his heart on the outside that afternoon. But he's the kind that's always in love, Nils thought, and woe to the little teacher with the big green eyes if some more elegant or more helpless female touches his fancy before she's had enough of him herself. Carl doesn't want a woman with feeling; he wants a woman with manners.

Perhaps I'm not doing him justice, Nils thought. Perhaps Carl has it in him to love a woman, as I dreamed of loving Mary nine years ago.

iii

He had just hit twenty when he first saw Mary, that summer of 1875, his first year in the Valley. Had there ever
been another summer like it? Could he ever again be as
brave, as lonely, as blind?

There had been two dozen families in Gold Mountain.
The old Tarpee brothers, the first whites on the prairie,
who had paddled canoes from Seattle in 1858 and struggled up the hill past the Falls to lay claim to ground in the
area later called Gold Mountain; the Tines, Agatha Tine
weighing three hundred and fifty pounds, scaring her husband, loving children; Pete and Lars Anderson, both of
them old prospectors who had had a great deal and lost it,
and now hunted and fished like braves with their squaws
at home to do the dirty work. The settlement of Gold
Mountain had been named after the Andersons' empty
dream. Tom Stump and his family, who never explained
where they'd come from the same way twice; Gifford
Greene and his many sons, most of them near babies
then; and a dozen odd more, many of them kinfolk to each
other. They were all there and all beginning to marry into
the neighbor's family when Nils arrived, an independent-
minded nineteen-year-old with a winter's wages at logging
in his pocket and a lot of ideas his father said were too big
for him.

"I made it from the bottom up," George Bengston had
told his son. "You don't have to. Logging's the natural
business for this country, not crops or cattle or mining.
Logging and fishing, that's what God put out here and we
was intended to use it. I couldn't stand the smell of fish
so I turned to the trees. This logging is going to get better
all the time and some day it will be yours, anyway. You

know how many feet I'm shipping out of Port Angeles this month? Stay here. Mine now, yours tomorrow."

"I'll take wages for the winter," Nils had said. "I want to get away from the Duwamish country and go farther in, where there's as much land as I want."

"How you going to get it?"

"I don't know."

"What you going to make with it when you do?"

"I'll find out."

His father grinned. "Mule-headed as his old man," he said, and turned to count out a winter's wages.

Who wants to start life where someone else has left off, Nils thought—never to be Nils Bengston but simply George Bengston's heir? So at nineteen he had found a spot where there was all the land he wanted, land so remote only a couple of dozen families had registered claims. All he had to do, then, was to figure out how he was going to get it.

He had begun, as they all had, by filing his claim to the quarter section allowed him by the homestead law. He hadn't known how this bight of land between Old Hi and the river was going to yield enough to satisfy him, or how this achievement, common to every settler in the Valley whether he be lazy or crooked or miserly, could be alchemized into something so much bigger it would set him above everyone else. But he wanted to be rich, he wanted to be strong, he wanted to be better—how often that wonderful feeling had burst through him in those days, telling him there was nothing he couldn't do. That he could grab life and squeeze and squeeze and never come to the end of his strength. There is no limit, he told himself, no limit at all while you're still alive, and let any man try to show me otherwise.

He had never, even at nineteen, expected it would all come at once. Nils was forward looking. That was his ad-

vantage and he knew it. He had seen so many other settlers
exhausted, or at least satisfied, simply by getting to the
Valley and proving up a claim. Their minds could stretch
no further. Their blood wasn't hot as long as their bellies
were full.

Nils was only nineteen and there were older heads on
the prairie before him, when he planted apple trees. No
one else had done such a thing.

"What for?" Tom Stump asked suspiciously, as if what
Nils was doing might take something from him. "You
don't have to do that to make your claim good. They don't
ask that. And what are you going to do with all them apples? I wouldn't break my back clearing ground for no apple trees."

The truth was that Nils didn't know what he would do
with the apples. He was just getting the land to give him
something back. In time, he found what foresight was
worth. He dried the apples and sold them at a good price
in Seattle. But that had been years later, years after he
first saw Mary.

How beautiful she had looked to him then, Chief Tom's
daughter whom the whites called Mary. It had been in
July, when the Valley Indians got into their long cedar
canoes and paddled fifty miles downriver to Tulalip for
the games. Nils had come down the hill to old Smith's
water-powered sawmill and the sound of voices attracted
him to the sloping bank at Black River. He watched idly,
conscious of the warm sun on his back and the hum of
crickets in the nearby field.

The Indians were getting into their canoes, five or six to
a canoe, with the squaws, as usual, in position to paddle.
Women and children, young men too proud to paddle and
the old ones who were going to stay behind, crowded the
bank. The *klootches,* the girls, talked gaily as they loaded
the canoes with baskets and the thick bedrolls woven out of

split cattail leaves. They were dressed in full elegance. Beaded moccasins, brighter, newer blankets, with some of the younger men in the highest style wearing white man's work clothes. They would be gone for many days, Nils knew, for it would take two or more to reach the meeting ground at the mouth of the river; and the games there, attended by tribes paddling in from every direction, would last almost a week. Everyone, even the women, would enter the games. Many a young woman would win over the braves in the canoe races. There would be big salmon barbecues on the shore, dances, ceremonials, speeches. Nils watched them embarking for this holiday. Suddenly he felt lonely.

Their voices sounded so happy, so full of anticipation. They blurred together in a warm hum. And then a young girl's laughter broke free, rising above all the others. It was a ripple of pure glee. Nils felt his throat tighten. He looked from brown face to brown face, unexpectedly anxious to know who it was.

It wasn't hard because she was standing up in a canoe, laughing because she was rocking it from side to side, while the fat mother or aunt or grandmother at her feet was scolding her and trying to look at the river and the cattail mats and the baskets and the girl all at the same time.

Nils guessed who she was, for he recognized the squaw at her feet as Rosa, second wife of Chief Tom. No one but Chief Tom's daughter would dare such tomboyishness with her. So this was the girl the whites called Mary and often remarked that she was pretty for a Siwash.

Nils felt a stab of hate for Tom Stump and others like him, who were ugly and ignorant but made kings of themselves by calling the Indians "Siwash." Mary was beautiful. Her body was straight and slender. Her black hair, in heavy plaits down her back, shone in the sun. Her face was delicate, with a narrow, rather short nose and a laughing mouth. It was the laughter that hit Nils so hard. He watched until the last canoe was loaded, sliding out onto the water to disappear soundlessly around the bend. Until he was alone on the riverbank with the old men, listening for the ripple from a moving paddle, a sound they all knew existed but none of them could hear.

He had been so proud of Mary. He had been different from the whites who couldn't see that one Indian might be better than another. "If he's got red skin," Tom Stump always said, "he's no good. I never have to look any further." Indians were the creatures who worked for you, whom luckily you didn't have to fight, as your father and grandfather might have earlier in territory to the east. Whom you married without ceremony if you were lonely and there weren't white women at hand, and would send back to the tribe should the time come, before you were too old, that there were some of your own kind to choose from. Such were the feelings of the Tom Stumps.

But Nils had promised Mary to love and keep her for the rest of her life. Such a vow was not part of the Indian ceremony, and Mary had smiled without understanding as it burst from his mouth. Nils had insisted on a legal marriage. It was his first statement of loyalty to Mary. "Legal" meant white, and the early settlers had laughed because he and Mary had ridden all the way to Squak to catch a traveling preacher. "She don't care, she don't know the difference," the older men had assured him, and only respect for their age and great knowledge on everything else had kept him from hitting them. His was a real marriage, a marriage on paper. Anything less would have been an insult to his feelings, as well as to Mary.

Those first two years with Mary could have been a dream. Even after the dream ended, Nils would remember Mary as she had been, and his heart would ache with nostalgia. An aimless, hopeless longing that brought nothing back. When he was awake the memory could not touch him. But at night in a dream he would see Mary as she had been, slender and laughing, running to him, touching him, promising she was real. Over and over he dreamed it and woke with hopelessness tight in his throat.

It was like dreaming of someone whose death you have been mourning. In daytime you knew she was dead. But sleep knocks down your guard, and she comes back to you, alive, beautiful, the product of your heart's refusal to believe she's gone. And she can prove she is alive. She touches you, speaks to you, laughs, even says, "See? I'm alive . . ." until you wake suddenly, ashamed because you might have cried out in your sleep.

But Mary hadn't died. The Mary of today had once more come back from her own people and was in the ranch house, waiting patiently. While the Nils of today lingered outside, dreading to go in.

In those first years Nils had lived like an Indian, not only because of Mary but because there were far more Indians than whites and it was they who worked for him, traveled with him, surrounded him. His house was the rough log cabin he had put together on his first homestead, but in the summer he and Mary moved into a house of mats tied over a framework of green willow poles. Mats Mary made as her great-grandmother had taught her, by pulling the sharp thread down the center of the cattail reed, weaving the dark green strips. He ate as the Indians ate—the roots of the ground, the wild animals of the woods, the berries. The Indians had no gardens, but for each tribe there were certain woods and prairies where they hunted food for their own people.

"How do you know where your places are?" Nils asked Mary.

She smiled patiently. "How do I know my own man from a hundred others?"

"But if there isn't enough?"

She replied simply, "It is provided."

He had loved to watch Mary settle the reed basket on her back for berry-picking. It was held in place by a wide strap around her head. Solemnly she would adjust it on her forehead, shift her shoulders from side to side until the basket rested comfortably across her shoulder blades. Suddenly she would become aware of him, and looking up, laugh like a little girl. As she picked the wild blackberries, she threw them over her shoulder into the basket. Nils had seen her returning with so heavy a load that she had to brace her neck against the basket's weight by putting both hands palm-flat across the back of her head. Even then, she would look up and laugh at him. The young Mary, Mary at fifteen and sixteen, had laughed a lot.

They dug roots that were like a thin, long carrot, and dried them as Mary dried the blackberries. They dried and smoked deer meat and salmon. Mary knew, as they all did, what were the proper times for spearing fish, the proper times for hunting.

"Indians know when the fish is sweet," she had explained. "Indians know when the deer is fat."

Mary had disdained a white like Tom Stump, who pulled salmon out of the river by the wagonload when they were coming up to spawn and then let half of them rot on the riverbank. "There's more in the water," Tom said.

"He eats soft meat," Mary remarked coldly.

Nils had watched Mary's people and learned from them. He saw them making a winter house, splitting a giant cedar with an elkhorn wedge, tying the overlapping cedar slabs together with long, slender cedar limbs that had been softened by heat from the campfire and later dried as hard as stone. Within these houses many families lived, each in its own section but always with a center area "for playing," as Mary told him. Each family had its own fire, with a trap door in the roof above to be pushed open with a long pole if the smoke were heavy.

"If it rains?" Nils had asked.

Mary shrugged. "We open it only a little."

"And get only a little bit wet?"

That had made her laugh delightedly.

Even in love Nils did not forget his destiny. He was cutting timber on his homestead and making money from its sale. He had cleared land for pasture. But his most pressing desire was for more land. He added another hundred and sixty acre tract acquired through preëmption. By mortgaging what he already had, he raised enough money to buy nearly four hundred acres from the Territorial University, to which certain lands had been allotted by the government. From year to year he bought homesteads others had proved up, for there were always settlers who quit because of hard luck or wanderlust. Or could be made to quit, Nils thought coldly, if they've borrowed money from you and can't pay it back.

With a few silver dollars in his pocket from the sale of timber, Nils bought up his neighbors' hogs.

"What for?" Tom Stump had whined anxiously, afraid all over again that someone was getting ahead of him. "You can't eat that much meat, what with deer plentiful, and the deer feeds itself."

"I'm going to dress them all in calico," Nils replied, "and send them to school."

In the fall Nils hired dozens of Indian farm hands and another dozen Indian women to cook for them. For three days the butchering went on, until every hog had been killed, cleaned, soaked in brine and hung over a slow fire of alder. Once cured, the meat was stored in the smokehouse for the winter. While Tom Stump and others like him couldn't think as far as thirty miles away, Nils had looked into the price of bacon and ham in Seattle.

"In the spring," he promised Mary, "we'll fill up the canoes with meat and paddle out to the city."

That first trip, above everything else in those first years, remained perfect in Nils' mind. There had been eleven canoes that year. Most of them Mary's cousins and half brothers had made, burning long hollows into the cedar logs with rocks heated red-hot in a camp fire. "Long time to build canoe," the Indians said, and Nils had smiled at their understatement.

Heating a big rock in a campfire, pushing it to the log with a stick, fighting to lift and move it to the right spot. Then scooping out the charred wood, scraping and digging with rocks roughly shaped like curved hoes the size of a man's hand. Then starting again to heat the rocks, to burn away another inch here, a few inches there. Thus the canoes for Nils' retinue had been made.

Nils could picture Mary as she had measured the progress the boys and men were making on a canoe. She would lean forward, one knee on the ground, her braids falling against her smooth cheek. She placed one palm gently against the inside of the canoe, the other at the same spot on the outside. Her dark eyes had looked dreamy. She gazed, not down at her hands or at the wall of the canoe, but straight ahead. Thus she judged the thickness of the canoe.

"I can't see how you can measure that way," Nils had protested. "You can't feel through it."

"We all know how," Mary replied simply, meaning that only a white man needs a measuring stick.

Mary had described that springtime trip to Seattle with "We leave when the salmonberries just begin to bloom. We come back when the berries are half gone." It was a peculiarly Indian way of telling the passing of time, though Nils hadn't thought of it that way then. The canoes slid soundlessly down the river. They were natural to it.

Unlike the unwieldy riverboats, they skimmed the treacherous riffles, darted easily away from uprooted trees or
derelict logs that occasionally broke across the course of
the river. They hadn't talked a great deal, he and Mary.
The canoes moved forward, past the dark timber. The sun
brightened the shiny water. Mary would turn, every now
and then, and smile.

They shot game for food. At night they cooked it over a
campfire built in the shallow declivities Mary scooped out
of the sand. And then they slept, their bodies wrapped together in a cattail mat. He would fall asleep in utter peace,
in the last half wakefulness still sensing the warmth of her
body. The river's gentle roar grew even softer, the cry of
the hootie owl even fainter, and he would be sound asleep.
He never dreamed then.

At the Sound they abandoned their river craft and
moved the load of smoked meat into the longer, heavier
salt-water canoes. Their food then was salmon and clams,
baked on the wide beach over fires of driftwood.

Seattle that spring of '77 was growing like an adoles-
cent with a childish mind and big feet. The crooked
wooden shacks still leaned over the water but throughout
the city the new buildings were of brick. Civilization's goal
—to forswear the materials of nature in favor of those man
makes for himself. Lake Union was no longer an outpost,
where a man might shoot a twelve-foot cougar without
much notice taken of it. Logs still bumped against each
other in the bay but more ships than ever before were
tied up at the foot of Mill and Main and Madison Streets.
It was still an Indian town, but the Chinese were moving
in. The railroad builders, hammering together the line
between the coast and the mountains; the little slant-eyed
cigarmakers and cooks and slave workers. Walking along
Washington Street, Nils had counted twenty-seven Chinese houses in a half a block. Angeline, the great Chief

Seattle's daughter, was selling little bundles of pitchwood to the whites from whom she still would not beg.

"It's changing and that's good," Nils had thought. "There's going to be a market here for anything I have to sell." And he doubled his asking price for the smoked meat.

Little Jake Stokes had been the man he sold it to, his neighbor Agatha Tine's husband before the big, heavy-drinking Martin Tine. Agatha had told Nils to see him. "He's a real good little man," she said fondly, folding her arms across her soft, enormous stomach. "He always said we would of spent the rest of our lives together if I'd stayed under three hundred pounds."

"He was your first husband?" Nils asked.

Agatha's moonlike face broke into a series of concentric circles. "No," she chuckled, chins quivering, "just the one before this one."

Behind his meat counter in Seattle, Jake listened to Nils and his dark eyes brightened. "I can see you ain't figuring on giving the meat away."

"You're the one who's going to sell it across the counter," Nils retorted. "Are *you* figuring on asking the least you can?"

"Do you really think you're giving me a fair price?"

Nils was only twenty-one. He felt he knew a good deal less than this bright-eyed little butcher but he'd be hanged if he'd show it. "There's no such thing," he said boldly. "There's only a selling price. Far as I'm concerned, that's to the penny what the buyer's got."

"If business weren't so good," Jake said with a narrow smile, "I'd try to tell you a few of the things you don't know. But why should I? The town is filling up. They're asking a dollar a dozen for eggs and people are buying them. So I can meet your price and still make money."

"In that case," Nils said flatly, "I'll go into partnership with you."

Jake's smile dropped. He swore softly. But before Nils and Mary left Seattle, the partnership was formed. Nils would buy cattle east of the mountains. He would drive them through the Pass, pasture them in the Valley, sell them in Seattle. Jake Stokes signed his name to it all, even to putting up the money with which Nils was to buy the first herd.

That partnership was Nils' first big triumph. Money from the sale of cattle would mean cash for more land. Land meant cash, first from the sale of timber, next as pasture for more cattle. A dollar makes two makes four makes eight . . . Nils lay on his back on the hotel bed in Seattle, arms folded behind his head, figuring. Life was moving faster now. He had made a little plan and its momentum was carrying him on to a bigger one. Nothing could stop him. Nothing. He laughed out loud, inexpressibly happy.

He hadn't been thinking of Mary. Strange, in those days, to have forgotten Mary even for a moment. A dull whimper startled him. She was squatting in the corner, her back against the wall. Nils saw that for some reason she was terrified.

It had been hard to discover why, for fear made the laughing Mary dull-eyed and incoherent. For an hour Nils paced the barren hotel room and questioned her, fighting his impatience, feeling ashamed of it. At last he came to understand. Mary wanted to run from Seattle.

There was bad sickness among the Seattle Indians. She had seen them that day, lying in their huts, too feverish to move away from the bodies of their dead ones. She had seen them run into the cold bay, come out near-dead to collapse on the beach. The Indians were fleeing, not even waiting to bury their dead. The pox . . . Mary hadn't called it that, but Nils guessed from her halting Chinook.

"We'll go home," he said gently, lifting her up in his arms. "The sickness will never touch you. I will keep you safe forever. Don't be afraid."

They had walked back to the Valley along the old Indian trail, expanded now to the width of a covered wagon. Brown sugar, black syrup, flour, parched coffee, were in the packs the Indian workers carried, fifty to seventy-five pounds to the man. Unlike a good squaw, Mary carried nothing. She had wanted to, though she was carrying a child by then and just beginning to show it. Nils had refused. For a few days in Seattle he had thought of her less than he should. He grasped this white man's way of making up to her, and carried her pack as well as his own. Then he felt better.

Mary had never again made the trip to Seattle. He tried, the next spring, to insist. But nothing he said would convince her that the city was not pox-ridden. Terror of going with him had driven her into blank, stupid silence. Finally, angry to the core, he had given up and gone alone.

He apologized for her, to himself. He knew that after they had left Seattle the smallpox had spread among the Indians to a killing epidemic. The largest part of the surviving Duwamish and Skagit Indians had fled, not even bothering to bury their corpses or with proper ceremony send them floating out to sea. In Mary's mind that made the city accursed. Nils apologized further with a white man's reasoning, closing his eyes to the fact that no Indian woman would consider it reason at all. That second spring Mary had Julie. Nils told himself that she would have come with him to Seattle if she hadn't had to stay home and take care of the baby.

And what a baby little Julie had been. Very round-faced, all Indian as far as hair and skin were concerned, but with a most un-Indian little nose and bright blue eyes.

Nils was absorbed, heart, mind and muscle, in his new business ventures that winter Mary had been carrying. He rarely thought of the baby's coming. The day Julie was born he was up in the Pass, driving a herd of white-faces through two feet of snow.

When he reached the cabin, Mary waited on him silently. She removed his boots, set out a hot meal, carried wood to the fire. Suddenly, through a haze of exhaustion, he had seen the change in her.

"Why didn't you say something?" he shouted.

Mary led him to the wooden box in which the baby slept. And what had seemed inevitable but relatively unimportant became, with that first glimpse of Julie, more important to him than anything else.

From the first, Julie was Nils' papoose. It was Nils, not Mary, who carried the baby, strapped to his back or in his arms, and later in a special seat tied with leather thongs to the front of his saddle. Mary relinquished the baby mutely.

Was it then, Nils had often wondered, that she began to change? Or was it as time passed, and no more children came, and she saw that the one little blue-eyed girl, as different from herself as the color of her bright eyes, was the last she would have?

Mary had once been quick-moving and laughing. Each year, even each month, she became duller. Little by little, she grew fat. Nils found himself wishing again and again that they might talk together—was it talking that he missed, or spirit? He had turned to Mary so often, hoping to see her dark eyes sparkle as they had before, to see her head lift with some strong emotion, to feel that she either loved or detested him. But she was merely placid. Dutiful, silent, hard-working, fat. Where had the Mary of that old dream gone?

Nils clenched his fists. What kind of a fool am I, he asked

himself, to be standing here in the dark crying over something I've lost, when across the way is a million dollars worth of hops and they're all mine?

Mary was back. For a while Julie had a mother, he had a wife. She was waiting for him. Her dark eyes would tell him nothing, ask nothing. He would see how fat she was, the way she dragged her feet in the old felt carpet slippers she always wore. "That's the trouble with them squaws," Tom Stump often said, "they're old before they're twenty." Hang the old miser, Nils thought, for ever saying anything I'd find myself remembering later. How old was Mary, since Julie was seven and had been born when Mary was fifteen? Only twenty-two years old. Only a few years older than that new little schoolteacher. And yet Mary's done with childbearing and squats in the corner waiting for old age. While the teacher is as big-eyed, as daring and as skittery, as a child.

Nils hurried toward the cabin. Mary would be waiting. He had no business out here, measuring her against Carl White's girl.

CHAPTER

3

i

It was night when Katherine Duncan and the captain's son rode into Gold Mountain. A crooked cluster of buildings hugged the black ribbon of the wagon road. Through the windows of the general store the smoky gleam of a kerosene lamp quivered against the shadow. Loud voices hurtled through the open door of a saloon. Elsewhere people slept; windows were dark.

In front of the store a peeled log lay across two or three fenceposts. Carl dismounted quickly and hitched the reins around the log. He nodded toward the building. "Nate Tarpee's trading post. It doesn't look it, but it's a hotel, too."

Anger had carried Katherine all the way from the hop ranch, but it had exhausted her, too. She meant to dismount briskly. She had even planned how to ask for a hotel room without betraying the fact that she had only once before done such a thing. But somehow with her hair hanging down her back, pretense seemed silly. She nodded wearily.

Carl was at her side, hands extended. "Here," he said, "let me help you down." She hesitated, reciting her refusal. Would it be proper for the new schoolteacher . . . With a sigh she slid toward him, let him lift her off the horse and set her on her feet. Across the slit of darkness they looked into each other's faces.

"I'm grateful to you," she whispered at last.

Without replying he took her arm and gently pulled it through his own. He led her into the trading post. Behind a rough-hewn counter a man with thinning hair and a long nose was unpacking a box of patent medicine.

"Nate Tarpee," Carl said. "Nate, the new schoolteacher, Miss Duncan."

Katherine saw the storekeeper narrow his eyes in speculation. Her self-confidence crumbled. She would have to say something . . . But Carl's voice went on smoothly. "Just for a day or two. Until she knows where she is to board out."

Nate Tarpee set down the bottle of tonic, pulled a key from his pocket and studied it carefully, both sides. "Yup," he said. He squinted at Katherine. "She got a valees?" he asked Carl, his eyes still on Katherine.

"It's coming up tomorrow with a load for the hop ranch."

"Well I don't know what kind of trappings we got for her to sleep in. Bertha's in bed and her stuff'd go around this girl three times anyway."

"Never mind, Nate . . ."

"Don't know what I've got to feed you, either. I can

make coffee. Out of anything. Barley, wheat. Done it many's the time. But Bertha's the cook, and Bertha's in bed."

"It's all right, Nate . . ."

"Well, come on then." Nate picked up one of the lamps, ordered Katherine toward the stairs with a jerk of the head. Whistling softly, he walked around the counter and across the room.

Carl faced her, holding out his hand. "Good-bye, Miss Duncan."

He was leaving. Katherine looked at him dumbly, stricken by the realization that she had been depending on him and that soon he would be gone. She felt suddenly that this was more than she could bear. She had to go back with him. He had suggested it himself. The *Viking* would leave in the morning; in two days she would be back in Seattle. She could be a housemaid for the family on Madison. She could be a clerk at the "San Francisco Store." As Peter Duncan's daughter she had known nothing but hard work anyway. With her mother, who could remember life in Boston, she had despised what she was and dreamed of being a gentlewoman. But what was the use of reaching for gentility, if that old childish fear of change was going to plague her all along?

For the first time Katherine saw the men at the other side of the store. They were in chairs tilted back against the wall, bootheels caught in the side rungs and thumbs hooked under their belts. Silently they surveyed her. The new schoolteacher . . .

Carl's posture was all formality. Lifting her chin, Katherine tried to copy him. "Thank you," she said stiffly.

"Coming?" Nate called from the stairs.

Katherine looked up at Carl in a last-minute plea for help. She saw his eyes, his whole face, change. "Listen," he said urgently, barely touching her hand. "The trip downriver and back usually takes a week. I'll be back here Monday. I'll help you get down to the boat and you'll be in Seattle before you know it."

That seemed impossibly far away. Katherine wanted to say, "No, now, right now!" but she nodded.

"Remember, I'll be back Monday." He turned toward the door.

In desperation Katherine took a few steps after him. He stopped. "Is there something I can do . . ."

Katherine held out her hand mechanically. "Good-bye," she said in a strangely hollow voice. He shook her hand, and she realized that they had done just that only the instant before. Along the wall the silent watchers were measuring her, perhaps laughing at her. In confusion she turned and followed Nate Tarpee up the stairs.

The room was directly above the store entrance, with windows opening on Gold Mountain's rutted street. Nate pulled a candle from his pocket, lit it from the lamp and, softening the end over the lamp's flame, set it on a saucer on the washstand.

There was a bed covered with a crazy quilt, a handmade table, a chair with a hand-hewn back and a seat of rawhide. On the washstand a big crockery pitcher covered with hand-painted roses stood next to a cracked white bowl. Beside it lay a bleached flour sack and a bar of orange-colored soap.

Nate was watching her closely. Katherine looked around the room, feeling that he expected it of her. Perhaps she should say something. She murmured, "This is your hotel?"

Nate chuckled. "Was for five years. If I had been the first white in the Valley I'd of done all right. Any time there's two of us the other fellow gets the best of me. I only run the place. It belongs to Nils Bengston."

Katherine felt a flush creep into her cheeks.

"Lock your door," Nate said, and went out whistling.

Katherine ran to the window. The bottom slid open easily. She dropped to her knees and leaned out, trying to make out the hitching post, the two horses, Carl. But there was nothing there. In a last spurt of panic she peered through the darkness in the direction Carl must have taken. Straining, she heard the rhythmic clop of horses' hooves in the distance. It was a muffled, lonely sound. She clutched the window sill, listening. The sound grew fainter.

Slowly she pulled herself to her feet and went across the room to the bed. The straw mattress crackled as her body pressed into it. I'll get up right away, she thought, and take off the dusty serge and wash my face with that orange soap . . . Tears came to her eyes. I'm afraid, she thought, I'm afraid and I'll never go to sleep . . . The hotel was silent as an empty barrel. From the saloon below came the sound of a man's drunken singing. A door slammed, shutting it off. Everything was still. The bed rocked gently on a sea of silence.

ii

It was the terror of her dream that wakened her. She was in Nebraska again. Or was it Kansas or Minnesota or Montana or Nevada? A little girl in a dirt house. Her mother was beside her. She couldn't see her mother's face, but she heard her crying. Somewhere her father was saying, "Naomi, I promise, the next place will be better. I'll get you a house with glass windows." Glass windows, glass windows, a house with glass windows—the words mixed together with the sound of her mother's crying. Katherine, the little girl, sobbed, "She wants a house with glass windows. *My mother* wants a house with glass windows . . ." Her father's voice stopped. He wasn't talking now, he was laughing. Deep, rumbling laughter that came from all around and in back of her. She began to run. The laughter followed. She turned to beat it with her fists, and the laughter grew. Then she saw him. Nils Bengston . . . "Stop!" she screamed. "Stop . . ."

Katherine awoke. She stared at the rafters, trembling with fear, wondering if she had called out loud. The hotel was still. On the washstand the stub of candle sputtered in a pool of wax. She had slept only as long as it takes to burn a candle; yet she was wide awake.

Katherine got up slowly, every movement of her body hurting. It had grown cold. Shivering, she pulled the quilt off the bed, wrapped it around herself and stumbled to the chair by the window. She lowered herself painfully. I'll sit up for a while, she thought, before I try to sleep again.

Which house had she seen in her dream? It had seemed real, and yet with the dream still vivid she could not say. It reminded her of the game her younger brothers and sisters had played. "Which house do you like best?" Felicity would begin.

"That one back in 'Brasky," Angus would answer.

"*He* don't even remember that one," from the scornful Teddy. "He *couldn't* remember it."

"Yes, I do!"

"*He* wasn't borned yet."

Katherine had always held herself aloof. A new home, a new baby every year—that way, she had once reflected bitterly, her father always has children young enough to believe him. When he told them they were going to pack up and this time it would be a wonderful place, their eyes sparkled. Yet in that next "wonderful place" they still had to sleep three in a bed, more for warmth than for lack of straw or cornhusks for the mattresses.

Once, when they couldn't buy flour, Teddy had been given the chore of grinding wheat through the hand coffee mill. For a week his thin shoulders had been hunched over the job, his eyes blinking with every hard crack of the kernels. Once ground, the coarse meal had to be put through again. At the end of a week he had finished, and saw with his own eyes what so much hard work had brought forth —no more than a two-gallon jarful. The next week his father was describing another place. "I can get it on a trade," he said, "and there's a good spring on it. I'll tell you what we'll do . . ." And Teddy was sitting on his lap, his arm around his father's neck. Only Katherine, the oldest, knew enough to doubt him.

Only once had her father been rejected by his younger children. Felicity had been a little girl of six or seven. There seemed to be nothing but corn in those days. Parched corn, in little, shriveled, pointed ears with rows as irregular as an old man's teeth. Like Indians they ground it into coarse meal, which most of the time came to the table as a thick, hot mush. Black syrup, grease, baking powder—that was all they could trade for then. When the year's cash spendings had been added, they came to thirty dollars.

Come Sunday, the family sat down to hear their father's weekly grace. "Dear God," he concluded at last, still looking heavenward over their bowed heads, "bless this poor house. Bless my faithful wife. Bless these children. In the name of Jesus, Amen."

He lowered his eyes. There was a moment of silence as the children watched intently to make sure he was through. He *must* be, their hopeful eyes said, or why would he say "Amen"? With a clatter they picked up their spoons. A hush fell as they bent over the steaming bowls. And at just that moment, without as much as a whisper to cover it up, Felicity added her bit to the grace. As clear as a bird call her sweet voice said, "And darn the mush!"

The other children's spoons stopped in mid-air.

"Felicity!" her mother gasped.

Color shot to the little girl's face. Tears came to her eyes. The defiance was out of her and she was hungry. She picked up her spoon, slowly dipping it into the mush.

"Naomi, I *promise* you . . ." Peter Duncan had made this plea again and again, each time as if his promise were totally unsullied. Katherine recalled the weary patience on her mother's face as she nodded. "Of course, Peter."

She doesn't believe him, Katherine had thought. She couldn't, after what he's done to her. He would sense it himself, and quickly go outside to find the little children. Through the cabin's open door Katherine and her mother heard him, saw the thin, dirty faces of Angus and Felicity and Tommy and Petie shine with belief in this, their favorite fairy story of all.

"We'll have a garden with so many things growing in it you can pick something whenever you get hungry. We'll get new clothes for you, and anybody who goes to school gets to have a pair of shoes. We'll have a real wood house, made out of boards. A house with glass windows . . ."

Katherine's mother sat lifelessly at the bench beside the rough-hewn table. Her hands lay in her lap as they had fallen when her husband released them—palms up, motionless. Her face, which matched Katherine's so closely, was gray with fatigue. "You shouldn't be angry with your father," she said at last. "You can't blame him. He believes it. He wouldn't say it to me if he didn't."

"A house with glass windows!" At the very thought Katherine had tasted the full strength of her bitterness. Such were the houses of rich people. The respectable, the stay-in-one-place people. Windows were for storekeepers and doctors and schoolteachers.

Naomi Duncan shrugged. "We don't *know* he won't get it."

"Oh, Mother!" How bitterly she had resented her

mother's loyalty. "Don't we? Don't we know that he won't?"

They had looked at each other in silence, the mother needing the illusion, the daughter refusing it. The mother lowered her eyes. "Boil water for tea, will you, dear," she said quietly. "It seems I never want my tea as much as when I'm carrying a baby."

Katherine turned toward the stove and reached blindly into the box beside it for a handful of quick-burning grass. Grass and cow chips, the makings of a poor man's fire. Why, she thought angrily, they aren't even from our own cows.

When I grow up, I'll be a schoolteacher. I'll be clean and respectable and someone else will lay the kitchen fire.

"Glass in *all* the windows, papa?" said Angus' little squeaky voice outside. "Front, side n' back?"

Katherine had had to close her eyes tight against the sudden tears. Her mother didn't cry. Then she wouldn't, either.

Katherine hugged the quilt tighter against the night cold. Through the window Gold Mountain was no more than a hole in the dark. She was alone. She felt alone, as she never had before her mother died. From the time she was old enough to know hunger from contentment and a sod house from a house with glass windows, from that moment she had been lonely. But it had been a feeling consciously shared with her mother. "I want to be just like you," she had whispered to her mother so often, and that meant to dream of the things her mother yearned for, to despise the things her mother hated.

Her mother had had a fine education. Thus the girl Katherine had wanted schooling more than anything else in the world and had resented her father for pulling them farther and farther from the civilized places where she could get it. Her mother had been a lady, whose finest dresses had once been fashioned by a French designer from New Orleans. Yet life made by her father's hands was rough, poor, wild. Knowing nothing else, she had not learned to be a lady, and she blamed him for that, too. Katherine stared sightlessly through the window of Nate Tarpee's hotel, and thought, I *will* be a lady, as Carl White believed me to be.

Carl had expected her to be displeased by the Valley. Katherine sighed. That was a tribute to be cherished. Like everything else about the captain's son—his strong sense of propriety, his courtesy, his assumption that dirt and coarseness would shock her—it was something to live up to. He had seen in her the quality her mother never quite lost, the air of having known something better.

Only once, Katherine reflected, once in eighteen years of marriage had Peter Duncan offered his Boston wife something of the life she had lost by marrying him. He had swapped houses and homesteads, mortgages and cattle and logs, as gaily as a boy trading jackknives and almost as fast. They had moved from desert to timberland and back again, buying sight unseen, lucky one time, hungry the next. Throughout Peter Duncan acted as if his promise were still good. The next place would be better, and at last, on the last trade he ever made, it was.

In return for a homestead on the Skagit and a quarter section of timber, he took a house in Seattle. That was only a year ago, Katherine thought with surprise, too little time for so many changes.

A year ago the whole family had been together, and her mother had been well. Her face had been radiant as she took her first look at that beautiful house in Seattle. "Be sure and wipe your feet, children," she had said absent-mindedly, like a little girl watching her elders divide up the barley candy. The house stood at the top of the hill overlooking Elliott Bay. It was made of real wood boards, cut at a sawmill—not a peeled log or a handsplit shake about it. More than that—it was painted white and stood two floors high, with an upstairs porch supported by six pillars sheltering a wide veranda below. And windows—glass windows—in every room.

Angus and Felicity and Tommy ran ahead. Naomi Duncan followed with Petie in her arms. Katherine and Teddy held back, disbelieving to the very last.

"An easterner built it," Peter Duncan told them excitedly. "A real easterner from Virginia. Wanted it like the houses he was used to. He ordered it built, but he didn't even move into it before he went to Frisco with a brig of timber, hit a bad storm and went down. I bought it off his son." He glanced at the children, estimating his audience. "I made a smart deal, too."

But he didn't look at me, Katherine remembered, when he said it.

The hallway had been as wide as a parlor. The newel posts were made of fancy carving, the hall windows contained leaded red and green glass. Above the parlor fireplace statues of naked ladies faced each other. Angus was at the glass windows, rubbing a stubby, uncertain finger down each pane. Teddy was in front of the fireplace, his mouth wide open. "It's yours, Naomi," their father kept saying, "yours, just like I promised."

After eighteen years in which nothing had been elegant or useless or beautiful, Naomi Duncan could only reply, "I wonder where you do the washing."

"A smart deal," her father had called it, but in time they found its weaknesses. Katherine had planned to give up her job in the dry-goods store and go back to school. Teddy had been talking about shipping out on one of the San Francisco boats. The night they moved into the beautiful white house, Peter Duncan admitted they would all have to work to keep it.

"Unless," he said vaguely, "we use what we got put away in the strongbox."

But the strongbox and its little burden of cash had come to be their only security. Katherine, Teddy, even little Tommy and Felicity, had worked to add to it. So Teddy laid aside his ambition to go to sea and Katherine told herself once more that it wouldn't be long before she could start training to be a schoolteacher. They all worked. Angus swept out the grocery at the corner of First and Marion, and took his pay in sausage and coffee beans and lard. Teddy split shakes and traded them for flour at the Busby mill. Felicity hired out to a wealthy family at the top of Madison, and Tommy ran errands for the San Francisco store. Carrying Petie, their mother did char work at a Mill Street hotel and Katherine went back to her job in the dry-goods store. Peter Duncan signed up to dig coal at the Newcastle mine.

He worked harder than any of us, Katherine thought. Why then should I blame him for what happened? Because he was so long in making the dream come true, or because he made it come true at all?

Katherine, Teddy, their mother and little Petie were the only ones at home when the house caught fire. It had happened so fast. The kitchen full of smoke, her mother's cry, Teddy's running footsteps and shaky call, "Katie! The house is on fire! Where's the strongbox?" Katherine had picked up Petie, run down the great curving stairway. Teddy was clinging to the carved lady who topped the newel post, his face stiff with fright.

"Run and call the fire department!" Katherine shrieked, only an inch from his face.

Naomi Duncan was in the hallway, staring at the smoke

billowing through the kitchen door. "I don't understand," she said dully. "How did it start?"

Katherine put her arm across her mother's back, gripping the thin shoulder. "Come on, Mother, hurry!" Petie was being squeezed by her other arm, and whimpered.

Her mother looked at Petie, then Katherine. "Did the lard spill onto the fire?"

"Please!" Katherine shifted Petie to a new position and pulled her mother toward the front door. "We've got to get out."

Naomi Duncan shook her head but she moved as the pressure of her daughter's arm directed her, in stumbling steps toward the door. They met Teddy on the porch.

"A boy that was outside is going after the fire truck!" He was gasping for breath but he ran past them and into the house.

"Teddy, come with us!"

The boy kept going. "The strongbox," he called. "It's in here somewheres!"

Katherine led her mother along the walk to the street. Hurriedly she set Petie down on the dirt. Then she turned to her mother, shaking her as hard as she dared. "Where is it, Mother? Think! Quickly!"

Naomi Duncan's thin, weather-browned face was vacant. "Is Teddy all right?"

"The strongbox, Mother. The box with all our money. Teddy's looking for it. Where did you put it, Mother?"

His arm across his eyes, Teddy hurtled through the door and across the grass. "I can't find it," he sobbed, shaken with a fit of coughing. "I looked all over and I can't find it."

Katherine's grip bit into her mother's shoulder. "Where, Mother?" she begged. *"Where?"*

Naomi Duncan looked at her helplessly. "I can't remember."

Katherine felt her throat tighten. "It's no use, Teddy, no use at all."

In the street four or five housewives had gathered, and a dozen children. Others were moving up the hill as fast as their ages permitted. A little boy pulled out of the crowd, running so hard he fell against Katherine, and clutched the folds of her calico skirt. "I called the fire department," he gasped. "They're coming. Bang, bang, cloppety, cloppety, clop . . ."

Katherine nodded mechanically. As mechanically her right hand patted her mother's shoulder. Little Petie was playing contentedly in the dirt, dreamily tasting what was stuck to the end of his finger. Teddy was staring back at the house, his eyes watering from the smoke. He seemed to be trembling on the finest balance, as if one desperate word might send him running down the hill or just as easily back toward the flames. Suddenly he broke into a run.

"Teddy!" Katherine screamed, losing all control of her voice. It was a maniac's voice, rising hysterically and breaking into a sob. "Teddy, Teddy . . ."

On the porch he flung up both hands, as if the gesture were supposed to tell her something, and disappeared through the door. Naomi Duncan stared after him. Smoke was beginning to pour out. Fat, round pillows of smoke puffed around and past each other and flattened into a cloud under the veranda roof. She pulled against Katherine's arm. "I'll get him," she said hoarsely.

Katherine clung to her mother. "It wouldn't do any good." Her jaw was so tightly clenched she could hardly swallow. "He'll come out," she said fiercely, "he'll be all right."

Over and over she said the empty words, holding her mother tightly with both arms. The crowd stared at them. The little boy who had called the fire department was dancing from one stranger to another, crying, "I ran all the way down the hill and all the way up the hill and told the firemen to come. I ran all the way down the hill and all the way . . ."

Please God, Katherine prayed, let Teddy come out safe.

In the distance, the fire bell clanged. Katherine turned to watch the crest of the hill over which they would come. The dashing, brightly painted wagons, the kingly fire horses with their arched necks and tremendous withers. Just a year before, she and Teddy and two or three of their smaller brothers and sisters had stood in front of the bakery at Third and Union and cheered as they pounded past in the annual Seattle fire cart race. Where were they now, when everything they owned was burning down and her brother was lost in the flames?

Teddy staggered to the door. He was swaying crazily and coughing. In his arms was the strongbox.

"Teddy!" Katherine cried. "Run!"

The boy stumbled forward, clutching the metal box with all his strength. He was doubled over it, his long thin arms overlapping across his ribs. Reaching them, he gasped, "I got it." Cough after cough shook his loose frame. His eyes squinted against the sting of the smoke.

And yet, Katherine mused, he had been grinning, as a man might . . .

The fire cart's bell clanged louder. The crowd turned toward the sound. Some smiled excitedly. As if to mock the sound, new spurts of flame exploded through the front windows.

Fast and hungrily the blaze licked into the framework, and still the building stood. Flames pouring through the windows swept skyward to gnaw furiously on the walls, and yet it did not fall. The big white house had been queen of the hill. Her windows looked out toward the glistening Sound, down on the rooftops of her inferiors. Katherine thought wonderingly, "She's larger, whiter, more elegant than all the rest, even now."

Teddy was hugging the precious metal box. Her mother stared impassively down the hill.

"It's coming!" a boy shrilled. The heavy thud of horses' hooves grew louder. The hill was steep. As cart and horses came into view, they slowed down. The horses snorted, their heavy necks arched against the strain. Their hooves beat up a cloud of thick brown dust.

"Never mind, Katherine dear," Naomi Duncan said.

"Hurry up!" Teddy screamed. "Hurry!"

Little Petie pulled excitedly on Katherine's skirt, his baby mouth rimmed with dirt.

"Oh, if father had only . . ." Looking at her mother's face, Katherine bit back her words. If father had only— what? He was twenty miles away, digging coal at Newcastle.

The spectators kept their distance from the Duncans. Their eyes traveled from the fire cart to the burning house, then turned curiously to the woman and her three children, as if to measure the size of the disaster in their faces.

"Never mind," Naomi Duncan repeated meaninglessly.

The firemen raced the horses up the sloping lawn before the house. Shouting, cursing, the men connected hose to water tank. More people—the idle, the old, the curious —had followed the clamor of the fire bell and gathered now in a semicircle around the dying house. Shopkeepers and children, housewives, with their aprons on, cluttered the dirt street. They fought to catch breath, gaped at the house, stared at Katherine and Teddy and their mother, and the baby playing so happily in the dirt. Poor woman, the glances of the housewives said. Such an elegant home, even if they were too poor to put anything into it. And they say the house was all they had in the world.

Katherine's mother looked straight ahead. How can

she stand so still and quiet, Katherine thought miserably, when her reward for eighteen years of wretchedness is burning down before her eyes? How strange we must look. Poor people off the Kansas prairie. Wearing patched-up cottons and scrawny from years of trying to fill up on potatoes and beans. They're wondering—How did we ever get such a house? Silently Katherine patted her mother's shoulder.

Thin streams of water spurted from the hose. The firemen sweated with the heat of the blaze. At the cart others pumped furiously, sweat dripping from their foreheads. "Harder!" the firemen at the house shouted. "Build up the pressure!" But the water was mere spit against a holocaust. It hit the building peckishly, like an insect trying to kill a bear. Steam rose from spots the water dampened. The flames recoiled, curled sideways from the helpless stream, then burst out stronger.

"It's burning down, it's burning down!" a little boy squealed, dancing down the road. "Look, look, look!" he sang, dancing by.

The firemen were yelling at each other, "Stand back! Everybody stand back!" The crowd was numb. Housewives with soapsuds drying at their wrists, children who had raced to see the fun and now stood frozen next to their elders, merchants who had run out leaving their shops unlocked—they were all voiceless with the knowledge that the final moment was about to come.

"She's going!" a man called.

The great white house trembled in her final agony. In a moment no longer than a gasp, her walls leaned inward, hung crazily at an angle. Then, the crash. The thundering, sickening crash as the whole building crumbled to the ground and the flames leapt up to engulf it.

"Aaahh . . ." the crowd moaned, sick with awe and delight. The fire horses whinnied, reeling backward.

"Mother!" Katherine put her arms around her mother. The sobs she had been stifling ached in her throat. She looked into her mother's face. The eyes were dry, the mouth straight, but there was a dullness to it, as if she had always known this would happen.

Teddy rattled the strongbox angrily. He had forgotten he was fifteen years old and tears poured down his cheeks. "This was all I could get," he sobbed. "I tried to think of what to take and I thought, this has all our money in it, this is what to take."

"You were right, Teddy." Katherine felt choky, but now that he was crying, she mustn't, for sure. "You did the right thing."

"But Katie!" Teddy, "it feels like it's empty!"

The two children turned to their mother. She didn't seem to see them. "Open it," Katherine whispered to her brother, "if it isn't locked."

Together they loosened the catch and pulled up the lid of the strongbox. Teddy's hand trembled as he picked up the piece of paper inside. "Their wedding license," he said, crying like a baby. "That's all there is." A wedding license, handwritten by a traveling preacher in Nebraska, to unite Naomi Fairfield with Peter Duncan.

Katherine looked helplessly at her mother. Dear God, she thought, she knew that, too.

Her mother's face seemed as flat and empty as her voice. "I was just thinking how lucky we are this happened on a school day," she murmured. "The children have their good clothes on."

Katherine led her down the hill and made tea for her in the kitchen of a neighbor's house. "Drink it while it's hot, Mother"—and Naomi Duncan obeyed. Like a frightened child she let Katherine undress her, wash her and tuck her into a strange bed. Katherine had seen then, for the first time, that her mother was again carrying a child, and her indignation against her father boiled up uncontrollably. She sat by her mother's bed, smoothing her hair, gently rubbing her back where it ached most, until she saw that her mother was asleep.

Two days later Peter Duncan returned from Newcastle. He began calling "Naomi, Naomi!" before he had closed the door behind him. He ran past the children, dropped to his knees beside their mother's chair and threw both arms around her. "Don't worry," he murmured, "I'll take care of you."

Perhaps that was the moment, Katherine thought, that I decided to leave home. She had turned away from the sight of her mother in her father's arms and walked out of the house. Until then she had believed that she could not leave. Her mother needed her, but stronger now was the urge to escape. I've got to get away, she had repeated over and over as she walked through the streets of Seattle. Away from promises and hunger, a new house and a new baby every year. Away—from him.

While her mother was ill, she could not leave. "She needs me"—it became her only excuse, for actually she was afraid of the decision she had to make. Fear was a familiar sensation. Fear of being laughed at, fear of being disliked and, most of all, fear of the unknown. The only relief came from bursts of temper, and these, like Felicity's "Darn the mush!" had changed quickly into shame at hurting her mother. All her life the world had been too big and had changed too fast. Like her mother, she wanted to draw its boundaries closer, to tidy and straighten them. "When mother is well," she had said. And then quite suddenly, only a month after the fire, her mother died.

Dry-eyed, Katherine dressed the body, painstakingly brushed and braided her mother's hair. Aunts and uncles from Oregon, the settled, steady Duncans whom Katherine had seen once and almost forgotten, came to Seattle in answer to their brother's letter. From the moment they walked into the shack Peter Duncan had found for his family, Katherine resented them.

"Your aunts, Nellie and Rebecca. Your uncles Ian and Angus." Peter Duncan ticked off the children with quick little jerks of his head. "Starting at the top, Katherine, Teddy, Felicity, Tommy, Angus, and we called the little one after me, Petie. They've grown some since you last saw them."

"We've been in and out of three houses since then!" Teddy's voice was changeful, and it betrayed him now, rising to an angry squeak at the end.

Aunt Nellie, the plump one with a sweet smile, nodded sympathetically. "You poor dears."

Katherine saw Teddy shy away from her kindness. "That's all right, we got along fine."

"We did not!" This from Felicity, in an indignant squeal. "One place had snakes and it was awful."

"Ugh, snakes," said Angus.

"You poor dears," their plump little aunt repeated.

"She makes me sick," Teddy hissed into Katherine's ear. "How long is *she* going to stay?"

Katherine studied her relatives. Her aunts, looking scrubbed and starchy, her uncles wearing dark suits and shiny black shoes, the symbols of prosperity. Their politely blank faces turned toward her father. They seemed to be waiting. They've been talking together, father and the relatives, Katherine thought. About *us*.

"Children, your aunt Rebecca and your aunt Nellie have very kindly offered . . ." Peter Duncan hesitated, turning to the relatives. They were smiling, hands folded in their laps. Aunt Nellie nodded brightly. ". . . have kindly suggested that we move down to Oregon and live with them for a while."

Katherine felt a warning twinge in the pit of her stomach. That was it, of course. What else could have put those empty smiles on their faces, those "you poor dears" into their mouths?

"All of us?" she asked flatly.

Teddy's voice broke in. "Not me!" he said. "I'm not going." There was anguish in it. Nothing any of them say, Katherine thought, is going to be right with Teddy. Nor with me.

Her father looked at his eldest son. "Peter and Felicity will live with Uncle Ian and Aunt Nellie," he continued mechanically. "Tommy and Angus with Uncle Angus and Aunt Rebecca."

The little children are to be taken away from me. He's already arranged that. And still he isn't facing me, Katherine thought, because there's more to it than that.

"You didn't say anything about me!" Teddy was standing as tall as his thin body would allow. His sandy hair bristled like the scruff on the back of an angry dog.

"I figured you and me and Katherine would stay together, maybe go down to California. They tell me there's real opportunity down that way."

"I won't!" Teddy looked all around the room, meeting every frown, defying it. "I've been wanting to ship out on the San Francisco boat. I would have last year if it hadn't been for the house." He turned to Katherine. "*You* know that. I can get on the boat now. You don't get me to go to California or Oregon or any place. I'm old enough to leave home and that's what I'm going to do." His voice softened. "Listen, Katie, you do it, too. You always wanted to teach school. Aren't you old enough, now?"

"Katherine has to go to California with me!" Peter Duncan's voice trembled. He's unsettled, Katherine thought wonderingly, because Teddy has bested him in front of his brothers. And he's afraid. He looked from one child to the next. "I'm going to be saving for a home, for all of us," he said. "Soon as I get it we'll all move back together again."

Aunt Nellie nodded briskly. "Of course you will, Peter dear."

"All in good time," Uncle Ian added.

And Aunt Rebecca murmured nervously, "The best of care . . ."

"Things will go real well in California," Katherine heard her father say. "More money down there, more jobs. We'll forget all our hard luck. This time things will be better."

This time . . . The old phrase, the old, old promise that was a lie. Katherine heard it with a feeling of wonder. He was smiling at the younger children, trying to cajole them into smiling back. But they stood in a motionless line, their faces solemn. He reached out to touch them affectionately. Even little Petie ignored his father's hand. He turned away to study the strangers who were to take him home. The silence in the room was heavy.

Peter Duncan faced his eldest daughter. "Well," he said huskily, "we'll let Teddy work on the San Francisco boat, if that's what he wants to do. But we'll go south, Katherine. You and I."

She wanted to cry out—No! I won't be trapped as my mother was, with each year growing wearier, more hopeless. I won't be beaten down to crying, as my mother once cried, "If I could just know, know so sure that nothing could change it, that I could always start the washing on a Monday morning." *He* always knew where the land was rich, the best of it waiting to be claimed. *He* knew where a man could make a fortune, in silver or gold or lumber or cattle. *He* knew the place, the place sunk deep in nowhere, where the houses are elegant and the saloons are cheap and this time everything will be better. In how many crude, heatless cabins had her mother listened to what he knew? How much had his dreams comforted her when she carried the washing down to the river and found nothing more than a dirty trickle?

Of his own accord her father had wrenched from her the only reason for taking her mother's place. The little children, her mother's little children—this round-cheeked little aunt and the thin sparrowy one would tub them and kiss them and see to their buttons. So it was for himself, not for them, that he was pleading. Take care of *me*, his soft gray eyes begged, your mother always did.

Katherine's voice felt thick in her mouth but it came out loudly. "No," she said, facing them all, "I won't go to California."

The words fell into a pool of silence. They echoed soundlessly, like ripples rolling toward the shore. The fixed smiles still fitted tightly over the faces of the relatives. Teddy was grinning widely, for in a way she had vindicated him. The little children were staring at the strangers, clinging to each other's hands.

Finally her father answered. "But I'll be all alone."

Katherine thought, he knows that will get their sympathy. It tells them he is helpless and lonely, that his daughter is selfish. He doesn't say things, her mother had always apologized, unless he honestly believes them. Was this the "honesty" for which her mother had forgiven everything, even his failure?

Then, at last, anger had come to her. She felt it break loose and clung to it triumphantly. Now, now was the time, and it might be short, for she could never stay angry long. Now was the time to defy him, to escape everything she hated and let this split second of frantic courage catapult her so far that she could never turn back. "You ruined my mother's life!" she cried at him. "But you're not going to ruin mine. I'm going to leave. You heard what Teddy said. I'm going to be a schoolteacher. I've always wanted to be a schoolteacher. Mother taught me how. She wanted me to teach school. She didn't want me to be a failure—" Katherine gasped for breath, added wildly, "like you!"

"My, my," plump little Aunt Nellie murmured. Thin Aunt Rebecca pursed her lips and shook her head.

Her father's face was white. "That's no way to talk."

Katherine kept on desperately. "You're taking my mother's children away from me. All you're worried about is who's going to take care of *you!*"

She turned toward Teddy. "He wants someone to *believe* him," she sobbed. "I won't!"

Sounds and faces had blurred together after that. Teddy was hugging her, whispering, "Don't be scared, Katie. I'm going to run away, too." One of the uncles said, "Quite a temper for such a little girl." "She favors her mother," both aunts seemed to say in unison, clicking their tongues. Her father was standing with his back to them all, staring out across the Sound. Felicity dragged Angus by the hand to present him solemnly to Aunt Nellie. "Angus wants to know," her clear voice said," if maybe now he's in the third grade, does he get a pair of shoes?"

Katherine had broken free of Teddy's arm and run from the room. There had been pitifully little to take along, for her few clothes had been lost in the fire. A shawl given to her by a neighbor, her past week's wages from the San Francisco store, a little castoff clothing. She stuffed it all into an old paper sack. While the voices of her aunts and uncles babbled in the next room, Katherine ran out the back door.

That night, for the first time in her life, she had walked into a hotel and asked for a room. The clerk squinted at her curiously. A little girl with red hair hanging down her back, an old shawl over her head and a paper parcel under her arm. She held out a fifty-cent piece. He looked at it, shrugged and took it. As Nate Tarpee had done tonight, he warned her, "Be sure to lock your door."

The night wind was rising. It came in gusts, rattling the poorly fitted windows of the Gold Mountain Hotel. The candle flame flickered and went out. Katherine sighed. In the dark she felt her way from the chair to the washstand and slowly began undressing for bed.

iii

The new day brought Uncle Julian with a riding horse and a set of instructions. He delivered them both absent-mindedly, with a look of perplexity in his pale eyes.

"Miss Duncan, Nils sent over this pony. It's yours." He scratched his head. "Now, let's see. The schoolhouse. That's going to be the old Wright cabin. It's over near the first hop shed. Wright's dead now, they tell me. Don't know what become of his wife. Seems to me she was a cousin to Nils' wife, though maybe not. She was a Klicki-tat. Nils' Mary's purebred Snoqualmie. Wright, he went gold hunting."

"Mr. Bengston has a wife . . ."

The old man's glance sharpened as he peered wisely at Katherine. "It's no wonder you didn't know it. She's over at the Indian camp more than she is at home. And Nils don't talk about her, out of loyalty."

Katherine interrupted briskly. "You were telling me about the schoolhouse, Mr. Sparks."

"Yes, yes . . ." Uncle Julian's old eyes clouded. "Old Wright. Did I say he's likely dead now? He went gold hunting, after Nils bought him out. Died because he couldn't find anything. Or maybe because he did. Who knows?" He chuckled, looked at Katherine apologetically. "I'm an old man, Miss Duncan. I talk too much. Well, now, about where you're to live. The Carlsons'll put you up. They'll have more children in school than any other family in the Valley, so they're bound to help out."

"Who decided that?"

"You sound like you know already." Uncle Julian's old eyes brightened. "Nils, of course."

"Always."

Uncle Julian nodded good-humoredly. "He's the decidingest man in the Valley. That's all right. He decided there'd be a teacher and he decided you'd do. You owe him that much."

Katherine snapped, "I don't care to owe him anything."

Uncle Julian's head went back in a quick, dry laugh. "No, of course not. But my dear young lady, you're going to, anyway. It's Nils who pays the teacher, right out of his own pocket."

"No . . ." Katherine stared at the old man. Nils hated schoolteachers, they had told her. Nils ridiculed schools and said they were made for ugly girls. He could keep the school from opening, they said. Why, then, was he providing the building and paying the teacher, unless it was to add to his power?

"I'll have to live at Carlsons'," she said doggedly, "because I don't know the Valley well enough to find a place by myself. I will *pay* them myself. But I won't take that horse!"

"She's a good little mare."

Katherine shook her head. "I won't accept her."

Uncle Julian's eyes narrowed. "From Nils?"

"Exactly. I don't care for his—manners."

"Ha, ha, ha." The old man's laughter trailed off weakly. "My dear young lady," he said wearily, "neither do I. Nils hasn't got as much manners as a bear has tail. But for some reason he's sent you a horse to ride and I'd take it, if I was you. Except for these little beat-up villages at Gold Mountain and Three Forks and Black River, there isn't a homestead within a mile of the next one. Carlsons live up toward the Pass, a good six miles or more from the schoolhouse. You'll want to get down to see the riverboat come in, too, and that's a good fifteen. On top of that, the woods can be a scary place for a woman, and if she's walking it takes a long time to get of them. On a horse you can let out a scream, close your eyes, grab ahold of the pummel and ride for the clearing."

Katherine looked at him uncertainly.

He winked, a long, slow wink. His shaggy white eyebrows seemed to quiver with it. His nearly toothless mouth was curved into a friendly smile. "After a week of walking, you'll be begging Nils for this horse," he said gently. "Look, daughter, wouldn't it be better to take it now and stay as high and mighty as you please?"

iv

"God bless Richie and Martha and Tom and Susan and Jane and Hiram and John." Jeb Carlson sighed, lifted his head, saw Katherine in the extra place next to the twins and hurriedly remembered his manners. "And bless Miss Duncan." He sat down heavily, as a man does who has been trying to pull stumps all day with only one ox.

The brown-eyed one named Hiram looked solemnly at the girl he had been told would be his teacher. "He almost forgot you," he said. "I wonder what would happen if he did?"

Katherine swallowed her smile. "Happen where?"

Hiram, who was seven, looked at her impatiently, as if he already doubted that she was prepared to teach. "In heaven, of course."

"Faith," Jeb Carlson called down the table, "tell your son not to ask so many questions."

Mrs. Carlson looked up wearily. "Hush, Hiram," she sighed. Her shoulders sagged forward again over the task of cutting up a smaller boy's meat.

"Oh, that's all right," Katherine spoke anxiously. These children were to be her pupils. Considering the number of them, it appeared they were going to be most of her pupils. Only John, who was five, would not be present when she opened school. They were all looking at her now, eyes round and solemn and hopeful. Catching Martha's eyes, Katherine smiled. Martha giggled.

"It is the duty of children," Jeb Carlson's voice roared suddenly from the end of the table, "to keep their eyes down and their mouths closed."

The silence was instant, but lasted only a second. Hiram's voice broke it. "But Pa," he said matter-of-factly, "how can we eat that way?"

Jeb reared to his feet.

"Please, Pa," his wife's voice pleaded.

Jeb sat down, slowly shook his head. "Children are a blessing. It would serve *that* one right if he was blessed with another one just like himself later on."

"Please pass the beans?" Susan's reedy voice seemed to rise to a question. Suddenly conversation was over and eating began.

Roasted smoked venison, new potatoes baked in the coals, white biscuits with wild honey that tasted of red clover, a pudding of dried apples and ground cinnamon. Katherine recognized the unaccustomed plenty. There was even butter on the table, firm from being cooled in the spring behind the cabin. She knew how seldom a family with one cow and seven children had butter on the table. The food was good. In the children's eyes Katherine could read the thought that it was good if only because it was so plentiful.

"Let the food that gives us strength give us strength to follow Thee. Amen."

With the last syllable of their father's final grace, the children swung their legs over the bench and raced for the open door.

"Hiram!"

The square little boy with brown eyes stopped as if reins had been jerked on him. "Yes, Pa."

"What were you whispering during grace?"

"Thank you God for the butter."

Jeb Carlson said, "Well . . ." Then he sighed. "It would be more to my liking if we said one grace at a time. But it was good, wasn't it, Son?"

Hiram nodded, moving experimentally toward the door.

"But you should have bowed your head."

"Pa, I was looking at *her*."

Jeb Carlson glanced quickly at Katherine.

"Let him go, Jeb," Faith Carlson said wearily. "He's only seven."

Hiram disappeared around the corner of the cabin. After him Jeb Carlson went, carrying a bucket. Katherine heard him calling the cow. "Co boss, co boss . . ."

Mrs. Carlson turned to her. She smiled faintly, as if she'd got out of the habit of it. "Hiram isn't the only one, I'll be bound. How old are you, dear? Seventeen?"

Katherine was caught off guard. She was nodding even while she was reminding herself to lie. She smiled. "Yes, seventeen," she said weakly. "But I told them twenty, to get the job."

Mrs. Carlson pursed her lips. "It don't make no difference out here, anyways. After some of the teachers we've had . . ." She hesitated, looked at Katherine, decided to hold her tongue. Nodding to herself she went to the hearth, lifted the steaming teakettle from the iron hook and poured water into a pan. "I don't often talk," she apologized, "but it's a pleasure sometimes. See that teakettle? It's made of copper, hammered by hand. My grandfather made it. My grandmother gave it to me just before we left Ohio. I've lost most everything else we had, but I did keep this kettle."

"How did you lose . . ." Katherine began the question even as she knew the answer. How had her own mother lost so much—her pendants and earrings, first, then her good clothes, cut and sewn by a French dressmaker at the time of her marriage; her cherished pictures and fancy work, and the furniture shipped upriver from New Orleans. And finally her looks, even hope . . . "You lost everything coming west?"

Mrs. Carlson nodded. "Coming west." She laughed suddenly. "Grandma's teakettle saved my life. A sneaking Indian came into our cabin once in Dakota. I hit him over the head with it. We always said if christening alone would do it, I'd turned one redskin into a Christian." She looked expectantly at Katherine, grinning like a naughty boy. "That there teakettle was full of boiling water."

Together they washed and dried the dishes, set a bowl of dough to raise overnight, swept the split cedar floor with a broom of twigs, put potatoes to soak for a new batch of yeast. Mrs. Carlson banked the fire under the blackened coffee pot. "Someday," she said, "I'm going to cook on a stove. They say it really saves your back." She straightened up slowly, her hands behind her pressing against the pain. "You were real helpful, dear. Shall we go outside and set for a while? I always sleep better if I've had a look at the mountain."

They settled themselves on the bench against the cabin wall. Mrs. Carlson's rough, red hands folded contentedly in the hollow of her skirt. "Isn't it beautiful?"

Beautiful—it was hardly a farm wife's word, yet she spoke it naturally. Reluctantly Katherine followed Mrs. Carlson's gaze.

The mountain's rocky dome over four thousand feet above cut up into the darkening sky. Its great bulk hung over them, black where the timber was heavy, pink where the setting sun colored the steep cliffs. The forest that blanketed so much of the Valley continued up the sides of the mountain, but irregularly, as if the huge rock had burst through it, pulling the cover of timber up its sides. As the sun dropped, the light changed and the shadows moved, like clouds changing their shapes before the wind.

"See? It never looks the same twice. I love that mountain." Mrs. Carlson smiled dreamily. "I wish you could have seen the way it looked to us the day we got here.

"We'd come all the way from Dakota. It'd been hot all the way, and so dusty you couldn't spit. We'd had sickness. We'd lost a wagon in one river and our milk cow got stampeded off with a bunch of buffalo. Half the children were sick from eating moldy grits."

She sighed, her eyes on the jagged outline of the mountain top. "When we come through the Pass, we were half-starved, half-dead, and you know what was in harness pulling our covered wagon? One old ox and a yearling heifer. Pray often and shave once a day, that's what Pa kept saying. That's what he did. Jeb's prayers got us through."

"You might say we were lucky, not being the first wagon through the Pass that year. It's only sixty miles but sometimes the first over in the spring take two—three weeks. Every tree that's fallen across the trail has to be cut out to let the wagons through. Either that, or stack branches deep enough on each side of the log so the wagons can drive right over them. And every washout has to be filled in.

"We were lucky, too, to keep our dog, him being such a good hunter. All the wagon trains before us that year had lost every one of their dogs, most often in a certain place where the road makes a switchback up above the south fork of the river. Right there our hound got a scent and took after it. Pa'd heard about trains losing their dogs so he took off right after him. It was a cougar, all right. He was eleven feet long. Pa missed him on the first shot but got him on the second. God was on Pa's side or he wouldn't have got that second shot. He was praying so loud I could hear him way back at the wagon."

She gestured toward the rim of mountains which enclosed the Valley at the east. "From here you can't see the road because of the trees," she said, "and when you come down from the Pass the trees keep you from seeing the mountain. You're coming down so fast the wagon wants to ride up on the ox's rump. They put their feet down with a slide and a jerk, the way a man does going downhill when he takes it all in his knees. You're dead beat and sick and maybe scared, because there's always talk about those eastside Yakimas and how they might send war parties through the Pass. Then suddenly, like stepping out of night into day, you hit the prairie. And there's this mountain, Old Hi, looking over you.

"The river was running along at the foot of it, singing like. The fields were as green as new grass. The trees were in full leaf and the air smelled of wild clover. We'd come two thousand five hundred miles, and all but one of us had lived through trials you'd of thought would kill us every one. There it was.

"I said to Jeb, 'We'll stay right here.'

"He said, 'Faith, we talked of going on to the coast.'

" 'No, Jeb, right here,' I said.

" 'Leastways, we ought to ride on to the settlement. Gold Mountain's only three miles ahead.'

" 'Jeb,' I said, 'I come two thousand and five hundred miles but I just can't make that last three.'

" 'I like it here, anyways,' Jeb says, grinning at me, and so we put our claim in to this very spot right here."

Mrs. Carlson's eyes filled with tears. "I looked up at that big old mountain and I cried and said, 'I didn't think we'd make it, I just didn't think we'd make it.' " She turned to Katherine. *"You* like it here, don't you?"

Katherine felt helpless in the face of such a plea. She hated the place, but could she throw that at a woman who had entrusted her with her love for it? "I want to live in the city," she said, turning away from Faith Carlson's warm, earnest face.

"Oh . . ." Mrs. Carlson's voice flattened as if Katherine had dropped a weight on it. "Then you'll be leaving the Valley as soon as you can. Anyway, try to do a good job of teaching while you're here. It's been hard on the kids, the kind of schooling they've had. One teacher beating them almost to death, the next one running away because the kids beat *him* almost to death. You don't get educated that way." Mrs. Carlson grasped Katherine's arm, shaking it with every word. "Miss Duncan, I want my children to read and write and believe in God!" For a long moment she held Katherine's arm. At last her grip relaxed and she patted Katherine in a motherly way. "Just try and do a good job," she said with a sigh, "even if you don't stay long."

V

Katherine lay with her head toward the open window. The flat shutter of cedar boards, hinged over the opening to be dropped down on cold or rainy days, was propped wide by a

stick of kindling wood. Cool night air poured through the
opening, blowing against her cheek. She pulled the com-
forter up under her chin.

The cabin was of cedar shakes, split by hand. The long
boards were ribbed with the grain, for they had been made
by a man with an adze and a sledge hammer. Those that
had been smoothed showed the cut marks where the draw
knife had bitten into them. A big kitchen with a fieldstone
hearth, a room at each end for sleeping, and out back a
lean-to for firewood and the milch cow—everything was
made by hand, cut from the giant cedars that had once
towered over the pasture land. Katherine touched the
rough wall gently, running the tips of her fingers with the
rough grain. The homestead house was two years old, but it
still had the sweet spice smell of cedar.

In bed with her was Martha. Across the room, but so
near she could hear their breathing, were the twins, Susan
and Jane. The boys were tucked into the other room with
the Carlsons, the smallest in a trundle that pulled out from
the larger bed. And they were all asleep. The night air
was heavy with sleep.

But Katherine was wakeful. Martha, sleeping beside her,
was her pupil. Across the room there were two more pupils. They already worshipped her, as she could remember
worshipping nearly every teacher she had ever had. They
promised this worship with every sigh and solemn glance
of their big eyes.

Thoughts at night are so different from thoughts in daytime—Katherine wished them away. Thinking alone in the
dark is like dreaming with a fever.

Carl will be back on Monday. I will leave on Monday,
Katherine thought. There is no contract, no promise to
keep me here. Nils Bengston himself has said he didn't
want me.

Martha's thin body rolled against her. Katherine pulled back, resenting the touch. And then she sighed, a sigh as shaking as a sob. Gently she reached over and caressed the little girl's head.

i

The schoolhouse had been a homestead cabin. It was small, because the man who built it had spent his strength on a two-thousand-mile wagon trip from Dakota and could think of nothing but abiding by the rules of the Homestead Act and getting in out of the rain.

His wife had insisted on a rough plank floor and two windows with split-cedar shutters. These were the adornments. The hearth where a lonely woman from Dakota once cooked had long since crumbled away. Chimney and fire pot had fallen together in a heap of stone as the clay which bound them gave way to the weather. The great cedars overshadowing the cabin had been cut, dragged by ox to the river, rafted, pushed down a chute beside the Falls and steered to Smith's mill at Black River. Around the cabin now were the civilized hop rows. Poles as tall as young saplings lined up in columns so long the ends of them melted together in the distant haze. The vines crawled to the top of them, spilling over with the weight of the ripening pods. In the wind the hop leaves rustled, whispering.

Such was the "school," Katherine thought, which Nils Bengston allows to exist. Only one concession had been made. There were three benches, narrow, splintery and backless, but still long enough to seat ten children apiece. And there were tables, matching the benches in length and roughness. Some former teacher whom Nils had "allowed" and then for some reason ceased to tolerate had abandoned a large slate.

Katherine inspected the school carefully. She had spent two days riding from one homestead to another, announcing the opening of school and listing the pupils. Three days remained before the morning she had designated as opening day. Alone in the dusty cabin, with the sun shining peacefully and her pony grazing in the clearing, she felt secure. The spirit of Nils Bengston might whisper, I've provided the school, I've hired you as its teacher. Now go ahead with the childish nonsense or quit and admit it's as childish as I say it is. But the days and hours which had yet to pass protected her. Thus far she had won, because the hour had not come when she might lose.

Like a good housewife, Katherine looked around to see what must be done. Eventually the hearth would have to be rebuilt, or they would all be too cold to study. As for school supplies, there were none. If former teachers had used books during their short tenures in the Valley, the books had disappeared as hastily as they had, and as completely.

The cobwebs were thick. Their dainty lacework sagged
with a burden of dust. But they hid no readers or geog-
raphies or spellers. Chalk, pencils, papers, maps, tablets,
all the physical bits and pieces of the schoolroom Katherine
loved the very feel of—they would have to come later.
First there was soap and water.

Katherine pushed back her sleeves, knotting them securely around her elbows. Picking up the bucket she had
brought from Carlsons', she walked to the river. There
was danger in worrying about how to teach a dozen strange
children with nothing but a jagged piece of slate and a
headful of untried ideas. But I don't have to do it right
now, she told herself. At this moment, at this very exact little moment alone at the schoolhouse in the sunshine, I
don't have to think about anything but scrubbing the floor.

She worked rapidly. There was peace simply in the
quickness of movement, in concentrating so thoroughly on
each lift of the arm and bend of the back. She carried the
crumbled hearth outside, stone by stone. With a handful
of sword fern she swept down the heavy cobwebs. She
whipped the soft soap into a fine suds, even in cold river
water, and scrubbed the tables and benches. The world
which had always seemed too big grew smaller as she
worked.

She began to hum. In a moment she was singing, keeping
time with each forward push on the scrub cloth. She hardly
thought of Monday. The schoolhouse was damp and soapy-
smelling, the benches and tables were in place and the slate
propped into position at the front of the room. The work
was done and Katherine had dumped the last bucket of
water and rolled her sleeves down before she remembered
that Monday was also the day Carl White was to return.

"I'll be back Monday," he had said. "I'll take you back to
Seattle then."

How could she have forgotten that promise, to which she

had clung so desperately during that first long night in Gold Mountain? In a week, Monday had become only Opening Day, the day she became what everyone in the Valley had called her from the first—Teacher. It was a title, as "General" or "Captain" or "Lawyer" was a title. Taking her hands in his, Carl White had promised to save her from this.

Katherine stopped humming. She had been singing one of her mother's favorite songs, but suddenly she couldn't remember what it was called. She dropped the hard maple bar across the school door, and unhitched the pony's reins from the alder limb. Wearily she pulled herself into the saddle. She hadn't felt tired until now.

ii

From the doorway Katherine studied the clearing around the school. Pride and panic tore her. She saw there were more children here than she had listed and certainly twice what she had expected. She had gulped down Mrs. Carlson's black coffee and wheat mush, and ridden out while the dew was still heavy on the prairie grass and the woods were cold and dark as night. Hours early, she had thought, but three little children had been earlier. The towheaded Andersons, Tillie and Judy, and their little brother Lars. They watched her owlishly as she propped the shutters open. They followed her from bench to doorway to yard. With self-conscious briskness she straightened things she had already put to rights and tidied where nothing could be more clean.

Soon other children came. Most of them rode ponies, two or three children to a horse. They gathered in the rough open space which the hop rows still ceded to the school. They whispered, pointed, giggled. When Katherine gained courage to approach them, they ran like fawns, peering at her silently from around the corners of the schoolhouse. She retired to the cabin, trying to walk casually, yet with so straight a back that they could not feel she was retreating. And there she remained.

At last the watch Mrs. Carlson had pinned to her blouse read half-past eight. It was time for school. The voices outside were shrill with excitement. Daring had come with the appearance of some older boys. With teacher at a safe distance, the meekest was a lion and the weak attacked the strong with impartial enthusiasm. Eight or ten children were wrestling, in lightly chosen groups of two and three.

Besides the watch, Mrs. Carlson had given Katherine a cow bell. Katherine picked it up, walked deliberately to the door. Her pulse was wild, as if beating time to the thoughts she had told herself to remember. Show no fear. Demand respect. Keep calm. She lifted the bell, brought her arm down with one great, determined sweep. The sound startled her. She blinked but kept swinging.

When she stopped, the schoolyard seemed paralyzed. The children were standing as they had been caught by the sudden clangor, staring at her speechlessly. The wrestlers looked up, still tangled together in the dirt. The big boys still leaned against the cabin, observing everything, mocking everything. Mouths were open with the last shout, fists were clenched for the last fight.

Gratefully, Katherine picked out the Carlson children. "Hiram," she said clearly, for the other names she had known so well at breakfast had fled her mind. "Hiram, would you please lead the line into the schoolroom? The others will follow, one at a time."

The little square boy named Hiram bounced forward, his round brown face twisted with a wide grin. Looking proudly from right to left, he marched toward the door. No one moved. At the door he turned, waving both arms like windmill blades in a cyclone. "Well, come on," he squeaked. "Or your ma'll give you a licking when you get home."

Miraculously the line formed. The children marched in. Even the big boys followed, two of them so tall they looked down on Katherine as they passed.

She had planned this day. She had lived through it a dozen times during sleepless nights beside Martha. She closed the door behind the last pupil. The wooden thud of door against frame hung in the hollow silence. A sigh shuddered through her body. She fought it down, and saw that her fists were clenched hard. Painfully she relaxed them. It was time to face the school, and herself as teacher. She turned around.

"Good morning, children," she said. Her voice was level, but a little too high. "We'll begin the day with the Lord's Prayer."

Several voices were distinct as they recited it. Several were puzzled. Their faces turned from one side to the other, their eyes lingering anxiously on the moving lips of others. All but the biggest boy mumbled dutifully and kept heads bowed.

"Now, the roll call. We will start over here. Each one stand in turn and give his name."

As each child rose to speak, Katherine nodded. "Thank you," she said quietly, writing the name into the notebook under "Present." Tommy Tine—that must be Agatha Tine's son. The Carlson children—Richie, Martha, Tom, Susan, Jane, Hiram—and right beside him, five-year-old Johnny, whom she had been too muddled to notice before.

"My brother wants to go to school, too," Hiram piped up hurriedly.

"He's only five, isn't he?"

"But he's smart!" Hiram's brown eyes were earnest.

"He should be six. Five is too young."

"I'm seven. I'm just starting. You didn't say I couldn't come because I was too *old*."

"He may stay," Katherine said weakly. "Next, please."

Bertha and Bobby Smith. The three identical Andersons —she had seen two at their homestead, but their round, pink faces were so much alike she couldn't tell which was the extra child. Then the Stump children, with hollow cheeks and a kind of hopelessness in their eyes. Sammy, Gerald, Susie and three smaller ones who whispered their names so fearfully she could not hear. Levi Barker—he was one of the taller boys, and he kept off by himself, surveying her solemnly from the end of the farthest bench. Liza Tarpee, eleven years old with pigtails. Emil Greene, who looked twenty. The last was a little, dark-eyed girl. She had been in the schoolyard, of course. At the end of a bench she sat quiet as a frightened grouse. "Julie," she said softly, as she took her turn. "Julie Bengston."

Katherine saw the darkness of her skin, the dull blackness of her thick braids. And yet her eyes were blue. Despite herself, Katherine thought—as blue as her father's. No other Indian or half-breed had thought to come to school. Only Nils Bengston's daughter would have come, to take her place among children whose parents scorned the "Siwash," to go to school while the hops were being picked.

"Julie Bengston," Katherine forced herself to repeat it. The little girl was watching her solemnly. She is so quiet, Katherine thought, so watchful. Even here at school Nils has his own way of being present.

iii

To Katherine the day had gone well, simply because it was almost over. The list of activities she had recited for so many days had not forsaken her. The picture she had formed of herself as teacher, standing before a roomful of respectful children, with praise for one and a deserved sharp word for another—the truth wasn't too ridiculous compared with it.

Even the complications of her own feelings hadn't kept her from being teacher. The sight of Emil Greene, who had only last week stoned her horse into running away with her. The little half-Indian girl Julie. The memory of Faith Carlson's hopeful smile begged her not to desert them. The room was barren and bookless, but she had managed to be teacher, anyway.

"I'll teach you another song. Everyone stand, please."

The girls jumped to their feet obediently, grinning for approval. The boys looked from side to side, hesitated a moment, then awkwardly followed.

> "It was upon a high, high hill,
> Two maidens chose their dwelling,
> And one was known both far and wide,
> Was known as Barb'ra Allen . . ."

Katherine sang it slowly, as her mother had always sung it and as her grandmother had taught it to her. The children watched, their eyes wide.

"Now slowly, from the beginning."

The children's voices followed hers, resting tipsily on some notes, falling hard on others. "It was upon a high, high hill . . ."

The school door swung open, hitting so hard against the wall that bits of dry bark and dirt fell in a cloud to the floor. Nils Bengston, the man who had laughed at her, stood in the doorway with his hands in his pockets.

Katherine stared at him despairingly. She had made herself teacher in a day. She had created order and found comfort in it. But here he stood, the man who mocked a schoolteacher and yet paid her out of his own pocket. Suddenly she felt bare, helpless and a little angry.

His big hands rested easily on his hips, the thumbs hooked over the trouser pockets. Ignoring Katherine, he turned his head slowly to survey the room. His blue eyes flickered as they rested on one child and then another. The children didn't move. Teacher and classroom were held immobile. He was in command, and the easy slope of his shoulders showed that he knew it. But he wasn't laughing now.

"Go on home!" he said suddenly. "All of you. Go on. Get!"

The motionless, silent children broke loose like a herd of frightened colts. Without a questioning glance at their teacher, they pushed past each other to the door. Four or five were already shouting in the schoolyard before Katherine recovered herself. She walked stiffly, but quickly, to the door, and turned her back to it. "I have not dismissed school," she said, fighting to keep her voice level. "Go back to your places, children."

The children hesitated. Right in front of her, so close the dry dung smell of his clothing swept down on her, was the big Greene boy. His eyes were surly but uncertain. Pressing against her skirt was little Johnny Carlson, who had begun to squeeze by but now suddenly reached for her hand, as if she might lead him to safety. The Stump children stared fearfully at Nils Bengston. Solemn as a preacher, little Julie Bengston looked on, waiting.

"I said, school is over. All through for today, and to-morrow, and the day after that." Nils menaced the crowding children with a gesture of his arm. They squeezed more tightly together, pushed harder against Katherine. His voice was low but cold. "No more school for a month and maybe not then. Now get out of this shack and run home or I'll sell every one of you to the Yakimas."

Their open mouths and scared eyes said it wasn't true, but they stampeded anyway. The Greene boy and Johnny Carlson and all crushed against Katherine, ripping her fingers loose from the door jamb.

"You'll get hurt, teacher," Nils Bengston said flatly.

Katherine looked at him numbly. But I won't move, she promised herself bitterly. I just won't move.

The Greene boy put his hands out to push her aside. His fingers had only grazed her shoulders when Nils Bengston picked him up by the shirt collar and the seat of the pants and threw him against the wall. Nils turned back to Katherine. "Didn't you know," he said quietly, "that you're not as big as he is?"

The Greene boy struggled to his feet. Whimpering loudly he crouched against the wall. Katherine stared at Nils. There was a hard knot in her throat and she was trembling. She noted crazily that his brows and lashes were very dark for so blond a man and that he had a long, thin scar along his jawline. Slowly, in the slow motion of a bad dream, she stepped away from the door.

The children fell out of the room. At the door the Greene boy turned to stick his tongue out at her, then vanished with a heathen yell. The schoolyard cleared.

"Yi, yi!" the oldest Smith child shrieked, whipping up the pony on which the three of them sat. The horse wheeled and disappeared down the trail. "Yi, yi!" came back from the distance, mingling with the faint clatter of hooves on the gravelly riverbank. Only little Julie Bengston remained. She walked past her father without a word. Her face smooth of expression, she crossed the yard and took a place near her father's horse. There she squatted, looking the other way.

"Aahh . . ." Nils Bengston exhaled deeply. He turned away from Katherine, as if there were no longer any necessity of facing her. "Miss Duncan, you started your school too soon. You can open it next month when the hops are in."

His tone was matter-of-fact. Katherine found her head clearing. As flatly as he, she replied, "If children are kept out of school to pick hops, they can be kept out to trap furs, or bring in the hay, or help with the butchering. In the end they are lucky to get three months of school a year."

"That's school enough for boys," Nils said easily, "and three times too much for girls." He looked appraisingly at the benches, the walls, the floors. "Quite a hard-working little housekeeper, aren't you? The shack looks tidy enough for church. At least, I suppose it does. Last time I was in church my mother carried me in her arms. They'd never have got me into the place if I'd been any bigger." He grinned, pleased with his joke.

Katherine's resentment sharpened. "I opened school today because it is the proper time to do it," she said in a voice which sounded three times louder than her own. "I will keep it open."

Nils continued to study the vista of hops. She waited, her chin higher than it need be and her back so straight it ached. At last he turned slowly to face her. He was still smiling. He shook his head. "No," he said quietly, "next month."

"No one person has the right to rule the lives of everyone else! Keep your own child away from school if you wish, but let the other parents decide such things for themselves."

Nils frowned. "Don't be a nuisance, Miss Duncan. For a week I've been looking for more hop-pickers. The crop is heavier than anyone had figured and every five, ten, or a dozen who might be picking and aren't are making it harder for me. So there's nothing for anyone to decide. I decided already." He laughed suddenly. "Julie will be here, though. Julie don't pick hops. So you and she can keep the school open, if you want."

Katherine could feel anger pounding in her throat. "Mr. Bengston," she said, "I understand you own a large part of this valley. I've been told that you are a very powerful man. I've been reminded that you pay my wages out of your own pocket and I'd better do exactly as you say. But I'm a schoolteacher, Mr. Bengston. You don't own *me*."

"I wouldn't know what to do with you," he said, grinning, "if I did."

Katherine gasped involuntarily. Mockery was the hardest blow of all. "This week I rode to every homestead and talked to most of the mothers and fathers in the Valley. They want their children to go to school, whatever your wishes may be. They promised me."

"And what would all their promises mean," Nils said quietly, "if I asked them to promise something different?"

"I'll go around to each one of them again!" Katherine's voice rose in desperation. "I'll tell them the school *is* open!"

Nils studied her silently. "You're not yet twenty," he said, "or I'm a poor judge. But a woman don't even have to be full size to be a troublemaker. This school is a little thing to me, Miss Duncan. I could have the building tore down tonight, if I wanted to. The riverboat's due in Black River and I could have you put on that and taken back to Seattle if I wanted to, too. But I've got plenty on my mind and I don't want to be bothered." He walked past her to the door. As if it were an afterthought, he turned and added, "Just remember, though, that I can get rid of you any time you start to get too pesky. So you let me do the deciding around here or you'll be out of the Valley before Thanksgiving."

The tears, the cursed, give away tears, were beginning to come now. Katherine shook her head desperately. She had meant to reply angrily that he couldn't send her back to Seattle, because Carl White was coming and she was leaving that very night anyway. Leaving the gloomy, wild, tree-covered Valley and the dark mountains pressing down on it. Leaving the leering Greene boy and the blue-eyed Indian girl, the Nelsons, Carlsons, Stumps and Smiths, and Mrs. Carlson with her worship of Old Hi and the pain she wouldn't admit. Leaving them all, with Carl White at her side to help her.

"Maybe someday you'll learn that the people here aren't like so many children you can lock up in the woodshed!" she sobbed. "I'm not only going to stay right here and teach school, but inside of two years I'm going to see that a real schoolhouse is built. You won't own the building, and you won't own the land that it's on. It will have books and tablets and pencils, and you won't own them, either! It will be a *real* school!"

Nils' eyes brightened with surprise. And then he shrugged. Like an Indian on the hunt, he walked soundlessly across the clearing, picked Julie up and placed her carefully behind the saddle. He didn't spend a glance on Katherine as he mounted and rode away.

Katherine closed her eyes, forgetting even now to wipe away the tears. She heard a sound and opened them. Hiram Carlson was standing before her, looking curiously at her face.

"I was hiding behind that cedar tree," he explained. "But I didn't know you were going to cry."

Katherine groped for the edge of her skirt, pulling it up roughly to wipe her eyes.

"He's big, isn't he?" Hiram reflected. "Bigger'n Pa. He must be twice as big as you are. Miss Duncan, can I ride home behind your saddle like Julie does?"

Katherine nodded fiercely. "I'll have to close up the school," she whispered. With a feeling that there had never been anything else to do about it, she made her big decision. More loudly, she added, "and straighten up for school tomorrow." Hiram took her hand. With the little boy silent beside her, teacher arranged the benches, closed the door and shutters, and barred the door securely on the first day of her teaching.

iv

Carl's hand reached instinctively for Katherine's, then hastily retreated. From vantage points at the other side of the clearing, two or three Carlson children were watching eagerly. There might be others in the cabin behind them. He brought his hands to his sides. "If it's a question of the fare. . ."

Katherine shook her head. "I hadn't even thought of that. Though it's true. I don't have enough money for the trip to Seattle."

"If you're hesitating because you don't have a position or a place to stay . . ."

Katherine smiled. "I should apologize to you," she said softly. "Because I haven't even thought of those things, either."

"Katherine . . ."

She looked up at him curiously. He had spoken her name so earnestly, throwing aside the little game of politeness they had enjoyed together. In real life you don't live by rules, she realized suddenly, you live by situations. And so he is calling me by my first name, as I have thought of him almost from the first. "Yes, Carl."

They looked into each other's faces. They were properly separated by at least two feet of the Carlsons' rough cedar bench, and more than properly chaperoned by a half dozen interested Carlson children. No one, Katherine thought, no one in the world can say I'm not being a perfect lady. No one need know how inadequate such ladylikeness seems to me now.

"Yes, Carl," she repeated, forcing herself to look down at her hands.

"Then you won't take the *Viking* tomorrow?"

"Not tomorrow," Katherine said slowly. "I don't feel I can leave right now. I've been here only a week."

"But isn't that enough?"

"Enough?" Katherine echoed the question uncertainly. Yes, of course it had been more than enough. And yet at the end of it she had shouted at Nils Bengston that in two years she would have her own schoolhouse. How could she explain that to Carl? She sighed. "I'll stay," she said, "for a while."

"Some day I'll have something better to offer you," Carl spoke jerkily, as if he were bowing at the same time. "I'm sorry I don't right now."

Katherine flushed. The implications were almost too serious to be thought of. Life in Seattle, where a lady walked on planked sidewalks and kept her skirts out of the dirt. Churches and schools and houses with glass windows.

"Will you come to the town meeting tonight?" she asked quickly.

Carl nodded. "If you'll let me accompany you."

Katherine looked at him wonderingly. His speech was too perfect. It left her groping for the perfect answer. She nodded. How handsome he is, she thought. So much finer a type than Nils Bengston.

"Would it be all right," Carl said huskily, "to take a walk?"

Katherine heard the plea in his voice and felt her color deepen. It seemed as if this were a play in which all the other actors knew their lines but her own had escaped her.

She managed to nod. She rose, smoothed her skirts and put her arm through his. He withdrew at her touch as if the intimacy shocked him. As quickly he pulled her arm hard against his side.

They walked in trembling silence, across the clearing, past the woodshed, into the dark clump of willows along the riverbank. The action of the play came alive in Katherine's mind. She saw them strolling together, knew how solemn and adoring his eyes were, knew, as Carl stopped, that he would put his hands on her shoulders, lift her chin, kiss her. His mouth was on hers. She submitted anxiously, placing her hands gently at the back of his head.

Carl stepped back. "Please," he said stiffly, "please accept my humble apologies."

Katherine nodded. He was correct, of course. She should be grateful to him for pretending she had resisted. But the taste of the kiss lingered on her mouth, and even deeper was the feeling of what another could have been. She was trembling, and prayed he wouldn't notice. The lady of the play came forward and spoke for her. "Shall we go back to the cabin?" she said primly. "The meeting will begin soon."

They walked with arms at their sides, a casual distance between them. Carl's eyes were cloudy, but Katherine saw in them only a gentlemanly degree of shame and a much greater sense of his own propriety. He is always so *right*, she thought enviously. He belonged to the world I've always peered at from the outside. But with every solemn step, Katherine's mind played traitor to her, and whispered, why, oh why, did he apologize?

Nils was amused by the sight of Uncle Julian calling the meeting to order. The old goat, Nils thought, sitting up there on Nate Tarpee's stool and banging the store counter with his fists. The old man's eyes watered heavily as he blinked at the crowd. The perfect judge, Nils thought. At his age he won't know one side from the other.

The lobby of the hotel and trading post was filling up. Benches had been placed in rows facing the counter. Nils was proud to have thought of that, for it gave the whole affair an official look. Flour barrels and coffee sacks and stacks of cured skins and kegs of nails and drums of kerosene had been pushed to the side. The round-bellied wood stove remained alone among the alien benches. The two or three sodden prospectors who usually killed the day in chairs along the wall had been shaken from their posts and were standing in the doorway, hands in pockets and hats jammed down over their ears, staring suspiciously at the unusual crowd. Women! their sharp little eyes said. Farm women were sitting in the store at eight o'clock at night with their good bonnets on and their hands folded proper in their laps.

"Town meeting?" one of the men shrilled at Nils. "I bet I had more fun at a funeral."

Nils leaned back, his powerful shoulders resting lightly against the wall. Uncle Julian was looking his way, no doubt wondering when to begin. Nils shook his head. The Carlsons weren't here yet, and their pesky little boarder. It wasn't his plan to hold the meeting without them and he was sure they'd come. "Important town meeting," he had told Jeb Carlson as he rode from homestead to homestead late that day. "It's your duty to come." Duty—that was the word that would bring the Carlsons. And that little green-eyed schoolmarm, too. In all her life, Nils reflected wryly, I bet she's never done anything just because she wanted to.

At last Jeb and Faith Carlson walked in. Right behind them was Carl White. Nils saw him holding the door wide with one arm and knew even before she appeared that the schoolteacher had come, too. Katherine Duncan entered slowly, holding her skirt with two fingers of each hand.

Her reddish hair piled on top of her head was half covered with a shawl. I know where your hat is, Nils thought to himself. You'll be leaving soon. I'll remember to give it to you.

The man at Nils' elbow whispered, "Is that her?"

"You know everyone else in the room. What a brainy cuss you are, Tommy, to figure that out."

"I just wanted to be sure."

"Good. I'm sure, too. Sure that the best part of making you a schoolteacher is that I won't have you around as a foreman." Nils caught Uncle Julian's watery eye. The old man's eyebrows rose. Nils nodded.

"Aahh," said Uncle Julian, loudly. "Ah, well . . ."

The assembly looked at him patiently. He wet his lips. As if surprised to find them wet, he brushed them with the back of his hand. The room was as still as an old well. "Silence, please," Uncle Julian said. He blinked at Nils, his head cocked a little to the side as if he were trying to hear some whispered instructions. "Friends," he said, "we are gathered here tonight . . ."

Nils leaned back, watching the faces as old Julian spoke. Though we are far from being an incorporated town, he was saying, we must look forward to the time when we are a real town. We must act, as townspeople do, together.

Several listeners nodded vigorously. Other faces were stiff with suspicion. They know who's behind this, Nils thought. But let them.

"We must join in our common purpose, dedicated to our common future . . ."

Wonderful words the old man knows, Nils reflected, when he warms up. But will he remember what I told him at supper tonight?

"The future of our children . . . The sanctity of . . . ah . . ." Uncle Julian blinked. He's coasting downhill

and almost at the bottom, Nils thought. Uncle Julian
sucked in a long breath. "We are here tonight," he said rapidly, "to meet the new schoolteacher."

Nils saw Katherine Duncan start and then control herself. He saw a surprised smile flicker across her face. Everyone in the room was looking at her. She turned to Carl,
murmuring a question. Uncle Julian looked dreamily
around the room, his thoughts a thousand miles or fifty
years away. Mrs. Carlson patted Katherine Duncan's arm,
"Well, now, dear, that is nice, isn't it?"

The time had come. Nils pushed his back away from the
wall and walked to the front of the room.

"Uncle Julian has made quite a speech," he said geni-
ally. "But it seems like he come to the end of it. So I'll help
him out. Folks, meet the new schoolteacher." With a sweep
of his big hand he indicated the young man who had been
at his side. "Tommy Hutchins."

There was a moment of frozen immobility. It broke, and
everyone swiveled to stare at the young man. Tommy
Hutchins smiled nervously. Nils saw Katherine Duncan's
white face, its primness shattered by disbelief. Carl put his
hand on her arm, and spoke to her. Her mouth tightened,
and she shook her head.

"What're you up to, Nils?" It was the voice of three-
hundred-pound Agatha Tine and it was pitched as if she
were calling the cows.

"Katherine, please let me take you out of here . . ."

Low as it was, Carl's plea carried across the room. But
still the girl was shaking her head. Nils grinned and faced
Agatha. "I'm seeing to it that the children of this Valley
have a schoolteacher."

Faces turned questioningly to Katherine Duncan. Seconds passed, and still she didn't move. They gave her up
and began to talk together.

Jeb Carlson got to his feet. "See here, Nils," he said awkwardly, "from all I heard so far people hereabouts are well enough satisfied with the teacher we already got."

Nils nodded. Young Tommy Hutchins was twitching at the back of the room, the color high in his face. Nils ignored him and said, "I'm glad to hear that. But I'm not sure Miss Duncan is as satisfied with us."

Katherine's head jerked up. For the first time Nils saw life come to her eyes. Jeb Carlson looked down at her, his face clearly puzzled. "Well, I . . ." he began, and sat down.

"Tommy, come up here and be introduced." Nils waved imperiously. The young man squeezed past the benches and faced the crowd.

"You all know Tommy," Nils said. "He's been around for a year. Tommy's got an extra fine education. Finished a year of high school in Port Angeles, he tells me. He's working at the ranch during the harvest but he'll be looking for a job after that."

Katherine Duncan's wide eyes were back on Nils' face. They looked black in her pale face. She's scared off, Nils thought, just as I knew she'd be.

"Being a man," Nils said deliberately, "Tommy is better fit for teaching, too. He don't look it but he can pick up a grizzly and hit a she-cougar over the head with it." Nils laughed. Several men echoed him, grinning at Tommy. Nils saw that Tommy was succeeding in meeting all eyes except those of the little schoolmarm. "So," Nils concluded, dropping the easygoing manner, "Mr. Hutchins will open the Gold Mountain school, the first Monday *after* the hops are picked."

The room was utterly still. Faces showed disagreement but no resistance. They don't like it, Nils thought, but they know who's paying, so as long as the teacher keeps still they don't even know how to protest. He felt disdain for their weakness. Pious and spineless, he thought. They were made to be pushed around.

Agatha stirred. "Well, if that's all there is to it, someone better go out front and give my horses the bad news that it's time they pulled me home." Grunting she got to her feet, rubbed her stomach and surveyed the group. "I will say this, though, before I go. If I was that little Miss Duncan, I'd be glad to leave a place where there wasn't one single mother or father that would get to their feet and speak for me."

"You talk too much, Agatha," Nils said. "If Miss Duncan had wanted to, she could have spoken for herself."

"I think I will!"

It was a weak voice, and not a very steady one. Nils wheeled around. Katherine Duncan was standing up, her back as stiff as an English general's. At the school she had cried, as a proud but angry child cries, bitter with shame at his own tears. But her eyes were dry now, and so big and bright they seemed to eat up her face. Nils was amused. Carl White put a high price on outside polish. What would he think of his sweetheart if she raised a ruckus?

"Miss Duncan?"

Nils knew she would ignore him. He grinned as she turned her back to him and faced the open-mouthed homesteaders.

"I have taught school in Gold Mountain for just one day," she said. "You are the parents of the children I taught. Is there any one of you who is dissatisfied with what I've done so far?"

The women shook their heads energetically. The men who owed Nils money or back rent or hayseed looked uncomfortably from the little teacher to Nils. Nils thought, how they wish they'd never come. Agatha Tine, upright as a new silo and just about as round, blurted out, "Dear, you done fine."

Nils leaned back on his heels and pushed his hands into his pockets. It was time to take the meeting back into his own hands. "I'm a parent," he said softly, "and I ain't satisfied."

Katherine looked at him squarely. "The parent of one child. But Mrs. Anderson is here, and she has three children in school. Here is Mrs. Carlson and Mrs. Smith, with nine school children between them."

Nils nodded. You never can tell about the little ones, he thought admiringly. "These Kansas farmers believe in planting often."

He watched her face for the color he knew would come to it. Little Miss Prissy, he thought, wanting to laugh out loud. Go ahead and talk. Everyone in the room but you knows how useless it is.

"I think the majority should decide."

From out of his daydream old Uncle Julian echoed fuzzily, "The majority . . . yes, the majority . . ."

Mrs. Carlson said, "She's doing fine. She should stay."

Carl pulled on Katherine's sleeve. "There is really no use . . ."

Nils felt a flash of irritation at the way Carl's hand fell so possessively on the teacher's arm. "You're right, Carl," he said curtly. "You always know when to give up."

Carl's eyes darkened. "This is a ridiculous meeting, Nils."

"You're right again," Nils snapped. He had expected to enjoy the evening, and except for Carl's presence, he had. "Let's end it." And he brought his fist down on the counter.

"Just a minute."

The teacher had pulled free of Carl's anxious grasp. She was standing with her arms across her breast, like a farm woman facing up to the mortgage owner.

"You called these people together, Mr. Bengston," she

said. "Was it some kind of a joke, or do they have something to say about who their teacher is to be?"

Nils' annoyance at Carl lingered. "I'm paying the teacher," he said flatly, "and I never buy anything I don't want."

Katherine gasped. Instantly Nils felt better. Looking at her white face and the funny, stubborn set to her jaw, he even felt like laughing. Surely she'd had enough. Now she can leave in a huff, all bristling with righteousness and hurt feelings, and Carl will be right there to tell her she was right. And to kiss that childlike mouth of hers. "Well?" he asked irritably.

"Well, well?" Uncle Julian muttered, peering toward the door as if he thought they might have moved it since he last walked through.

Katherine breathed deeply. "Mr. Bengston, I need the job."

Nils shrugged. "And so," with a gesture of the thumb over his shoulder, "does Mr. Tommy Hutchins."

"It was my understanding that I was to receive fifty dollars a month, for every month the school was open."

Nils grinned. "Have you figured out what I owe you for today?"

Her eyes sparked but she continued levelly. "I assume Mr. Hutchins has been promised the same sum."

"He's worth it."

"But you would like to spend less for—for a school teacher." Katherine turned so as to address everyone in the room. "*I* will do an equal amount of work for forty-five dollars a month."

Little exclamations rippled across the crowd. Uncle Julian murmured. "When I was a boy in western Pennsylvania . . ." Tommy Hutchins said, "Look, Nils, I thought you said this afternoon that the thing would be all settled before we came."

Nils grinned mightily. This wasn't what he had planned but this was good. "It was, Tom, it was. Only thing is, that girl has gone and unsettled it." He stepped aside and with one big hand pushed Tommy Hutchins forward. "You're the one who wants the job," he said, enjoying himself thoroughly. "Go ahead and bid for it."

The faces moved curiously from Katherine to Tommy Hutchins. "In western Pennsylvania," Uncle Julian began chasing the shadow of an old memory.

Tommy Hutchins pulled himself up. "I would teach for forty-two fifty if I got room and board with it."

"Forty dollars a month," Katherine flashed, so quickly the heads hadn't turned her way, "and room and board."

Tommy Hutchins looked at Nils. Nils shrugged, keeping his eye on Katherine. "Well," he said to Tommy out of the corner of his mouth, "what are you going to say now?"

Mrs. Carlson pulled Katherine down and whispered in her ear. Tommy opened his mouth to speak, but Katherine spoke first. "Forty without board and room," she said quickly. "I'll work for the board at Carlson's."

Tommy Hutchins stammered, "Thirty-eight dollars a month, but that's only because I need a job."

"So do I!" Katherine retorted. "Thirty-seven dollars and fifty cents!"

Tommy looked to Nils, but Nils' face was blank. The Carlsons and Smiths and Andersons were whispering and taking no pains to hide their smiles. Agatha was patting her stomach as if she'd just enjoyed an entire roast grouse. One of the loggers was chewing hard and looking about uneasily for a place to spit. Tommy tapped Nils' arm. Nils ignored it, studying the ceiling.

Katherine's voice was louder now. Like a man who runs the last few steps up the mountain, for fear he won't get to the top, Nils thought. "Am I to understand," she said, "that I am to be the teacher at Gold Mountain?"

Tommy looked sullenly at Nils. Nils grinned. "Well, is she, Tommy?"

"I guess she is . . ."

The voices broke loose. Everyone pushed to his feet. A bench fell backward and hit the floor with a splintering crash. Some walked out without a word to anyone, still wondering what they had come for. Others collected in a friendly group around Katherine and one by one shook her hand. At the door they turned back.

To see how I'm taking it, Nils thought, and the laughter that had been begging for release all through the meeting poured from his throat. Hands in pockets, he laughed until the last shocked face had turned away and the last good farmer's wife had pulled down her bonnet and departed. Then he turned to Tommy Hutchins.

"Man," he exclaimed, "you let her take your job away for fifty cents a month."

Tommy said stiffly, "I didn't like the way things were going."

"Neither did I!" Nils roared. "Neither did I!" and he laughed some more.

Tommy hurried out of the empty store. Nils beckoned to Uncle Julian. "Let's go home, old man."

Uncle Julian nodded. "That's the first time I ever saw you let someone else take things out of your hands."

"You have your sharp spells, don't you?" Quite suddenly Nils felt bored and tired. "I could have sent her packing. Maybe sometime I will."

"Heh, heh . . ." The old man wheezed when he laughed, making a sound like a child pumping a broken reed organ. "But you didn't."

Nils strode silently through the door, the old man at his heels. Uncle Julian was a nuisance and that smooth-faced Carl White was a nuisance and this whole affair of the school was a stupid way for a man with the biggest hop ranch in the world to spend his time. In the street he loosed the reins from the peeled log that served as a hitching post. He could see the Carlsons' wagon, disappearing to the east. Carl and his sweetheart, he thought peevishly. A hundred to one he won't kiss her without asking her first. Lovemaking by the rule book. She's never known what it is to be weakened, and lost, and helpless with love.

In a thoroughly bad mood, Nils flung himself into the saddle and turned down the dark trail toward the ranch.

CHAPTER

5

i

Old Uncle Julian thought he knew how the little school-teacher felt. Only children and old people see that Nils is kind. And God knows you have to love him to understand his weaknesses. He sighed. The sun filled the barnyard and the old rocking chair was as comfortable as a bed. He would go to sleep presently with the calls of the hop-pickers— "Ticket! Ticket!"—coming to him from the distant field like occasional bursts of an old familiar song.

"Ticket!" the Indians called when their reed baskets were filled to the top. Down the row the white field bosses would come, carrying on their shoulders the slanting wood trough with the boards which stuck out as handles at both ends. A ticket for a full box, to be cashed in at the end of the day for two big, round silver dollars—that was what they worked for: "Ticket . . . ticket . . ." Indians called in high, nasal voices. Pick fast so they don't settle and pack them lightly in the box—the Siwash know the tricks of it, Uncle Julian thought with a smile. Chinese pickers packed the hops down neatly—and starved.

"Ticket . . ." The old man closed his eyes against the sun, still smiling. The crop is free of the hop louse and the price is holding up. Nils is getting rich today. I wonder how many of the little teacher's pupils are out there helping him do it?

It had been amusing, that town meeting the night before, though Uncle Julian couldn't quite remember why. He had a general feeling that several very funny things had been said and occasionally they came back to him. But he couldn't force himself to catch them firmly, at least not in a rocking chair in the sunshine right after a good meal. Anyway he couldn't remember things any more, not the things that happened today or yesterday. Today's events appeared before him briefly, and retreated, mocking him from a safe distance. His mind felt tired.

The new teacher—that was it, of course. Gold Mountain was a fine spot for a girl her age, and one with such a scaredy look in her eyes. How could such a girl handle a pupil like the Greene boy?

Uncle Julian sighed again. He enjoyed sighing, for the act was a voice of nostalgia. It was a physical bridge to the days an old man can only sigh over, the days he could remember so sharply that he could smell and feel and hear the odors and touch and sound that went with them. Teachers, he thought, are getting to be women. It was hard to convince himself that it really mattered, one way or the other, what would happen to the little green-eyed Duncan, she being a woman. There were always women and there was always trouble. In his seventy-two years of ricocheting from one to the other, old Uncle Julian had even ceased to distinguish between the plain ones and the pretty ones, for whom in earlier years the agony had seemed worthwhile.

A teacher was a teacher. You have to have them, Uncle Julian supposed, as soon as your country begins to fill up with farmers. Farmers don't travel light, carrying little more than a gun and marrying the women at hand. Farmers marry white women and white women want their children to better themselves. It had been that way in western Pennsylvania, where he was born. It had been that way in Ohio, where he married. And now, with the new century only sixteen years away, it was changing to be that way even in the Washington Territory.

Uncle Julian didn't resent it, as some of the others did. He didn't go shouting that the hunting was no good any more and the good land was grabbed off and there were getting to be too many laws. He didn't resent anything any more, short of having someone steal his gun or call him a liar. He'd had eight years of schooling himself, sixty-odd years before in western Pennsylvania, and he didn't really agree with Nils, even if Nils was the boss of Gold Mountain, that you don't teach school unless you've failed at everything else and you don't go to school unless you're too lazy for anything else. Nils' mind was young and his fist was quick but an old man has his own thoughts. Who had told him to write to this new teacher, anyway, if it wasn't Nils himself?

Of course, Julian knew, Nils was full of soft spots when it came to getting something for his daughter Julie. Despising schoolteachers on the one hand and on the other going out looking for one to teach Julie—that was Nils. That had been Nils, for years.

"Why you so set on teaching her to read?" that lardhead Tom Stump had asked Nils. "Ain't she half-breed?"

Uncle Julian, for all his habit of not remembering, had no trouble recalling what Nils had done to Tom. Beat him to sleep, and left him all bloody for his wife to pick up and drag home.

There had been other "town meetings" besides the one the night before. If Nils sometimes let the Carlsons and Hansons and Smiths have the first word, he always had the last one. Or had until last night, when that little girl with the red hair on top of her head got up to say her piece. Uncle Julian chuckled. Tom Hutchins was a weakling, and Nils had even less use for weaklings than he did for school-teachers. Others had been surprised that Nils let the school-marm beat down the man he'd picked, but then, others didn't half know Nils, for lack of trying. Nils liked strength wherever he found it. He admired temper, though he himself was so strong he didn't need it—he bent things to his way without it. Some might think he had failed at the town meeting . . . Julian chuckled softly. Nils didn't know failure. Unless . . . The old man squinted thoughtfully. Unless there was failure in the end of his marriage to Mary.

For Mary had left him again, and this time old Indian Doc brought word from the Indian camp that she wouldn't return. Some sense of his own failure had kept Nils from going after her, Julian judged. He hadn't loved her as he once thought he would—that was Nils' failure, and he didn't try to deny it by searching Mary out and forcing her to come back. There was honesty in doing nothing, and there had been honesty in Mary's leaving without a word to her daughter Julie, as if the child had always belonged only to her father.

"Will you stay here?" Uncle Julian had heard Nils ask, "or will you go to your mother?"

The little girl's eyes begged her father for the right answer.

"I'll get," Uncle Julian had murmured. "Leave you two to talk it out."

Nils' big hand pushed Julian back into his chair. "Stay here," he said gruffly. "Keep me from saying the wrong thing."

Julie whispered at last, "Maybe she'll come back?"

"It don't look like it, this time." Nils squatted on his heels so as to look into her face. "Julie, baby, I know how I feel about you. I got to know how *you* feel. I can take you to Mama. What do you want to do?"

They wouldn't believe it, Uncle Julian had thought at the time, those people who are afraid of Nils. They wouldn't admit that Nils Bengston, who takes what he wants, would have the conscience to give up what he loves most.

Julie's face was only an inch from her father's. Solemnly, she said, "She doesn't seem like my mother any more."

Nils straightened up slowly. "All right, Julie. We'll stay here together." He turned to Uncle Julian. "No need to tell the whole Valley Mary's gone." And later, after Nils had taken out separation papers at the courthouse in Seattle, he warned Uncle Julian all over again to keep his private affairs, and Julie's private affairs, to himself.

"I'm no talker," the old man had snapped the day Nils admitted that Mary had left for good. Uncle Julian would have said a good deal more, but just then Julie reached up for her father's hand, Nils swung her up into a tight, silent embrace, and his face, looking blindly toward Julian over the little girl's shoulder, was so shattered by defeat—or was it loneliness?—that Julian's retort dried up in his throat. Nils was a giant of a man, and meant to be strong. If he ever goes down, Uncle Julian had reflected, I hope I'm far away from the sight and sound of it.

ii

Uncle Julian was a small man. Perhaps that was the reason why, when he first saw Nils, he had been more impressed by his size than by anything else. Sixty years of living had taken Julian from Pennsylvania to Ohio to Utah to California to Oregon City to Seattle. In those years, when the world was opening up for people who got there first, he had never been the first at anything, but he'd been there second often enough to try his hand at a good many occupations and to live well. In Seattle he had an old man's job at the bakery, and a little house and a plump wife, both of which were as comfortable and unbeautiful as old shoes. Julian wasn't proud of anything except that he had reached the age when he was no longer expected to do anything first or even well.

He met Nils Bengston in a market decorated with the sign, "Stokes, Grady, and Bengston. Meats. Founded 1869." Stokes, a wiry little man with bright black eyes, was wrapping up a piece of beef for him when the back door slammed open against the wall.

"Take it easy, Nils," Stokes said without looking up. "It took a dollar's worth of hardware to fix that door the last time you broke it."

A silver dollar clanked onto the marble counter and rolled to fall against the meat. "There's your money, Jake," a big voice said, "but isn't that the second time you've collected a dollar for fifty cents worth of hardware?"

Jake Stokes grinned wryly. "From you, Nils? Collect twice from you?"

Julian had really looked at Nils then. Nils was big. He carried himself as if he knew how big he was, but at the same time as if he'd never had to stoop for anyone where he came from.

"My partner," Stokes said briefly, pushing the silver dollar aside with the back of his hand. "Bengston."

Julian nodded.

Nils faced him squarely. "Well," he demanded, "what's yours?"

Julian wondered why he felt forced to answer. After all, there had been nothing out of the way about the question. I'm twenty-five years older than you are, Julian had an impulse to say, as if that would establish his right to answer Nils or not to answer him. But he replied, "Julian Sparks," adding, a little pettishly, "though you won't remember it."

"Glad to meet you, Mr. Sparks," Nils said, surprising him with his deference. They shook hands.

Julian picked up his package of meat. "You live in Seattle?"

"Snoqualmie Valley. Ever hear of it?"

Julian shrugged. "I might have."

Stokes laughed. "You see, Nils?"

Nils' grin didn't entirely vanish, but his face seemed to harden. "That's all right. I don't want too many getting interested until I can see a little clearer what's in the bottom of the pan. Well, everything's cleaned up so I'm heading back."

"Good-bye, Nils."

Nils waved his hand. "Good-bye, old-timer," he said, "when you get tired of buying your meat in somebody else's butcher shop, come out to the Valley." And the door slammed behind him.

Old-timer. That had hit Julian hard. Fifty-eight years old and a big Swede from the mountains makes me old with the wave of his hand. "Anything ever happen to trim that fellow down a little?"

"Not yet," Stokes said dryly. "And with his brains and muscle and luck, maybe it never will. That guy," he added slowly *"might* end up the richest man in the Territory."

And he called me old, Julian thought irritably.

iii

During the next five years Julian had been reminded occasionally of Nils and the Snoqualmie Valley, by a word now and again from Stokes. "Nils was asking," Stokes had said once, "if you was an educated man."

"Now why," Julian exclaimed, "did he want to know that?"

Stokes shrugged. "If he asked, he had a reason."

Then Julian had been in the post office one day, sending a letter from his wife Kate to her sister back east, when a long, thin man with a wide-brimmed hat pulled down hard over his ears strode past, carrying a leather pouch by a strap over one shoulder.

"Headed for Snoqualmie," the postmaster volunteered. "Goes by horse to Black River, Squak prairie, then on to Snoqualmie. Been carrying the mail out that way for almost three years now."

"They get mail out there, eh," Julian had mused, remembering with a tinge of malice how Nils Bengston hadn't wanted too many people in the Valley. "Good number must have settled down there since I last heard about it."

The postmaster smiled. "There's not a settler between Cedar River and Squak," he said, "Nor between Squak and Snoqualmie. You could carry all the mail in your pants pocket, if the government would allow it."

"How many folks are there?" Julian insisted.

The postmaster narrowed his eyes thoughtfully. "Whites, you mean?"

Julian nodded.

"Twenty-five, thirty. That is, both in Squak Valley and Snoqualmie Valley, put together."

What was that fellow Bengston doing these days? Julian had wondered. But he hadn't wondered long. In two minutes he was thinking instead that Kate had baked a wild blackberry pie that afternoon. Kate was a good wife. Kate, and old age, had brought him peace.

And then only a few months later Kate died.

She died quietly, not ailing at all beforehand. "Julian, would you get me a glass of water?" she had asked him, and he had been so surprised by the request that he did it instantly, with a shiver of premonition making his hand tremble as he lifted the dipper and tried to carry it across the room without spilling too much on the floor.

She tried to drink, gasped and fell forward. He wasn't sure how long she lived. Maybe a few minutes, maybe an hour. After he had carried her to the bed and covered her with the old crazy quilt, he stood looking at her, stunned into helplessness. It hadn't been original, Julian knew, to get drunk. Hadn't men always met the challenge of disaster that way, if they were lucky enough to have the price? An hour after Kate was buried, Julian was on the waterfront, and as far as he ever knew he stayed there until Nils found him.

Nils came to him like the brightest figure in a delirium. He had known him instantly, even known his name. But looking up, the face seemed to ripple like lake water under a gust of wind, and the mouth moved grotesquely, without speaking. Julian kept murmuring, "Where's Kate?" And then the warm, quivering blackness closed in.

When he awoke he was in a hotel room, and Nils was with him.

"I got drunk," he said weakly.

"You're more than that. You're sick," Nils said. "Lie down."

He had awakened many more times. Not out of a drunken stupor, but into those brief moments of clarity which break through the heat of fever. Sometimes Nils was there, sometimes he wasn't. Nils was a compassionate giant, bringing cold water, smoothing the covers. Even in delirium Julian had felt surprise at Nils' kindness.

In their first conversation, Nils said, "You better come out with me to the Valley."

Julian shook his head weakly. "I've got a house in Seattle."

"You want to go back to it?"

Of course he didn't want to. He groped for another reason. "I've got a job. In the bakery."

"A job, a job . . ." Nils' blue eyes narrowed disdainfully. "I'll give you a job."

And so Julian had exposed the bottom reason, the one he hadn't wanted to dig down to. "Young man," he said, "young man, I've done my part of breaking ground and neighboring with the Indians and proving claims. You aren't the kind to figure anyone else has ever done anything, but maybe I've done more than you will ever do. And I'm not trying to pioneer any more. I'm sixty-three years old, and I'm tired." He closed his eyes and pretended to go to sleep.

But of course he had gone with Nils. It was nine years since the summer day he had tied his old saddlebags on the back of one of Nils' horses and followed him across the hills to the Valley. He'd been too sick and confused, right up to then, to wonder why Nils bothered to take him along. For there hàd been a reason. Nils had definitely offered him work, for all his self-sufficiency implying that he needed him.

On one of their stops Julian had asked him why. "What do you need with an old man like me? What do you figure I'll do worth paying for?"

"There are going to be accounts to keep, letters to write. You've had education. You talked like it. And you're the kind I can trust."

Or the kind you can bend around your finger? Julian thought, and remembering Nils' compassion, felt ashamed of himself. Heaven knows, Nils had saved his life. "I don't need to get paid," he said impulsively, "as long as I have a place to sleep and enough to eat."

"You'll get paid," Nils said, adding flatly, "just what you're worth."

Julian snorted. It was all right with him if this ambitious young man had no use for gratitude. That would ease the pain of owing him something. "You don't say," he chuckled. "And how do you figure I'll be worth anything?"

In nine years in the Valley Julian could remember only that one occasion in which Nils had seemed to say something he didn't want to say. "I might as well tell you," Nils replied. He forced himself to look straight at Julian, but his eyes showed what it cost him. "You went to school, didn't you? You can read and write and keep figures?"

Julian nodded. "You asked me that a couple of times before. Like I said, yes, I done some of it."

"I can't read or write." And then Nils jumped onto his horse and rode through the timber as if a pack of wolves were upon him, leaving Julian to mount and follow as best he could.

iv

Uncle Julian laughed softly. For nine years he had written Nils' letters and read Nils' newspapers, a barricade between

Nils and the chasm of his own ignorance. The people to whom it mattered had never discovered that the big man of the Valley could neither read nor write. Those who knew were illiterate themselves and, except for Agatha Tine, put so little value on education that it would never strike them to miss it in Nils. But Nils missed it. Strange, Uncle Julian thought, and laughed again. The teachers we've had in Gold Mountain have never known. Maybe they haven't lasted long enough to guess.

Three months—that was a fair average, the old man reflected. The last one, now, the one before this little Scotch-English girl from Seattle. Uncle Julian had put her on the riverboat at Black River himself. He could still see her, teetering up the gangplank with a wicker suitcase in one hand, her bonnet askew over one big red ear, and with the other hand threatening him with an umbrella. She'd scolded him every step of the way, and he the one who had taken her down the hill on the back of his horse. A face like a weasel with a bellyache, the old man thought contentedly—that was Miss Clara Beane. God was good to help them get rid of her.

God, the Greene boys and the old Indian graveyard. Bless those idiot Greenes for thinking of that.

It was an old graveyard, which some earlier generation of Snoqualmies had placed close to the river. Searching for a high spot, they had stretched out the bodies of their dead in the tops of the cottonwood trees. To one of them, perhaps one of their finest braves, they had given special honor. He had been carefully placed in his cedar canoe, bolt upright, staring bravely ahead, with a long musket braced to lie across his lap. It hadn't been hard for the Greene boys, and maybe some of the others, to figure out that if they hid in the graveyard and made the right sounds at the right times, Teacher Beane would be scared out of her leggings when she walked past.

Julian had laughed when he heard about it. In fact he wasn't sure that he hadn't made the mistake of laughing in front of Clara Beane. But what matter, Julian thought. There's been eight or nine schoolteachers in the Valley already and none of them ever lasted. And none of them will, as long as Nils is the power here and Nils put so little value on learning.

There was the teacher who claimed he had been to high school. Nils' daughter was six then, and Nils had hired him on the spot. Julie and the three little Wright children, whose home was the schoolhouse now, and a couple of little Indian boys, who were Julie's cousins on her mother's side, were in that first class. School was held in the back of the Gold Mountain trading post. That teacher lasted three weeks, Julian recalled. At the end of that time the pupils got up and walked out.

Little Julie had led them straight to Nils. In a solemn group they approached him, Julie in the fore.

"That teacher," Julie explained, "told us zero times two makes two and zero times three makes three and zero times anything makes something."

Nils had hesitated. Being puzzled, he laughed. Just as suddenly, he grew angry. "See what I mean about those schoolteachers?" he had shouted at Julian. "How stupid can you get when you're educated? I know better than that and he's taking my money. Sixty dollars a month because he went to high school. Who talked me into getting a schoolteacher, anyway?"

Of course no one had. It had been Nils' idea and as they both knew there would have been no schoolteacher if it hadn't been. Julian shrugged. "Send him away."

"*Send* him! Don't you suppose he'll have sense enough to be gone when I get there?"

He had. In fact, as Julian remembered vividly, Nils had never caught up with him though he'd saddled up and ridden all the way to Squak prairie. "If anyone ever talks schoolteacher to me again," Nils said later, "I'll chase him up Old Hi and break his head over the point of it."

But the next year there had been another teacher in Gold Mountain. Perhaps Nils had consented because some of the other settlers had children and wanted schooling for them, or perhaps because Julie had asked. The new teacher had stayed until the morning he took a stick to little Jimmy Wing, one of Julie's cousins. Teacher had hardly touched Jimmy when Julie and the six or seven other girls in the school attacked. They scratched his face, pulled his hair, pushed him over and took off his shoes and pants. Then they hit him with the shoes until both eyes were blacked and he was cut and bruised in a dozen other places. No one had to ask that teacher to leave the Valley. Like Clara Beane, he had boarded the *Viking* at Black River the first time she touched land.

Julie came home from school that last day with a vest button proudly clutched in one hand. Solemnly she handed it to Nils. Julian watched Nils laugh until he cried.

Uncle Julian settled his hands comfortably about his stomach. His mind whispered that it was time to go to sleep. Yes, when this little teacher left, they'd have to look for a man teacher. A man, maybe, who could stand up to Nils. Not an old man, like himself, or a weak one, like that youngster Tommy Hutchins. I drove Miss Clara Beane to the riverboat myself, the old man thought wistfully. And she shook her umbrella at me. I wonder who will make the ride with Miss Katherine Duncan? He smiled, because he had suddenly remembered her name. I can remember, he thought, at times. His head fell forward. His mouth drooped open with the first gentle snore.

In the hop field, an Indian called, "Ticket! Ticket!"

6

i

Katherine had taught school in Gold Mountain for only six weeks when she saw the wisdom of Uncle Julian's advice to bring an umbrella, if she had one. The golden fall ended with the cry of the last hop-picker. It began to rain.

There was the persistent, quiet rain, which dripped musically into the rain barrels at the corners of the cabin. There was the furious rain, whipped to lashing gusts by winds which seemed to come from every direction. Wind dashed the lowering clouds against the mountains, and they broke into rain. Wind came down from the Pass, carrying the rain with it. Some days it did not seem to rain, but the clouds would settle so deep into the Valley that mist dampened the clothing and beaded itself along the eyebrows and hair.

Katherine kept the school open, though so few children had come during hop season that it was hard to say whether she or Nils had won. Agatha's boy Tommy hadn't missed a day, nor had Julie Bengston. The Carlson children had been as faithful as they could, but even they had picked hops for two weeks.

"I'm real sorry, teacher," Faith Carlson said. "No one wants the school open more than me and Jeb. Most of all I hate to have the children pick hops because it's one more time we let Nils Bengston have his way. But we've got to have a little hard money set aside for the winter." Like an Indian family, all the Carlsons except five-year-old Johnny had worked during the harvest.

Johnny had cried because he couldn't go along with the others. It was Hiram, the seven-year-old, who quieted him. "Listen, John," he said soberly. "I've got to pick hops but you get to go to school. While I'm gone you can be the boss of the school in my place."

"The boss?" Johnny squeaked, the tears drying as if they had never been.

"See?" Hiram exclaimed. "See my little brother happying out his cheeks?"

For a few hours the pickers were working the rows so close to the schoolhouse that their calls broke into the lessons. Three of the Stump children appeared suddenly at the open window. Their pale faces lined up on the sill, like tomatoes set out to ripen. Katherine smiled at them. They stared in silence. Suddenly a woman's voice shrilled, "Where you kids at?"

"We'd ruther be in school," the biggest child whispered, and the three dropped from sight and scampered back into the field.

Katherine had steeled herself against trouble with Julie Bengston. But there was none. The little girl was distant but attentive. Her mother had gone off and left her for good, the settlers were whispering, though Katherine knew none of them dared discuss it openly with Nils. It served him right, they said vaguely, as if Mary's leaving Nils were his just punishment for refusing to leave her, as they had so often advised him to do. Katherine suffered during such conversations, for she could not think of Nils without antagonism so uncontrollable that the walls of her comfortable little world were wrecked by violence and she was left exposed and helpless. She didn't want to think about Nils at all, or even about Carl White, for thoughts of him were disturbing in another way. She loved and admired him, but when he sent word that he would have to miss a few of the *Viking's* trips into the Valley she had been light-headed with relief. Carl would raise the question of her leaving the Valley, and for some reason she didn't want to be forced to answer it. She had begun a job; she wanted to finish it. She wanted to be Teacher, and only Teacher, to let hard work build such a high enclosure that her feelings about Nils or Carl or anything else would be shut out completely.

Katherine told herself that her promise to build a real school in two years was spoken in anger and no one, least of all Nils Bengston, would take it seriously. Building a new school was a goal for the teacher who was in the Valley to stay. Not just for the winter. Nor for only a few months, or a year, or a year and a half until Carl White took her back to Seattle for their wedding.

But there were lesser goals, and these Katherine allowed herself to think upon, like a woman who has refused the cake but reaches for tiny flakes of frosting. First, she had won over Nils and held the job. She had kept the school open. Next, the fireplace, so that school would be possible in cold weather. The bigger boys had rebuilt it in a day and chopped and stacked two months' firewood.

With these things done, Katherine began to make a list of accomplishments to come. Not, she promised herself, because she planned to stay forever. To prove it she headed the list "School year of 1884-85." This notebook was at the Carlson home, tucked under the rafter above her bed. When the work was done at night she sometimes sat alone at the long table, her back to the dying fire and a bit of candle melting slowly in a cup in front of her. It was a time to write a little, to think a great deal. She went to bed when the fire was out and the cold began to creep into her fingers.

Books—those were at the top of the list for "School year of 1884-85." With the schoolroom filled once more after hop-picking, she talked to the children about the books they might have at home.

"We ain't got a book," the oldest Stump child replied, flushing miserably.

"Lots of people ain't!" Hiram Carlson offered loyally.

"Haven't," Katherine corrected.

"Haven't," Hiram echoed.

Little John nodded wisely. "Lotsa people ain't got what haven't."

But when the children explored the forgotten corners of their homestead shacks and lean-tos, they found books, and they carried them to school as proudly as yearling hunters dragging home their first venison. There were five Bibles, all with birth and wedding and death dates written in the front. "Containing the Old and New Testaments; translated out of the Original Tongues; and with the former translations diligently compared and revised" —such was the title of one of them, but under it, in a clear, round hand, was written: "Mary Anderson. Born at Fort

Lincoln on July the 14th, 1878. Returned to God August the first, 1878. We held services on the trail in Montana territory."

On the shelf next to the Bibles was *The French Student's Companion* by a professor in the Albany Female Academy. There was a first reader, a history book, a copy of the journals of Lewis and Clark. Then a book called *Chauncey Judd: or, The Stolen Boy. A story of the Revolution.* It was rain-spotted but the bold figure of a minuteman, one hand under his coat and the other ready at his musket, still embellished the cover. *Golden Thoughts in Pen and Pencil*—this one contained two petunias, pressed and dried so long ago that they crumbled into dust when Katherine opened the book. Down the row a large volume in gold-embossed leather stood out from the rest. *Poetical Quotations, from Chaucer to Tennyson,* Katherine read, "published in Philadelphia in 1876." This last had come from Tommy Tine, carried to school in a careful wrapping of washed gunny sack. Yet Tommy had never been to school before and fat, good-natured Agatha could neither read nor write. To whom had this elegant book belonged, published in a far-distant eastern city only eight years before? How little, Katherine thought wistfully, how very little any of us here know about each other.

Thus the Gold Mountain school had acquired a shelf of books, however useless some of them might seem to be when the job was to teach the alphabet to a clutch of little Swedes and an Indian girl. Next on the list Katherine had written "School supplies." She ordered them from Seattle, and when the day came that they would arrive on the *Viking* Katherine saddled her pony and rode down the Valley to get them. There would be pencils and tablets and grammars and spelling tablets, but also there would be a baseball and bat.

It was a long ride in the rain, and Katherine was wet

through by the time she was half way to Black River. But thinking of the order, she smiled happily. The grammars and tablets were for all the good little children, the Carlsons and Nelsons and Andersons and the rest. But the baseball and bat was for the bad boy, Emil Greene.

They had told her that if the Greene boys came at all, they wouldn't stay in school longer than a week. Emil alone had come, but Emil had stayed.

"I ain't coming to school no longer," he had told her almost every afternoon.

Each time she had agreed, "Good-bye then, Emil."

"You can't make me come to school. I'm sixteen," he added after school one day.

"I couldn't make you come to school if you were only six," she replied steadily.

"Well, then," he muttered.

"Well, then, good-bye, Emil."

He hesitated, looking down at her as if he were trying to make up his mind whether or not to break her in two. Katherine forced herself to smile.

Emil growled, "I guess you didn't hear about me."

Katherine's heart jumped. For a moment panic won out and she stared at him dumbly.

"About all the things I done," he said louder, stepping toward her.

"Can you handle a shingle bolt?" Katherine asked. It was a wild stab but it reached him.

Emil stared at her. "Sure! Sure I can. Ask 'em over at the mill. Ask them there what kind of a shingle weaver I was this summer. They'll all tell you."

"You do look strong," Katherine said quietly. "Well, good-bye, Emil," and she turned and walked back into the schoolhouse. Emil, somewhat subdued, had been in school as usual the next morning.

She had been proud too soon of conquering the bad boy. The first morning she laid a fire in the new hearth, smoke poured back down the chimney, filling the cabin and setting the children to coughing. Tears in her eyes, Katherine rushed to open the door. Someone was laughing loudly. Even in her flurry Katherine identified the voice as that of Emil Greene.

She lined the children up in the schoolyard, in rows just like those they kept at their benches inside.

"She's got to close the school, she's got to close the school . . ." That was Emil Greene's hoarse whisper from the back row. The others, still blinking with smoke, watched their teacher dutifully.

"Someone has stuffed something up the chimney," Katherine said matter-of-factly. "Is there anyone here strong enough to climb on the roof and pull out whatever it is?"

Levi Barker, one of the older boys, raised his hand. Emil Greene stared resentfully at Levi, looked back at his teacher and then bolted toward the school. The children waited in heavy silence while Emil pulled himself onto the roof and removed a great wad of dirty rags. Their eyes were round and wondering. Emil threw the rags to the ground, jumped down and returned to his place in line. The children's eyes rested expectantly on Katherine. Emil's sullen face said —now for the lecture.

Katherine ignored him. "While we're out here," she said, "I'm going to tell you about a plan I have. We're going to have a baseball team. Tomorrow I'll send to Seattle for a ball and a baseball bat."

Emil Greene hadn't missed a day of school since. Katherine laughed, telling Carl about it later.

But Carl had seen nothing laughable about it. "Baseball is a man's game."

"Don't you see, Carl, the game itself isn't important. It's

taming that wicked Greene boy, keeping him in school . . ."

"You can't make a silk purse," Carl retorted flatly, "out of a sow's ear."

"Why not?" Katherine asked, and felt ashamed because her voice was anything but genteel. "In a way my school is filled with sow's ears."

"I suppose you'll be on this—this baseball team?"

Katherine had smiled, knowing she was tormenting him but for some reason enjoying it. "You can look for me," she said softly, "on second base."

Carl had been irritated. It was irritation she knew would vanish at the merest touch of her hand, or at any sort of an apology. Yet she had neither touched him nor asked to be forgiven.

Their meetings were less frequent now, for Carl was spending more time at school and had been working as well as an apprentice in a Seattle law firm. It was a month since that last meeting, a month since he had said good-bye, his lips still tight with disapproval. A simple little, "I'm sorry, Carl," a look of acquiescence instead of defiance—but she hadn't been able to give in that much.

And so he had gone back to the *Viking* with only a tense, "I hope things go well during the next month," riding across the Carlsons' clearing without even turning to wave as the trail bent toward the woods. He hadn't kissed her good-bye. And yet, like a naughty child, she still wanted to laugh.

The rain had stopped. Humming to herself, Katherine leaned back in the saddle and let the pony take her down the familiar trail. In among the giant cedars the air was warm and aromatic. Carl had said he wasn't coming for several weeks. When he did, she would be careful not to offend him and he would be too polite to remind her that she ever had. Meanwhile, no need to worry about their next meeting. There was plenty of time, plenty of work.

On Monday she would take the tablets and the baseball bat to school. It would be weeks and weeks before the snow would be heavy enough to keep the children away from school. Things were going well. "School year 1884-85"—she had failed at nothing on her list, so far. Impulsively she reached forward and ran her hand along the pony's neck. She had all but forgotten to whom the pony belonged, and how defiantly she had once refused it.

ii

By the middle of December even Katherine had to admit that the school should be closed. There was no arguing with the early snow, which mere determination could not clear from the wagon roads and trails. There was real danger to the children who pushed through drifts half as tall as they were, to arrive at school wet and shivering and an hour or more late. For those who lived in the true wilderness, like Levi Barker, the journey was impossible.

"I could talk back to Nils Bengston," Katherine said to the Carlsons. "But I can't do anything about the weather."

"I don't think you were supposed to," Faith Carlson said.

"No. But if I can't teach school, what will I do?"

"You can stay here with us." Faith and Jeb Carlson said it almost together.

Katherine shook her head. "Thank you. But we need hard money, don't we? We always do. I can't live here without putting in my share."

"Just until you can start school again."

Katherine gestured toward the nearest shutter. It was tightly barred with a length of split cedar. But the east wind had driven the fine snow around the edges and through the invisible cracks. It lay in a feathery white ridge along the sill. "How can we know when that will be? Remember you were telling me about the school principal who had to work on the railroad half of every year? And last year the teacher at Squak earned a living splitting hop poles. I can't do those things. But I'll have to think of something different."

"You got spunk, Miss Duncan," Jeb Carlson said.

Katherine smiled. "No," she said, "but maybe if I stay here long enough I'll learn to get it."

It was Agatha Tine who helped her find a job. "It's just like Faith Carlson to ask you to live off them," Agatha said. "But they ain't got shoes to go around. Why don't you come down here. I'll give you room and board if you teach Tommy and me to read." She chuckled. "If you teach me, don't think you won't earn it."

"I'd help the Carlsons more by paying them room and board than I would by moving out."

Agatha grinned. "Good girl. All right, then, you're out for a job. A paying job. Can you cook?"

"I was the oldest of six children, not counting the ones that died."

"That's right." Agatha laughed. "The way you talk sometimes, I keep thinking you're one of those delicate city girls. Someday people around here are going to forget about the wrapping and look inside the package. Maybe some of them will be surprised." She settled herself comfortably, hands clasped across her stomach. "There's that shingle mill Nils opened up on the South Fork last spring. There's fifteen, twenty men working there now, and three days ago their cook took a notion and made off for Alaska, along with what cash he could find in among everyone else's belongings." She stopped, her bright little eyes fixed hard on Katherine.

"Would I have to ask Mr. Bengston for the job?"

Agatha nodded slowly. "He's the one."

Katherine spread her hands in her lap, studied the rough skin, the burns from hot skillets, the fingernails broken from carrying cordwood, the cracks and chapping from using the coarse yellow soap she and Mrs. Carlson made. "I don't like to," she said, "but I will."

"He's not the skunk you think he is," Agatha said. "*I* know Nils."

"And *I* don't care to," Katherine said flatly.

Chuckling, Agatha rolled across the kitchen to the pantry shelf. "Before you go back to Carlsons I'm going to fill up your saddlebags. There's some jars of veal meat, some real dates Jake sent me out from Seattle, some pickled crab apples and a nice smoked slab of bacon. Faith won't want to take them. Tell her I gave them to you. Tell her they're for Christmas. Tell her I'm on a diet." Holding her stomach she laughed uproariously. "Now she'll believe *that*, won't she!"

Old Indian Doc was in the barnyard when Katherine rode into the hop ranch. She dismounted quickly, conscious of the glass windows in the ranch house and the faces that might be behind them. Since the day her runaway horse had dragged her into this same yard she had come no closer to it than the trail to Black River which ran past a quarter mile south. There, right in front of her on the barn wall, was her hat, the little bit of vanity she had bought instead of an umbrella and lost along with her pride that terrible day three months before. Rain had softened the straw and made the dyes in the ribbons run together. When snow came it had settled on the ribbons and frozen fast; it glistened in the wintery sunlight, mocking the shape of the hat that was to have made her look like a lady.

Nils had put it there—Katherine was sure of it, and for a moment she forgot everything but how much she hated him. Like an angry terrier, she grasped the tasseled ends of her shawl, pulled it off her head and shook it so hard snow sprayed in her face.

The old Indian approached her. Looking from Katherine to the hat and back again, he giggled, covering his toothless mouth with his hand.

Katherine looped the reins around the hitching post. "Mr. Bengston?" she said stiffly.

The Indian spoke rapidly in Chinook, but he pointed toward the house. Nils and Julie and old Uncle Julian lived alone now. Katherine had heard a dozen contradictory reports on how they were getting along without Mary to cook and wash for them. She wanted to ask if Uncle Julian and Julie were there, too; she felt weak at the prospect of facing Nils alone. But Indian Doc had turned his pointing finger to the silly, snow-encrusted hat on the barn wall, and was repeating some question she couldn't understand. "Oh, leave me alone!" she snapped at him, like a crotchety grandma slapping at a mosquito. Strengthened by annoyance, she made her way to the house.

At her knock, the door opened suddenly and Julie was in front of her, her face bright with an unusual smile. "Teacher!" she breathed.

Katherine smiled, fully as glad to see Julie as Julie was to see her. "How are you, Julie?"

"I'm doing the washing all by myself," the little girl said breathlessly. "Mama isn't here any more."

"Julie!"

It was Nils' voice, a sudden roar from a corner Katherine couldn't see.

Katherine flushed. She had never seen Nils' Indian wife, and hadn't expected that her absence would make this meeting with Nils any worse or any better. But it was worse, somehow, for there had been pride in Nils' angry command. Pride was a feeling she understood. Despite herself, Katherine felt a twinge of sympathy.

"Let her in, Julie!"

The little girl hesitated, confused by her father's manner, but she opened the door.

The great fieldstone fireplace filled the end of the room. Elsewhere Indian mats were spread, with a hand-split table and three or four handmade chairs with cowhide seats making up the white man's furniture. On a stool next to the fire sat Nils, elbows on his knees and a crooked black cigar in his mouth.

Katherine advanced to the middle of the room. She had planned what to say, but she had not expected to recite it standing up. Nils' blue eyes were curious and amused. It was Julie who darted across the room, pushed a chair forward and said, "Please?"

Nils grinned. "My, ain't she polite?" But he didn't move.

"Thank you, Julie." Katherine sat down carefully, collecting herself while she shook the snow from the hem of her skirt. Nils' gaze was so steady, so—uncompromising. She forced herself to meet it directly. "Mr. Bengston, the school is closed temporarily because of inclement weather, as you know."

Nils nodded. "Is that what you call it?" he said mockingly, pointing at the snow heaped up against the bottom half of the windowpane. "And so you're out of a job."

Katherine flushed. That miserable color in my face, she thought angrily. It's one thing I can't control. "I see you already know."

Nils laughed out loud. "Who would know better than me?"

Of course he would remind her that the school building was his, the wages came from his pocket, the job had come from him in the first place; and yet for weeks Katherine had almost forgotten it. In a way, it wasn't true any more. The building and money were his, yes. But the school, the children's acceptance of the school, their love of school, even to his own little daughter Julie—this was something Nils Bengston couldn't touch. Katherine felt pride stiffen her backbone. "You also know, then, that I need another job, until spring, when I'll reopen the school."

It gave her some satisfaction to see that Nils was surprised. "Go on back to Seattle," he said bluntly. "You've never belonged out here anyway. Your friend Carl will help you find work."

"I'll stay here."

She said it quickly because she was growing angry at him, as always. She resented it. Anger was a personal thing, it came from the heart.

"This is no place for you," he repeated. His voice was harsh. "You belong in Seattle, where men bow when they meet a lady and you wouldn't have to ask for work from a man who won't get off his chair for nobody."

Katherine said in a rush, "I'd like to go to work cooking for the men at the shingle mill."

Nils stared. He pulled the cigar from his mouth, studied each end of it, tossed it into the fire. At last he looked back at her.

"Would you please tell me what the wages are?" Katherine knew she spoke with telltale haste, but she managed to hold her head up and keep her hands sedately folded in her lap.

"Ten dollars a week for cooking three meals a day," Nils said slowly. "And your board and room."

"It's not far to Carlsons'. I'll sleep there."

"If you don't put breakfast on the table by six o'clock tomorrow morning, you don't get the job."

A shiver of triumph was beginning to run through her. It rose to a wonderful light-headedness. She stood up, adjusted her shawl and walked to the door. She felt his eyes on her every step of the way.

At the last moment she remembered Julie. "Good-bye, Julie," she said, giving the little girl the smile she dared not turn on her father. "And thank you, Mr. Bengston."

Nils was still watching her silently, and he still hadn't moved. At the door, Katherine turned back impulsively. "I surprised you, didn't I?" she said lightly, and hurried out.

iii

Fried ham, wheat mush, platters of fried eggs, hot cakes and molasses, baking powder biscuits, fried potatoes, pie, coffee. . . . Katherine got up at four o'clock every morning, reciting victuals as if they were part of a dream she hadn't had time enough in bed to finish. Her eyes burned and her mouth was dry with lack of sleep. She washed quickly, gasping as the cold water assaulted her face. She hadn't time to arrange her long hair in the elaborate dress she had worn as Teacher. She brushed it fiercely, and let it hang in long braids down her back.

With the shawl wrapped around her thin body and securely knotted at the waist, she picked up the lantern and Mrs. Carlson's big, black umbrella, and hurried to the shed to saddle her pony. She moved quickly but in the trance of half-sleep, like a serious-minded ghost with an important tryst. She was never fully awake until she was in the saddle, the lantern in one hand and the umbrella in the other, and the pony was walking through the woods toward the shingle mill.

After breakfast she began the baking. Apple, blackberry, prune, pumpkin pies—many of the loggers would eat a pie a day. Then there was bread, made from the sponge

of sourdough she kept in a crock in the cooler, and dough-
nuts for the men to soak in their coffee. She cooked beans
every day, with chunks of fat pork dropped in first at the
bottom of the iron kettle. Nils brought meat to the
kitchen in the form of halves and quarters. Because she
wouldn't ask him to cut it for her, Katherine had been left
alone with two hundred pounds of hog and the choice
between cooking it whole or going after it with a carving
knife and carpenter's saw. She cut it herself, tears of anger,
despair and weariness dropping onto her hands.

As a schoolteacher she had gained hard muscles and a
few pounds. As a mill cook, the muscles grew even harder
but there wasn't much else to her except bone, freckles,
heavy red hair and eyes too big for her face. The day she
met little, wiry Hi Barker at the trading post he said,
"Nate's just about to put me on the grain scale. He's betting
I won't make a hundred. You better get weighed, too,
teacher. It looks to me like you're gradually disappearing."

"She don't dare eat what she cooks," said Nate. "She
knows what's in it."

At first it seemed to Katherine that the three meals at
the shingle mill overlapped. If she did not pound the big
copper dinner gong on time, the men walked in anyway,
threw themselves onto the benches and banged the table
with their fists. In the kitchen she would stack pork chops
on platters, tip the bean pot into a big bowl, scoop up the
gravy, praying that it was all cooked through. They shouted
if the food was late. They had as much or more to say if it
was raw.

By the end of the first week, Katherine's dread of that
shouting, her deeper dread that Nils might walk in, had
made a thorough mill cook out of her. The food was on the
table at six in the morning, twelve noon, and six at night.
Always, thought Katherine, the hands of the clock are
straight up and down or just straight up.

On her way to the door to ring the gong she glanced methodically at the table, checking off each item. Milk pitcher. Mustard pot. Jelly jars. Pickles. Like a starter pointing the gun that would open the horse race, she picked up the mallet and beat the dinner gong.

The whine of the great circular saw would die away. The donkey engines would cough, spit and stop. Covered with grease and sawdust, the shingle weavers and bolt haulers and kneebolters and packers pushed past her to the table. Sawdust coated their hats, stuck in a fine red dust along their eyebrows. They smelled of sweat and cedar wood, odors imbedded forever in the very fabric of their clothes. There was no shouting now. Katherine went back to the kitchen. Not a voice was raised except to call for the coffee pot or another bowl of beans. When they had finished, they kicked back the bench and walked out.

They moved quickly before the meal. Afterwards they dragged their feet, thumbs hooked under their suspenders and the top pants button open for comfort. They worked from seven in the morning until six at night, for twelve and a half cents an hour. Two days wages paid for food and bunk.

Every week new men came to camp, others left. "You can tell how long a man will stay," her father had said, "by the size of his turkey." Katherine smiled whenever she thought of Peter Duncan's old rule. A "turkey" was the bedroll, the carpetbag, the sum of a man's moveable possessions. In its size and kind you read his character. She had come to the Snoqualmie Valley with a wicker suitcase, three dresses, a red flannel petticoat and a heap of underthings made from bleached muslin and boiled flour sacks. How long was *she* going to stay?

When the last man had eaten and gone, Katherine took her only rest of the day. She scalded the teapot, carefully measured two pinches of tea into it, poured in the boiling water. Putting pot and teacup on the table at her elbow, she dropped wearily into the kitchen chair and closed her eyes. The steam engines would start up again. Their chugging was deep and rhythmic. Then the scream of the saw as it bit through the wood. A shout, occasionally, from one man to another, too muffled to mean more to her than a sound. In time, the noise was peaceful. She drank her tea slowly, holding the cup in the palms of both hands so as to warm her fingers.

It was unusual for anyone to come into the dining room except at mealtime. When Katherine heard the thump of boots one morning after breakfast, she set the teacup down quickly. Whoever it was, he was headed for the kitchen. It couldn't be Carl. The boat wasn't coming upriver, in this weather. And why would Nils come, since there were plenty of supplies? But the thought of Nils was disturbing. She stood up, nervously wiped her hands on her apron.

The man appeared in the doorway between dining room and kitchen. It was an Indian she had never seen before. His clothes were ordinary enough—jeans and a heavy shirt and boots—but his hair was long, stringing out below his dirty felt hat like a black mop dropped carelessly over the top of his head. He was grinning foolishly, and mumbling a combination of Chinook jargon and English swear words. He moved toward her, hands outstretched.

Katherine backed away. Fear made her heart pound and her mind go blank. "No, no," she said, "get away . . ."

He seemed to be talking steadily. His gestures grew more dramatic, but even more senseless, as he advanced.

"I'll scream!" Katherine cried, but it didn't interrupt the mumbling flow for a second. Who will hear me, she thought desperately, with the engines puffing and the saws whining? Down in the mill a man had to shout to be heard by someone only three feet away. Perhaps a scream would excite him even more, bring him on her in one leap. If

she could talk to him . . . Her throat ached but she said,
"Please, if you want something, the boss is over in the mill.
Go see the boss . . ."

Her words sounded foolish, even to herself. She was
pleading with him, but clearly he wasn't listening. Instead he seemed to be pleading with her. She backed away
still further. He followed her. Her back hit the edge of the
table. Keeping her eye on the Indian, she reached behind
her, groping for a weapon. "You want money?" she asked
him. "Go away. I'll get you some money."

He was only a few feet away now. Katherine felt along
the surface of the table, searching frantically but afraid
to turn her head. The Indian was a giant mass, a grinning,
chattering mass, barring her way to the door. "No, no!"
she shrieked, losing the last of her self-control. She ran
from him, toward the stove. Skillet and bean pot and ket-
tles blurred together in her eyes. There was the meat
block, the knife with the big bone handle lying next to
the ham. She had dropped it there only an hour before.
She grabbed blindly, and turned to meet him. But he
hadn't followed. He was standing just where she had left
him, and at last she had silenced him. He was staring at
her in sheer amazement.

Her confidence returned. With pulse pounding in her
neck and throat she moved to drive him out of the kitchen.
The object was heavy in her hand. She stepped toward him,
waving it in the air. Miraculously, he backed up. Boldness
swept through her. "Get out of here!" she screamed, ad-
vancing like an angel with a fiery sword, "or I'll kill you
with this!"

He looked more puzzled than terrified, but he moved
back.

"I'll stab you!" she shouted, in a frenzy of courage.
"You come near me again and I'll kill you!"

He stumbled, halting abruptly in the doorway. As suddenly, Katherine's courage disintegrated. He had stopped, he wasn't leaving, he might come at her again—she lost her wits entirely. The weapon in her hand was forgotten. Her arm seemed paralyzed by it. Right at her elbow was a stack of flapjacks, still warm on the griddle at the back of the stove. With her left hand she scooped them up and whirled to take aim. He was standing there, his mouth gaping. "Get out, I said!"—and she put her body behind the throw that sent the whole stack of hot cakes across the room.

They were out of her hand when she saw him duck, falling to the floor as if he'd been shot between the eyes. They had landed with a soft splash before she saw what she had hit. It was Nils Bengston. Nils had walked in, unheard because of the rumpus. And Nils had got the hot cakes, squarely across the face.

The silence throbbed like a pulse beat. Nils lifted one big hand and brushed the spatter out of his hair, off his cheek. The Indian was sitting flat on the floor, legs straight out and eyes round, like a frightened baby. Nils looked down at him. "Well, hello there, Jimmy. You begging again?"

The Indian replied with a burst of jargon.

Nils nodded sympathetically. "Too bad. The lady didn't understand." He turned to Katherine. "I see you haven't met Jimmy. He's never done anything bad, except beg for food. He's always hungry." Nils rubbed his cheek with the back of his sleeve. "I'm glad you decided to give him pancakes, instead of beans. You might have given them to him in the kettle, hm?"

The Indian got to his feet. Nils gestured toward the door, issuing a curt order in Chinook, and he fled.

Katherine looked up at Nils. She was still trembling. "He just wanted . . . something to eat," she said, feeling hysteria bubbling through her.

Nils nodded. His eyes were bright. "When I come in, you were yelling you'd stab him to death." He pointed to Katherine's hand, still clutching the weapon with which she had been ready to defend herself. "Were you going to do it with *that?*"

She lifted her arm, stared at the object she had been clutching so hard. It was the big soup ladle. The carving knife with the heavy bone handle lay untouched on the meat block. The ladle, it seemed, had been handier.

She looked back at Nils. He was smiling, with his eyes sparkling and his teeth white in his tan face. The whole thing suddenly seemed funnier than anything that had ever happened to her before. Katherine began to laugh. Nils laughed, softly at first, more loudly as he watched Katherine's face. For a long time, with the saws whining outside, with the soup ladle hanging crazily at Katherine's side, they looked into each other's face, and laughed together.

iv

Katherine tried to listen carefully, for she knew this was a real proposal of marriage. How often Carl had regretted that he couldn't take her away from the Valley. How romantically he had promised, "Some day . . ." It had been all wishing, and she had agreed without reservation because in it all there was nothing to say yes or no to. Now Carl was holding her hand, and his words were so exactly what she had expected to hear some day that she almost forgot she must reply.

"I hope I'm not presuming," he was saying. "We *do* understand each other, don't we, dear?"

She nodded. "Oh, yes, Carl," she said very warmly because she was afraid she hadn't been listening closely enough and might have missed some question. She felt ashamed of her absent-mindedness. To make up for it she pressed his hand harder than she meant to.

"You will, then." Carl pulled on the reins. The big work horses stopped obediently and the wagon settled into the ruts. Carl's arm encircled Katherine. He bent and kissed her cheek. "Have I told you that I love you?"

"Yes, oh yes . . ." She spoke fervently, but she was glad he couldn't see her face. The truth was that she couldn't remember. Hadn't he said he loved her? Hadn't she said she loved him? Surely their kisses, their promises, had meant as much without a name tag. She thought suddenly, he sounds a little silly, and was immediately ashamed of herself again. "I love you," she said, "very much."

He kissed her, and for a moment the dreadful urge to doubt him, and to doubt herself, was stilled. She lay passively against his shoulder, accepting his kisses but restraining all desire to kiss him back. Her lips lay beneath his as sweet and virgin as a child's, for she had learned it was only the sweet and virgin that he wanted from her. Desire in the girl he was to marry, the shiver of awakening passion that had once—only once—made her cling to him —he had been shocked by it. She had felt it, and drew away, furiously ashamed. After that she never forgot the part he expected of her. In his arms now, she felt nothing more than a pleasant warmth. I wonder, she thought, if this is all there is to it? And she knew instantly that it wasn't.

He was talking to her. Katherine flushed. He was waiting for an answer, and once more she hadn't heard the question. She looked at him, seeking reassurance. The serious face, the dark, thoughtful eyes, the kind mouth and gentle hands—of these things the Carl she had loved seven months ago had been made. They were Carl's now. September until March—he couldn't have changed. Had she?

"I'm sorry, Carl," she said hastily. "What did you ask me?"

"You were thinking of something else."

He was accusing her, and of course he was right. "I'm sorry," she repeated. "I'm to open the school again Monday morning and there are so many things to think about." She felt guilty at using such evasion. This was Carl, whom she had just promised to love.

Carl pulled her around gently to face him. "Katherine, I've asked you to come to Seattle with me. I've asked you to marry me this week, and live in the home of my parents until I have finished my training and can pay for a home of our own. Is this your answer, that you've been thinking about the school?"

Katherine felt a wave of unhappiness as she looked at him. No, he hadn't changed. He had known her mind as surely as he ever had. How could she defend herself, except with another lie? She should be clinging to him joyfully, telling him he had made her utterly, completely happy. But she was uneasy.

His proposal hadn't made her happy. It had only confused her. Worst of all, she felt a twinge of pity, because she knew how clearly he could see it. Her face was full of it. Embarrassment, confusion, a sense of duty and a wish to please, but not ecstasy, not love.

"Not now, not so soon," she whispered. "It's only that I wasn't expecting . . . it so soon." She put her hand on his arm, and then wished that she hadn't, for it was such an obvious gesture of comfort. "Later," she said. "Carl dear, I do love you. I always have, from that first awful day at Snohomish City when I was going to run away from the boat instead of getting on it, and I bumped into you. You remember. Did I ever tell you that you stopped me from running away? I would never have come to the Valley at all, if it hadn't been for you." She was talking too much.

She knew it and stopped abruptly, looking anxiously into his face.

It was different. It was shadowed with new wisdom she hadn't seen in it before. We are both changing, she thought, and I believed it was only I.

He smoothed back her hair, as grave and careful as a mother. "Later, then," he said quietly. He picked up the reins and slapped them along the horses' backs. The spring wagon rolled forward, creaking softly. "Now," he said, keeping his glance away from her and straight down the road they were traveling, "tell me all about school, and your plans for reopening it."

So Katherine began to talk and talk, though suddenly all she really wanted to do was to cry.

CHAPTER

7

i

Katherine packed her lunch for the box social with utmost care. It would go to Carl, of course. If it were filled with gold nuggets, no one in Gold Mountain would think of outbidding the man who had spoken for her. For Carl, then, or for the new school building, to which the bidding money was to go, her hands moved delicately, appreciating their task. Besides, Carl was watching. He sat on a three-legged stool by the open door.

"I'm so glad you got here in time." Katherine shook the Indian reed basket, squinted critically at the inside. "This will do," she added absently. "I haven't got a box."

"It was luck that I made the trip this week at all."

Katherine glanced up quickly. But his face showed no hint of displeasure. She smiled, and meant it. Carl so often seemed displeased that she was relieved whenever she found she had only imagined it. "Perhaps I should have written you about the social."

"No matter," he said stiffly, "since I arrived without invitation anyway."

She flushed. Then he *was* angry. Had there been a time during the past year when she had completely measured up to the standards he set for her? She must be a lady, he often reminded her, suggesting that there were ways in which she wasn't. In the way she sometimes let her hair fall loosely down her back. In the speed with which she had learned to mount and ride a horse, like a young Indian. In her costume, which had been without a proper bonnet or gloves, without lace, ruffle or finery, for the whole year. In all these outer things he saw a loss of dignity. "But no one in the Valley finds anything wrong," she had often protested, and he shamed her with his reply, "They don't know any better. *I* do."

She picked up a clean dish towel, shook it hard and spread it as a lining inside the basket. For the hundredth time she resolved not to apologize to Carl. "I didn't think of it as a party," she said. "There have been so many different affairs, all through the summer, for raising school money. This is just another one of them."

"It may seem that to you. But at a box social men bid for the lunches, and their supper partners are the girls whose boxes they win."

Carl was being deliberately patient. It inspired Katherine with a ridiculous desire to stamp her foot. "Of course." Her hands worked furiously with the lunch basket.

Carl came to the table. "We are engaged," he said quietly. His hand touched her elbow, asking her to look at him. She turned. "If I hadn't come, would you have gone to the social and sat as a partner with another man?"

"I am the teacher," she said stubbornly, but her voice had lost its boldness. Carl was hurt. According to his code— and hers, too, for hadn't they always looked at things in the same way?—she had slighted him. Besides—and this was worse—she had been something less than a perfect lady.

"I'm sorry, Carl," she said. Now she had apologized, as she had done so often, and so often sworn never to do again. His face softened; she knew he would never refer to it again. But she would remember. Once more she had apologized, and the apology had curdled in her mouth.

"I've made apple turnovers," she said, "and some little venison pies. There are some sandwiches of smoked pheasant. Mr. Carlson hung several birds in the smokehouse when he cured that last deer. Eggs are scarce." She knew she was prattling like an old woman, but she went on, "Our best hens are getting broody so I couldn't make spiced eggs, as I had planned. Then there is honey bread, and a little pot of fresh creamed cheese."

Carl lifted one hand. "Whoa!" Katherine halted with the last sharp intake of breath. He was smiling. He was neither scolding her nor pressing her with the question which seemed harder to answer every time he asked it. She felt such a wave of relief that she faced him and lifted her face for a kiss.

His arms went around her, and he held her tightly against the musty wool of his lapel. She felt him tremble. Once she had been ashamed of feeling too much; now she felt nothing at all. His hands pressed her anxiously, as if he sensed her detachment and was trying to bring her closer. With curiosity she noted the heavy beat of his heart. The Carlson children will be running into the house about now, she thought, yelling that it's time to go . . . "Carl," she whispered uneasily.

"You've been in the Valley for over a year now," he said. He spoke hurriedly, as if he had to say it all before she left his arms. "I've asked you many times to come to Seattle and marry me. You've always answered, not just now, later." His arms tightened convulsively. "How much longer do I have to wait?"

Here was an intensity of feeling she had often longed for. And yet the question turned her cold. Guiltily, she hid her face against his shoulder.

"Katherine," he pleaded, "Katherine . . ."

Her mind ran blindly from the necessity of answering him. She lifted her face, and he kissed her hungrily. From the distance a child shouted. Another answered from some spot near the cabin. The children were coming in.

Carl released her so suddenly he seemed to have jumped backward. "Your hair," he said hastily, "is—is disarranged."

Katherine stood still, feeling awkward and numb. Her hands went to her hair and dutifully smoothed it back from her face. Why be disappointed in him, she asked herself, when a moment ago I was disappointed in myself? Now that the children were here, there would be no chance for questions she couldn't answer, kisses she didn't share. Gratefully she went to the cabin door, and waved the children to come in.

ii

The box social was held on a Sunday at the schoolhouse. Since the day was warm even for the middle of September, the men moved the benches out into the yard, and those who could sit still at such gatherings took places in the shade of the big cedar and alder trees. Katherine's desk, a

table one of the settlers had discarded when his family got
too big to find places by it, was set in the center of the yard.
By four o'clock it was covered with the lunches.

Some were in Indian baskets, like Katherine's. Two or
three women had been able to boast and packed their
lunches in shoeboxes the like of which everyone had seen,
but few bought, at Nate Tarpee's store. One lunch was put
up in an old sewing basket, another in a clean flour sack
with a girl's satin sash tied around.

Puffing enormously, Agatha Tine lowered herself from
her spring wagon, and trundled across the clearing to de-
posit a lunch packed away in a milk can. "Whoever gets
these eats is going to have to share with me," she wheezed.
"So nothing else was near big enough to hold it all." She
spotted Nils in a nearby group of men. "How about it, Nils?
You bid for my lunch and I'll promise to eat with one hand.
Anyways, I finished off a meal just before I come." Laughing, she moved toward the benches under the trees.

Old Uncle Julian blinked up at her, hands and chin resting comfortably on the piece of cherry wood he was using
as a cane. Next along the line was Faith Carlson, with little
Johnny, now six years old, stretched out asleep with his
head in her lap. Agatha looked appreciatively from one to
the other. "This is where I belong," she said, turning to
lower herself onto the bench. "In among the old men and
the lucky women."

Faith frowned. "I don't know as you have to holler it.
Nobody knows but Jeb and he says it don't show."

Agatha chuckled. "What kind of an eye has a man got
for things like that? Why not holler it? I'd be proud."

Faith nodded wearily. "I *am* proud. I'm just too tired
these days to show any of my better feelings."

The crowd at the box social represented Gold Mountain
prairie so thoroughly that it was easy to see who was absent.
The tight little groups of men, the lines of women on the

benches, turned to identify each newcomer and to cat-
alogue the missing. There's Nate Tarpee and his wife Bertha, their silent glances said. She don't get out much but
they say he don't encourage it, the way she likes her chaw
of terbacker. . . . There's Hi Barker, bless him, and his
son Levi. Could it be he come without his fiddle, or is that
it over there under the wagon seat? . . . Look at that
wagonload of Stump young 'uns. She's nursing one right
now, but what do you bet she's already carrying another.
It'll show when she stands up. If Tom does what he did
last time, he'll put in the first bid for every lunch, and
never raise his voice otherwise. . . . Let's see, Andersons,
Nelsons, Smiths, Carlsons. . . . And there's Nils Bengston holding little Julie by the hand while he talks to
that crowd of shingle weavers. Right next are a dozen
loggers Nils has working in his woods. Now what would
bring them traveling no-goods to a box social if it wasn't
orders from Nils? . . . Teacher was the last one here. She's
got real pretty the last year. Who'd of thought that scary-
looking little girl would finish out her first year, least of
all start a second by raising money for a new schoolhouse?
The captain's boy's been courting her all year. Oh yes,
there he is, right behind her, and don't he dress like a
gentleman from Seattle!

Agatha leaned toward Faith Carlson. "Who's the sweetheart of the social going to be today?"

Faith smiled. There was always one girl at a box social
whose box lunch caused a special flurry of bidding. She
wasn't always prettiest, and whether or not she was a clever
cook had nothing to do with it. But the eyes of the young
men would be caught by her, and they would make a game
out of paying her attention. Some would start it, others
would follow, until the girl was in an agony of blushes and
laughter. The older girls, who could remember when such

court had been paid them, would smile, their hands lingering possessively on the arms of their own men. They would
be critical or tolerant. They would laugh softly or sigh
with nostalgia. While the others, the men and women
who had long ago got over envying the young, laughed
with the game. Faith looked over the crowd with an expert
eye. "The boys seem to like that oldest Anderson girl."

A girl whose head was covered with pale yellow ringlets
had been surrounded by four or five boys. They were teas-
ing her, each fortified by the presence of the others. She
giggled, tossing her blond head.

Agatha said, "That's Belle, ain't it?" She studied the girl
critically. "Yep, there's bound to be some real lively bidding when her box is sold."

"If they know which is hers. You aren't supposed to tell."

Agatha guffawed. "Ain't you the innocent, Faith Carlson.
What do you suppose keeps the young men busy before the
bidding starts, if it isn't going around asking every pretty
girl which box is hers?" She punished her stomach with a
hearty slap. "For myself, I think that little red-headed
Katherine Duncan is far and away the prettiest female
here. She's ragged as the rest of us, but she's got style."

"She's the teacher!" Mrs. Carlson sounded genuinely
shocked.

"Sure she is," Agatha retorted, "but God gave her a pair
of big, beautiful eyes and the kind of hair men can't wait
to get their hands into. Teachers are supposed to be old
maids but that one don't look to be built for the part."

"Miss Duncan is engaged."

Agatha's little eyes rested speculatively on Carl White.
"Yes, I know. He told me, way last spring, but I don't see
no ring on her hand. And you still ain't heard them talk
about a wedding date." Agatha squinted wisely. "What's
that mean, to be 'engaged'?"

"To be promised," Faith Carlson snapped. Her pain had grown worse with this pregnancy and Agatha's good nature irritated her.

"Huh! When I first come to the Territory a girl was 'engaged' just as long as it took the preacher to get to the house after she said yes."

Nate Tarpee walked to the middle of the clearing and whopped the table with his fist. His long black hair had been carefully parted and plastered down with water. In one hand was a wide-brimmed black hat. He banged the table again, and the hum of voices quieted. Surveying the crowd, he twirled the hat several times at the end of a long forefinger. His face was expressionless as he flipped it into the air, ducked his head forward and straightened up, hat squarely on his head. Someone laughed. Frowning with mock fury, Nate turned toward the sound and shook his fist. At that, everyone laughed. Nate's long, sallow face cracked into a grin. "Well," he boomed, "now that you're awake, let's open up the bidding."

Nate made a good auctioneer. Having a sharp eye and a sure instinct, he knew which lunch belonged to Belle Anderson, which one the teacher had put up. He set them both aside for the last. He talked constantly, shouting, gesturing, pleading, confiding. When the bids were quick, his words rolled from his tongue so fast they shed their meaning. "It's for the school, itsfortheschool . . ." he chanted. "Be good to the school. Buy this lunch and be good to your stomach."

The men bid lightly, with a grin and a shrug of the shoulders, for most of them had already set aside a certain amount of money for the school and they enjoyed the game of letting Nate Tarpee tease it out of them. The lunches brought two dollars, four dollars, sometimes six or seven. At last only two remained. Nate Tarpee picked up the one every male under forty knew belonged to the pretty Belle

Anderson. It was said that Belle had been spoken for by a young woodsman from Black River. Tim Naughton, his name was, and he was here now, the center of a tight knot of his fellows.

The lunch was wrapped in a white cloth and tied around with a wide pink sash. Nate held it high, turning it to examine side, top, and bottom.

"Two dollars!" someone shouted. "Two dollars for the ribbon, five for the whole lunch!"

Another man yelled from the back of the crowd. Everyone laughed. Nate ignored them all. He turned the lunch around once more, even more slowly than before. He sniffed it loudly, rolling his eyes. The loggers began yelling. In their center, young Tim Naughton grinned self-consciously.

"All in good time, men, all in good time," said Nate.

"One million dollars!"

"The shirt off my back."

"If you could eat with your eyes, old Nate'd be full up."

"Start the bidding, you bow-legged swindler."

Nate bowed and a woman giggled. Belle Anderson, her face a bright pink, looked at everyone in the crowd but Tim Naughton.

"I have here," Nate began, "a rare jewel."

The bidding went fast at first. Secure in the fact that Belle's intended would have to win the lunch in the end no matter what it cost him, every man in the crowd got into it. "Two dollars!" one man called who hadn't but a dollar in his pocket. "Three!" another shouted, though he'd won a lunch three minutes before and had already pulled his supper partner behind a wagon and kissed her. "I'll give four!" said a third man, gesturing coarsely at the other two.

The bids leaped up a dollar at a time. There was so much loud joking, with two or three men blowing kisses toward the blushing Belle and several more challenging each other over the heads of the crowd, that the voices were almost indistinguishable. At five dollars the pace slowed and the bids went up fifty cents at a time.

Nate nodded, pointed, called, his ear alert for the highest number. "Eight dollars!" That was from Tim Naughton himself, and it stood out boldly from the bids of those less serious than he. It would be the last bid. Nate knew it and so he bellowed, "Now we're getting started. Now we're bidding. Eight dollars! That's fine for an opener. Do I hear ten? Do I hear ten?"

The answer burst out suddenly from the midst of the shingle weavers. Chuck Dwelley, his name was, and he had already lost two fingers though he was only twenty-four years old. "Down in Squak," he drawled, "we wouldn't think of taking a lady's box lunch for less'n twelve. So that's my bid."

The shingle weavers, brothers for every piece of finger that ever went down the chute, grouped behind their challenger. Around Tim Naughton the loggers closed in and began talking together in quick, low voices. The older men and women looked excitedly from one camp to the other. It was clear everyone else was out of it now.

Nate Tarpee rubbed his hands together. Belle Anderson blushed anew. The tittering of the other girls went on feebly for a moment, then stopped.

"Twelve!" Nate announced with a great show of disinterest. An ordinary bid, his long face said, a very ordinary bid in any auction *I* ever steered. . . . "That don't seem like . . ."

"Fourteen!" Tim Naughton interrupted. The loggers wheeled around, watching the weavers.

Chuck Dwelley laughed. "Is that all?" he said. "A girl would sure be unlucky to get herself a logger. I'll make it twenty!"

Man, woman and child caught a sharp breath and stared at the shingle weaver. His hands were in his pockets, he was resting back easily on his heels. His friends were lounging in the same position. No one in the crowd had ever heard a higher price offered for a pretty girl's lunch. Whispering started up. Who would have guessed that young fellow from Squak even knew Belle Anderson. Or did he? Everyone knew that to push the bid from fourteen to twenty, without even leaving an open door at all the figures in between, was an act of daring. But the weavers were looking at the loggers and grinning. We work in the mill, you work in the woods. You say we get high pay for staying under a roof and juggling little shingles and we say you're ignorant roughnecks without a brain between you. Twenty dollars, their grinning faces said. Why, that's nothing to a weaver!

Young Tim Naughton was frowning uneasily. His friends looked at him. He murmured something, shrugged his shoulders.

"Twenty," Nate warned, the hand that was high over his head keeping the bidding open. His eyes were on Tim Naughton.

Every logger in the little group pushed his hands into his pockets. Hurriedly they pulled out their money. A stack of three silver dollars. A handful of coins. A greenback, creased where it had been folded into a tight little square.

"Do I hear another bid?" Nate shouted. "Just one more before the end."

A logger waved at him frantically.

The shingle weavers laughed. "Mr. Auctioneer," Chuck Dwelley called, "is it allowed to raise my own bid?"

The loggers were sorting out the money, awkwardly counting it into Tim Naughton's hand. One of them reached back into his pants pocket, fishing anxiously through its empty depths. In the distance Belle Anderson bit her lip and turned alternately pink and white. Tears filled her eyes.

"Going, going . . ."

"Hold up!" the loggers yelled. Tim Naughton advanced, his hands cupped under the pile of money. "Twenty-seven dollars and thirty cents!"

Nate whirled, pointing his forefinger into Tim's face. "Going going gone!" he shrilled, so rapidly the all-important words melted together.

Chuck Dwelley drawled, "Hey, wait a minute . . ."

Tim Naughton dropped the money on the table and grabbed the lunch. The men cheered and the women laughed as he loped across the clearing to Belle Anderson's side. She was laughing now, though her cheeks were wet.

The shingle weavers thumped Chuck Dwelley's back, and doubled over with laughter at how they'd cost the loggers every cent they owned.

Carl stood up. "They've had their fun," he said to Katherine. "We'll buy your box outright, and save the bidding." He held out his arm.

A lady walks on her fiancé's right arm. It was the mannerly thing to do. But Katherine was conscious of Agatha, grinning wryly. Of Mrs. Nelson, arms akimbo, frankly judging her every gesture. She thought of the loggers and the shingle weavers, who laughed easily and mocked everything. Of Old Uncle Julian, who called Carl "the gentleman from Seattle." And Nils was still there, close by the table. She got up, pretending not to notice Carl's arm. "Yes, let's walk a bit."

"Katherine . . ."

She turned guiltily. Was he insisting for the sake of courtesy, or to claim her in front of everyone? "Oh, yes," she murmured. Her color rose unhappily as she slid her hand through his arm. In silence they walked through the crowd to the table.

Nate was just leaning forward to pick up her basket. The weavers and the loggers had wandered off, and many of the others had left to claim their partners. The fragrance of coffee drifted across the clearing. The women were boiling it on the schoolhouse hearth. Some of the men had gone back to playing horseshoes. There was a metallic clink of shoe against pin and a quick burst of laughter.

"No need to put this up for bidding," Carl said to Nate. He dropped a five dollar bill on the table and picked up the lunch basket.

Nate shrugged. "It don't matter to me. You'd of got it anyway." He picked up the bill. Yawning, he stuffed it into the canvas sack which contained the rest of the money.

"I'll bid ten."

Katherine's hand jerked from its hold on Carl's arm. She turned toward the voice and faced Nils Bengston.

He was smiling, not at her but over her head at Carl. There was no smile in his eyes. "Ten dollars," he repeated. "You ready to go better than that?"

Carl's voice was cold. "See here, Nils, I've bought the lunch. The bidding is closed."

"The bidding was never opened." He looked at Nate Tarpee. "O.K., Nate, you're the auctioneer. Take back that lunch and put it up right."

Nate shrugged uneasily. "Nils, you already bought a lunch. It cost you six-fifty. What do you want with another?"

Nils answered Nate, but he looked down at Katherine. "We got to build that new school, don't we?"

Katherine pulled her glance away from Nils. Her hands were trembling. She let one clutch the other, trying to steady them. She had better luck with her voice. "This is ridiculous!" she said quite clearly.

Nils chuckled. "Twelve dollars, then," he said. "That'll do more for the school than Carl's five, won't it, Teacher?"

Carl stepped forward. "Miss Duncan's lunch is not for sale!" He jerked a ten dollar bill from his wallet and threw it on the table. "Fifteen, then, to close the bidding. It's all I have."

Nate stammered, "Going going gone . . ."

Carl said to Nils, "You can outbid me, but Miss Duncan would refuse to be your supper partner anyway."

For an instant Nils looked thoughtfully at Carl. Then he grinned, dismissing him entirely. "I'm glad we got your friend to loosen up a little," he said to Katherine, "for the sake of the new school."

Carl exploded, "Blast you, Nils!"

Katherine, not Nils or Carl, heard the first shout. It came from the oldest Smith boy, who had been too sick with a fever to come to the social. He was here now, riding a pony bareback and with nothing much on but a cotton shirt and a pair of jeans. His face was flushed with fever and the effort of riding hard. "Prairie fire!" he gasped as the pony galloped into the clearing. "It's burning across our place, headed north and west!"

Katherine looked dumbly from Nils to Carl. Nils could have forgotten them. Anger, amusement, deviltry were wiped from his face. "Prairie fire!" he shouted. He cupped his hands to his mouth. "Prairie fire heading this way! Every man get home fast, pick up every bucket you got and ride for the Smith place!" He began to run.

All around them, the men and boys began running, too. As Nils reached his horse and leaped into the saddle, the first box wagon was headed for the trail.

"Jennie, Tommy, Max . . ." a mother called. "Jennie, Tommy, Max . . ."

"Into the wagon," Jeb Carlson shouted, carrying Johnny over one shoulder and dragging Hiram with his free hand. Faith Carlson limped painfully behind, her body heavy with the new child.

"Prairie fire . . . prairie fire . . ." Young Tim Naughton was racing toward his horse, the bright pink sash from his sweetheart's lunch draped idiotically across his chest.

Hi Barker ran toward his wagon, Levi right beside him. "Wagon's too slow," Hi called to his son. "We'll unhitch the team and ride on their backs. Them draft horses will pass up every cayuse on the trail."

"But Pa, your fiddle's in the back."

Hi Barker hesitated, then said gruffly, "If we don't stop the fire, I won't be here to play it," and he began to loosen the harness.

Prairie fire at the Smith place—Katherine thought suddenly, Why the next homestead north and west of the Smiths' is the Carlsons'! She whirled on Carl. "Quick, unharness the team. Faith and the children would be better off waiting here anyway. We'll ride as the Barkers are doing. We'll get there faster."

"Fighting a prairie fire is no job for a woman." He tried to take her arm. "Here, I'll help you into the wagon. When we reach Carlsons', I'll go out with the men."

Katherine shook herself free of his protective arm. "Where do you think I come from?" she blazed at him. "A—a city? I've seen prairie fires. The more hands on the bucket line the better. I'm going to help." She grabbed his sleeve. "Please, Carl," she pleaded, trying to pull him toward the wagon. "Take the harness off the horses. We can go faster!"

"A woman, racing bareback on a workhorse? Katherine, you're the teacher here!"

Katherine peered into Carl's face. He just could not see. She looked desperately around the schoolyard. Not ten feet away the Greene boy, her seventeen-year-old pupil, was tightening the cinch around his pony's belly. She ran to him. "Emil, may I ride behind?"

The boy grinned. "Sure, Teacher." Katherine grabbed

the rim of the saddle, and he boosted her onto the horse with one hand.

"Katherine!" Carl called, running toward them. "Come back immediately!"

"Should I wait, Miss Duncan?" the Greene boy asked, in the voice of an obedient school boy.

"You may go," his teacher gasped, throwing her arms around his waist, "and Emil, the faster the better."

iii

It was the river that saved Gold Mountain. The trading post and the hotel. The blacksmith shop, the boarding house and the grist mill. Lean-tos, cabins, the lop-sided shack and the abandoned building rotting under its false front—they were all preserved for the next generation because the river happened to run only a hundred rods away.

But the homesteads south and east of the settlement were not as well protected. The Smith cabin burned to the ground. The wind rose, blowing down on the prairie from the east, and by the time the men had collected buckets and raced to the fire the Carlson place was in flames.

The homestead lay at a sharp bend in the Middle Fork, so that the river ran along two sides. The fire, a crackling, darting line of flame that was over a quarter mile long, swept forward at an angle from the other side.

The Greene boy kept his pony at a full gallop most of the way. Katherine held on around his waist, hugging him as a frightened bear cub hugs its powerful mother. The smoke was heavy when they were still a mile away. As they neared the Carlson place, Emil Greene began slapping the reins on each side of the pony's neck. "Yi, Yi!" he hollered at the sweating cayuse. "Yi, yi . . ." The smoke was sharp and he began to cough. Katherine felt it sweep into her nostrils, down into her throat. She lowered her head, half burying her face in the boy's back.

They could see the fire from a spot where the trail followed an inside curve of the river. Emil pulled the pony up. There were other horses here, some free, some loosely tied to the trees nearest the water. "Looks like we don't dare ride in further," he said. He sounded like a conscientious fifth-grader apologizing for the way he'd done his lesson. "Better leave the pony and run for it."

They hit the ground at the same time, and began to run. The smoke became more unbearable with every step. Katherine stopped. She grabbed Emil's arm and motioned to lie down on the ground. With a quick jerk she opened a tear in her petticoat, quickly ripped a long strip off the bottom and tore the material in two. "Here, tie that across your face." They knotted the pieces of petticoat at the backs of their heads, and ran on.

The meadow Jeb Carlson had cleared so painfully with one ox, was a field of fire. The new barn he had built only two months before was in the center of it, a peak of flame. But a strip of pasture still lay between the fire and the house. Along its edge the bucket line had formed, the last man standing up to his knees in the river.

It was Tim Naughton, the silly pink satin ribbon still tied around his chest. The ends of it were wet from dragging in the river. "Other end of the line!" he gasped. "Need help at the other end of the line." He lifted his hands like a baseball player, caught the empty bucket the next man threw. With one sweep he bent down and filled it. The next man leaped across the intervening space and lifted it from his hand. Tears from the smoke streamed down his face and he ran as awkwardly as a wounded bull moose, but he held the bucket gingerly, scarcely spilling a drop.

"Other end," Katherine said, blinking to take her direction. The line from the river was single. Nearing the fire, it fanned out. From there on there was no set pattern to it, for the front of the fire was broad and there were very few men to police it. With Emil beside her, Katherine ran as Tim Naughton had directed.

The last man at the far end was Nils Bengston. His face glistened with sweat. Soot had streaked his cheeks and settled on his blond hair like black hayseed. He glanced at her briefly, then at Emil. "There," he said, jerking his head toward buckets which lay on their sides behind him. Katherine recognized them as the ones Jeb Carlson had kept in the new barn. Someone—Nils?—had got into the barn and pulled them out. She picked one up and took a position some ten or twelve feet to Nils' left. Emil grabbed another, ran back to exchange it for a full one.

They moved rhythmically. The instant the weight of a full bucket pulled on his hand, the man up front lowered his head, ran through the smoke. Aiming as carefully as he could he threw the water along the edge of the flame. Back to the man at the head of the water line, he dropped the empty bucket, reached for the full one.

Nils ran to Katherine. "This wind is tricky. You stay well back of me." He was shouting, though he was so close she had to tip her head to see his face. "You pass the buckets. I'll go up to the fire and empty them."

She nodded. Smoke was so thick she could not speak without choking. She reached out blindly, and Nils dropped an empty bucket into her hands. Suddenly he grinned. "Good girl," he seemed to be saying. She turned and ran to Emil, dropped the empty bucket, took the full one from his hands.

It was harder to run with a pail of water than she had expected. She was fighting for breath when she reached Nils. His big hand touched hers as he took the water from her. Lightly, the handle of the empty bucket fell across her palm. She turned and ran back.

There was no time to it, no day, night or hour. The first wave of exhaustion passed, and Katherine felt strong and light-headed. Then weariness swept back, and she worked grimly, pleading for a little more breath. She and Nils and Emil raced toward each other through the yellow smoke, met briefly, turned and ran apart.

They did not shout it to each other, but they knew that the fire was gaining. With each frantic glance over her shoulder, Katherine saw they were closer to the house. The wind was tricky, as Nils had said. For a while the creeping fire would lie low along the ground, and then with a sudden gust from the east it leaped forward. Then the pitiful buckets of water were useless against it.

More men arrived to fight the fire and the line closed in a little more with each new addition. The rhythm of the bucket line remained unbroken. Swing to the right, grab a good hold, swing to the left, let go when he has it, pick up the empty one, roll it down the line, swing to the right . . .

"She's breaking through!"

Katherine heard Nils shout. She stopped in her race toward Emil, and turned back. With her eyes all but closed against the smoke, she could just pick him out, a dark giant in an eddy of smoke. In confusion she ran toward him. Before she reached him she saw there was fire at her right where the next man in line had been standing only a second before. She wheeled around, trying to get her bearings from the position of the house. The house was lost. She stared helplessly, like a child suddenly separated from its mother. The wind, fierce and capricious, turned the smoke aside for an instant, and she caught a glimpse of the house. It was directly in back of her, as she thought. But between them was a roaring wall of flame.

She turned back. "Nils!" He appeared almost miraculously. He was bare to the waist. The shirt in his hands was charred and his arms were singed. "You moved," he gasped. "I looked for you. Make for the river."

Obediently she began to run. His arm stopped her, thrown around her hard and jerking her backward. "No!" he cried against her ear, "not that way. It broke through and the house is going." He whirled her around roughly, with one hand pushed her forward. "I got to get Emil. You can make it alone. But run, girl, run!"

She ran. Her long skirt sagged where she had torn it. One foot caught in it and she fell to the ground. She jumped up, beginning to run again. The skirt caught on a snag and she went down once more. She could hear the fire behind her, hissing like a wildcat. With the wind behind it, it was moving as fast as a horse could run. She struggled to her feet. Panic turned her feet to lead. You can make it, he'd said. Her feet in their high button shoes raced with a will of their own. Across the field, through the long dry grass, down the slope—with a sob of relief Katherine felt the gravel of the river bank press into the thin soles.

She looked back. The fire could have been no more than a few feet behind her. She watched with sick fascination as it ripped down the grassy slope, sputtered and died in the stretch of wet sand only a few feet away. People were shouting, some of them very near. She meant to turn and look for Nils, to see if he had found Emil Greene and carried him to safety. She should look for Jeb Carlson, for the Barkers, for Carl. But she didn't do any of these things. For a second or two she looked straight ahead, a strange dizziness creeping through her brain to lodge in a great black mass at the back of her eyes. Then she fainted.

iv

Everyone agreed later that Katherine was lucky not to be drowned. With the unconscious Emil Greene over his shoulder, Nils reached the spot on the river bank only seconds after Katherine dropped. He set Emil down in the sand, lifted Katherine out of six or eight inches of water and stretched her out beside Emil. With handfuls of water and a few sharp slaps, he brought the boy to.

Emil began coughing helplessly. "Watch her," Nils ordered. Emil nodded. Grinning, Nils disappeared down the river bank.

They said the Smiths and Carlsons were lucky, too, lucky to be alive. Both families lost their homes, their barns and sheds, and everything in them except the livestock. Nate Tarpee moved a few barrels and sacks around and found room for the Smiths in the back of the trading post. The Carlsons moved into an abandoned homestead shack that was part of Nils Bengston's shingle mill.

"It's lucky the good weather is holding," Faith Carlson said. "It's hard to hold a good house-raising in the rain." But she didn't call it "lucky" that her pain had grown worse. Patiently she lied to herself, saying that these later pregnancies were always hard. But she let Katherine tend to the cooking and mind the children. Only when Jeb came near the cabin did she force herself to get up, and with a second, even harder effort, force herself to smile.

The dates for the house-raisings were set. Every family in the Valley joined in. The men cut logs, split the shakes, trimmed and shaped and cut with adze and frow, axe and drawknife. The women brought food and clothes for the children and squares for the quilting bee. The last of the hops had been picked, dried, baled and pulled by four-horse teams to the storehouse near the Black River boat landing. So the crews of foremen were free, and Nils brought them along to help with the building.

The day the Carlsons moved into their new cabin, Mrs. Carlson was too sick to sit up. She rode to her new home in the back of the box wagon, carefully wrapped in layers of borrowed quilts. "I'll be up by Thanksgiving," she promised the children. They looked at her solemnly, a puzzled little crowd in a semicircle around the big new bed.

"Promise?" Hiram asked.

"Promise," she said.

He turned to his little brother. "She promised, John," he explained. Relieved, the little group broke up and raced outside.

Katherine hid her face by busying herself at the kitchen table. With hands that had grown quick and sure, she laid a cooking fire. If Faith Carlson could so promise, if Faith could smile fearlessly at her husband, what grounds were there for her own uneasiness? Pray constantly, the two of them said, and shave once a day. There was comfort in work and in that way, Katherine thought ruefully, she had more to take comfort from than most.

She measured the lard out into the big brown mixing bowl, quickly cutting it into the flour. Clothes had to be made, for they all had but one covering apiece. Nate Tarpee had given them yarn for sweaters and there were castoffs from all over the Valley to be cut down to size for the children. On top of this, there was another week of school, and then Thanksgiving.

The children would be frightened if they did not have a real Thanksgiving. To let the holiday pass, or even to let it be a little less or a little different, would be instant notice that their mother was gravely ill. No, she would have to manage it. The pumpkin pies, made with honey. The mincemeat ground from venison and fruit rinds. The roast pheasant, the ham, the pickled apples . . .

A bit of flour sprayed across her skirt. With the back of her arm, she brushed it off. This was her only dress and she hadn't even an apron. She thought suddenly, I wonder what Carl would think if he saw me.

Her throat tightened, as it always did nowadays at the thought of Carl. She hadn't seen him since the day she had disobeyed him, riding away on the back of Emil's cayuse. She had heard later that Carl worked in the bucket line. "Carried more water than any two of the rest of us," Jeb Carlson told her. "And then he got back on his horse and rode down to Black River." Carl had gone back to Seattle on the *Viking*, but he hadn't returned with her next trip nor with any trip since. On the day of the fire Nils Bengston had tried to make him wait, Jeb told her, but Carl wouldn't listen.

"What did Nils say to him?" Katherine asked, for she couldn't, wouldn't, ask Nils himself. "What could have made Carl go off like that?"

Jeb shook his head. "Couldn't of been anything Nils said. I was standing right there. Nils was arguing that Carl ought to stay and take care of you. 'She's down there on the beach, stretched out cold,' Nils told him. 'Somebody ought to take care of her. It ought to be you.' But Carl wouldn't answer him, except to say the *Viking* was due to pull out."

"Then Carl knew where I was."

Jeb nodded. "Yes, he knew." Having told her, because she had asked him and he was a truthful man, Jeb was uneasy. "It ain't like Carl to run off without doing what he ought," he said. "He saw me standing there, he knew I'd go down and watch over you."

But it hadn't been a good excuse, and as time had passed it hadn't improved. Katherine pushed angrily on the dough for the Thanksgiving cookies. According to his code, Carl had been justified in his anger, but there was no code in the world that made it right to run away. If he had come back, if he were in the room right now, she would not apologize. For the first time, she would not bring them back together at all if their only meeting ground was her apology. Once she had cared for him enough to say anything to save his pride. She didn't now. Another step had been taken, another moment had come, another bit had been stolen from the imperfect whole.

8

i

If Hi Barker said it would rain before Christmas, it would rain. Katherine had never doubted it. The crickety little fiddler had an instinct for changes in the weather. While other prophets tested their rheumatic joints and said it was sure to storm, Hi cocked his head to one side, sniffed, listened as if there were sounds too high or low for anyone else to hear, and told you exactly what the weather would be.

The first time Levi came to school with one of his father's predictions, Katherine nodded absently and dismissed it. The children were wearing jackets and there was a fire in the hearth, but Hi Barker said they were in for a hot spell. Katherine was fanning herself with a spelling tablet the next afternoon, schoolhouse shutters and door wide open, when she remembered Hi's words. She laughed, thinking that he must be some kind of wizard. A not-quite-human, music-making sprite, but a good one. No wonder they had named the mountain for him.

Rain before Christmas—that had been bright-eyed little Hi Barker's reply the very day the worst blizzard of years broke across the Valley. Now it was the day before Christmas, and the snowdrift that had piled up to the eaves on the east side of the Carlsons' barn was reduced to a dirty gray mound, forlorn in the middle of a mud puddle. Gone was the snow-white Christmas many farmers from the Middle West had been anticipating so sentimentally. It didn't look like Christmas in Minnesota now. There was no reason to be reminded of that last holiday season in Kansas, or the days when you took a sleigh to grandma's house across the glittering prairie of Nebraska. No turning back, even in memory, from the new and sometimes brutally unfamiliar country. The giant trees, the swollen river, the hard, wind-driven rain, the damp and the dark—this could be no other place than the timber country of western Washington.

Katherine lifted a log from the pile next to the hearth and laid it on the fire. The children were all outside—there wasn't a youngster in the Valley who would think of staying in the house because of so ordinary thing as rain—and when they came in for supper they would have to be dried out somehow. Christmas Eve. Katherine looked at the room wistfully. Whatever there was of Christmas in it, the children had made themselves.

Richie and Martha had cut the tree and nailed it upright between two pieces of firewood. All of them, even little tow-headed Johnny, had made its decorations. Scraps of ribbon, bits of red calico, a little string, paste made from flour and water—they had used these precious things. On the tree were strings of holly berries and popcorn, "snowballs" of cotton, and stars that looked like almost anything but stars, cut from lined theme paper Katherine brought home from school.

"Stars of Bethlehem," the brown-eyed Hiram called them, and once started on cutting them could not be stopped until every scrap of paper was gone. Then he insisted on putting all of them on the tree. He could reach only the lower branches. The older children obligingly hung their decorations up above. With its lower limbs white with stars and stars alone, and its upper ones so crowded with berries and cotton and popcorn that the green scarcely showed through, the tree looked like an overdressed woman with her petticoat dragging. The children admired the tree unreservedly, except for Richie who seemed a little puzzled. Hiram quizzed Johnny remorselessly as to which of the stars were best and why.

"I like that one," Johnny would reply, so eager to please that he pointed to four or five.

"That's un-possible." Hiram picked up Johnny's stubby hand, pulled up the pointer finger and adjusted it properly. "Now show me the absolute best."

Johnny giggled, looking delightedly at what Hiram was doing to his hand. "You tickled!"

Hiram frowned. "John, pay good attention!"

Instantly Johnny sobered. Without a glance at the tree he flung his arm out dramatically. "That one!"

Hiram seemed impressed by his little brother's posture, but puzzled as he analyzed his choice. He squatted a little so as to sight down Johnny's finger toward the tree. "This one?" he asked, touching a paper star with one finger.

Johnny nodded energetically.

Hiram looked critically at the star. "The absolute best?" he mused. He shook his head slowly. "No, John. This one has too many points. We'll have to start over again."

Little Johnny looked longingly over his shoulder.

"Pay good attention, John!" Hiram warned. "Now, think hard. Which do you think is the absolute best?"

The Christmas goodies were lined up on the shelf next to the fireplace. The children had had a hand in their making, as could be seen at a glance. Cookie cutters were a luxury no Valley homesteader owned unless they were inherited treasure saved somehow during the long voyage west. Since sugar went into it, cookie dough was a treasure in itself. Katherine had divided it between the children and let them cut shapes out of it freehand. Richie's angel was easily recognized. Martha's Christmas trees were symmetrical, almost, or as Martha put it, "Perfectly even, on one side." The triangles, circles, rabbits, dogs and reindeer which the other children made were all clear enough, until one got down to the handiwork of Hiram.

After earnest discussion he had convinced Johnny that six was a little too young for shaping cookies. Johnny hadn't agreed at all until Hiram presented the wooden potato masher and told him he "was allowed" to crush the rock candy into the crystals which were to be sprinkled on the cookies. Johnny pounded contentedly while Hiram preëmpted his share of the dough, and made stars out of all of it.

Stars out of cookie dough were an even greater problem than stars out of theme paper, and when they were baked most of them looked like blistered circles. But Hiram went to the shelf every quarter hour to admire them. His happiness was unmarred until he was told that eventually they would have to be eaten. Then his tears were so overpowering that he had to run outside so no one would see him cry.

The matter of Christmas presents had troubled Katherine the most. Since the fire there hadn't been an extra board or nail or length of goods around the place. Jeb had been cutting timber for Nils; not a cent of his wages or Katherine's could be spent for anything but necessities.

How many Christmases, Katherine reflected, have I prayed for a doll and found that my only present was a suit of long woolen underwear? There is no poverty worse than the poverty of owning nothing silly. She had bought suits of underwear, seven of them, at Nate Tarpee's store, paying half and promising the rest when school reopened and she would receive wages. But she had made rag dolls, with embroidered faces and white petticoats starched stiff as crinoline. She had bargained with Indian Doc, whose knotted old hands were deft at wood carving. If he carved and painted small war canoes for the boys, she would give him a plug of chewing tobacco. Nate had given her the tobacco. "But don't tell Berthy," he said. "It's the last in the place and she had her eye on it."

Thus Katherine believed the problem of Christmas presents had been solved, until the day she found Martha in tears because she had nothing to give her mother.

"I know just how she feels," Tommy sobbed sympathetically. "Because I feel so bad myself."

Faith Carlson was in bed, as she had been almost continually since the fire, but she slept fitfully. Katherine herded the children out of the cabin and into the woodshed.

"Now," she said to the assembled seven, "we will decide about the Christmas presents for your mother."

Their faces were sad and wise. Only little Hiram and Johnny screwed up their foreheads thoughtfully, as if presents were actually a matter of choice, not of money.

"We can't buy anything," Richie said.

Tommy wailed, "I feel so *bad!*"

Katherine said quickly, "But you can *make* something."

Tommy quieted and his eyes widened with interest. Richie looked doubtful, but he watched her hopefully. Martha exclaimed, "Oh, Miss Duncan, could we make something for the new baby?"

So for some time they discussed the new baby.

Most of all, Johnny wanted to know where it was. Hiram silenced him with a superior, 'Inside of Mama, of course. Where do you think you came from?" Johnny was too astonished to say anything more. Each child decided what his present would be—a toy made from spools, a dress, a shawl, a pair of booties, a crayoned picture, a stuffed bear, and from Johnny, a riding horse.

Hiram exclaimed, "Oh, John! You can't *make* a riding horse!"

Johnny's mouth trembled threateningly.

"That's all right, Johnny," Katherine put in. "Maybe you can't, but somebody makes them."

Richie got up from the keg he'd been sitting on. "I'm going to get started." The other children followed, all of them happy with their secret projects.

Like the tree and the cookies, the presents were now awaiting the day of celebration. Tonight being Christmas Eve, there would be prayers and songs and a simple supper so that every edible involving sugar or raisins or honey or butter or other precious materials could be saved for the next day. Katherine sighed. Thanksgiving, with their mother sick abed, had been hard enough, perhaps because Faith had promised her children to be well by then. She had made no promises about Christmas, and the children seemed to know they should not ask her to. There was to be a new baby in February—they understood that and accepted her illness as one of the adult mysteries connected with it.

Only Richie could remember that the other children had been born without these long months of pain. Katherine

saw that he was afraid, saw that like her own brother Teddy
he would keep it to himself. Faith Carlson had succeeded
in deceiving her husband. Perhaps, Katherine thought,
because she tried so hard. She seemed to collect her
strength all day for the time when Jeb would come in from
the woods and ask her how she felt. Even her color improved and her eyes brightened. With Jeb to see her she
actually looked different. Tomorrow Jeb would be home
all day.

Faith appeared at the bedroom door. Her face was gray.
She steadied herself with a hand at each side of the door
frame.

Katherine started. "Faith, whatever . . ."

Mrs. Carlson walked slowly across the room. In her full
muslin nightdress her body looked grotesquely out of pro-
portion to her small head and narrow shoulders. The pil-
low had flattened the hair at the back of her head and the
braids had been loosened by her tossing. She reached the
rocking chair and lowered herself heavily. "Don't worry,"
she said unevenly. She was gasping for breath. "I want
to be up for Christmas Eve. And I'm going to get up tomorrow morning and stay up all day." She took several
long, quick breaths. "Except for going to the church service
at the trading post. I don't think I could . . . stand the
trip in the wagon. Too bouncy . . ." She tried to smile.

"Really, Faith, you shouldn't."

Faith said wistfully, "Oh, Katherine, not for Christmas?"

Of course Christmas was different. Gay, sentimental. A
time to love and a time to forgive. Katherine turned her
back to Faith and busied herself with putting the plates
out for supper. Carl had neither written to her nor come to
Gold Mountain since the day of the box social and the
fire. The Carlsons, bless them, had never questioned her.

Being a good deal less sensitive, Agatha Tine had.

"Where's that eleegant fiancy of yours?" she asked, pronouncing the words with a little pout. "Jilted you, did he?"

"He is very busy," Katherine had replied, "finishing his law course."

Agatha grinned. "Proud, eh. Well, when he gets done with that course," and she winked broadly, "come on down and tell me how your engagement is coming along."

Katherine reached angrily for the mush bowls. With far more speed than was necessary she set them out along the deal table. Agatha had been right, of course. She was "engaged," but forgotten. She had a "fiancy," but no one to love. She turned, and taking the spoons from the shelf, dropped them on the table with a clatter.

"Daddy's coming!"

That was Hiram and Susie, heralding their father's coming with simultaneous shrieks. Another child called, "Is Daddy coming?" and three others, standing out in the yard in the rain, yelled, "Yes Daddy's coming!"

Katherine kept her back to Faith. She knew what Faith would be doing and right now, at this particular moment of weakness, she could not bear to see it. She would be smoothing back her hair, hastily replaiting her braids. She would straighten her shawl and feel anxiously at the ruching around her throat. When the sound of his voice meant he was nearing the door she would sit up straight, moisten her lips, smile. . . .

Katherine made herself pick up the pile of spoons and one by one set them beside the bowls. Christmas, she thought, Christmas, alone.

ii

The wind rose as the sun went down. It whined through the cedars so angrily that the knock on the door was al-

most lost in the sound of it. Frowning, Jeb pushed his chair
away from the table. "Now who, in this storm . . ."

Katherine felt a warning jerk at her heart. If it were . . .

Jeb opened the door. Wet through, his jaw clenched
and body tensed against the raw wind, was Carl.

Katherine's hands flew to her hair. It was loose around
her shoulders, for she hadn't had time to braid it. Her dress
—panicky fingers felt of the skirt, reminding her that this
was the one she had cut from a faded cotton of Mrs. Nelson's.

"Come in, come in!" Jeb was saying, his hand on Carl's
elbow. He peered into the darkness. "Where's your horse?
You *did* ride out from Seattle?"

"I put him in your barn." Carl was shaking with cold.
He still hadn't looked directly at the group around the supper table.

Jeb smiled. "Lucky for us you were putting something
in instead of taking something out," he said jovially, "We
can't hear a sound in this wind."

Katherine meant to rise, but sat frozen to the bench.
How will I look to him? she thought. What will he think
when he sees me.

"First of all you warm up, and then you'll have some hot
food." Jeb turned toward the table. "Faith . . . Katherine . . ."

Carl turned his head slowly. "Mrs. Carlson," he said politely, inclining his head. "Katherine . . ."

He was looking at her at last. She tried to smile. Like a
sleepwalker she got up and went to him. The children's heads swiveled slowly as she passed. She extended
her hand. "I'm glad to see you, Carl," she said, and flushed
because her voice was only a whisper.

"I'm glad to be here," he said stiffly. His hand felt cold,
but no colder than her own. Quickly she looked away.
"Come over by the fire, and dry out . . ."

During the hours that followed Katherine blessed the number and noisiness of the many Carlsons. But at last all the children were in bed and asleep, and Jeb was saying good night as he helped Faith to bed and closed the bedroom door. Silence was heavy as Katherine and Carl looked at each other, adjusting to the reality of being alone together. It was the moment Katherine had yearned for; yet from her first glimpse of him in the doorway tonight she had dreaded it.

Carl's dark eyes were intent upon her face, asking something of her. In confusion, she turned toward the hearth. "I'll put more wood on the fire."

Carl jumped forward. He took the log out of her hands and dropped it onto the heavy andirons. Dusting one palm against the other, he turned to her.

Like a docile child, she waited for his kiss. He looked down at her, only a shadow of space between them. Her body tensed. The faintest shiver flickered through her, as if someone had blown suddenly at the back of her neck.

Carl cleared his throat. "Katherine, there are several matters we must talk over."

The moment lost its intimacy. Carl walked away, turned with his hands clasped together behind his back. It's to be a business meeting, Katherine thought, not a love scene. She nodded. "Yes, Carl."

"When I last saw you . . ." He hesitated, searching for a word, the right word.

"Yes, Carl."

There was a trace of mimicry in her voice, though she hadn't meant it. His pose cracked and he stepped forward and took her hands. "Katherine," he said huskily, "don't mock me."

She flushed. His dark eyes were hurt and all the pride was gone from his face. It was a kind of loss he couldn't

stand as well as other people. Suddenly she had to comfort
him. "Carl, I wasn't mocking you. I couldn't."

"There is so much to talk about," he said. "All the things
I've been thinking about, the questions that have been tormenting me since that day."

She said softly, "That day of the box social and the prairie fire."

He drew his breath in sharply. For a moment his eyes
searched her face. His hands relaxed, he sighed, and the
relaxation seemed to spread through his body. "Yes," he
said quietly, "that day." He dropped her hands and turned
to stare into the fire.

The unspoken question hung in the silence. It might
have been a physical object which Carl had dragged from
hiding and flung down between them. Do we love each
other and are we to marry? It was that simple, so terribly
simple that neither of them could say it. In all the time
since she had last seen him, Katherine had never voiced it
to herself. It hit her now, brutal and clear. If they understood each other, as she had once imagined they did, that
was the question they must answer together. If somewhere
during the struggles of the past two years that understanding had been lost, then it was the question she would have
to answer for herself. Instinctively she tensed, ready to defend herself. "Well, Carl?"

He burst out, "Why did you ride off in—that way? Why
have you refused to leave the Valley, when originally you
wanted nothing more than to get away from it? How can
you have allowed yourself to—to lower your standards of
conduct, and appearance . . ." He wheeled to face her.
"Katherine, how . . ."

Katherine lifted her chin. This at least is familiar, she
thought. He stepped forward and pulled her into his arms.
It was so unexpected that she clung to him, comforting him

with little mechanical pats on the arm. "My dear, my dear," he said hoarsely, "don't try to explain anything. I know now that it doesn't matter."

While he kissed her Katherine thought, Why, he has forgiven me! She wanted to protest. In his arms, how could she?

He released her. Before she could speak he pulled a little box from his pocket and opened it quickly. A diamond solitaire in a setting of yellow gold sparkled with the reflected firelight.

His eyes were on her face. Dumbstruck, she looked at the ring, then at him.

Carl laughed. "I wish you could see your face! It's a picture. You really *were* surprised." He picked up the ring and dropped the box into his pocket. Smiling he lifted her left hand and carefully slid the solitaire onto her finger. "You should have had this a long time ago."

Katherine thought, courtly compliment, or a rule of etiquette? And then Carl unknowingly answered her. "It isn't proper to be engaged without it."

Katherine let him take her in his arms, and waited obediently for the proper kiss.

iii

Determined as she was, Faith Carlson was too ill to get up Christmas morning. The children opened her presents for her, and spread their handiwork for the "new baby" all over the coverlet. Jeb asked if her pain was worse, and she denied it. "All of you go ahead to church," she insisted. "The sun's shining. It's a nice day. It'll be three months before Brother Bill gets back this way again and I don't want the children to miss him."

So Katherine put clean shirts on the boys and fresh pina-

fores on the girls and Jeb loaded them all in the back of
the wagon. Katherine sat next to Jeb. Carl, who had slept
overnight in front of the fireplace, rode behind.

It had been his own idea to attend services with the Carlsons. "Brother Bill is close to illiterate," he told Katherine
privately, "but the church service does give us an opportunity to appear together."

As on other special occasions, Nate Tarpee had moved
bales and barrels to create space for the church service.
The store's peculiarly varied assortment of chairs, benches
and stools was lined up as "pews" facing the "pulpit,"
which was Nate's store counter. Out of consideration for
Brother Bill the bottles of whiskey, the beer keg and mugs,
the boxes of cigars and tins of pipe tobacco, had been
stowed in the back room. Even the big brass spittoons, the
post's special refinement, had been removed from sight,
though Nate had always held that this worked a hardship
on many members of the congregation, among them his
wife Bertha. "More people would come to church," he complained, "if they could spit."

Most everyone came anyway, for though Brother Bill dis-
approved of many of their pleasures, he was widely admired. Two or three times a Baptist evangelist had
appeared and held mass baptisms in the river; it was gen-
erally felt that his kind of religion "didn't take," simply because some of his conversations were notably ungodly.
A Catholic priest came occasionally to the Valley; except
for two Irish families in Three Forks, his followers were
Indians. Best known and most widely loved was Brother
Bill, whose last name of William was heard so little (some
of his devoted followers didn't know it) that few remembered it was the reason for his being called "Bill" and that
his first name was really Theodore.

Brother Bill was a Methodist, though more than half of
the people who came to hear him were not. For one hun-

dred and sixty-nine dollars a year he walked a circuit of some hundred and fifty miles. Nils Bengston, who said the man was a fool to earn a living that way, had once proved it by figuring that Brother Bill received twenty-five cents a mile. "A quarter for every mile," Nils put it, "and not a cent for preaching." Brother Bill was tall, though not as tall as Nils, and he was built wide and heavy. And he had a temper. People in the Valley said it was just as well that he and Nils had never been in the same room together, and unless Nils got the fear of the Lord in him, they weren't likely to.

Brother Bill slept in barns, and sometimes preached in them. His friends along the circuit fed him and gave him a bed, if they had one, but there wasn't a single settlement big enough to provide him with a church. At one time the people of Black River had thought they could at least give him a horse and buggy, and began a collection for it. When he heard of it from Hilke Orvaag, Brother Bill devoted the last thirty minutes of his two-hour sermon to refusing it.

There were so few trails wide enough for a buggy that he would be forced to neglect parts of his district that were the hardest to reach. The easy way was not the true way to serve God. And he had another reason. If he had a horse and buggy, he explained, the young men would want to borrow it Saturday nights to go visit their sweethearts. Knowing young men and their girls and the distances which separated them, he was sure the horse and buggy would never be returned on time for an early start on the Lord's work. So he had continued walking. He followed Indian trails, wagon roads, pack and sled trails, sometimes nothing but blazes. Fallen logs, swamp, rivers and creeks impeded his progress. He once admitted that he had often followed bear trails rather than crawl through the brush on his hands and knees.

No one knew whether Brother Bill had heard Nils Bengston's cruel calculation of the value of his service. But the

first people in the Valley—the ones who had seen Brother
Bill limp into Black River when the only family in town
was the one that kept the post office, those people—who
heard the third sermon Brother Bill had ever preached—
knew that one hundred and sixty-nine dollars a year seemed
like enough to Brother Bill because at first he had covered
the same circuit for nothing.

"How are you going to live?" the people at Black River
had asked him that first Sunday. "We can't pay you."

"Like Sherman," Brother Bill had replied with a grin,
"when he marched to the sea!"

iv

"And Lord don't let no bitterness come into our hearts.
Open up our eyes to what's right, like you always done. In
Jesus' name, Amen." Brother Bill looked up from the final
prayer. His straight black hair was hanging in his eyes.
Blinking a little he smiled, and the service was over.

The congregation stirred slowly. The men reached for
their hats and quickly jammed them down to their ears, as
if they had just found they were undressed. The woman
rose, breathed deeply as if to inflate their bosoms.

On the bench where the Carlsons sat, Katherine began
helping little Johnny into his jacket. She saw Carl get to his
feet but she had no inkling of his intention until he cleared
his throat. It had become his way of declaring that he was
about to speak. She looked up at him, suddenly frightened.
"Carl . . ."

But he had begun. "Miss Duncan and I wish to take this
opportunity . . ."

Katherine looked at little Johnny Carlson, at Mrs. Nelson's broad face, at the familiar shelves and the old stove,
at Brother Bill. Everything was so familiar, yet so unreal.

" . . . to announce our betrothal . . ."

Carl's hand was on her elbow. She didn't move, and the hand became demanding. Slowly she got to her feet. She was conscious of the fact that one hand was still clutching stupidly at the other to hide the ring. Around her the faces jumbled together in a patchwork of odd-size mouths and eyes and teeth. She felt her mouth stiffen into a smile. Over her head Carl's voice said, "Thank you." He released her elbow, and she dropped to the bench. She was trembling.

Brother Bill began to speak. The smiling faces floated before her. Now Brother Bill was standing at the trading post door like a city minister, shaking the hand of each person who passed through. On the plank sidewalk outside, the churchgoers lingered. Carl's eyes were on the crowd outside. He seemed to be counting them. "A good gathering."

He held out his arm, properly bent so that her hand might rest on it without the intimacy of actually touching his body. Like a pair of dolls, they walked to the door.

Brother Bill shook her hand solemnly. She heard herself say, "Thank you," and realized in amazement that she was smiling. Carl moved forward. She stumbled, caught herself, and felt the wooden smile clamp harder over her face.

Mrs. Nelson was the first to congratulate her. "We'll be real sorry to lose our schoolteacher," she said in her flat, loud voice. "My, ain't that a big stone."

"We all want the best for you, Miss Duncan."

"Going to give up being a schoolmarm, eh? Well, who can blame you?"

"Congratulations, that's what I say, congratulations!"

"I sure wish Mary was here to see that there diamond."

She was acting a part but somehow she had got into the wrong play. In the flurry of their well-wishing, the dreamlike confusion evaporated like a mist. This moment was real, sickeningly real. The night before Carl had put a ring on her finger, and she had not refused it. How could he know her feelings, if she had been too much of a coward to tell him?

Carl was saying, "You're right, Mrs. Nelson. We've always planned on living in Seattle."

"I suppose you already set your wedding date?"

Carl patted Katherine's arm possessively. "This is the last trip I'll make to the Valley without taking her back with me."

"Well, well," Mrs. Nelson said, looking sternly at Katherine, "I was hoping maybe she'd finish out the school year."

"Great guns, Nellie," someone behind her objected, "wasn't you ever young and in love?"

Katherine looked at her hand, as still on Carl's arm as if it had been put out for display. She had never felt such cold, bottomless despair. Who arranges our lives, she thought, that at this particular moment I should know for sure that I don't love Carl, that I never will?

V

The moment Katherine walked into the Carlson cabin she knew something was wrong. The children's voices had been loud enough to give Faith plenty of warning. She should be sitting in the rocker by the fireplace, tidying herself for Jeb.

Katherine found her lying in bed. Her eyes seemed sunken, staring at Katherine without understanding. Katherine touched her cheek. The skin was tight and hot. Faith whispered. Katherine leaned over her and heard her repeat, "I'm dying."

"No!" Shocked, Katherine pulled up the quilt and tucked it around her. Faith was stoical. It was unbelievable that she had given up. "You're going to get better," Katherine said flatly, and ran outside.

The horses were still harnessed to the wagon. Running across the clearing, Katherine called, "Don't unhitch them, Jeb."

Jeb stared, one hand on the breastband.

"Faith . . ." She stopped, gasping for breath. "Faith isn't . . . well. I'm going for the doctor."

Jeb protested, "Nearest one is Doc Meade. I can't let you drive fourteen miles to Black River. I'll go."

Katherine shook her head emphatically. "You go in and sit with Faith."

Jeb stammered, "The sky looks bad. It could storm. If it does, that hill by the Falls . . ."

Katherine put a foot on the step, jumped quickly onto the wagon seat. "It won't storm," she said, as flatly as she had told Faith that she would not die. "Stand back, Jeb," and she took the reins in her hands.

"Anyways I ought to saddle up your pony," Jeb said. "If a storm breaks you can't get a wagon up that hill."

Katherine pulled the horses around sharp. "It won't storm," she repeated doggedly. "And you know Doc Meade can't ride since he broke his leg."

"Katherine . . ."

Katherine leaned down and looked directly into Jeb's puzzled face. "Jeb, you *have* to stay here. It's you she needs now, not me."

She saw his jaw tighten as he understood. "Gee ap!" she called, and slapped the reins hard along the horses' backs.

Jeb had not hurried the horses on the way home from church, and so they were fresh. The wind and sun had dried up the worst of the mud—that was another blessing. Katherine glanced anxiously at the sky. It was clouding over. If it rained . . . She shook her head angrily. "Gee ap," she urged the horses, "gee ap . . ."

She rode through Gold Mountain with scarcely a glance to right or left. Straight ahead was the old Indian trail through Squak and on to Seattle, the trail Carl had taken only an hour or so before. To the right was the wagon road past the hop ranch to Three Forks and down the hill past the Falls to Black River. She turned onto it.

The woods were dark. For the first time she realized she had come away without a gun or a lantern. There had been so many cougars . . . Grimly she held the horses to a walk. Cougars or not, it wouldn't do to tire the team out now.

She passed the hop ranch, and was in the woods on the other side when a man's voice yelled, "Whoa there!" It was Nils Bengston, in a heavy, gray-white Indian sweater, his head bare and a gun across his arm. He was holding two dead grouse by the feet. It struck her that hunting was a strange and lonely way to be spending Christmas.

"I can't stop."

His grin faded as he ran toward her. "What's wrong?"

Even as she was explaining, he dropped the birds and the gun into the wagon and vaulted in after them. With a sideway thrust of the shoulders he shoved her out of the driver's seat. Somehow the reins got into his hands. He snapped them and the horses broke into motion. Five minutes later he said curtly, "I'll go with you."

They scarcely spoke all the way to Black River. In every clearing they looked up at the sky. Clouds were piling up, and the wind was rising.

"Will it rain?" she asked him.

He shrugged. "It's bound to."

"If it would only hold off until we get back up the hill . . ."

He grinned. "It would help. I'd hate to carry that horse doctor all the way up."

"It's turning cold."

"That all the coat you've got?" He gestured toward the

old brown jacket she was wearing. It had belonged to one of the Anderson boys, the only coat among all the castoffs that hadn't been too big for her. Katherine nodded, pulling her shawl over her head and drawing it more tightly around her shoulders. Nils' face had such an unusual softness to it that she looked away quickly, frightened that he might see too much in her own. His next words saved her. "Just as well Indian Doc finally pulled your hat off the nail. It wouldn't have looked stylish with that outfit, anyway." He laughed.

Nils could always laugh. Katherine glared at him and felt better.

They had just turned into Black River when rain began to fall.

"It's raining!"

"That's happened here before." But she saw the way he turned to study the blue-gray clouds piling up to the east.

Katherine said anxiously, "But it isn't raining hard."

"It will." He pulled the horses up in front of the weathered board house that was Dr. Meade's. In one motion he dropped the reins into her hands and leaped to the ground. "I'll drag him out fast, if he's here."

Nils went in without knocking. In only a few minutes the door opened again and Dr. Meade came out with Nils behind him. He was a squat, sandy-haired man with long uneven mustaches and a big nose. An old satchel was in one hand and he was buttoning his coat with the other. Despite a bad limp, he moved quickly. "Hullo, Teacher," he said gruffly, pulling himself into the wagon by the strength of his arms.

Nils spoke to the horses, turning them back. The doctor settled himself with a grunt, balancing the satchel on his knees. "Mrs. Carlson pretty sick, is she?" His frown pulled his eyebrows parallel to his mustache.

Katherine nodded. "She has a high fever. She hasn't been right since the fire but today it was different."

"Pains coming regular?"

Katherine whispered, "I didn't like to ask."

The doctor guffawed, appealing to Nils as his thumb gestured toward Katherine. "What do you think of a girl who will start out alone on a twenty-eight mile trip with a snowstorm about to break, but she doesn't have the nerve to ask the woman if she's going to have a baby?"

Katherine stammered, "The baby isn't due until February."

The doctor shook his head slowly, "When it comes to that, the doctor's guessing and the mother's guessing. The time to come is something only the baby knows."

The rain was harder now. The wind beat it against their faces. Katherine leaned forward, crossing her arms across her chest in self-protection. The half-dried mud puddles were beginning to fill up. In the deepest ones the wagon wheels caught for a moment, rolled forward with a loud sucking sound as the team jerked hard against the traces. "You said snowstorm," Katherine said to the doctor accusingly.

He shrugged. "What do you think, Nils?"

Nils grinned, though the rain was streaming down his face. "I think August will be hot and dry."

They turned into the woods, and the rain was suddenly softer. But the trees were crying with the rising wind. Here the mud was worse, for the sun had shone too briefly to reach in and dry it out. The wagon lurched into each treacherous rut, swaying awkwardly as the horses pulled it out. No one tried to talk. They braced their feet to steady themselves and swayed with each dip of the wagon. Looking sideway Katherine saw that the doctor's face was calm, or at least resigned. Nils could almost have been smiling.

Shivering, she hunched her shoulders, clutching at the ends of her shawl.

The road had turned out of the woods and was climbing the hill beside the Falls when it began to snow. Katherine felt the first big, wet flake land on her cheek and brushed it off with the back of her hand. They were all soaked through. Now without the protection of the heavy timber they would freeze as well.

"Snow," she said grimly.

"Snow," the doctor agreed. "What did you expect?"

The ascent was steeper now. The horses were straining to keep the wagon moving. In every rut it stopped. Harness squeaked and the wagon groaned as the animals lowered their heads and fought the weight. At last it would rock forward and roll unevenly for a few feet more. The snow was falling fast. With the wind behind, it made an impenetrable white wall. Nils was blinded by it but he ducked his head low, slapped the reins frantically and yelled at the team.

The hill seemed to rise endlessly. Hidden by the swirling snow, the Falls thundered at their left. At last the burden was too great. The horses stopped, rebelliously lifting their heads. Their bodies were streaming.

Nils stood up and handed the reins to the doctor. "They pulled us longer than I thought they could," he shouted against the wind. Snow covered his bare head and had frozen in a white crust along his eyelashes.

"You drive, doc, we'll push." He jumped to the ground.

Katherine was shivering so hard she hardly understood Nil's meaning.

"Hey, you!" he bellowed, motioning to her to get down.

Katherine got to her feet. Numb and dazed by the cold, she picked up her skirts and stepped from wagon to step to muddy ground. She could see Nils' head and shoulders at the other side of the wagon. He grinned at her. "What's the matter, Teacher," he shouted. "From all I can see of you it looks like you fell in a hole." The wind screamed against them. "Get ahold of that step and push! Like this —one, two, three, shove . . ."

Katherine grabbed the metal step. Nils called, "One, two, three, push . . ." and she threw herself forward. With the first step she felt her shoe go ankle deep into the soft mud. "One, two, three, push . . ."

Nils' voice was fainter. The wagon moved suddenly. Katherine lost her balance, clutched desperately at the cold step. "One, two, three, push . . ." Nils' voice seemed to come with an effort. "Keep it up . . . like that . . ."

Katherine counted silently. One, two, three . . . One shoe had come loose. She looked down at it helplessly, counted, pushed. With the next forward lurch of the wagon, she felt the shoe sink even deeper into mud. The wagon seemed to be rolling. Frantically Katherine pulled her foot free of the shoe, and ran along beside it. The wagon settled into a new rut, stopping so suddenly that she threw herself against the hard metal step. She looked over her shoulder. The shoe was ten steps down the hill. "Again, one, two, three . . ." Nils called. Katherine pushed.

The wind ripped one end of the shawl from her shoulders and slapped it against the wagon wheel. The wheel turned and the shawl went around the axle, jerking Katherine backward and almost throwing her under the wagon. Gasping, she righted herself and grabbed the step. The shawl was gone.

"My shawl!" The wind drove the words back into her mouth. She kept pushing. There was nothing to do but keep pushing. The shawl dragged under the wagon for a time. Katherine saw the corner of it as the wheel went over it, burying it forever in the mud. One, two, three, push . . .

Foot by foot, they moved the wagon up the long hill. Throwing her weight forward, gasping for breath, counting, moving, shoving again—it became a series of mechanical actions. Katherine did them with her eyes closed. At the top of the hill Nils called "Whoa!" She collapsed against the wagon, her eyes still closed. "Well," Nils' voice said. "So that's what you're doing. Sleeping."

She opened her eyes. He was right in front of her, and he was smiling.

"Lost your shawl?"

She nodded wearily.

He looked at her feet. "One shoe come off?" he asked, in a strange voice.

She pointed down the hill. "A mile back."

His smile made her heart jump. "We don't see much of each other," he said quietly, "unless the going is rough."

She would have refused if he'd asked her, but he didn't. He swept her into his arms and lifted her onto the wagon seat. "Doc, you move over and put your arms around this girl and warm her up," he shouted at the older man, "or I'll do it myself."

The doctor moved and Katherine leaned against him gratefully. Nils climbed up and took the reins. Face hidden in the doctor's coat, eyes closed, Katherine thought— it's true. When things have gone badly, it hasn't been Carl who helped me. It's been Nils. Nils, Nils.

vi

For three days the doctor stayed on at the Carlson place. Except for the children, who moved around the cabin like frightened mice but slept well at night, there was very little rest for anyone. Jeb Carlson lay in bed fully clothed, but jumped to his feet at his wife's every move or sound. Katherine sat in the rocking chair by the hearth, napping only when she couldn't stay awake. No one saw the doctor sleep at all. Nils went home at night, returned each morning.

All of them, even little Johnny, seemed to know when the crisis came. The doctor had gone into the bedroom and closed the door. They waited outside, eyes on the pitiless door. Hiram came to Katherine so silently that she started at the pleading touch of his hand.

"Mama's going to die!" he sobbed suddenly. He was the little bull calf who never needed sympathy, the proud little rooster who turns to no one, but he let Katherine pick him up and hold him in her lap.

"No," she whispered, her throat aching. "No, no, no . . ." The chair squeaked softly as she rocked back and forth.

When the doctor opened the door at last, he was carrying a baby. It was concealed by yards of white cotton flannel but the new born baby's wail was unmistakable. Jeb jumped up.

"The baby's alive," the doctor said gruffly. "Your wife is, too. Better go in and see her." He turned to Katherine. "Ever take care of a premature infant? Know how to keep its bed warm enough? Heat up some fieldstones, wrap them, line the crib with them. Know anything about the milk?" He threw the questions at her.

Katherine rose slowly, with Hiram clinging to her hand. "Doctor, will they really . . ."

The doctor sighed and for the first time Katherine saw him smile. "The baby will live, if you're a good nurse. And so will the mother," he added, shaking his head, "though I'll never know why."

Nils stepped forward. "I'll go out and pick up some field-stones. And if there's anything else . . ."

The doctor exploded, "Well, isn't anyone going to ask me whether it's a girl or a boy?"

"Well, what is it, a boy or a girl?" Nils yelled back.

"It's a boy!" the doctor roared.

"Well then it ain't likely to turn into no schoolteacher," Nils said calmly, smiling at Katherine, and went out to get the fieldstones.

vii

Katherine turned her hand slowly from side to side, watching the wintry sunshine pierce the diamond solitaire and flash out again. It was the first time she had dared rest, except to fall asleep for an hour or so out of necessity. And it was the first time she had thought about her engagement ring. Only four days earlier Carl had opened the box and proudly slipped it on her finger. Yet she knew that in those four days they had been separated forever.

She leaned back against the barn wall, tilting her face to the sun and closing her eyes. Being new since the fire, the barn smelled sweet with cedar pitch, and even sweeter when warmed by the sun. Exhaustion, now that Faith and the baby were safe, was a pleasant sensation. The doctor was packing his bag and would soon leave for Black River. Nils was in the barn, hitching up the team so as to drive him there. Jeb was asleep, the children were playing. It was good, just for a few minutes after one job was finished and before the next would begin, to be all alone in the sunshine, doing nothing, thinking nothing at all.

Thinking had grown more complicated. Until recently it was Carl she consciously closed out of her mind. Whether it was because she couldn't make up her mind how she felt about him, or because she knew and lacked the courage to tell him, she hadn't wanted to think about Carl. Now for the past four days she had been near Nils, bound to him by their intimate common purpose of saving Faith and her baby. They had spoken very little but Nils' presence had

been as comforting as the crackle of the cedar logs in the
hearth and the sight of a well baby sleeping peacefully in
his cradle. As two people working together on a life or
death task, they were anonymous, and Katherine had not
been afraid of him. But the job was done. The urgency had
dissolved. She was once more the schoolteacher and Nils
was the dominating king of the Valley who hated schoolteachers in general and ridiculed her in particular. If you
liked Nils, you bowed down to him. In old Uncle Julian
Katherine felt she saw what happened to anyone who admired Nils. Nils didn't need anyone; he was built to have
people need him. A woman who loved Nils would be lost
forever, as her own mother had been lost through the gen-
tler domination of her father. Katherine had pulled free of
her father just in time, saving nothing but a scared little
redhead with just enough grit to keep the world from
knowing how desperately scared she was. In a year that
rebellious child had made herself into Teacher. Teacher
was a whole person. If she loved Nils, if she even thought
of him . . .

Katherine's body stiffened defensively, the wonderful
sleepiness jolted out of her. She mustn't think about Nils.
Once it had been the existence of Mary, his Indian wife,
which branded such thoughts as wicked; even when people
whispered that Mary had been no wife to Nils for many
years, that only Nils would be too proud to admit it. Now it
was a matter of fact, not of hope or pride or wishfulness. At
last Nils and Mary were divorced. It had been listed in
the *Post-Intelligencer,* printed proof of something everyone
in Gold Mountain had known for years. Not Mary, then,
but Carl's ring, winking in the sunshine, stood between
Katherine and Nils. She stared at it, fighting down the
sense of disloyalty it aroused. She couldn't marry Carl.
Why had she refused to recognize the real reason, unless
she was afraid of it?

At the other side of the barn Nils' voice spoke to the horses. Katherine's right hand flew to cover the ring, like a frightened mother bird protecting her young. In a moment the doctor would come out of the house, Nils would leave, and she hadn't said a word of thanks to him in four days. She should get up, walk around the barn, speak to him. She recited the actions, like a person who lies in bed in the morning and dreams that he has already accomplished the dread chore of getting up. The horses snorted, the wagon creaked as they jerked it into movement. Nils' voice said, "Whoa . . ." and then, as she had known all along he would, he came around the barn.

He stood between her and the sun, looking down at her with his hands on his hips, and to Katherine his face was in shadow. She said quickly, "I've been wanting to thank you, Mr. Bengston."

But he had his own ideas of what they were going to talk about. "I see you got a new ring."

The protective right hand pulled back, disclosing the diamond. Katherine flushed. How silly I'm acting, she thought angrily. As if I hadn't known it was there. She forced herself to look up into his face. "An engagement ring."

"I don't go to church. But I heard about it."

It was hard to make out Nils' expression, with the sunlight in her eyes. But it wasn't amused, as it should have been—didn't Nils always laugh at everything?

"Yes." She didn't love Carl, but Nils thought she did and had accepted the ring on her finger as proof of it. Katherine uttered silent thanks that she had not yet taken it off and returned it to Carl. "Yes, it is beautiful."

"Carl knows the right way to treat a lady." His voice sounded strained. "But I bet he don't know how to love one."

Color flooded into Katherine's cheeks. "That's nothing for you and me to be talking about!" She meant to be outraged, but her voice caught, and she knew she sounded more like a little girl trying not to cry.

"There isn't any polite way to love someone," Nils said. "And you can't love out of duty, or because you promised you would."

"I don't know the—the subject of your remarks," Katherine said stiffly, "but I don't want to hear them. I had intended to thank you for helping Faith and Jeb. That's what I'd like to do." She stood up. "Thank you very much, Mr. Bengston. You've been helpful."

Instead of leaving, Nils came so close Katherine had to look up to see his face. She was trembling—would he notice? "Please leave!" she burst out. "I wanted to thank you, and have it end that way. Why do you always spoil everything?"

"When you really love someone," Nils said quietly, "it eats into you. You can't stay away. You can't move a foot or a hand without thinking about them. If they're away from you you drive yourself crazy trying to remember exactly how they look and how they move and what they say. Let them be a thousand miles away, you look for them all the time."

Katherine fled to the protection of anger. "If you're talking about yourself, I'm not interested. And if you're talking about Carl White, or about me, I say you're presuming. You've been very kind and I hate to leave you in anger but . . ."

Nils raised his hand. *"I'm* leaving," he said. "I won't be back, unless you send for me."

"I'm sure there will be no reason for that!" She was shaking so badly she knew he must see it. Now was the time for Nils to laugh—she was braced for it. But he didn't. For a second he looked down at her and then he simply turned and walked away. Katherine sat down on the bench. The doctor came out, climbed into the wagon, and Nils and he drove away. The sun dropped slowly toward the dark trees. Shivering, Katherine got up and went inside.

9

i

Nils watched the men loading a wagon with the last of the season's hops. The oxen blinked patiently as each nine-hundred-pound bale was dropped. The wagon's heavy timbers groaned, the double yokes jerked down on the oxen's necks. The hops had been picked by hand, spread and turned in the kilns by hand, pressed into bales by hand. The men were sweating to load them and the ox teams, four beasts to a wagon, would sweat to get them the Valley to Black River. From riverboat to seagoing vessel, thus the third crop would go. From the ranch of Nils Bengston into the beer bottles of England. Nils frowned. Other years had been better. But curse those who were prophesying that every season would be worse than the last.

There had been more than a thousand Indians at the pay table this year—did *that* sound as if there were nothing to pick? The great herds of ponies, the horse races and sing gambles and games of two-card Monte; the young Indians in jeans and the half-naked old ones, with long hair and moccasins and a blanket—they had been the same this season as before. The silver dollars had been stacked just as high, and the Indians had as usual spent a good many of them for bottles of Jamaica ginger. Again this year Nate Tarpee had succeeded in selling the Indians several bottles of bluing, with instructions not to drink it until they got back to camp (or at least, out of the store). Where were they looking, what did they see, these cussed long-faces who sniffed for the scent of failure like hounds after bear?

His foremen came to him with anxiety so thin on their faces that their grins showed through. They said the hop louse had hit the ranches up north. They said the crops were so sickly two of the owners figured on planting potatoes next year. They said they'd heard hop prices weren't going to be as good as they had been—the English dealers were buying in the East. They said—Nils muttered angrily. They said what they'd always said, because they had always hoped it was true—that this time Nils Bengston had outreached himself. And they were as mealy-mouthed as ever.

The driver cracked a long whip over the heads of the oxen, bellowing a string of profanities. The animals lowered their heads and moved with a slow, thudding gait.

The last of the crop—but it had been a good crop, if a smaller one. The weather hadn't been right all year. It had been dry at the wrong time and rainy at the wrong time. Why didn't they think of that, instead of screaming "Hop louse!" when not one of them could show him a vine eaten

by aphids? As usual the long-faces were the ones without an acre or a dollar of their own. They were the ones
whose wages always go for what they have already eaten.
Theirs were the flat bellies during the winter.

Nils thought, But *I* had eight hundred acres of hops this
year, and they yielded sixty to seventy-five boxes to the acre.
There is so much livestock here that we grew a hundred
and fifty acres of hay alone. Potatoes, carrots, turnips, on-
ions, pears, prunes, plums, berries—we raised, we sold them
all. The year's apple crop alone was bound to hit above
five thousand bushels. Could anyone match that?

Thinking of the apples made him smile. They came from
the trees he had planted when he was a heedless kid of
nineteen. He'd been as poor as Tom Stump, who laughed
at him for borrowing money so he could buy the tiny trees.
Tom hadn't been the only one who laughed. Tom wasn't
the only one who was still poor while he, Nils, was rich.
What had he seen that Tom and the others were blind to?
Nothing, perhaps, except that you can't get rich and be
safe at the same time.

The loan that bought the apple trees had come from his
father. It was the first loan, the smallest one, and the last
he'd asked of him. There had been Seattle banks willing
to take a chance on him when he wasn't yet twenty-one
years old and none of them since had had to press him for
payment. Every mortgage had been bigger than the last,
but he had grown steadily richer. The others would have
stopped years before. They would have paid off their debts
and settled down forever with what they had. They were
too easily satisfied. Nils grinned. Half the people in the Valley owed him money. What would they think if they knew
he was so heavily indebted himself that one crop failure
could ruin him?

Some would worry about him. Some would be gleeful,
right down to the holes in their shoes. Most of them

wouldn't believe it, and this was the remarkable fact that gave him courage whenever he was forced to think of the possibility of failure himself. He had bought worthless stump land and made it rich as pasture. He had bought timber, a sawmill at Black River and a shingle mill at Gold Mountain. He owned buildings in three villages, farms all over the Valley, a hotel and a store. He had handled them all as he had those little apple trees whose fruit brought him the first cash he had; he spent all income immediately as a down payment on something bigger. No, most people wouldn't believe Nils Bengston could fail. He didn't believe it, either, because he never had.

He wasn't like poor old Captain White, who had staked his life on a tub of a riverboat. They were building a railroad now. It had already reached Union Bay on Lake Washington and they were saying it would get to Bothell by Thanksgiving. Snohomish Junction would be next, then Squak, then Black River. In a year or two there wouldn't be a living on the river. Ten years from now the little children wouldn't know the sound of the riverboat whistle, bleating as she came around the bend like an old ewe with the sniffles. Riverboats will soon be gone, Nils reflected, but there'll never be a time when men won't want their beer. No one could be safer, then, than the owner of the biggest hop ranch in the world.

ii

Julie came up so quietly that Nils was startled by the touch of her hand. "Well, Julie," he said, sweeping her off the ground so that her eyes looked directly into his.

She could laugh, though seldom with anyone else but him. There had been times when they were alone together that she had laughed until she rolled on the ground, her

knees pulled up against her chest in a spasm of utter delight. But when she was solemn, as she was now, her face
was a smooth, tan circle. The mouth barely moved to speak
and only the blue eyes, the light and variable eyes of the
white man, could give her away. They were shining now.

"I have come home from school."

Nils felt his smile stiffen. Since those days spent at the
Carlsons he had seen Katherine only when a meeting could
not be avoided. He had had time, in the long months since,
to prepare himself for the sight of her. Yet he winced at
the mere mention of the school. I *have come* home from
school. Julie said it so precisely. It reminded him that before Katherine came she had learned to say it the wrong
way—from him. I just come home. That's what he would
have said. Nils frowned. Well, what was the difference?

He hugged Julie impulsively. "You like school, baby?"
The words were out before he remembered she had asked
him not to call her baby.

"We're going to have a new school."

"I've been hearing that for two years," Nils said
brusquely. He hugged Julie tighter, bargaining for an extra
minute before he would put her down and she could look
at his face. I know Katherine is in the Valley. I know what
she looks like, I know the sound of her voice. I have seen
and memorized everything about her, and set it aside.
After all this time, he thought, I shouldn't be licked just by
thinking about her.

Julie gasped, "A school with glass windows." She
sounded as if he were squeezing the words out of her. Nils
lowered her to the ground. "With glass windows? Is that
what your teacher said?"

Julie nodded solemnly. "So we don't need to light the
lanterns, even in winter. The windows will let in light, and
whenever we want to, we can look out at the mountain."

"Did your teacher say that, too?"

"Which part?"

"About the mountain."

Julie nodded again. "Teacher loves the mountain."

Teacher . . . "What else?" Nils said quickly. "What else is going to be in that new school of yours?"

"Real desks," the little girl said. "Everybody's going to have his own."

"Is that so?"

"Pencils and new books."

"Yes . . ."

"A regular big wood stove with a round tin chimney."

"You don't say."

"Teacher says maybe we will have a globe."

"What the deuce is that?"

Julie said patiently, "A big, round ball—that's the earth. All the countries are painted on it."

Nils muttered, "Oh, I seen those. Well, what else?"

Julie's voice dropped to a whisper. "Teacher didn't say for sure, but I think there's going to be two toilets. One for girls and one for boys!"

Nils stared at her in his effort not to laugh.

Julie asked anxiously, "Don't you believe it?"

Nils nodded. "Oh, yes, I believe it."

"Father, will you come to the program?"

"I don't know nothing about it!"

Julie clutched his hand. "But we just decided about it today! There's going to be a program at the school."

"What kind of a program?"

"Mostly we're going to recite and sing." She tugged at him eagerly. "I'm going to say 'Tell me little housewife playing in the sun.'"

Nils said roughly, "I never heard it." He took Julie's hand in his. "Let's go to the horsebarn. I've got to look at the teams."

"Father, *everybody's* coming. Teacher's going to tell

about the new school. If you aren't there, she'll wonder . . ."

Nils broke in angrily, "She won't wonder about a thing! I got something else to do, something important."

Julie pulled her hand free. Her eyes rested on him for a moment, then she turned away and walked toward the house. Nils knew she would not mention the program again.

He wanted to call her back. Julie would obey, but he knew how proud and how tongue-tied they both would be. She could not understand his indifference and he could not explain it. What was the poem—"Tell me little housewife playing in the sun . . ."? Julie would recite it for the others. Others would listen, others would clap their hands and smile because she had done so well. Then Katherine would tell about the school. The others would be there to hear her. The glass windows, the real desks, the big wood stove with the round tin chimney. Others would promise to help her, others would applaud. Perhaps even Carl would come out from Seattle, for the first time since the Christmas Sunday when he had made public his claim to Katherine. But he, Nils Bengston, would be missing, the man who loved her as no one else could.

iii

Elsewhere in the Territory people were talking about statehood. In Black River they were talking about the railroad. But in Gold Mountain, they were talking about Teacher's new school.

Every few weeks there was some sort of an event "for the new school." There were box socials, school programs, a quilting bee one week and an auction of the quilts the next. With each the school fund grew, sometimes only by a dollar or two. Those who had no money gave butter or eggs or a calf. Nate Tarpee squeezed such donations from one family, wheedled another into buying them, and turned the proceeds over to Katherine.

"Pulling ourselves up by our bootstraps," Agatha called it. "Make something and sell it back to ourselves. I'll never be able to look at that school without seeing hams and butter and box lunches and quilts, and little teacher running around with a shiny nose and her braids coming loose."

Late in the fall of '86, more than two years after Katherine had arrived in Gold Mountain, help for the school came from an unexpected source.

It was Brother Bill's day to preach in Gold Mountain. After the service he approached Katherine. "I've been hearing about the new school."

Katherine smiled. "Every three months for two years?"

Brother Bill looked down at her sternly. "Doubt is a sin." He cleared his throat and pushed the long black forelock out of his eyes. "Someday I hope Gold Mountain will have a real house of worship, as well as a real school."

"Why, of course!"

Brother Bill's homely face cracked with surprise. "Of course?" he echoed.

"I've thought of it often."

"Once the school is built . . ."

Katherine nodded energetically. "That's what I've planned, too."

Brother Bill studied teacher's bright, small face. There was such intensity in the big eyes. He sighed, and a wide grin took the place of the ministerial frown. "Now who was going to commit the sin of doubt," he said. "If I'd thought I would have known that you'd have a plan like that." He forgot his sternness altogether and boyishly stuffed his hands in his pockets. "You're going to need a good carpenter. I was building houses in Seattle long before I knew whether Genesis come first or last. I know you'll help with the church. So I'll put up your schoolhouse."

Katherine said conscientiously, "Money for the school has come in very slowly. It may be years before we can collect enough for a church."

The cowlick had thrown the long lock back in Brother Bill's eyes, but he ignored it. "It looks like God wants the schoolhouse first. He'll show us the right time for the church."

Thus it was decided that Brother Bill would be the school's head carpenter. The lumber would be cut at Nils Bengston's water-powered mill at Black River. Brother Bill would be coming around about the first of February and again about the first of May. On this second next hike around the circuit he would stay long enough to get the school building well started. Others could finish.

That night Katherine took down her notebook from the rafter above her bed. By candlelight, she turned to a new page and printed carefully: "School year 1887-88. Classes will be opened in the new school building."

Over the winter there were more events "for the new school," as the weather permitted. Brother Bill reappeared in February. With Katherine he wrote the list of materials which would have to be bought in Seattle. Nails, school desks and the big tin stove with the round chimney—these would be transported by the *Viking*. Windows and doors would come from the Dave Denny mill in Seattle. They would be shipped across Lake Washington, through Squak slough and Squak lake to the village of Squak; it would be fifteen miles along a rough wagon road from there to Gold Mountain.

"It will take some good ox teams to haul that lumber up the hill from Bengston's mill," Brother Bill said. "Who's got them?"

"I don't know." The untruth seemed doubly wicked

when told to Brother Bill. Katherine blushed. "The only good teams are at the hop ranch."

Brother Bill frowned. "I'm not on the best terms with Nils Bengston."

"He donated the land for the school." She said it too quickly, but having begun his defense she could not abandon it. "He has also given one hundred dollars in cash and some of the lumber is to be free. He's been very helpful." Her voice faded. Nils had offered nothing to her directly. For more than a year they had scarcely spoken to each other. Whatever he had been willing to do for the school had been promised through Julie.

Brother Bill asked, "Is the school to be built with money that comes out of a saloon?"

Katherine's face burned. Brother Bill's antagonism to Nils was reasonable and she should not be hurt by it. "Not from a saloon . . ."

Brother Bill was at his full height. "What else is money that comes from the growing of hops?"

Katherine could not answer. Soon Brother Bill had gone, the list of building materials in his knapsack. Weeks later Katherine realized that he had not said he would ask Nils for the oxen.

Then *she* would have to ask him. For weeks the thought disturbed her. She had vowed to stay away from Nils, just as she had vowed not to abandon her school and her children in order to run away from him. And yet this was a chance to see him, not across a room, not riding past, not from a window. May came, and still she had neither gone to the hop ranch nor sent her request by Julie.

Before she did, a cattleman riding east from Squak brought a message to the school. It was a note from Brother Bill, who wrote he would be there in three days, and figured on starting work on the school immediately.

She would have to talk to Nils herself. The excuse was

reasonable. There wasn't time any more to ask her conscience what was "loyal" to Carl, and what wasn't.

Katherine dismissed the class hurriedly. Heart pounding,
she watched the last child disappear down the trail. The
shutters were already closed, the door was barred. She
raced across the schoolyard to where her pony was grazing.
The bridle hung from the saddle horn. She did not wait to
put it on him. With one leap she was in the saddle and
had the halter rope in her hand. She spoke to the pony,
turning him toward the hop ranch. She and Emil Greene
had not gone half as fast the day they rode to fight the
prairie fire.

iv

Nils saw her coming. He had just come from the hop fields,
where crews were setting the poles. The sight of her went
through him like a tremor. He'd go to the barn. Whatever
brought her here, someone else could talk to her. But he
didn't move. In the field he had been testing the soil, rubbing it through his fingers; his hands were caked with dirt.
He thought of how dirty his hands were. They felt separate
from the rest of him, as awkward and as uncertain as he.
He'd go into the house. Under Julie's bright gaze, and with
Uncle Julian, a wise old witness, he could meet Carl
White's girl and show no more than he should. Still he did
not move. Katherine was near now. She was reining the
pony in, with the other hand throwing the unruly red curls
back from her face.

Nils walked toward her on wooden legs. She should say
something. He looked up into her face and panic hit him
at what he saw. Dear heaven, he thought, we feel the same.
Whether she's Carl White's girl or whether she isn't. And
she doesn't know what to say any more than I do.

He put his hand on the pony's neck. "He was always a good horse," he said huskily. "A lot of horse for an Indian pony."

"He's a fine horse."

"I'm glad you didn't send him back." What a stupid thing to say! She'd had the beast for almost three years. She'd even thanked him once, in that proud little way of hers. "Uncle Julian figured you might."

"I didn't," she said, half whispering.

Her mouth was trembling. We can't keep looking at each other, Nils thought angrily. Our faces are too bare. "You need a horse." His hand fell awkwardly on the bridle. She hadn't waited to put it on the horse. His throat constricted at this sign of her eagerness. "You ride real good. As good as a man." It looked as if there were tears in her eyes. Nils stepped back abruptly and thrust his hands into his pockets. "You come for something," he stated brusquely, turning away from her.

Her voice was small as a child's. "I came to ask for the loan of your oxen."

"What for?" He kept his eyes on the trail as if he were watching for someone.

Her answer came out in one breath. "Brother Bill's coming three days from now. He's going to start building the school. He needs the teams to haul the lumber up from the mill."

Nils' old resentment of the evangelist stirred. It was a good feeling. "My oxen wouldn't take a step for no preacher!"

"Oh, but I'm sure Brother Bill could . . ."

"Not him!" Nils frowned. "Three days from now, eh? He figures on hauling the lumber Sunday."

"Well, no, I'm sure Brother Bill wouldn't work on Sunday."

Nils' gaze jerked back to Katherine's face. He had been

holding back so much. Gratefully he poured his feeling out
against Brother Bill. "Why not?" he roared.

Her eyes flickered.

"Why not?" he repeated.

"It's the Sabbath. He will be holding services. On Monday he'll begin work on the school."

Her mouth wasn't trembling and her eyes had cleared.
She never backed away from a fight, Nils thought. He could
bear to fight with her. He grinned suddenly. "He ought
to have the lumber ready," he said. "So I'll haul it myself.
On Sunday."

Katherine began to object, and stopped herself. But the
unspoken question lingered on her face.

"Well?" Nils said. "Anything wrong with that? According to Brother Bill I'm headed straight for hell anyway. I
might as well haul a little lumber on the way down."

"We planned to hold the service in the schoolhouse this
time. There'll be a dedication prayer afterward outside
where the new building is going to be."

As Nils thought that over his grin widened. "You mean
you wouldn't want me and my oxen to come rolling in and
break up your fine prayer meeting."

Her chin was high and her nose was in the air. God bless
her spirit, Nils thought, and his feeling for her came back
so hard and sudden it hurt.

"Exactly!" she said, stiff as the preacher himself.

He wanted to sound mean. He wanted to get riled. *They*
wouldn't work on Sunday. He would. He'd haul the lumber
on the Sabbath and make hypocrites out of them all for accepting it.

Nils cursed them silently, the good, the nice and the penniless. He grasped at anger and felt it shrivel into nothing.
"Katherine . . ."

Her eyes went real wide. How green they were—he
had almost forgotten. And that crazy splatter of freckles

across her nose. His size had always given him confidence but now it seemed like a weight he could not move. A sense of hopelessness swept through him. "You'll get the lumber. It will be there by Monday morning."

"Thank you."

She was looking at him in a way he couldn't endure. He felt himself move toward her, saw her lean toward him, felt the shock of her soft mouth against his. But he hadn't moved, and neither had she. Carl White's girl . . . but he always took what he wanted, wasn't that what they said about him?

"Why don't you get out of here!" Nils blurted out. "Haven't you got no place to go?"

He shouted the last words over his shoulder as he walked toward the barn. He walked fast, looking straight ahead. The pony gave a snort of surprise; she must have pulled him around suddenly. Then the sound of the pony's hooves, trotting away down the dirt road. "If I was only sure," he cried out loud, "if I only knew . . ."

V

Three days later the people of Gold Mountain gathered to break ground for the new school. Solemnizing the occasion, Brother Bill gave an extra long sermon. Then the congregation rose. With Brother Bill in the lead they walked across the clearing to the spot where the new schoolhouse—the real school with glass windows—was to be erected.

Brother Bill had just raised both hands and asked them to bow their heads in prayer when a string of oxen appeared at the bend in the road. They were pulling one of the hop ranch's long flat wagons and it was piled high with lumber. The driver was Nils Bengston, bareheaded, his work shirt open at the throat, and laughing.

Every bowed head twisted sideways as the devoted tried to peek at Nils Bengston while Brother Bill prayed. The evangelist's voice faded as he reluctantly lowered his hands.

"Hello, Bill!" Nils shouted. "I got your lumber."

The oxen seemed to move more slowly with every step. Brother Bill looked from his flock to the wagon and back again. "We'll have our prayers," he said sternly, "when he's gone." Two or three of them nodded. The rest were looking at Nils. It was doubtful that they had heard the minister at all.

Brother Bill held his position, his hands at his sides and his shoulders square. The minutes ticked away painfully during the long silence attending Nils' approach. The oxen came so slowly that he was certain several times that Nils had stopped them. At last Nils actually did pull the oxen up.

They were so close the animals could have butted the edge of the group but Nils yelled anyway. "Now where's this stuff supposed to go?"

Brother Bill felt a tickle of sinful anger. "About three hundred feet straight ahead," he said, his eyes on a spot just over and beyond the heads of the congregation.

Nils clucked at the oxen, but they didn't move. He slapped them with the reins. The beasts didn't seem to notice.

Someone in the group called, "Speak to 'em, Nils. You know how."

Oxen traditionally obeyed nothing but swear words. Bill knew it and so did everyone else. Brother Bill glared at the man. Nils was standing up in the wagon, his feet planted wide apart and his bare head tilted back with silent laughter. He was daring all of them—anyone could see it. Brother Bill fought for command. "I'd like to remind everyone that this here is a prayer meeting!"

Nils answered, "Sorry, Bill." He jumped down from the wagon, gently patted the neck of the lead ox. "Please," he said. "Please, for God's sake?"

Brother Bill roared, "I will not have blaspheming on the Lord's Day!"

Nils yelled back, "Well if you'll tell me what day you *will* have it, I'll come back and unload this lumber for you!" He crossed his arms and leaned against the ox. "All I said was please."

"You're breaking up our meeting!"

Nils shrugged.

Brother Bill's body stiffened. His temper was his worst sin. He knew its slow rise and terrible strength. "Mr. Bengston," he said, lowering his voice, "you aren't helping me to lead this meeting."

"Brother Bill, you ain't helping me to unload this lumber."

"Can't you make them oxen move?" the evangelist retorted, voice rising.

"Why sure! If I can talk to them the way they's used to."

Brother Bill pressed his lips together frantically. A man chuckled, a woman giggled. He could beat Nils Bengston in a fist fight or die trying, but he couldn't bandy words with him on the Sabbath. He faced the congregation. "We'll go back inside the schoolhouse, until . . . later."

Like a distraught cowdog Brother Bill loped around the fringe of his flock, motioning them toward the old cabin. It was a warm day, and the shutters were open. As the congregation filed in Brother Bill hastily closed them on the side near Nils.

Nils called, "Whatever you're going to say in there, you better say it loud!"

Brother Bill closed the door with a bang.

They had been whispering. The sound died as they faced their preacher. He saw that some were ashamed, some indignant, and one or two of the men were all but laughing. He thought of the days before he got the call, when the only way to treat a man who laughed at you was to lick him with your bare hands. He thought of the times he'd done it, of the days when money could make him forget how unhappy he was and a bottle of liquor could make him forget anything. His long, rough fingers combed through his hair. "Let us pray," he said unsteadily. "Father in Heaven . . ."

A jumble of swear words broke into the prayer. Nils was shouting at the oxen in a way the oxen understood. Brother Bill raised his voice. Unencumbered by the fear of God, Nils' was stronger.

Hastily Brother Bill ended the prayer. "We will sing!" he called, loudly enough to inform Nils himself. He sought a hymn that would be fast and loud. "Onward Christian Soldiers!" he announced, and began singing without waiting for anyone else.

For a moment they stared at him dumbly. Their preacher was straining his throat with "Going as to war, With the cross of . . ." Outside Nils was cursing the oxen at the top of his lungs. One by one the group began to sing.

Brother Bill's throat ached. His arms beat the air desperately, urging them to sing louder and louder. When they came to the end of the three verses they knew, they sang right on into the first and went through them all again.

Their faces were red with the effort, their bodies strained forward. Their eyes shone as they followed Brother Bill's flailing arms. They went through the hymn a third time. Some stopped for breath, gasped two or three times and went on singing. The fourth time the tune was lost in the shouting. Sweat stood out on their red faces. "Onward! Christian! Soldiers! Marching! As! To! War!"

Brother Bill's arms stopped their frantic directing. One by one the singers gasped to a halt. Brother Bill listened, body rigid and arms in mid-air. There wasn't a sound from outside. Still they waited, the group as motionless as he. In a moment they heard the slap of board on board. The oxen had moved. Nils was unloading the lumber at the far side of the clearing.

Brother Bill sighed. "I will declare Thy name unto my brethren," he said quietly. "In the midst of the church will I sing praise unto Thee." He ran his fingers through his hair and grinned. "That's from the book of Hebrews." Half his followers were still gulping for air. But they were grinning, too.

vi

Brother Bill began the school in May and the men of Gold Mountain worked on it through the summer, a few hours here, a few there, as time permitted. Thanks to the box socials and the twenty-five cent ham dinners and all the other projects Teacher had organized for two years previously, there was money for everything. "School Year 1887-1888" would indeed begin in the new building, just as Katherine had once written in her notebook. By the first of September they would need nothing but books. To raise money for them Katherine planned one last project, and it was to be different from any of the others.

The railroad had moved forward slowly, from Union Bay to Bothell to Woodinville to Squak. It would be in Gold Mountain early in 1888, if what the railroad men said was true. Trains were already running to Black River, and track had been laid along the south bank of the river all the way to the Falls. The people of the Upper Valley had already learned which section foremen would take them up the hill on a hand car for twenty-five cents apiece.

With summer came the Valley's first sightseers. On a

warm Sunday fifty or sixty people from Seattle would come out for a look at the Falls or just for the ride itself. Among them were sportsmen, city people who astonished the Valley by fishing and hunting simply for the fun of it. Hilke Orvaag, complaining that he couldn't feed the Sunday tourists unless he built new tables, gave Katherine a new idea. She and the mothers of the school children would prepare a Sunday dinner, serving it out-of-doors to the people who came out on the excursion train. As teacher, Katherine wrote the railroad with the idea of persuading its director to post signs in the passenger cars on the day of the dinner. She was unprepared for the response.

Ever since the road had been extended as far as the Falls, the company replied, some sort of promotion had been under discussion. They had now definitely secured the services of a professional tightrope artist, for a performance the first Sunday in August. A special excursion train would proceed not only to Black River but all the way up the grade to the end of the track in a clearing above the Falls. There the excursionists would enjoy the spectacle of a famous daredevil making the perilous crossing on a wire stretched across the river. If the mothers of Gold Mountain could be prepared to serve dinner to, say, eight or nine hundred people, at, say, fifty cents a plate . . .

Everyone in Gold Mountain worked for the school that first week of August. The men split logs to make the long plank tables on which the dinner was to be served. They set them up under the maples where the land above the Falls sloped gently towards the river. Hogs were butchered and the boys went out after deer. In every kitchen in Gold Mountain women baked bread, pies and meat. On the big day they loaded it all into box wagons and drove down the prairie to the picnic site.

When the excursion train came around the bend and

squeaked to a halt, the women were waiting behind the tables in a close and silent line, like badly outnumbered soldiers sworn to hold or to die. They had baked two hundred pies and as many loaves of bread. If all the roasts of venison and baked hams and chicken and beef and sausage had been weighed together, it would have come to a quarter of a ton.

Their faces were drawn. Even Agatha's moon-shaped face had a thin look about it. But their aprons were unspotted and starched so stiff they rattled.

As it turned out, the train had brought a thousand people, and they found nothing wrong with the food. In fact it took them less than an hour to eat it all up. Then the promised entertainment began.

A wire had been stretched across the river and tightly fastened to platforms raised four or five feet above the ground on either side. The platforms were reached by simple wooden ladders. As the time for the act drew near, the crowd thickened along the river banks. Hundreds of Indians had collected silently, their eyes flicking from the dinner tables to the indefinable white man's folly above the river. Farmers, loggers, prospectors of the Valley mingled with them, as curious about how Teacher's big doings were getting along as they were about the performance.

At last a well-dressed man climbed to the top of the south platform and began to talk. The crowd recognized him instantly as the barker. They listened but with the air of people who believe only what they see. One false step, the city man was shouting, and this man could be dashed to his death on the rocks three hundred feet below. Gold Mountain knew that. Another reason to doubt that he would actually get out on that wire, their glances said. The performer bowed automatically every time the barker raised his voice. The Valley people waited patiently for the proof.

At last the barker stepped back. The tightrope walker leaned down and someone below the platform handed him a straight-backed kitchen chair. With this in his hand, he slid one foot cautiously onto the wire.

There wasn't a sound but the rumble of the Falls. Among the spectators there was hardly a movement. The man moved along the wire. With each step away from the river bank the silence among the watching people grew more intense. The river swept under him, crashing over the precipice. He hesitated, swaying slightly, then took another step.

In the middle of the river directly over the Falls, he stopped. Crouching, he tested the wire, pushing down on his insteps so that he bounced gently. Then he straightened up, facing first one bank and then another in an appeal for applause. The clapping was faint and died out abruptly, as if the spectators had forgotten what they meant to do.

The performer bowed, his face stiff with the showman's practiced and meaningless smile. He tested the wire again, sliding a little from side to side. Then he struck a pose. Now, now I'm about to do it, the posture said.

He held the chair with one hand and with the other began to unbutton his coat. Before the awestruck crowd he removed the coat and hung it on the chair. Then, very slowly, the shirt. Finally, the trousers. One foot, then the other, hung in the air for a long and terrible minute. All his clothes were now draped over the back of the chair. He stood before them, swaying slightly, naked but for a pair of pale blue tights.

He posed again, lifting one free hand. A long "Aahh . . ." rippled across the crowd. Quite suddenly, as if he wanted to stay their applause, he balanced the chair on the wire and sat down.

While he rocked back and forth, the crowd went wild. They hooted, whistled, clapped, shrieked. When he got up and slid hastily along the wire to the platform, they applauded even louder, as if getting back to safety were something remarkable in itself. The roar of voices outdid the roar of the Falls.

The tightrope walker put the chair down on the platform. Automatically his body stiffened in the position of the artist accepting acclaim. Arms lifted in a graceful arc, feet turned out like a ballet dancer's, back straight, head up, smile. Thank you, thank you, it said, and at the same time, louder, please. He held it while the crowd screamed approval. One, two, three, four, five, six, seven, eight, nine, ten. He dropped the pose and the smile, turned and scuttled down the ladder. Hilke Orvaag was standing at the foot of it. The performer seemed to trip. Hilke's square hands shot out to steady him.

The man was shaking from head to toe. His face was pasty white. Staring at Hilke's ruddy face like a man trying to see something a mile away, he muttered, "I need a glass of beer."

Hilke looked quickly over his shoulder. "Could you need it more than me?" he asked. He put an arm around the man in the pale blue tights. "In the wagon," he whispered. "But my wife don't need to see us." Grinning happily, Hilke hurried the trembling daredevil away from the scene of his triumph.

vii

It was all over. The tourists had climbed back into the train and the little black locomotive had pushed it down the grade. The people from Kalakwahtie had gone home by canoe and wagon and the people of Three Forks and Gold Mountain had headed home one by one, thinking already of the evening chores.

It was quiet again, and the shadows were lengthening before the afternoon sun. The women sorting out dishes and bowls and roasting pans at the picnic tables were too weary to speak. Their aprons were crumpled and their hair was in their eyes. In a wide circle around them Indians waited silently for the scraps. They came forward at a nod, took what the women handed them, crept back to the watchful ring.

Nils was alone at an empty picnic table. One by one the wagons were leaving. He should be in his own, and halfway home. But he waited, because he could not see Katherine. She should go home with the Carlsons, but there was Faith. And there was Jeb, waiting in the wagon. Could she have left with someone else?

Nils shook his head. He would have seen her leave, and he had no business thinking about her anyway. He shouldn't have come today. They didn't need his help. He had tricked himself into believing they did. He'd told himself the sight of Katherine couldn't hurt him; or that if it did now, each meeting would disturb him less than the last and that was the only way to get over it. He had studied the crowd of Seattle people, expecting to see Carl White among them. That would mean seeing Katherine and Carl together, and he had thought that would be the kind of bitter medicine he needed. But Carl hadn't come, and the sight of Katherine alone shook him so badly he wondered that when he first loved her he had felt so little by comparison.

This watching her from a distance—Nils hated himself for being such a beggar. He had known all along that he wouldn't even talk to her. When it was all over she would climb into the wagon with all the Carlsons. He would watch her until the road turned and they were all out of sight. He had pictured it, prepared himself for it. Perhaps that was why he was waiting so uneasily. She must appear, climb into the wagon, go. Then he could begin his lonely ride home.

The Nelson wagon rolled away, then the Smiths' and the Andersons'. Besides himself there were only the Carlsons now, with Jeb stirring impatiently on the wagon seat.

Faith Carlson began calling the children. They appeared from all directions and climbed into the back of the wagon. Nils heard the elder Carlsons talking together. Then Faith questioned one after another of the children. Suddenly Nils was frightened.

He walked quickly toward the Carlsons, his fear doubling as he saw how gratefully they turned toward him. Faith resented him, Jeb would have liked him but didn't dare. It was wrong that they were so eager to see him now.

"Have you seen her?" Faith called even before he'd reached them.

"Not for a while. When did you last . . ."

Faith exclaimed, "Not since the train pulled out!"

Little Johnny sang, "The train, the train! *Choo* choo choo choo *choo* choo choo choo . . ."

Jeb looked at his wife. "Faith, you don't suppose . . ." It was clearly a question he did not expect Nils to understand.

Faith shook her head firmly. "Her leave the *school?*"

Nils winced. They knew her best and they knew it was the school that kept her here. He owned the biggest hop ranch in the world. In a few years the ranch would pay off his debts and he'd be one of the richest men on the Coast. He had everything in the world, but nothing Katherine would see as reason for staying in the Valley.

"Have you looked for her?" Nils gestured up the slope toward the woods.

"I remember she did say something about she'd like to rest quiet for a few minutes." Faith turned to the children. "Not a one of you seen her, for sure?"

They shook their heads. Johnny jumped up and made a locomotive with his hands. *"Choo* choo!"

"I'll find her."

Jeb was at his side as he walked along the river bank, then turned up the hill and circled back through the maples. Neither of them spoke. They found Katherine in the long grass at the far edge of the clearing. Her shoes were off. They stood side by side at her elbow, unbuttoned and toed in as if a pigeon-toed girl had just leaped out of them. Her hair was loose and her apron was crumpled up under her head. She lay on her side with her hand on one arm and her knees drawn up, and she was sound asleep.

Nils and Jeb sighed almost simultaneously, then they looked at each other and smiled.

"Well!" Jeb whispered. "It don't surprise me she fell asleep. After all she's done the last few days."

"I'll take her home."

Nils spoke softly. But there was such urgency in his voice that both he and Jeb were startled. Jeb's smile faded. For the first time in his life Nils felt as if he might be blushing.

"Yes, I will, Jeb. I'll take her home," he repeated. Instinctively he tried to keep Jeb from replying. A commanding forefinger pointed in the direction of the wagons. "No need to wake her up yet. You go home with your family."

Jeb said uncertainly, *"We* could wait . . ."

"I'll take her home!"

"It makes a long ride for you."

"Jeb, I want . . . I've got to talk to her."

Jeb looked at him thoughtfully. Nils faced Jeb, daring him, even asking him, to guess the truth. Jeb knew Katherine as well as anyone in the Valley. He knew Carl White. Nils stood in front of him, grim but defenseless, waiting for Jeb's judgment. His feeling for Katherine was plain, if Jeb could see it. And if he could, what would his opinion be of a man who fell in love with another man's girl?

Jeb said at last, "I guess you got a right to talk to her, if you want to."

Jeb wouldn't try to judge another man. Nils thought, I should have known he wasn't the kind that would. "Thanks, Jeb," he said softly. "I guess you know . . ."

But Jeb did not want to know, if knowing put him to the test of judging. He backed away. "It don't seem right to wake her," he murmured. He hurried down the hill toward the wagons.

Nils sat down in the grass next to Katherine. The sun dropped slowly, the shadows lengthened. The rocky cliffs of Old Hi turned pink with the late afternoon glow. The scratchy voices of the crickets grew louder and the meadowlark's song turned melancholy. Nils' eyes were on Katherine. He pulled a stalk of grass, chewed on the soft end, threw it away, pulled another. As one hour slid into another, he sorted out his thoughts and endured the struggle between conscience and desire.

The sun fell behind the ridge. The trail through the heavy timber would already be dark and dampness would rise from the river. Gently Nils picked up the sleeping Katherine and held her in his arms.

She stirred and opened her eyes. They were dull with fatigue. "I fell asleep."

"Don't wake up." Her head fell back against his shoulder. He carried her down the hill, walking more carefully than he ever had in his life. In the wagon he pulled her close and put his arm around her. She was awake, but she did not pull away. They rode the many miles back to the Carlson farm in sleepy silence.

In the barnyard Nils jumped to the ground and held out his hands. Katherine hesitated, looking down at him like a child wakened from a deep sleep. At last she leaned forward and let herself drop into his arms. He held her, his face against hers. Her hand touched his. It was cold. His own hand closing over it felt the cold stone of the engagement ring. He put her down, wheeled her around toward the house and gave her a gentle push. "Go to bed," he said hoarsely, but watched until the door closed safely behind her. Then he got back into the wagon and let the horses take him home.

10

i

Tommy Tine, Agatha's son, sat on a log in the sunshine and decided that the way things were going the day promised to be just about perfect. First off, there wasn't any school, so a fellow could come down to watch for the *Viking* without playing hooky. Not that Tommy was given to playing hooky, especially. Since Miss Duncan had started teaching almost four years before, only a real emergency, like the first snow or an extra good fishing day, had ever dimmed his faithfulness. Even then it wasn't as if he'd planned it. More that he just happened to change his mind somewhere along the road between home and the schoolhouse. He'd never lied about it afterward. "Didn't go to school today, Mother," he'd say, walking right into the kitchen with his string of fish. She never punished him. "Well you better clean them things outside," she'd say, "I don't want to find no salmon tail in my sugar bowl." But she looked so hurt he always wished he hadn't done it. His mother wanted him to be as bookish as Grandfather Martin had been, the one who signed the papers when the Washington Territory was made. Tommy knew she was already saving up for a pair of eyeglasses. He hoped he'd learn to read well enough to use them. He didn't like to disappoint her. So he was glad there was no school today, and he could come down to meet the *Viking* and still go home and look his mother in the eye.

Then there was the weather. Being June it was more likely to be rainy than clear. As his mother said, "We got a right to the sun during July and August but in June, it's doing us a favor." Today the sky was pale blue and there wasn't a cloud to cross over the sun even for a minute. The sunshine ate right into you. It warmed the top of your head and thawed out your joints. It made you happy without knowing why and sleepy all the time. The robins chirped, the meadowlarks sang, the hayfields smelled sweet. Last week the log he was sitting on would have been soggy with rain. The wetness would have soaked through his jeans in no time. His fingers picked lazily at the bark. It was dry and warm, and came off in little rust-colored chips. Tommy sighed with pleasure.

There were so many things he might do today. He could go fishing. He could burn out a little more of the cedar canoe old Indian Doc was showing him how to make. Or he might go find Julie Bengston. Julie always had fine ideas, like building a dam across the creek or hunting for periwinkles. He thought about them all. It was fine to think about them while you sat on a log waiting for the riverboat and did nothing. Because if he didn't move until sundown, if he left the fish in the river and the periwinkles in the swamp pools and the canoe untouched in the woodshed, the best part of this perfect day was still waiting at the end of it. Tonight there was a dance at Black River.

Hi Barker would come down from the mountain with his fiddle. If Hilke Orvaag's hotel didn't burn down, they'd still be dancing at breakfast time. People would come by wagon from Gold Mountain and Three Forks. They'd paddle upriver in canoes from Kalakwahtie and the farms below.

Tommy stretched out on the log and closed his eyes. The dance tonight—he might even whirl around a few times himself, if Julie Bengston would try it with him. Fishing and periwinkles, Miss Duncan standing in front of the class, the sound of a fiddle playing, the smell of warm cedar needles, Tom Stump yelling with his arms beating the air . . .

"Toot!"

Tommy rolled off the log with a thud. That one short wheeze, like his mother trying to call him when she was out of breath—that was the *Viking's* whistle when she came around the bend. The riverboat was here at last, and he had been asleep.

He rubbed his eyes hard with the back of his hand. At the foot of the hill a crowd had gathered around the boat landing. In a minute the *Viking* would be alongside and they'd be shoving her cargo out and a fellow would find plenty to look at. Suddenly Tommy spotted Teacher, waiting for the boat along with all the ordinary people. "Gee!" he said, and ran down the hill toward her.

Tommy skidded to a stop right at Teacher's side. Grinning broadly, he said, "You're here, too."

"Yes, I am." She smiled at him, but to Tommy it seemed

like a shaky smile, as if she were thinking of something else
and was maybe even a little scared.

"Yep, you're here," he repeated. She wasn't acting natural. It made him uneasy.

"I done that extra lesson at home," he volunteered.

"*Did,* Tommy." She was looking at the *Viking*. She didn't
even look at him when she talked.

"Did," he mumbled, kicking the dirt with a boot heel.
He liked Miss Duncan fine. The only teacher he'd had before her had given him a first reader and every time he
finished it had made him start over again at the beginning.
He had hated the book so much he hadn't even learned to
read it, and his mother had twice washed his mouth out
with yellow soap because he had called the teacher a
pukey. But Miss Duncan was different. After two years in
her school he was in the fifth grade, and he'd had a new
book every year, not a single one of them a "reader." He
liked Teacher too because she wasn't . . . Tommy's mind
stumbled when he tried to find the word for what she
wasn't. She *was* like Julie Bengston. She rode a horse like
a man and played baseball with the kids and she didn't
giggle or cry. She didn't talk grown-up, closing you out as
if being young meant you weren't quite smart. Tommy's
heel stirred the dirt angrily. Miss Duncan had never acted
. . . secret. But she was now. He took a few experimental
steps to the side, watching her closely to see if she would
miss him. She didn't. She was staring at the deck of the
Viking, so still it was like she was holding her breath. Her
face looked funny and stiff. In disgust, Tommy turned and
as noisily as he could, walked away.

But he couldn't abandon the riverboat, even for a
thoughtless woman. He slid through the crowd to a vantage
point on the river bank next to the landing, a perfect spot
for looking.

There was old Captain White. He and the man stevedoring for him were already pushing boxes down the plank. There was the captain's son, but he wasn't working this time. In fact, Tommy couldn't remember when he had last seen him on the *Viking*. He was dressed up good enough for a funeral, Tommy decided. Tommy's eyes followed him admiringly. Young Mr. White walked down the gangplank. He seemed to know just where he was going. He didn't look right or left. He went up the hill through the crowd with no more than a nod to anyone. Then he stopped, right in front of Tommy's teacher.

Tommy's stomach contracted unpleasantly. Sure he'd heard the women talking about him and her. "Funny kind of 'engagement' when he ain't been to see her for eighteen, nineteen months," they said. "But she's still wearing his ring." Tommy had taken it all for female talk. It just wasn't possible that Teacher would think of doing something so— so common, as getting married. He watched Carl White extend his arm, saw his teacher smile as she took hold of it. She didn't look like herself. Her smile, her gesture as she put her hand on his arm—suddenly Tommy saw her as just another woman. Teacher, who was to be admired, had crumbled and fallen away. Mr. White and Miss Duncan were walking up the hill now. Very slowly, like they were talking over secrets. Tommy clenched his fists and felt all riled, as if something bad had happened. "Gee whizz darn!" he blurted out.

He bit his tongue guiltily and looked around. He hadn't meant to say anything out loud. No one seemed to have heard him, except one man he hadn't seen before and he was grinning. It was only Julie's father. Tommy gulped with relief. "Oh, it's you, Mr. Bengston. I didn't know you was here too."

Mr. Bengston was all right. He always said the words Tommy was forbidden to use and he wasn't likely to report a simple little Gee Whizz Darn. His mother complained that he had a big heart and a hard head but the way she said it, it sounded like a compliment and that's the way Tommy had always taken it.

Mr. Bengston said, "I like to watch the boat come in, same as you, Tommy."

But he was looking up the hill, where there was nothing to see right now but Mr. White and Teacher, walking together toward town. He had been grinning when Tommy first saw him, but Tommy thought uneasily that for Mr. Bengston, who laughed at everything, the grin hadn't lasted long at all.

"You going to the dance tonight?" Tommy asked. He wanted desperately to draw Mr. Bengston's attention back to the landing.

But the question failed. Still watching Carl White and the teacher, Julie's father said slowly, "I don't know, Tommy. I don't know if I dare."

Tommy looked at him dumbly. Mr. Bengston was so big. He was strong, the strongest man in the Valley. What he'd said didn't make sense. It was one of those grown-up remarks. Behind it lurked the whole unpleasant, secret grown-up world. Tommy turned his back on Mr. Bengston, gluing his eyes on the *Viking*. He wouldn't look up the hill. He wouldn't look at Mr. Bengston. It seemed all of a sudden as if the sun had gone down.

ii

Carl was thinking of the people around them. Katherine saw it in every motion he made. In the way his steps were measured as he walked up the hill from the *Viking*. In the way he allowed no recognition to break across his face, though she knew he had seen her even before he got off the boat. In the way he held out his arm, saying, "You're looking well, Katherine."

Couldn't he smile? Katherine surprised herself by feeling irritated. Not guilty or worried or excited or any of the other emotions she had been suffering ever since his letter had come the week before. They had not seen each other for two and a half years. The whole world had changed in that time but—"You're looking well, Katherine." "I'm feeling fine," she said curtly.

"You brought the wagon." He didn't pretend it was a question. He was stating a fact, so flatly as to deny the possibility that it might not be true. He never had approved of her riding astride, especially when she had become so hard and skillful a rider. His intonation brought back every quarrel they'd had, and her irritation doubled. I wanted to be nice to him, she thought. Why won't he let me?

"Shall we go?"

They walked up the hill. For the first time Katherine wished she had told Carl everything she had to say in a letter, and sent it to Seattle months, or even years, before. If he could stay away from her for two and a half years, why had she imagined she owed him something? His letters had come at regular intervals, almost as if he had marked the dates on the calendar well in advance. His reason for staying in Seattle had been good—he had to finish his studies. But would a man in love consider that any reason at all?

She had begun so many letters to him and destroyed them all with a feeling of shame. Writing a letter and sending back his ring could be made to sound very honest and proper, but she had felt it would be cowardly. What was "honest" about running away from the moment when she would have to explain her feelings to his face? And so at last she had written, "If you can make the trip without interfering with your studies, I would like to talk with you."

Weeks later his answer came. "My studies are finished now, and I am employed full time by the firm of Bryce & Bennet. I agree that there is much to talk over. Can you meet me in Black River when the *Viking* arrives there a week from Saturday?"

This, then, was the moment she had felt only a coward would avoid. They had met, smiled politely, and were walking arm in arm. Was this the time to say, Carl, I do not love you. I cannot love you. Thank you for everything, but . . . Kindness urged her to reach back two and a half years to the last time they had been together. By acting natural she would assure him that nothing had happened since. But so much had happened, so much which in his deep self-interest he didn't even suspect. "You are working for a law firm?" she said stiffly.

He nodded solemnly. "As I wrote you, the name of the firm is Bryce & Bennet. For a time I will serve as an apprentice."

Katherine thought, why is it hard even now to tell him I don't love him? Because "I don't love you" is an admission that somehow I *haven't* measured up? I was asked to love, I tried to love and failed? Or is it just that I know how proud he is. If Carl doesn't love me, it will still hurt him to be rejected. It would be easier for both of us, she thought, if he had come to tell me that he no longer loves me. He would do it so kindly.

Carl was saying, ". . . fifteen dollars a week. Many apprentices aren't paid at all."

She nodded. "That's fine. You should be proud." Now, when he was in the midst of describing his success? Was now the time?

"It will give us a modest living."

Her hand tightened convulsively. "I can't go to Seattle!" Once she had been ready with every kind explanation. She hadn't expected to need them now. Confused, she repeated the stupidity. "I'm sorry, Carl," she murmured, "but I can't go to Seattle."

Of course he would misunderstand. Why wouldn't he, when she had blundered around the truth? "Katherine," he said stiffly, "I believe you heard what I told Mrs. Nelson after the Christmas church service two years ago. I said that was the last time I'd leave the Valley without you, and I meant it sincerely. For three years you have postponed our wedding date because of this . . . little school of yours. Your school has separated us long enough. The school year is finished now. There is no reason why you can't come with me."

She grasped at the unimportant error. "Oh, no, the term isn't finished *here!* There will be classes all through June and July, to make up for the time the school had to be closed over the winter."

"Let Nils find another teacher!"

Color rushed to Katherine's face. He blamed everything on the school. Their long separation, the unhappiness that had developed between them before that. She wanted to cry out at the injustice of it, but the strength to do it deserted her. He was wrong, all wrong. Now could she begin to tell him? Later, later, her mind cried silently, I'll talk to him later. "The wagon is right over there," she said unsteadily. "In front of the hotel. I wonder who those men are beside it?"

Carl frowned. "They were on the boat. Loggers. Undoubtedly looking for a ride to Gold Mountain." He turned to Katherine. "I'll refuse. If we are alone, we can talk."

Katherine stammered, "We shouldn't refuse!"

Carl shrugged. "Very well, later then."

Later, yes, later, Katherine's mind cried in silent reply.

iii

The dance began at nine o'clock, more or less, and would
end at dawn, unless the fiddler caught still another wind
and played on. The dancers left home after evening chores
and were often late for the morning ones.

Being hungry or sleepy was no excuse for leaving early.
Everyone brought food. The kitchen table in Hilke Orvaag's hotel was loaded with roasts of ham and venison,
crocks of sauerkraut and pickles and bright yellow butter,
and loaves of bread. You could eat whenever the idea took
you. Chairs and benches lined the dance floor. By midnight many an old man would have dozed off sitting up,
hands on his cane and chin on his chest. A dozen children
would be stretched out on the benches, one leg drawn up
close, the other falling off the bench, their heads resting
comfortably in their grandmother's laps. The only disturb-
ance was the silence when the fiddler stopped to rest a while
and the dancers went outside for a breath of air.

Hi Barker had never played better. Everyone was saying
it. "Hurray for Hi, hurray for old Hi!" Levi, who never
danced, sat on a stool behind his father. Every smile they
gave Hi as they danced past, every affectionate nod made
the boy's eyes shine with pride. Even little Johnny Carlson paid his tribute. The younger Carlsons were lined up
on a bench, their mother and father at one end and Katherine and Carl at the other. Hi had just wound up a fast
reel.

At last he handed his violin to Levi and began to stretch
his arms and fingers. That meant he would rest a while.
Katherine turned to Carl. In the afternoon she had
dreaded talking to him, but since then it had been even
more unbearable not to be able to. Then there had been

the crowd of children, the chores, the evening meal, the many preparations for the dance.

"Carl, we've been wanting to talk," she said. "Hi has stopped playing. Shall we go outside?"

She took his arm. Quite suddenly the music began again. Carl stopped. "It looks like old Hi doesn't need a rest yet." He pulled Katherine around to face him. "And it's a waltz."

Katherine exclaimed, "But I'd like to talk . . ."

"We can talk while we're dancing." Carl led her onto the floor with a slow, even glide. "*I* can do more than one thing at a time. I'll do the talking. The *Viking* leaves first thing in the morning. We'll have breakfast with the crowd and get on the boat right afterward."

"Carl, I can't!"

He glanced at her dress. It was of brown and white gingham, with full sleeves and two rows of ruffles around the bottom. "You'll look fine, even in Seattle," he said confidently. "You don't own anything worth riding all the way back to Carlsons' for. We can say good-bye to everyone in the morning." His quick gesture was tinged with distaste. "They're certainly all here."

Katherine stiffened. Now, while he had irritated her. "Please, Carl," she said, "may we leave the dance and go outside?"

He looked startled. His smile was gone so quickly she might have knocked it off his face. "If you wish."

Katherine walked across the dance floor and out the front door, Carl behind her. At least, she thought, Nils isn't here to see. Others would notice, nudge each other, smile, but she need not go out into the dark with Carl with Nils' eyes following her.

Outside the air was warm, and sweet with the scent of some invisible Balm of Gilead tree. Spears of lantern light from the hotel windows cut across the darkness.

"Yes, Katherine?" Carl's voice was anxious. It sounded like the Carl she had once talked with during the trip inland from Snohomish City, the boy who knew insecurity and self-doubt and hopelessness. Katherine thought, will I end up by pitying him? She walked out of the irregular circle of light and turned to face him.

They seemed to have fallen into a pocket of blackness. Carl's face was indistinct, but she knew he was looking down at her, waiting. He was afraid. She could feel it as surely as if an uncontrolled spasm had made him clutch her hand. All the tactful phrases, the reasons that were not reasons at all, flashed across her mind. She had such a simple thing to say, and had thought of so many complicated ways to avoid saying it. Carl was waiting.

Would he be angry? Would he destroy her with his retort, in the fury of his injury trying to hurt her as much as she had hurt him? Katherine drew a deep breath and spoke quickly. "I can't marry you," she gasped. "Because I don't love you."

He did not move. In the quivering silence she pulled the diamond ring from her finger and extended it blindly. "I kept wearing it, because it didn't seem right to take it off without your knowing." His hand was there, and she dropped the ring into it. "Carl, I'm very sorry."

"You might have written."

"Carl, I'm sorry. I tried, but a letter seemed a cowardly way to tell you. If you had only come out."

"I was exceedingly busy." His voice was steady. He was a stranger whom she had not hurt but only inconvenienced. "The work that kept me away from you was *important*."

Another slap at her notion that "her little school" was important, too. He was telling her that it was the school, only the school, which had made them strangers to each other. And he believed it. A sigh shuddered through her, escaping in the barest exhalation of breath. After all, it had been so terribly easy.

"I want to thank you, Carl. You have helped me in so many ways."

"Nothing at all." His voice was muffled, as if the darkness choked it off.

She said anxiously, "No, truly, I am grateful to you. For your kindness, when I first came to the Valley. For all your advice."

For loving me. The words came to her, but she held them back. If she didn't love him, what right had she to remind him that he had once loved her? "For everything . . ." Surely there must be something more to say.

"Good-bye, Katherine." His arm moved. Mechanically she responded, and they shook hands. "Good-bye, Carl." He was about to go.

"Oh, Carl," she cried out, "if only . . ."

He turned back. "If only?" There was no eagerness in his voice. There was nothing at all.

The last bit of her old feeling for him died like an echo. She shook her head. "I guess—oh, I don't know."

"Good-bye, then." Even in the darkness she could see the polite inclination of his head.

"Good-bye." She stood still, listening to his footsteps as he walked down the wooden sidewalk in the direction of the *Viking*. The sound ended abruptly. He had stepped off the sidewalk into the dirt street. Still she waited. Hi Barker's fiddle twanged faintly in the distance. It was all over. He was gone. For the first time there was a painful lump in her throat. She walked unsteadily toward the hotel.

The light through the hotel windows made a pale circle on the sidewalk outside. Just at the edge of it Nils Bengston was standing.

Katherine gasped. He hadn't been at the dance. She

had been so thankful for that. Now Carl was gone, it was all over. Her teeth were chattering as if she were cold.

Nils moved toward her. He was so big he seemed to be falling down on her. With his next step a pale streak of light fell across his face. The mouth was hard, the eyes black.

"Nils." It was an anguished whisper. She put her hands up to steady herself, to push him away?

"You didn't kiss him good-bye."

Her hands touched his chest, clutched the rough shirt. She looked at him helplessly. "It isn't fair . . ."

In a mighty sweep his arms pulled her against him. For an instant her body tensed and her hands pushed desperately against his chest. But the secret desire stirred. It spread through her relentlessly. Through her body, down her arms to the fingertips . . .

Nils kissed her mouth. The shock of feeling was so strong that she could not turn her head away. Her hands crept up to his shoulders, while he kissed her cheeks, her forehead, the soft hollow of her throat.

Inside the hotel Hi Barker's fiddle played a final flourish. "Form your squares!" the old man's voice sang out, and in a second the violin began the fast bright tune of a square dance. *"Honor* your *partner . . ."*

Katherine pulled away. Nils held her, with her hands pressing uselessly against his chest. "My darling girl," he said huskily, "don't ever run away from me again."

She couldn't speak. *"Now* every*body* circle *round!"* came from the dance floor. She looked up at Nils—the wide eyes, the blunt nose, the hair that had grown so long it curled back behind his ear, the strong mouth. He was a strong man, and yet she had never been so helpless against him as she was in loving him.

"Ladies keep a-going and the *men* turn back . . ."

She tried to pull free. In one kiss she had told him her

feelings as clearly as if she had whispered them in his ear, but she fought against him with an instinct to save herself. In the distance Hi Barker's scratchy voice sang, *"Pa's* in the pantry, *cows're* in the hay, *take that pretty one* and *bring her this way* . . ."

"Nils . . ."

His hands were gentle, but she might as well have tried her strength against an iron bar. In her fight for independence she had told herself that loving Nils she would be lost forever. Now, weakened by his touch, just his physical size and strength were overpowering. He was strong, he was rich, he was invulnerable. She had seen, in her mother, what love did to a woman, but what could it add, or take away, from Nils?

"Chickens in the bread pan *kneading up* dough, *heel* and toe and *away* we go . . ."

His hands drew her closer. One slid under her chin, tilting her head back. He leaned forward, his face blurring as it neared.

"No," she whispered, stiffening against him.

"If you love me . . ." he said, almost against her mouth. For a moment Katherine seemed to stop breathing. Everything hung in balance. To love him forever, or pull away. Then the moment was gone. He was kissing her, and she was clinging to him hungrily, while the fiddle twanged in the distance and Hi Barker's singsong voice called, "If you *love* that girl don't *tell her* a thing, *grab* a partner and *start* to swing . . ."

iv

As Nils rode home he tasted a sense of triumph such as he had never known before. It will be the biggest, finest wedding the Territory has ever seen, he kept telling himself.

I'll build the biggest house in the Territory. I'll buy her store clothes from Seattle. If she's set on keeping up the school, I'll build her a new one. A big one, much bigger . . .

The moon was nearly full. In the barnyard he unsaddled his horse by moonlight, whistling softly to himself. He led the horse to the boxstall. As he opened the door he heard the low whimpering sound of a child crying.

"Julie!"

The crying grew louder at the sound of her name. "Father . . ." she sobbed, lost somewhere in the dark corner of the stall. "Father . . ."

Nils fumbled for a lantern, lit it and turned the flame up to see her face. Julie was crouched in the corner, her back against the wall. Indianlike, her face had gone blank with fear.

Nils went to her quickly, laying his big hand on her shoulder. "What's the matter? What're you doing out here?"

Her body was cold and tensed so hard she was shivering. He pulled her to her feet. "Julie, tell me. Why are you here? Where's Uncle Julian?"

She whispered, "I don't want to go inside."

Years ago he had seen Julie's mother as mute with fear as Julie was now. He shook her. "Why not?"

She crumpled suddenly. "Mama came back!" she sobbed. "And she's terrible sick."

Nils stared at her. "Mama came back . . ."

"Don't make me go inside!" Julie was pulling on him with both hands. "I don't want to catch it. Please, father, please . . ."

Mechanically Nils pulled a red handerchief from his pocket and dried Julie's face. "No," he said, "you don't have to go back to the house. I'll bring you a blanket and you can sleep in the loft."

"She's got the pox fever!" Julie wailed. "Father, I'm scared!"

Suddenly Nils felt exhausted. If I could just lie down and sleep. "It's all right, baby," he said over and over again. "Everything's going to be all right." And he patted her head, repeating the empty promise, while within himself he felt nothing could ever be all right again.

CHAPTER

11

i

The epidemic of smallpox swept through the Indian shacks along the river. The people of Gold Mountain rode past quickly and were pursued by the sounds. The wailing of a widowed squaw who paced along the beach, crying her sorrow to the skies for day after day and week after week. The gutteral chant of the doctor as he treated his patient, the sudden screech, the long moan, when another one died. The white settlers shivered and prayed.

As coastal Indians always had, the Valley Indians looked for a cure in their sweat houses. They dug them into the mud of the river bank, like industrious farmers building potato cellars. Around the shallow hole they piled fieldstones some two or three feet high, laying rough boards across the top as a roof. A bonfire blazed nearby. They heated large stones in it, and with heavy green poles rolled them into the sweat house. Water was poured onto the red hot stones, and cedar branches spread over them. Naked, the feverish Indian crawled through the low door and pulled it tight behind him. When the heat and steam had become insufferable, he burst through the door and leaped into the river.

Whatever disease the white man had visited upon them —measles, smallpox, influenza—the Indian treated it in the same way. Gold Mountain's white children grew used to the sight of a naked brown body plunging into the icy river, a cloud of steam pouring from the open mouth of the hovel from which he'd come. They leaped into the water in two's and three's, crazy with fear. They splashed around helplessly, out of their heads with fever. Most of them crawled out to die before old Indian Doc could begin his chant.

The Snoqualmies buried some of their dead as the Catholic father had taught them, in graves made sacred by the cross he had made of saplings and planted in the center of the burial ground. Others carried the bodies to the hill above the river, stretching them out on the upper limbs of the tallest trees or burying them on the highest ground. It was a spot the white boys had often visited in search of blue and white burial beads, but they stayed far away from it now. The whites who saw the mourning processions hurried away, as if the very sight of them might pass along the fever. There had been hundreds of Indians on the prairie above the Falls. No one knew how fast they were dying. No one cared, except to pray that the plague would not touch him.

At the hop ranch the hired help had recognized Indian

Mary's disease the moment she walked into the barnyard.
They had fled like field mice before a hungry owl. Bedrolls
lay cold in the bunkhouse, spiders spun webs over the
clothing on the nails along the wall. The Valley knew that
only Uncle Julian had stayed, though the last of the foreman to saddle up had tried to drag the old man along
with him. "You've seen smallpox," the foreman said. "It
ain't a pretty way to die." But death in that form hadn't
seemed half as close to Julian as the death that shadowed
him every day; death for an old and ailing man lay in the
next step, the next bite, even the next breath. So he stayed.
There was the biggest hop ranch in the world, only three
months from harvest time, and Nils Bengston was trying to
run it alone, with the help of a senile old man, a little
girl and a dying wife.

For the first time there were people who felt sorry for
him. What right had that Indian woman to come back,
they asked each other? Mary had left him so often and
finally deserted him altogether. It had been four years since
she had been Nils' wife; everyone knew there were "papers" dissolving the marriage at the district court in Seattle,
though it had been a couple of years before Nils would
agree to ask for them. Now, eaten with pox fever, she had
turned to him. "Nils ought to send her packing," the whites
agreed. "She ran off to her own people. Why don't he make
her go back to 'em now?" But they knew he hadn't. "He's
crazy," they said to comfort themselves, because they felt
sorry for him and it was an unusual feeling to have toward
Nils.

No one dared visit the hop ranch. Some slowed down at
the spot where the road passed the entrance, peering toward the buildings to see what movement there might be.
But they never saw anything; the long storehouses, the
kilns and sheds, the barns, woodhouses, the farmhouse,
the rows of bunkhouses, looked deserted. Death seemed

close even by daylight and the rider always leaned forward in the saddle and spurred his horse to a gallop. No one but Nate Tarpee had ever talked with anyone at the ranch.

Riding past the entrance he saw Julie, peering at him from behind a stump. At his approach she darted back into the lane.

Conscience, and curiosity, stirred him to call out, "You sick?"

Julie shook her head.

"Your Pa sick?"

Julie shook her head a second time. "I'm not supposed to be out here."

"You lack for something?" His horse took a step toward Julie. The movement put her to flight. "Want me to leave off something for you here at the road?" he called after her, but she was running toward the house.

Nate hesitated, his hand uncertain on the reins. But he had seen smallpox. "Leave the big Swede be," he muttered, with an uncomfortable tight feeling in his throat. "Let him run his two square miles of land by himself. He can do it." And he turned his horse and rode away as fast as he could.

ii

On the tenth day Mary died. Miraculously, Julie and old Uncle Julian were well. Nils had ordered them to eat and sleep in one of the bunkhouses, and to stay as far from him as they did from Mary. He alone cared for her, until day and night, even time and place, ran together in the confusion of weariness. He did not know exactly when she died. He had fallen asleep in a chair. He awoke suddenly, thinking she had cried out. "Mary?" he whispered. His

body felt heavy; it seemed to take all his strength to stand
and walk to the bed. There was a sharp ringing in his ears.
He shook his head angrily to get rid of it. "Mary?" he said
again, and then he saw that she was dead.

He looked down at her, and a violent shudder went
through him. He had hardly known this woman he had
cared for. "We'll go home," he had told her once. "There
the sickness will never touch you. I will keep you safe forever." For ten days of hell he had kept some kind of faith
with that promise, uttered so many years before to a young
Indian girl he could only half remember. Loyalty—he had
felt he owed her that much for not loving her. This was
the end of it. Her face was swollen hideously. Disease had
bloated the nostrils, the mouth, the cheeks. . . . The taste
of bile rose in Nils' throat. He swallowed, fighting against
shudders that seemed to be attacking him in a series. He
must bury her, he told himself, and it should be done right
away. It was no time for mourning. He dared not even go
close enough to Julie to tell her that her mother was gone.
He pulled the gray and red blanket over Mary's face,
turned and walked heavily to the barn.

He found shovel, boards, saw, nails, a hammer. With
great pains he fashioned a coffin. The work went slowly.
The feeling of heaviness grew worse with every moment;
moving at all was an almost insurmountable problem. He
concentrated on it, watching his hands fixedly. He sawed
the boards, nailed them together, tested the joints for
strength. When he was through he loaded the box onto the
back of the wagon and went back into the house. Dread
of the task slowed him down; fear of not finishing it
speeded him. As gently as he knew how he wrapped Mary
in all the blankets on the bed, and carried her out to the
wagon.

The effort made him weak and he began to tremble. He
lowered her into the box, nailed the top boards into place.

He despised the weakness that had hit him, and began to race against it.

The burial spot must be as far from the ranch buildings as possible. That was the only clear thought his mind would give him. He hitched the team to the wagon, drove them straight across a field of sprouting oats to a rocky spot high above the river. The water had never risen this high, and the nearest dwelling was miles away. She would not be disturbed here. In the distance were the apple orchards which he had planted when Mary was a young girl, a laughing, slender, chief's daughter, who once had teased her stepmother by rocking the canoe.

Nils paced off the grave, and began digging. The surface dirt was thin. Underneath were the round boulders of an ancient river bed. He bent his back against the weight of them. Sweat burst out on him, and his strength seemed to leave him with it. He worked frantically.

At last the hole was big enough. He lifted the coffin onto his shoulder, lowered it into place. He was trembling. Hurriedly he groped for the shovel, scooped the dirt onto the box with frantic, unsteady sweeps of his arms. The hole was filled, and the last shovelsful made an uneven mound above the grave. Nils' teeth were chattering; he clenched his jaw and still could not stop the sound. It was done. He threw the shovel into the back of the wagon, and clutched suddenly at the bang board, leaning forward against it. Shudder after shudder ripped through him. He held on tight, wishing angrily for the strength to curse out loud. The worst of it passed, and he pulled himself onto the wagon seat and turned the horses home. It was done. He rode with his elbows on his knees, head down, eyes closed.

In the barnyard the horses stopped by themselves. Nils straightened and stared witlessly at the house and barns. He hadn't been asleep, he was sure of it, but he couldn't remember the ride home. His head throbbed painfully.

The thought kept hammering at him that he would have to burn his clothes and bathe before he got near Julie. If he scrubbed himself hard, if he destroyed everything he'd worn, even his boots, perhaps he would not carry the sickness to her . . .

He stood up, rocking unsteadily. Right away, he thought, right fast before Julie comes near. Let the horses stand in harness for a while. He saw the door of the bunkhouse open and Julie step out.

"No!" he shouted. It seemed as if his voice weren't carrying at all. "No, stay there!" He lifted both hands to wave her back. She hesitated. He would have to get down from the wagon, call her again . . . "Baby . . ." Nils took a step, but his legs didn't hold him. He grabbed for the dashboard. His fingers touched it and slid away as his great body crumpled and fell unconscious to the wagon floor.

iii

Katherine and Faith Carlson were in the kitchen when Julie rode in.

Faith exclaimed, "My goodness, it's Julie Bengston. Why . . ."

Katherine ran to the door. "Where are the children?"

"In the woods," Faith said distractedly. "Or the shed, maybe. Oh my goodness, I don't know."

"You watch for them. Keep them away. I'll talk to Julie."

It didn't take Julie long to tell Katherine what was wrong. She didn't explain why she had come to her teacher rather than to others. "*You* help us." She made the request as confidently as if she were asking for the right answer to an arithmetic problem.

Katherine nodded with all the authority of a teacher before her class. "You go back home," she said firmly, "and stay with your father. Cover him over with a blanket. Be sure he doesn't get cold. I'll get the doctor."

Without a word Julie wheeled her pony around and raced back along the trail. Katherine ran into the house for a shawl, then across the clearing to where her pony grazed. Jeb had the wagon in Gold Mountain. No time now to worry about how she would get Dr. Meade up the hill to the hop ranch. She grabbed the halter rope and leaped onto the pony's smooth back. It was the second time she had gone for a doctor. Only this time Nils could not help her.

In Black River she found Dr. Meade in back of the hotel, bandaging a gash on the leg of Hilke Orvaag's big bay horse. The doctor was on his knees. He squinted up at her through bushy black eyebrows. "Well, it's the teacher and she caught me doctoring a horse. I'm not ashamed of it. They pay up faster than some humans. Who's having a baby, Miss Duncan? I hope you forgot your ladylike sensibilities enough to ask the right questions this time."

"Nils Bengston is sick."

The doctor tied the bandage with a quick little jerk, and got slowly to his feet. *"Nils* is sick." He knew what it meant. Hilke, standing beside him with his mouth open, knew, too. "Aahh . . ." The doctor sighed. His satchel stood open on a stool. He went to it and scowled at its interior. "Mmm."

Katherine burst out, "Doctor, will you come, please?"

The doctor looked at her sideways. "I have a lot of patients, Miss Duncan. They're not all horses. Most of them I can do something for and every now and then I save a life. There's almost nothing I could do for Nils."

Katherine cried, "But you're the only doctor!"

The man nodded. "That's just it. Who will take care of all the other people?"

"Then you don't go to see Nils?" Hilke Orvaag asked incredulously.

"Of course I'm going!" the doctor bellowed suddenly. "You know I never turned anyone down in my life. I just don't want this young lady to think she can ride down here and drag me up to Gold Mountain every two years." He scowled at Hilke. "Saddle that big black of yours. I been riding some and it don't seem to hurt my leg any worse than falling in and out of ruts in some old farm wagon."

A loud sigh escaped from Katherine. "Thank you, Dr. Meade."

The doctor wheeled toward her. "Why are you so anxious about that big bully of a Swede?"

Katherine flushed. Hilke was staring at her. Suddenly his face broke into a knowing grin and he hurried toward the barn. The doctor's eyebrows seemed to be pointing at her accusingly. "I . . ."

"Never mind," he said curtly. "I'm not interested in your personal follies." He closed his satchel with a loud snap. "You haven't been to the hop ranch?"

Katherine shook her head.

"Not near Nils?"

"No."

The doctor nodded. "Good. Now you get on your pony and ride back to Carlsons' and don't you go near that ranch, even if you love that man enough to die for him. He might not live to appreciate it." He thumped his pockets energetically. "Fever pills, yes. Eyeglasses, yes . . ." He glared at Katherine. "Well, go on. I can find my way up the Valley. Good-bye."

"Good-bye." Katherine walked away reluctantly. She turned back. "If there's something I can do," she said in a small voice. "If there's any way at all I can help . . ."

"He's not going to have a baby," the doctor snapped. He looked at Katherine's face and his voice softened. "My dear girl," he said gently, "there's nothing you can do. Nothing at all. But you could do a lot of harm to all those little Carlson youngsters if you didn't stay away."

The doctor's sudden kindness was unbearable. Katherine burst into tears. "I love him!"

The doctor's hand touched her shoulder. "I'll tell him," he said simply. "Now go home."

iv

Dr. Meade arranged the strips of side meat in the big iron spider and reflected that the practice of medicine involved so little of what he had learned at medical school. He'd graduated after eleven months. The wonderful thing about higher education, he mused, is that so much of it sticks with you even after you're smart enough to forget it. If he was a good doctor now it was because he had learned so much since college. And because he could cook, shoot straight, speak Chinook and had no use for liquor. He grinned. How would that have looked on his diploma?

He set the spider over the coals, pushing it back and forth on its long legs until it rested evenly on the hearth. Come to think of it, who cared what was on his diploma, or even whether he had one? The Territorial Legislature —he laughed. He had paid two dollars at the county auditor's, shown his diploma and signed his name. So much for the law. He wasn't nursing the legislature, he was nursing people, as he always had. He'd been a post doctor in Idaho, a doctor in the range country of Montana. The Valley was a civilized place by comparison.

Wherever he'd been, his patients had trusted him. You do, the doctor thought wryly, if there's only one doctor and you've ridden from ten to eighty miles to get him. They didn't ask where you'd studied, and the two dollars you paid the county meant nothing to them. Old Mark Bliss

was called "doctor" simply because he had strong hands.
The "rubbing doctor," they had named him back in Idaho,
and paid a silver dollar for a healing rub. Years before little Mrs. John Tobias had put two medical kits in the wagon
when she and her husband left Iowa for Oregon. Those
kits made her the "doctor" for the whole train and she'd
been mending and healing and delivering infants ever
since. Lucy Grant hadn't gone to medical school to learn
about bread and milk poultices, which she prescribed for
every ailment known to man, but she'd never lost a child-
birth and she was as deeply trusted as he, even if she was
a woman. Patching a man's head after the Indians had
lifted his scalp, cutting off frostbitten toes without anaesthetic—no, they hadn't said much about that back east in
medical school.

The doctor picked up a long hunting knife. Potatoes
were roasting under a thin covering of hot ashes. One by
one he speared them with the point of the knife and dragged them to the edge of the hearth. If I'd married, he
reflected, I wouldn't be such a good cook, and that would
mean that in cases like this I wouldn't be such a good doctor. Nils was far too sick to eat. He was in the bedroom
with damp towels over his forehead, if he hadn't already
thrown them off in the delirium of his fever. But that little
Julie had been hungry when he came and too grieved by
her mother's death to feed herself properly. Old Uncle
Julian had become too witless to think of food when he
wasn't hungry himself. Julie was sure to eat, once he got
her started. At the moment feeding the child was a doctor's
job as much as worrying about what to do for her father.

He didn't know, and that irritated him. He knew many
a doctor who would have soothed himself during the past
few days with a little whiskey. But that was one of the four
ways in which Doc Meade had lived up to his oath and his
diploma and himself. He scarcely knew the taste of liquor.

Not that he hadn't administered it, if there was a reason. The day, for example, when Luther Anderson fell from his hayloft and broke his legs in so many places a country doctor would hardly know where to put the splints. Doc Meade saw that if the man was to walk again, he would have to be treated in a hospital in Seattle.

The eldest Anderson boy drove the wagon. Dr. Meade and the groaning Luther were in the back. It was a long ride over a trail so rough that most wagons broke down at least once before they got to Seattle. Doc had carried a quart of whiskey in his satchel that day, and praised heaven for having it. The man had been in severe pain. Whenever he regained consciousness the good doctor forced open his mouth and poured half a tumbler of whiskey down his throat.

"My legs!" the man would moan as he awakened.

"Liquor is the servant of man," Dr. Meade replied, and tipped the bottle into his mouth. He had often said later that by the time they reached the hospital the doctors could have transplanted Luther's arms and legs without anaesthetic and Luther would have smiled.

The meat was beginning to sizzle. The doctor shook the pan a little, to see it didn't stick. Then he went to the bedroom door.

Julie was squatted beside her father's bed. Her eyes were round and blank. In pain and in fear, the doctor thought, the Indian comes out strongest. He should scold her for sitting by her father. But what was the use, when she had undoubtedly been near him the week before? If it was smallpox . . . The doctor frowned. There wasn't anything on his diploma that said he couldn't catch disease. In thirty years of practice it seemed as if he'd had everything his patients had ever had, except a baby. If it was smallpox, he and Nils and Julie and the old man Julian might easily die together.

But was it? Nils had been ill for two days now. His fever had been high, his pulse quick. In his rational moments he had complained of headache and pains in his back. But there was no rash. Perhaps it was too early, but if the dusky red spots had not appeared by morning . . . The doctor sighed. Then it wouldn't be smallpox. Nils was wasting with the fever; he was out of his mind most of the time. Whatever the illness, such a fever might easily kill him whether or not the doctor knew what to call it.

"Get up, girl, and wash," he said gruffly. "I'm hungry but I won't eat unless you do."

Julie went outside. Obedience, a natural sense of courtesy—they are strong in her, the doctor noted, and besides she's a hungry little girl. He picked up a potato with the tip of his hunting knife; with a second knife cut off the crusty black covering. When he opened it on her plate a delicious steam rose. He used his hunting knife to scoop butter from the crock and cut it into the potato. With the same long knife he speared several strips of side meat and carried them from the hearth to her plate. He pushed the knife's point through a cold biscuit and held it out to her. She pulled it off and began chewing on it. In the same way, the doctor filled his own plate. They ate in silence. Julie's plate was empty before his.

"Now go to bed," the doctor said. He didn't believe in deceiving people, but the little girl's wide, unhappy eyes made him tell a downright lie. "Your father's going to start getting better tomorrow. I want you to be wide awake so you can help take care of him." When Julie was asleep, the doctor pulled a chair up next to Nils' bed and settled himself for the night.

By noon the next day he was sure Nils did not have smallpox. But he was plainly failing. The doctor watched him anxiously, cooling him with damp towels and trying to force a little lukewarm tea into his mouth with a spoon.

Convulsions, a coma—it would be one or the other, the doctor thought, unless the fever broke. Nils talked deliriously, then lapsed into half-consciousness, his mouth moving and his eyes fixed blindly on the ceiling. That poor little schoolteacher, the doctor thought. What a confession it was for her to say she loved him, and now he's going to die before I've had a chance to tell him. The doctor was feeling for Nils' pulse when Brother Bill walked into the room.

He put Nils' hand down gently and turned to the big evangelist. "What are you doing here?" he whispered.

"I got to Black River this morning. They told me Nils was dying of the smallpox. I walked up right away."

The doctor shook his head. "Not smallpox."

Brother Bill looked down at Nils. "What is it?"

Doc Meade shrugged. "I don't know. I suppose *you'd* say God alone knows."

Brother Bill said simply, "Yes, I would." He moved toward the bed.

The doctor stepped in front of him. "Stay back, Bill. No use in your . . ."

Brother Bill got past him without actually shoving him aside. "I come to pray with him." He pushed his hair back from his eyes and got down on his knees beside the bed.

"Get out of here, Bill. I don't know what this fever is, but it might be something you could catch."

"You're here, Doc."

"Because I'm a doctor."

"Haven't you ever caught anything?"

"I've had everything," the doctor snapped. "But it's my business to be here."

Brother Bill said, "The man's dying. That means I got more business here than you have." He nodded solemnly toward the bedroom door. "So *you* get out. If you stay you got to get down on your knees. I'm going to pray."

The doctor looked from the evangelist's big, homely face to the unconscious body of his patient. At times doctoring isn't even a matter of medicine, he thought bitterly, and they didn't teach me that in medical school, either. He bent one knee and wearily let himself down to the floor. Bill's prayer began. "Our Lord in heaven . . ." The doctor rested an elbow on his knee, and covered his face with his hand.

V

Nils came out of the semicoma briefly that afternoon. He turned his head and looked at Brother Bill, though his eyes did not seem to focus clearly.

"Can you hear me, Nils?"

Nils' voice answered him weakly. "Quit your shouting. My head aches."

"I'm glad you're awake. Will you pray with me now, Brother Nils?"

Nils' breathing was so labored that his voice came out unevenly. "Am I that bad? Doc think I'm dying?"

"You should be prepared."

"Where's Doc?" Nils' voice had fallen to a whisper.

"Sleeping in the next room. He ain't more than cat-napped the past two, three days." He cleared his throat. "Pray with me, Nils."

Nils closed his eyes. "So I'm dying."

"You've been a sinful man, Nils Bengston. But God receives all those who repent."

Nils' lips barely moved. "You trying to get me into heaven, Bill?"

The evangelist nodded. "Heaven is the life after death, where all is beautiful and good."

With a sudden movement Nils pulled himself up on one elbow. "If everybody gets changed I wouldn't know my friends." He fell back, exhausted by the effort.

Brother Bill looked at him uncertainly. "Well, it don't say exactly that everybody's *changed.*"

"If they ain't, then heaven's full of stupid people." Nils' eyes were bright. The pupils had dilated so wide the eyes looked black. He was breathing hard. With a great effort he put both hands behind him and pushed himself to a sitting position. A shadow of his old grin flickered across his face. "It don't sound good to me, Bill," he gasped. "I changed my mind. I'm not going to die."

Brother Bill felt the demon of his temper stirring. "God will decide whether you live or die," he said loudly, "not you. I come here to pray with you. Now bow your head like a Christian."

"I'm not going to die!" Nils repeated weakly. "I'd rather own the biggest hop ranch in the world."

"Bow your head!"

Nils stared glassily at Brother Bill. "Nobody's going to pray over me," he whispered, "least of all a twenty-five-cent walking preacher."

That was too much. Brother Bill had often heard Nils' estimate of him: twenty-five cents a mile but not a penny for preaching. For the first time in years the temper got away from him completely. "Bow your head and pray!" he bellowed, threatening Nils with both fists, "Or with the help of God I'm going to beat your ears off!"

The shout brought Doc Meade running to the room. He saw Brother Bill leaning over the bed, his face white with anger, and Nils sitting straight up with a wide grin on his face. "Dear Lord," he murmured, as if he had come in specifically to lead off the prayer. He went to the bed and felt Nils' wrist, his forehead, his heart, but even as he did it he knew the fever had broken and Nils would live.

CHAPTER

12

i

The last day of school was to be a July fourth program. Every pupil would be in it. The big Smith boy who had given up chewing tobacco in order to sit through class. The little three- and four-year-olds, who attended the first grade because their mothers didn't want to fuss with them at home and kept right on attending it until they knew by heart all the pictures in all the books. The "good students," like Julie Bengston and Levi Barker and Tommy Tine.

The program was to be held in the new school, and for that reason was like none Gold Mountain had ever anticipated before. It called for a new dress, if possible. Mothers dyed buttercloth or ripped up dresses of their own if they couldn't afford to buy a length of goods at Nate Tarpee's store. For the new schoolhouse was as different as silk is from homespun. It had a store-boughten look.

Instead of a dirt floor, one walked on smooth planks. The old wood shutters had been replaced by real glass windows. There was a big, potbellied stove with a tin chimney instead of a crude hearth of fieldstone and clay. In the old school a thirsty child had had a choice between the river or a bottle of water brought from home. A row of jars had stood on a bench at the back of the room, with initials scratched into each metal top. Now there was a well, and a shiny bucket of water with an equally shiny dipper hanging from a nail above. There were even two outhouses, one for girls, one for boys. No question but what the new schoolhouse was one of the best in the county. How many had blackboards the size of a wall and real sheepskin erasers?

Julie and Tommy Tine were to say one of the longest poems, or so Teacher had said before Julie left school because of the smallpox. Nils heard of it from Tommy's mother, Agatha, who arrived at the hop ranch with a wagonload of food the same day Doc Meade left it. "I passed Doc on his way home this morning," Agatha said. "He said you wasn't bad sick any more but more'n likely you'd soon be bad hungry. It's a good thing I come. You look skinny as a garter snake and just about as strong."

Before she left she had filled the cooler with smoked ham and venison, butter, two or three round hard loaves of bread, a couple of pies and preserves to last a winter. She had declared that the ranch was well rid of the lily-livered cook who ran off with the foremen; he put so little by he must have been planning to starve them anyway. She had also passed along the information that Doc Meade had had a message for Nils and forgot it. "Nothing important," the doctor had promised her, with a sharp look in his eye. Also, she concluded, there was a school program in a couple of days, and Tommy couldn't be in it unless Julie was, because they were to say a poem together.

"I'll send Julie back to school tomorrow," Nils said.

"I'll come over, if you need someone to fix for you."

"When I want a woman around here," Nils retorted, "I'll pick her out myself."

Agatha snorted. "Too bad you had to go and get sick, with the big school program only two days away. You'll miss it."

"I never missed school, or any part of it."

"Ha!" Agatha eyed him narrowly. "It just calls attention to your ignorance, to act like you're proud of it."

"I'm ignorant," Nils snapped, "but I'm rich. I got the biggest hop ranch in the world. I can afford to hate school."

"And schoolteachers." Agatha's little round mouth closed tightly as she scanned his face.

"You're a fat old busybody." Nils lay back and closed his eyes. "If my legs would hold me, I'd go to the program, just for Julie's sake. That'd be the only reason. Miss Duncan is a bright one, and a good one, for being a school-marm, but me and her don't look at anything the same way and we never will. I'm tired, Ag. Now that you brought me all that good grub, why don't you go on home?"

"I'll tell you about the program afterward."

Nils shook his head warily. "No hurry, Ag, no hurry."

ii

Katherine stood at the window, watching the road on which the wagons would soon appear. The school desks had been crowded together in the middle of the floor and benches from the old school placed along the walls for the parents. Everything was in place. The globe, the American flag, the Bible for the opening reading and the harmonica with which to start the songs. American flags, cut, pasted and colored were pinned on the back wall; the front wall, which was taken up entirely by a blackboard, was appropriately decorated with crude chalk drawings of minutemen and their muskets. All in readiness, Katherine thought, even to Teacher's new dress.

She touched the soft folds of the skirt affectionately. It was made of green delaine, a light wool muslin with a little leaf pattern woven right into the fabric. It was the first good dress she had made since she came to the Valley. Her mother had often spoken of the delaine dresses she had worn before her marriage, fashionable dresses that had one by one been lost or worn out and never replaced. Katherine had planned this new dress for months. In the very beginning she had decided that it must be of delaine.

The sin of pride—Brother Bill would call it that, Katherine thought. But it seemed as if she had always had an uncommon need for her pride. She had chosen a course four years before and kept to it, but pride had protected her, spurred her, goaded and strengthened her, every step of the way. The first was taken the day she defied her father and all her aunts and uncles with the announcement that she was going to become a teacher. A skinny little seventeen-year-old with scarcely five whole terms of schooling behind her—it had been a crazy, a proud, thing to do. Yet the best of everything she had done since had been accomplished in the same way, as if she had found a pattern that day she stared down her elders, a pattern that was her own. Decide on the impossible, and be too proud to give it up.

Pride had built this new school, but it was a good kind of pride, the kind even Brother Bill approved of. The shared feeling of a hundred neighbors, which built good things and brought good people together. "Teacher deserves it," the Valley people said, like parents tolerating their child's whim because she's been such a good girl. No one had dreamed there could be such a school here, but teacher had worked hard and done it in four years. It would be closer to the truth, Katherine thought wistfully, to say that I've done it in twenty-one.

For this new school and even her delaine dress was an answer not only to Nils Bengston who had once said he'd send her back to Seattle, or to Carl White who had begged her to give it up, or to ignorance or poverty or anything else in the Valley that had stood in her way. To Katherine this day was part of the lifetime of Katherine Fairfield Duncan, born twenty-one years ago in a sod house in Kansas.

"School" had been such a changeable word. Once it had meant the neighbor's kitchen, where a mother born in Boston ransacked her memory for the bits of learning she passed on to a class of Katherine, Teddy and five children of her own. For a few weeks it had been part of an old fort. The outside walls of the school had been splintered and pock-marked by the impact of hundreds of bullets, and the pupils had played in the charred remnants of the other buildings. School in a barn, in a kitchen, in a sod house or an abandoned log cabin. Teachers who ended the term to butcher the hog or work along a trap line or boil a year's crop of maple sugar or give birth to a new baby. Schools without books, without pencils, without heat, where the winter wind cut through the unchinked walls so that your mind felt as stiff as your fingers and toes. From now on the children of Gold Mountain would have a school that was a school and something more, a teacher who was a teacher above all else. That had been the goal, glimpsed when she was too young and untrained even to receive a proper teaching certificate, and kept before her ever since because she was too stubborn to settle for anything less. That's where pride had taken her, straight up the road toward the impossible. The people of Gold Mountain had gone with her, determined as she was to give their children something they had missed themselves. We have come a long way, Katherine reflected, glancing around the sunlit school room. So far that in a few years no one will remember what it was we struggled so hard to leave behind.

A wagon appeared around the bend of the road. Katherine felt a sudden tight sensation in her stomach. Squinting, she tried to make out the driver. Mr. Nelson . . . She sighed. She did not expect Nils to come. She had told herself repeatedly not to think about it. But thinking of Nils was as unavoidable as thinking at all; she thought about him hardest when she was reminding herself to put him out of her mind. He was still in bed, but he was well enough to send for her and she had made up her mind to go to him if he did. But he hadn't, and that seemed to prove that even when he was physically weak and ailing he felt no need of anyone outside himself. He had kissed her. Was that why she was afraid to face him? Katherine straightened her bodice with a nervous gesture, and went to the door to welcome the Nelsons.

One after another the families of Gold Mountain arrived. The children's faces were shiny. The girls' hair had been brushed from their faces hard enough to pull their mouths into a smile. The boys smelled of soap and shoe grease. Many of them had new haircuts, with a white strip showing between their summer's sunburn and their new hairline. The children raced for their own school desks while their parents found places along the wall. Katherine was about to open the program when still another wagon came into the yard. In it were Nils Bengston and Julie.

Katherine whirled around and flew to her desk. "We'll begin," she said in a choked voice. No one heard her, but at least she was away from the door so she would not have to

meet him. She picked up a ruler and rapped it sharply on
the desk. "We'll begin," she repeated more loudly. The
children closed their mouths and faced her, every one a
perfect student now that their parents were here.

The door opened. All heads turned toward Nils and
Julie. Katherine's gaze followed reluctantly. Julie's face
was bright with a smile. Nils stood behind her. His face
was pale and there was a boniness to it which illness had un-
covered. But he still looked like a puzzled giant, his shoulders hunched forward as if the room were not quite big
enough. Katherine felt a wave of heat flow into her face.
She nodded silently.

Julie took her father's hand. "Over here," she whispered. Nils let Julie lead him to a place at the back of the
room. With her eyes on Katherine's face Julie put a solemn good-scholar look in place of her smile and took a seat
in the middle of the room.

He came after all . . . Katherine picked up the Bible.
Her finger felt for the place mark. Will he speak to me
afterward? she thought. What will he say, what will I say to
him? She looked blindly into the open book. No moment
in her four years in the Valley had been quite as hard as
this one, when she must hold the book though her hands
trembled, read aloud though her voice shook, and face
the crowd in front of her, though Nils was among them and
she could think of nothing but how much she loved him.

iii

The duet sung by Julie Bengston and Tommy Tine was
the last number on the program. Julie jumped up at
Katherine's signal. Nils looked at her, suddenly anxious
about how she would appear. He analyzed her dress and
the dresses of the other girls, and concluded that it was all

right even if it was red. Her stockings—he stared at them, wondering why he hadn't noticed before. Wide, bright stripes ran all the way around them. In a flurry he peered at the legs of the other little girls. Two of them had striped stockings just like Julie's. He had to repress a sigh. For years he had trusted Agatha to buy Julie's clothes. She had done all right.

Tommy Tine's face was pink and his ears looked enormous and very red. He had slid down in his seat so far that he seemed to be resting on his shoulder blades. Katherine repeated the signal to stand up and come forward. He stared at her blankly and didn't move. Agatha's face was as red as his. She was pulling in her breath to yell across the room when Julie reached down and took Tommy by the arm. She whispered hoarsely, "You get right up, Tommy Tine, or I'll never speak to you again." With a long groan Tommy stood up and followed Julie to the front of the room.

Katherine picked up the mouth organ and sounded a note. Julie's sweet, clear voice repeated the sound obediently, but Tommy was staring over the heads of the audience as if suddenly fascinated by something at the back of the room. Julie's elbow nudged him lightly. He jumped and began to sing.

> "Fair lady, I will buy you a penny's worth of pins,
> To pin up your laces and many other things,
> If you'll walk, walk with me, anywhere, anywhere,
> If you'll walk, walk with me, anywhere."

Tommy stopped abruptly. Instantly Julie lifted her chin and sang:

> "Kind sir, I won't accept of your penny's worth of pins,
> To pin up my laces and many other things,
> Nor I won't walk with you, anywhere, anywhere,
> Nor I won't walk with you, anywhere."

This time Nils could not hold back his sigh. "Aahh . . ." he said out loud, sliding down on his spine and shoving his hands into his pockets. She knew *her* part of it, all right. If she had made any mistakes, you couldn't tell it.

> "Fair lady, I will buy you a pretty golden chain,
> To hang around your neck when you trip across the plain,
> If you'll walk, walk with me anywhere, anywhere,
> If you'll walk, walk with me, anywhere."

Tommy's voice trailed off and his glance wandered over the room. Julie sang out brightly:

> "Kind sir, I won't accept of your pretty golden chain,
> To hang about my neck when I trip across the plain,
> Nor I won't walk with you, anywhere, anywhere,
> Nor I won't walk with you, anywhere."

Tommy was looking out the window.

"Tommy!" Julie hissed.

"Fair lady, I will buy you a silk gown five yards long!" Tommy exclaimed. He stumbled, forgetting. He wheeled around to look at Katherine.

"To trail the ground . . ." she whispered.

"To trail the ground!" Tommy shouted.

Quickly Julie sang, "Kind sir, I won't accept of your rich silken gown, with five long yards to trail along the ground . . ."

Nils grinned. Julie knew it better than Tommy, anyone could see that. Better not to say anything about it to Agatha. His gaze moved to Agatha Tine. It's a shame, he thought, but he was grinning.

> "Fair lady, I will give you the key to my chest,
> Gold or silver, whichever you love the best . . . "

And Julie answered saucily, "Kind sir, I won't accept of the key to your chest . . ."

As Julie finished Tommy seemed to come to life. He

stood up straight and frowned mightily. "Fair lady, I will give you the keys to my heart," he sang out, directing the offer in the opposite direction from Julie.

He must be coming to the end, Nils thought. He's like a horse riding for the barn.

"To keep with you forever until death do us part . . . "

"Kind sir, I *will* accept of the keys to your heart,
To keep with me forever till death do us part,
And I'll walk, walk with you, anywhere, anywhere,
And I'll walk, walk with you, anywhere."

Tommy and Julie stood before the crowd with bright, expectant looks on their faces. They were out of breath. Nils brought his hands together in a resounding clap, and everyone else followed. Nils looked around proudly, noting how many people were smiling at Julie.

The program was over. As Katherine stood up and thanked them all for coming, Nils' preoccupation with Julie ended abruptly. The children fell over each other in their effort to get their wraps on first and to be first out the door. Their parents got up slowly, smiling to themselves. Katherine stood at the door like Preacher Bill, and no couple left without stopping to congratulate her.

At the back of the room Nils let one person after another push past him. He hadn't an idea in his head of what to say to her. He felt bare. Anger and deliberate laughter had always been handy when he needed protection, but he couldn't even begin to arouse them with his whole being shouting that she was beautiful. What could he say to her? "I love you. I've been trying not to for well on to four years and it doesn't work." When he kissed her at the dance in Black River, he had kissed with feeling he had never known before, and she had shown feeling as strong as his own. He couldn't have been mistaken, but that was weeks ago. She hadn't come to him, she hadn't said it was the same, now. Julie touched his arm. He looked at her confusedly.

"Father, everybody's going!"

"Oh, sure." Katherine was waiting at the door. She had spoken to everyone else. "Sure," Nils repeated mechanically.

Julie's hand pulled him down. "Everyone else said something nice to Teacher," she whispered urgently.

Nils walked to the front, Julie jerking his hand to make him move faster. But he went in slow motion, his feet dragging, his eyes on Katherine's face. Katherine didn't move. How green her eyes are, he thought, like river water when the sun goes through it. "I . . ."

She was so very still. Her wide eyes looked at him solemnly. "I want to thank you," he began. Her mouth—he found he couldn't stop looking at it. The lower lip was rounded, moist along the rim. He had kissed her.

Katherine moved, picking up a pile of papers and hurriedly pulling one out. Nils saw that her hands trembled. "This is Julie's last English composition," she said, in a tight little voice. "I thought you'd like to read it."

Bitterness flooded through him. He wanted to hurt her, to destroy her with one devastating word or one murderous blow. His throat tightened so he could hardly speak; for the first time since he had got out of bed and dressed for the program, weakness returned. He gritted his teeth, forcing himself to stand without support. Anger would have been comforting; this feeling of nakedness was unbearable. "Miss Duncan," he said at last, "I can't read or write."

Julie whispered, "Father, you're supposed . . ."

Nils answered her by bolting through the door and across the schoolyard to the wagon. With Julie stoically silent beside him, he turned the horses onto the road and whipped them into a trot.

The wagon creaked alarmingly, jolting in and out of the sun-baked ruts. Under his breath, Nils began to curse. With each word his pulse quieted and his strength returned. The hop ranch buildings were only a few rods distant when Nils jerked the horses to a halt. Julie's startled voice said, "Father, what are you doing now?" Nils growled wordlessly and turned the horses back the way they'd come. "Forgot something," he gasped as the wagon slammed in and out of a hole, and he lay the reins hard across the horses' backs. The return trip was as fast, as tense and as silent as the departure had been. In the schoolyard Katherine's pony was still tethered to an alder. Nils threw the reins into Julie's hands, and leaped to the ground as if he'd never known a sick day in his life.

He ran across the yard and pushed the schoolhouse door open so hard it hit the wall with a crash. Katherine was at the desk. And then she was in his arms.

He kissed her in a frenzy. "Sweetheart," he whispered, "sweetheart . . ."

The summer sun shot bright shafts of light into the room. Outside the horses whinnied. Her mouth was soft. He kissed her cheek, and felt her breath warm against his ear.

He stopped kissing her but he could not let her go. He held her gently, and talked to her over her head. "You got a pretty dress," he said. "The color of your eyes. Did you know it was?"

She nodded, her chin rubbing against his chest.

He grinned. "Too bad you're such a dried-up little old schoolmarm. Heart like a stone and head full of letters and numbers. Poor little thing. Don't even know she's got beautiful big eyes."

Katherine giggled, somewhere below his lapel.

Nils kissed the top of her head. "I love you, Kate."

"Not Kate!"

Laughing, Nils tilted her head back and kissed her on the mouth. Her hands tightened on his shoulders. He kissed her again. Her lips parted and she seemed to melt into him. He kissed her throat, and caught the sweet odor of her body. Suddenly he held her at arm's length. "Did that Carl ever kiss you?"

Katherine's eyes widened. "What do you mean? We were engaged. But he never called me Kate." Katherine burst into laughter.

Muttering angrily, Nils drew her back into his arms. "Then I will."

She drew back. "Julie . . . Isn't Julie outside?"

"She'll wait." But the mention of Julie reminded him of the composition paper. "I can't read or write," he said flatly.

Katherine nodded. "That's what you said."

Nils said brusquely, "Maybe you guessed it before."

"No."

"I could learn."

Katherine's eyes filled with tears. "Would you?" she asked softly. "Why?"

"I want to marry you."

They looked at each other. After a moment Katherine tried to speak, and then only shook her head and smiled. Nils sat down on the nearest bench and pulled her into his lap. "I'm going to learn how to read and write," he said. "And I'm going to build you a house. Then we'll get married. We'll have the biggest wedding in the Territory."

Katherine laughed. "You have a house."

"It's not big enough," Nils said curtly. He frowned at her. "Did you ever live in a nice house?"

"Once," Katherine said wistfully, "in Seattle, before I came here. It burned down."

Little by little, she told him about the big white house on the hill. The house with glass windows in every room, with the carved newel post and the crystal lamps and the naked goddesses over the mantelpiece.

Nils listened attentively. "I'll build one just like that," he said when she finished. "Only bigger."

Katherine shook her head. "No. That kind of house was my mother's dream. For many years I thought it was mine, too. But it isn't. Just an ordinary house . . ."

Nils held her tightly by the shoulders. "Listen here, Kate. I own the biggest hop ranch in the world. An ordinary house isn't enough. I'll build you a house they'll talk about in Seattle. When it's done, we'll get married." He grinned. "Engaged in the morning, married that afternoon."

Katherine's mouth opened to object. He kissed her. "The biggest house in the Territory."

She shook her head but Nils saw that her eyes were sparkling. "How about learning to read and write? Are you going to do that better than anyone in the Territory, too?"

Nils frowned. "How long does it take?"

"That depends on how hard you work at it," Katherine said soberly, a smile twitching at the corners of her mouth. "And how bright you are."

"It will take a year to build the house. Maybe more, to furnish it right. Do you think I'll be writing and reading in that time?"

Katherine shrugged. "I don't know. Who's going to teach you?"

Nils shook her. "You are, by golly."

"During school hours?"

"No!" Nils howled. "After school. At night. Any other time."

"Well, I don't know," she said, grinning wickedly. "I might not have the time."

"We can start right now."

Katherine's head tilted sideways as she looked up at him. He leaned forward but she slipped out of his hands and went behind the teacher's desk.

"Sit right there," she commanded, pointing to the school desk in front of her. Nils sat down, forcing his tremendous body into the little desk.

Katherine picked up a piece of chalk and wrote a series of letters on the blackboard. "Now," she said briskly, turning to look down at her giant pupil, "pay close attention. This is the letter A . . ."

In time Julie got cold and came into the schoolhouse to see what had happened. She saw her father doubled up in a sixth-grader's desk, slowly reciting the ABC's.

13

i

The house Nils Bengston built for teacher was fabulous
from the moment the first shovel of dirt was moved for the
foundation. The people of Gold Mountain watched a hanging garden of Babylon, a sphinx at Giza, a gem-studded Taj
Mahal, spring from ground that had cost two and a half
dollars an acre.

It was just like Nils to build a house like that, they all
said. There were dwellings like it in Seattle, and some
claimed to have seen its twin in San Francisco. But everything about Nils' house for Katherine was bigger, more

long list of properties in Three Forks and Black River with my name on them. I've got a sawmill and a shingle mill. I'm in the logging business and the hop business and the cattle business, and I sold five thousand bushels of apples last year. When I come to the Valley I had two pair of britches and a winter's wages from rafting timber. Have I got money enough? Ha! Are you trying to tell me I don't know what I'm doing?"

He laughed at Agatha, ignored the Nelsons and Andersons, outshouted Nate Tarpee, and would not listen to Katherine at all.

Katherine's uneasiness was sharper than anyone else's. This extravagant house was for her and she was afraid from the moment the studdings were erected. There were great square pillars, heavy enough to support a medieval castle.

Nils would not show her the plan. "Bad luck to let a lady see her wedding present ahead of time."

Katherine retorted that he didn't believe in bad luck, or good luck, for that matter. Hadn't he often said "luck" was something a weak man talks about to explain why he'd failed?

Nils' answer was to pick her up and swing her around so that she had to clutch at him like a child riding pickaback, or fall to the ground. "I'll show you where the rooms will be," he said, bracing her legs around his waist, his big hands holding her by the ankles.

"Nils!" she gasped, looking down to see if her petticoats were showing.

"Now this is the front door," he said, ignoring the protest, "and this is the—the foyer, or something."

Nils' education kept apace with the building. He appeared at the schoolhouse two or three afternoons a week, his primer and speller strapped together and tied to the back of his saddle. The first time several of the bigger boys lingered in the schoolroom, pretending to be busy with extra lessons, Nils picked them up two at a time and threw them out the door.

As a scholar Nils proved to be slow or quick, depending on his private opinion of the subject. While he was studying from a first-grade primer, reading was difficult. He said the story was silly. When Katherine gave him copies of the *Times* or the *Press* or the *Post-Intelligencer,* he turned to the financial columns and learned rapidly. Arithmetic was easy from the first. He had always kept hop ranch accounts in his head and had often corrected the errors old Uncle Julian made on paper. He could read market reports and shipping news in the newspapers while he was still stumbling over the Sermon on the Mount and the Twenty-third Psalm.

"You learn only what you want, and no more," Katherine scolded.

"Does that make me a fool?" Nils asked, grinning. "I'm only doing this because I want you."

"If you studied what you don't like the way you study what you do like, you could teach school."

Nils choked. "Woman, if you knew what I used to say about schoolteachers."

Month moved into month, and the wonder of Nils Bengston's house for Teacher grew. Round turrets were built into the four corners of the house, each topped with an elaborately carved cupola, each of a different design. The building bristled with wrought ironwork and wood carving. By spring it had been painted white, and work on the inside began.

Oak, marble, crystal. Blood red wallpaper with golden plumes. Overstuffed furniture with heavy oak carving and upholstery of fine black horsehair or deep red velvet. As each new addition was made, Katherine's apprehension grew. She told herself she should not listen to the others, for Nils himself was confident. Why should she feel that he was wrong and those without confidence were right? Besides, no one could stop him. He *would* build this house. It was a natural expression of his desire for the biggest of everything, as if his physical size required a world bigger, more daring than anyone else's.

"School year 1889-90" in Katherine's notebook had just begun when the first load of furniture arrived at Black River. It had been shipped in on the *Viking*, each piece of it so heavily crated that the box weighed as much as the contents. That afternoon Nils stopped at the schoolhouse.

He came through the door like a man who has never known the barrier he couldn't push aside. The children waited gleefully for him to kiss Teacher. They'd seen him do it and Teacher's face was already bright pink as if she were afraid he might.

"Class dismissed," Teacher said in a particularly firm voice.

"Sure, kids, go on home," Nils commanded, waving "shoo" at them with both hands.

They scuttled through the door, then looked back to see if he were really going to. Grinning, Nils kicked the door shut with the toe of his boot.

"Nils, really."

He pulled her into his arms and kissed her. *"Really,"* he whispered mockingly and kissed her again. "Yes, *really."*

"Where is your primer?"

He grinned at her crookedly. "I didn't come for no reading lesson."

"Any reading lesson."

"Don't be so prissy. I got something for you."

Katherine looked at his empty hands.

"Not here. Lock this place up and come with me."

They rode through the hop fields toward the river. The house was visible from a distance. Its fancy cupolas pointed skyward like church spires, high above the roofs of the stables and barns and sheds nearby. Its white paint glistened in the afternoon sun.

"In the house?" Katherine called.

Nils nodded. "A surprise."

They tethered their horses to a fine brass hitching post, walked through the iron gate to the house. Gardeners had been working. Grass had been sown the moment the outside construction was done in the spring, and now they had clipped it to unnatural smoothness. Shrubs had been planted to form alleys and circles and other patterns, and had been trimmed in various geometric shapes. Katherine knew Nils was proud of them because he had brought the Italian gardener all the way from Portland. Nils opened the door for her.

The hallway was full of heavy crates. Only one of them had been opened. "Here it is," Nils said, pulling her past the boxes into the parlor.

It was an organ. Katherine looked at it unbelievingly. Scrolls and fancy lattice work adorned the sides and every inch of the massive back and top were carved. Brass candlesticks were attached to fancy brass arms fitted into holes in the woodwork, and swung over the keyboard in a half-circle. Gently Katherine took hold of the carved knob and slid back the panel which hid the keys. The ivory had the sheen of old satin.

"Oh . . ." she breathed. "Oh, my . . ."

Nils looked at it as admiringly as she. "Just think," he said, "it come all the way around Cape Horn."

Katherine's eyes were misty as she smiled at him. Nils had often said that a donkey had more music in him than he did. The organ was wonderful to her because it was music; to him because it had come twelve thousand miles. It was the finest gift he could buy her because it had been the hardest to get.

"Miller Organ Company," she read softly, her finger tracing the ornate gold lettering. "Lebanon, Pennsylvania."

"Cost three times as much to send it," Nils said jubilantly, "as it cost for the danged thing itself."

A feeling of apprehension shook her. "Nils, the cost. I'm worried."

Nils frowned. "Why?"

"I keep hearing . . ."

"Who have you been listening to?" he burst out angrily. "You sound like one of my foremen."

Katherine stared at him. Why did he protest so bitterly? "Perhaps they don't know what they're saying . . ."

Nils shrugged. "Maybe they do and maybe they don't. I've never had a foreman," he said, one hand tightening into a fist, "who didn't take a nickel's worth of truth and cover it over with a dollar's worth of lies."

"They said there were lice on the hops."

She waited for the burst of laughter or the fit of anger. But he only shrugged again, not quite facing her. "There are."

"No!" She had heard people talk of the diseasing aphids ever since she came to the Valley. The danger had grown in her mind until now it seemed to be the most dreaded thing in the world.

"We're spraying the fields," Nils said. "We'll get rid of them."

"But the crop . . ."

"It's a good crop. Maybe the biggest we've had. We won't miss what we lose to the lice."

Katherine cried out, "Nils, is that true?"

He turned toward her and lifted her chin with his forefinger. "Do you like the organ?"

She nodded, too choked to speak.

He kissed her gently. "Do you like the house?"

"Oh, darling . . ."

He looked straight into her eyes. "Katherine, if you love me, let's get married."

"Yes," she whispered. The ache in her throat was unbearable. Nils might fail; the realization hit her hard and grew instantly into certainty that he would. But he was grinning again, as Nils Bengston, who had never failed at anything, always grinned. He wanted her to marry him. Nothing, nothing, not a single gloomy whisper or the faintest shadow of fear would be allowed to spoil that.

"Right after the hop harvest," he was saying. "We'll wait till the Yakimas have gone back over the mountain and the rest of the pickers have cleared out and the last bale is on its way to England. Then we'll have our wedding. Right here. The biggest, the fanciest wedding in the Territory. Maybe, by then, in the State. Washington becomes a state and Teacher becomes a bride."

Katherine tried to smile. Instead she hid her face against his chest. "Can you read your book straight through?"

"Almost as good as little Johnny Carlson," he said, laughing.

Right after the hop harvest—would Nils be laughing then? Katherine put her arms around his neck and held him tightly. "Please God," she whispered, fighting back tears, "if only . . ."

"What was that?"

She lifted her face. "Kiss me," she answered in a husky voice. He bent his head. Clinging to him, Katherine closed her eyes.

ii

Nils felt the package he had stuffed into his coat pocket. Still there, he thought, though there was no reason at all why it shouldn't be. He walked up the plank and stepped onto the deck of the riverboat *Viking*. Old Cap White was inside at the wheel. Nils waved absently. He was uneasy. It was such an unusual feeling that he hardly knew how to manage it. It was vague, it was baseless, but it was persistent. He frowned, both irritated and puzzled. He'd heard things in Seattle that weren't good news for the owner of a hop ranch but he'd had problems before. Trouble had always stirred him up, not depressed him.

It was the way Seattle had looked, he told himself. A hundred and twenty acres burned to the ground, every business house in the city leveled except a few on the east side of Second Avenue. They were rebuilding it. Even without a wharf or a warehouse in which to store supplies shipped into the stricken city, the buildings were going up fast. Half the stores were still tents; the gift bulging in his coat pocket had come off a packing box counter in a canvas store. But what of it, Nils thought impatiently. Seattle people were hopeful, not gloomy. Why was he so down at the mouth?

He walked across the deck to the railing. Leaning forward on both hands he stared at the gray river. He felt nervous because he had made a trip to Seattle in the midst of the hop-picking season. That might be it. But that didn't make sense either. He had ridden to Seattle every week of every hop-picking season the ranch had seen. The Indians must be paid in silver dollars and he didn't trust anyone else to pick up that much money and carry it for twenty-eight miles. He had driven a box wagon containing three or four thousand dollars all the way out from Seattle alone, with nothing but nerve and a one-shot rifle to protect him. He'd never felt a shadow of the feeling that nagged him now. He was . . . worried. Nils guffawed. He hated the word. Worry—that was a disease that attacked the minds of weak men and old women. He cursed softly and went into the cabin to talk to the captain.

Old Captain White was puffing at the *Viking's* controls. The boat pulled away from the wharf, easing out slowly into the current. The captain's beard had grown white in the past few years and his black eyes seemed to have sunk deeper behind his high cheekbones. The scowlike *Viking* shuddered as she hit the full force of the current. Grunting, the captain pulled the wheel around and steadied it against his belly. "Upstream," he muttered. "Never did like this trip upstream. Don't get the chance to keep my pipe lit like I should."

Nils grinned. The old captain was getting crotchety. Nils' own uneasiness disappeared instantly. "I'll take the wheel for you, Cap."

"Keep your hands off." The old man braced the wheel with one elbow, twisted sideways to reach for his pipe. "How come you didn't take the train?"

"I did, going in."

"Sure, sure," the captain said accusingly, waggling his head.

"The railroad's hurting you, eh? Business poor?"

"Business is dead." The old man shrugged. "Why would a sensible person ride with me, when the train makes a straight thirty-mile trip in only three, four hours?" He gestured toward the deck. "How many passengers you see out there? Five, six? How much freight? The kids don't even come down to meet the boat anymore."

"You must of seen it coming?"

The old man snorted loudly. "Sure, I seen it coming. It had to happen. I know I got to die some day, too, but that don't mean I'd like someone to put a bullet through me."

"It's too bad, Cap." Nils looked affectionately at the old man. It *was* too bad, but wasn't he working against the captain as much as anyone else? Last year the hops had been shipped by riverboat. This year they would be loaded right onto the spur line and sent to Seattle on the railroad. Times had changed. If change had made a failure out of Captain White, it was his tough luck, but maybe it was his fault, too. Nils despised failures, but he liked the old man. "Look here, Cap," he said gently, "what are you going to do? How are you fixed?"

Cap shrugged. "I can't even sell her for what she's worth. Too old, too flat, that's what I keep hearing. Even the river's working against me, it looks like. She's filling up so bad there's hardly a clear channel. That's what happens when you cut the timber." Frowning, he tried to relight his pipe. "I'm going to tie this good old tub up along the bank somewheres," he said simply, "maybe down by Kalak-wahtie where you can see Mount Rainier now they got the big trees down. I'll live on her. I got enough put away for beans and coffee. I can grow my own tobacco."

Nils frowned. Cap was giving up, and for some reason his own uneasiness returned. "Carl can help you."

The captain squinted up at him. "Uh," he grunted. "Maybe you didn't know he went down to Frisco, first steamer that left after the fire. He said that was the end of Seattle. He's married, too. Anyways, Carl and me don't look at things eye to eye. I wouldn't want to shame him." Suddenly the captain's eyes sparked. "Say, you took his girl away from him, didn't you? Getting married in a couple of weeks, ain't you?"

Nils nodded. When the old man spoke of Katherine and Carl together, he felt shooting pains of jealousy. If the captain had been younger or had anything like a smile on his face, he would have cracked his jaw. "I hope things work out for you, Cap," he said brusquely. "It won't seem right when the *Viking* don't pull into Black River any more."

"Don't cry over me," the old man snapped. "You're worse off'n I am."

Nils was startled. If he had been sitting peacefully in the hop ranch yard and an Indian arrow had come out of nowhere, striking him, its feather tip quivering with the impact as the first waves of pain went out through his body . . . "What are you talking about?"

"What have I got to lose?" the captain asked sourly. "An old sidewinder of a boat. I'm too old to want much, anyways." He squinted at Nils. "But you're an ambitious man."

"You sound like one of my foremen." Instantly Nils realized that he had once said the same thing to Katherine. If the whole world was beginning to sniff failure . . ."From the day the first plant showed through the dirt they've been promising me there would be lice in the hops," Nils said. "Now we got a little of it. That don't mean the ranch will fail. We can take care of it. We *are* taking care of it." He looked closely at the captain. "Now just why," he went on, angry now, "would that make me so bad off that you have to worry about me?"

The old man shrugged. "If the *Viking* was to sink right here and now it wouldn't hurt the Valley a bit, because there's already something come in to take its place. But if the hop ranch was to go under, it would be a terrible loss to everyone."

"Go under?" Nils shouted, letting his anger take over completely. "Because of a few lice, when we got a crop so big . . ."

The captain waved his hand. "Don't keep shouting hop lice at me," he said calmly. He took his pipe out of his mouth and frowned at the cold bowl, his little eyes crossing slightly as they looked down his nose. "There's more than one way to kill a cat."

Nils watched the captain working over his pipe as if there were nothing to equal the job in importance. A sign of age—Nils felt sorry for him. His clothes were shabby, his back humped, his once powerful shoulders were losing their strength. His boat was aging and so was he, and to-

gether they would rot on the bank at Kalakwahtie. No
wonder, Nils thought, that he's looking for someone else
to feel sorry for. His anger at the old man vanished before a
pleasant feeling of superiority. Old Captain White was
like a memory of his youth. A symbol, a picture, a beloved
character out of earlier, different times. Nils thought of
Katherine. But not of better times, for he had never had
so much before. His ranch, his millions, his house, and
now, his wife . . .

His hand went instinctively to his pocket, feeling the
outline of his wedding gift for Katherine. It was a pair of
little gold slippers, sparkling with stones of many different
colors. He had wanted them for her so badly that he hadn't
been able to hide his eagerness and their price had been
fantastic. Every saleable item in Seattle was costly now, either because all others of its kind had been burned up or
because it was one of the few things that hadn't been. The
slippers would be Katherine's wedding shoes. They were
extravagant and therefore just right for the wife of one of
the wealthiest men in the Territory, the mistress of a
thirty-room house. Nils' fingers pressed against the package, feeling the jeweled studdings through the wrapping
paper. The existence of the shoes, the feel of them, was
reassuring. The shoes were real. The captain's fear, his own
uneasiness, were as unsound as a bad dream. He nodded
at the old man and went back on deck, his hand clamped
tightly around the slippers.

iii

Nils Bengston's house for Teacher had been built with oak
from Minnesota and marble from Vermont and crystal
from Boston, but Gold Mountain regarded Teacher's wedding day as a thoroughly Gold Mountain affair.

November first was the date. Preparations began weeks beforehand. Since Katherine had no relatives in the Valley, the dozens of families whose children she had taught took possession of her wedding day. Ceremony, dress, food—Gold Mountain jealously took all those matters unto itself.

In years past many a young couple had postponed their wedding for months until the preacher came through. Others had ridden thirty miles to Seattle so that some strange minister might bless their union. But this, the Valley knew, was no usual affair, and so Jeb Carlson made a fifty-mile horseback ride to catch up with Brother Bill and see that he would appear in Gold Mountain in time for the ceremony.

Agatha Tine took charge of the food. Some of the other women worried about what should be served in a mansion such as Nils had built, but to Agatha a wedding supper lighted by crystal chandeliers was a feed, just like any other. Cakes, cookies, roasts of meat, turkeys and chickens, crocks of potato salad and pickles—and plenty of all of them.

Only a few things were brought in from Seattle. The champagne, because having read a newspaper story about a party in San Francisco, Nils insisted on having it. The satin and lace for Katherine's wedding gown, the candied fruits for the wedding cake, a string of pearls for the bride . . .

"What shall I send for?" Nils asked Katherine again and again. "Don't you want something more?"

"I have everything."

He looked down at her, gently put his hands on her shoulders. "You can have anything you want," he said. "You got to tell me because I'm nothing but a backwoods logger and I just don't know."

She shook her head. "Nils, truly . . ."

"Jewelry?" he asked anxiously, just barely shaking her. "If they haven't got it in Seattle, they'll have it in Frisco. I'll send for it. Some kind of dress goods? You think the house needs more furniture?"

She smiled. "No, no, no . . ."

He looked into her face, frowning in his intensity.

"What do *you* want, Nils?"

He looked surprised. He glanced around the richly furnished drawing room, through the long windows to the hop fields stretching forever and ever outside. "What could I want for?" he mused, still looking through the window. He turned back to her and pulled her into his arms. "I've got everything," he said, holding her tightly. "The biggest hop ranch and the littlest wife."

There were no wedding invitations. No one tried to make a list of guests. Everyone in the Valley understood that he was invited whether he lived in Gold Mountain, Three Forks, Black River, or Kalakwahtie, whether he owned a Sunday suit or would have to come in denim and logging boots, whether he could look Nils Bengston in the eye or still owed him money.

For the first time in a year Katherine tried to reach her father. Again she failed. If her letters to him were delivered, he did not answer them. He had always talked easily, written with difficulty. She wrote to her aunts and uncles in Oregon, and they replied as they had before. They had seen him only once in five years, when he had been talking of silver mining in Colorado. God's will be done, they wrote, and all the children were doing fine.

They could not come to the wedding, of course, for the trip was too long and too dangerous. But Katherine's intended had been generous indeed in sending the fare and they'd use the money for clothes, a more sensible way to spend it anyway, didn't she agree? Teddy's letter had a different ring to it. The steamship company had transferred him to San Francisco, where he was a clerk in their business office. He'd been married for three months now and his wife was carrying a child but they'd both be in Gold Mountain for the wedding if they had to build their own raft.

"He's all right," Nils said when Katherine read the letter. "I'll send him money for the trip."

"Nils, he wouldn't take it."

Nils frowned. "No?"

Katherine shook her head firmly, "No."

Nils grinned. "The Duncans sure made their kids ornery."

"Proud."

Nils shrugged. "What's the difference?"

Katherine's eyes snapped. "Don't you know? Is there anyone more proud than you?"

Nils burst out laughing. When she tried to slap him he kissed her. "I'm not proud," he said against her ear, "I'm just rich."

iv

Katherine dressed slowly for the wedding. She was alone in the big master bedroom. Faith Carlson, Agatha, Hannah, Julie Bengston, Mrs. Nelson, and a half dozen other women had left her so that she would rest for an hour or so. They were in the kitchen now, undoubtedly arguing about whether it was time to come upstairs and waken her.

She smiled wistfully. She had tried to sleep. She had lain back in the huge four-posted spool bed, pulled the coverlet up to her chin and dutifully closed her eyes. But then the fears that had been plaguing her were worse than ever. Faces she didn't want to see danced in the darkness. Words she wanted to forget sang monotonously in her ears. Agatha, Faith and Jeb Carlson, the hop ranch foreman,

Nate Tarpee, everyone, everyone had heard it. Everyone
was whispering it.

Something terrible had happened to Washington hop-
growers. Nils Bengston's crop, the one which could set him
straight or make a pauper of him, had been dried and baled
and shipped to Seattle, but it was still there. Why, if Nils
had found a buyer?

Nils refused to discuss it. Hop ranches from the Skagit to
the Duwamish were going under. Growers were getting less
than one hundred dollars an acre for hops when every acre
they grew on had been cleared for five hundred or more.
The Chinese were buying up hop ranches and wealthy men
were going into bankruptcy. But Nils laughed and said,
"November first is my wedding day. Only thing I'm worried
about is whether me and Brother Bill get in a fist fight before he gets us properly married."

Katherine tried to think of the way Nils grinned, the way
he laughed, the way he picked her up and kissed her and
told her not to sound like a foreman. He owned the biggest
hop ranch in the world, he would soon be the wealthiest
man in the state of Washington, and she would be mistress
of the most elegant house west of the Mississippi, so smile,
he said, and kiss me.

But he had made extra trips to Seattle this past week. He
answered all her questions by pointing out how harmless
the hop lice had been and what a large crop they'd had, but
his voice was rough when he cut off her queries about where
and how he would sell it. Meanwhile there were whispers,
broad hints, sympathetic or curious glances. No one knew
anything for sure, but no one could keep silent. People
spread the disaster news swiftly and anxiously, like thieves
passing along stolen goods. It was no use trying to sleep with
her mind so full of it.

Under the soft coverlet Katherine's body lay stiff as a
cedar post and every time she closed her eyes they snapped

open again and she found herself staring sightlessly at the gold drapery overhead. Nils said he had nothing on his mind but his wedding day. He made her anxiety seem ridiculous. Offering sympathy would be calling him a liar. Unless he came to her . . . Katherine threw back the coverlet and got out of bed. Perhaps her fears were truly groundless. No one but Nils knew whether the whispered reports were true, and Nils laughed. She went to the huge gilt dressing table by the window and sat down.

The mirrors showed how pale she was. With thumb and forefinger Katherine impatiently pinched her cheeks. Then she loosened her long braids and began to brush her hair. It came to her waist, and snapped with each long stroke of the brush. In two hours, she thought, we will be married.

Her wedding gown was spread over two chairs, the veil and train of lace across two more. On the dressing table was a Juliet cap of pearls to which the train would be attached. Katherine put the hairbrush down and picked up the cap. She turned it around thoughtfully. A cap of pearls. Had it been some childhood dream of her own which made her choose such an ornament, or an old wish of her mother's, absorbed so long ago that it had become a wish of her own? Suddenly Katherine saw her mother's face. The picture was sharper than that of the faces of Agatha and Faith whom she had seen less than an hour before. The deep worry lines across her forehead, the weary set of her chin, the look of hope and then hopelessness, about the eyes. "If I could just know for sure," her mother might be saying, "that I could do the washing of a Monday morning."

Katherine looked around the room, from the marble fireplace to the beautiful mahogany bed, to the gold-framed mirror and dark red carpet. "A house with glass windows," she could hear Angus pleading in a shrill little boy's voice. "Papa, did you say we'd have a house with glass windows?"

The shadow in the corner was herself, a little girl with a pale face and angry eyes, carrying an armload of dried cow dung to start a fire for her mother's tea. "Some day," that little girl was sobbing, "some day I'll have a real house all my own."

Katherine got up and went to the window. The men were outside, Teddy and Nils and Brother Bill and Jeb Carlson and others who had been helping with the preparations. Their women were in the kitchen. Katherine frowned. With Nils was a stranger, or at least a man she did not know, whose face had a puzzling familiarity to it. There would be many here today whom she might know only by sight. Why should the presence of a stranger be so disturbing? And yet an uncomfortable tightness settled in her chest. They were talking earnestly. She studied them, her pulse pounding out a warning. A friend of Nils,' a traveler, perhaps a cattleman from Kittitas. Teddy appeared, joining Nils and the stranger. Then Jeb, then Ole Nelson. They formed a silent circle, hands in pockets, faces solemn. The stranger talked, talked, talked.

Nils was listening. The picture was wrong. All at once, Katherine knew why. She had never seen Nils so motionless, so silent. She had never seen him listen for so long without once laughing.

Katherine whirled away from the window and ran to the bedroom door. Leaning over the bannister she called, "Faith!" Below a door opened, closed, there were running steps along the hall. Faith stood at the foot of the stairway and looked up at her.

"Faith."

Faith was crying.

Katherine stared at her. She felt cold, almost numb. "Faith," she said in a hollow voice, "will you come up here a minute?"

Faith climbed the stairs slowly. She walked past Katherine and into the bedroom. Katherine closed the door with exaggerated care and leaned against it, holding tightly to the doorknob. "Who is that man?"

Faith shook her head. "I don't know exactly. He rode out from Seattle."

"He's in business with Nils in some way."

"Oh, I don't know just how," Faith sobbed. "Oh, Katherine."

Katherine said doggedly, "He came to tell Nils something about the hops."

"Yes, yes." Faith covered her face with both hands. Tears came through the fingers, spotting the bodice of her dress.

Katherine took hold of Faith's wrists and pulled her hands down. Faith's plain face quivered in her misery. "Faith, listen," Katherine said. "You've got to tell me what they're talking about, whatever you heard. Soon I'll be talking to Nils. I've got to be ready."

Faith fought a new wave of sobs. She looked blankly at Katherine, collecting herself with an effort.

Katherine's hands tightened on her wrists. "Tell me!" she said harshly.

Faith's body shuddered with the last sob. "Something happened to the price of hops," she said dully. "The man come to tell Nils they can't get but six cents a pound for them. I heard Nils say it cost eight cents a pound to grow them."

Katherine released Faith's hands, and they dropped lifelessly. "I'm not sure," Katherine said huskily, "that I quite understand what that means."

"Jeb says Nils got a dollar and a quarter a pound last year."

"Aahh . . . "

Tears came back to Faith's eyes. "The wedding," she cried, "the beautiful wedding."

Katherine turned and walked to the dressing table. She

picked up her brush and mechanically began pulling it through her hair. "I'd better start getting dressed for it."

"We're not going to have the wedding!"

Katherine wheeled around to face her. "The wedding, the party, the champagne, the dancing, every bit of it." She waved the hairbrush at Faith. "Now go wash your face and take off your apron and get ready. Don't let Nils see you looking like that!"

"If he's lost everything, everything . . . "

"He hasn't!"

Faith cried, "Oh, Katherine, the man said . . ."

Katherine said sharply, "I don't care what the man said. This is my wedding day." She waved the hairbrush, brandishing it like a man holding a lion off with a saber.

"I'll help you dress."

Katherine shook her head. There was such a painful lump in her throat that she couldn't say much more. "I'd like to be alone for a while." She touched Faith's hand. "Faith, I'll have to talk to Nils. I've got to think what to say."

Faith turned and ran out.

Katherine sat down at the edge of the bed. A moment before she had had to fight to keep from crying, but she was past that now. Crystal and marble and satin surrounded her, and Nils had lost everything. Think, she told herself, think. Everything depends on whether you can help him now.

If he has lost everything, she thought in anguish, can I help him without losing him?

V

For an hour she sat there, measuring herself against the crisis she had to meet. She thought of so many things, so many which had nothing to do with Nils or the failure of the hop ranch or even with herself as she was now. Think, she told herself, think.

Nils had failed. The cornerstone of his little empire had been knocked out and when debts were paid and property sold there would be nothing left for him but rubble. Failure, which he despised so deeply that anyone who had ever failed was to him despicable—on his own wedding day the worst of all possible things had happened to him. To anyone else it would have been a lighter blow.

But it was not so with her. For me, Katherine reflected, nothing could be as terrible as the loss of Nils himself. Nils' world had been destroyed; hers had not been touched. Now, at last, she was the stronger of the two.

He needed her now; he had only wanted her before. But needing another person, even the woman he loved—could Nils be humbled to that degree without hating her? "No one ever cut him down to size," old Uncle Julian had said. "Lot of people would like to, but I'm not one of them. Nils is a big man. He was built to be king. If he was to be cut down I don't think I'd like to see it." This, then, was the true shape of the crisis. Katherine sat on the edge of the big bed, still as a doll, asking herself if she could meet it.

How ill prepared she would have been when she first came to the Valley. She thought back over the dreams she had cherished, the little-girl dreams, the petulant, unhappy, never-fulfilled dreams of her mother. She had had only one ambition then, and that was to live in a world in which nothing unexpected could happen. Like an extension of her mother's pathetic plea to know for sure that she could always start the washing of a Monday morning, the younger Katherine's world was to have been a neat and proper place. It was to be hemmed in; by making it smaller and smaller, neater and neater, the fears of her youth were to be closed out forever.

No child would spend a week putting wheat kernels through an old coffee grinder. No little girl would roam the prairie looking for cow chips. There would not be this house and then that one, coming so fast one after another that a child could not say where he came from. Such were the materials with which she had built her dream, the negative desires, the things she prayed would not be.

When she came to the Valley five years before, she had looked at everything through the mist of this dream. As she had all her life, she saw only the things that were not good enough; she had understood no experience but the experience of disappointment. She had hated and feared Gold Mountain because even more than the hateful places of her childhood it was crude and poor and terrifying. That Katherine Duncan who had spent her last dollar on a pair of silly pink gloves because they would make her look like a lady, rather than on the umbrella which would have kept her dry—*that* Katherine could not have helped Nils, for she hadn't been even a big enough person to love him.

But now, now at the moment of crisis, she had five years in the Valley behind her. Five years of preparation, begun the day she got wet enough to admit she should have bought an umbrella instead of the pink gloves. Perhaps she had never been truly helpless, but she had been obsessed by an old-maidish conviction that she should be. Gold Mountain had taken that out of her. Everything that had happened to her here, the good and the bad, the tragic and the trivial, stood solidly behind her now. Nils' Katherine was not that scary creature with the pink gloves, Nils' Katherine was the girl whom Gold Mountain had trained to be equal to him.

She was the girl who stood up in a public meeting to bid against a man for her job; who had cooked in a logging camp and attacked an Indian beggar with a stack of hot cakes and a soup ladle; who had taught a second grade full of sixteen-year-olds; had learned to travel alone with a lamp for light, an umbrella for rain and a gun for everything else. *She* could help Nils, and it was time to do it.

She slid off the edge of the bed, quickly pulled on a soft flannel wrapper, and going to the top of the stairs called down to ask for Nils.

vi

Nils, who always slammed doors, closed the bedroom door quietly. Katherine waited for his usual greeting—one great sweep of an arm which pulled her against him, a quick "Hello, Kate," and a grin just before he leaned down to kiss her. But he did not move to touch her. He had always carried himself carelessly, as if to contradict the braggadocio of his size. But his shoulders were almost too square now, his posture too consciously upright. Hands and face were still. He showed nothing at all, except in his eyes.

Katherine felt her throat constrict, fiercely fought down the desire to cry out. She went to Nils and taking both his hands, pulled him forward to a pair of chairs. She sat down, forcing him to sit opposite her.

"You don't know what to do," she said simply.

"They waited a long time. But they always said I'd outreach myself someday."

They—Katherine recognized the "they" he had spoken of so often. The nameless ones whom he imagined were always waiting for his failure. Nils had done a lot to prove how wrong "they" were. "How bad . . . is it?"

Nils said dully, "It couldn't be worse."

"This year's crop can't be sold?"

"I'll end up paying $50,000," he said in a strange, hoarse voice, "for the pleasure of growing it."

"But your other property, such as the sawmill and the timber claims and the store?"

Nils looked directly into her eyes. "Kate," he said, "I don't own them, not half as much as the banks in Seattle."

"Mortgaged . . . "

Nils grinned crookedly, though the misery was in his eyes. "Everything. With the hop ranch doing so well I knew bankers who would loan me money on Old Hi."

Katherine grabbed his hands. "Nils, you didn't mention this house."

Nils frowned. "It wouldn't help. They don't like to loan money on a house. Not productive, doesn't earn anything. And a house like this, way out here?" He gestured toward the gold-framed mirrors, the golden brocade, the mahogany woodwork. "Even if I was to get a mortgage on it, it wouldn't begin to pay off what I owe. They're already figuring on what they're going to do with the hop ranch when they take it over."

"Then the house *is* free and clear? They won't take it, too?"

Her excitement puzzled him. Some of the unhappiness went out of Nils' face. "Well, yes, just the house itself, maybe a little strip of land around it."

"You could let them take the hop ranch, take the hotel and the farms and the shingle mill and all the rest . . ."

"Let them?" Nils said dryly. "They don't have to ask permission."

"But you'd still have the house."

Nils grinned. Katherine saw that her voice and manner were shocking him into aliveness. "Why yes," he said, "I'll still have the house. Not a bad place to starve in. Why do you keep talking about the house?"

He was wide awake now, trying to figure her out. How could she ever have thought there could be trouble bigger than he was? She jumped up, sat on his lap and threw her arms around him. "Then my idea will work," she said excitedly. "I wasn't sure because I didn't know about the mortgages and things."

"I never heard you talk like this before," Nils said gruffly. "What do you know about mortgages?"

Katherine giggled. Her feeling of relief was almost unbearable. "My father brought more of them home than he did meat and potatoes." She kissed him, and with her face hidden against his shoulder said quickly, "We'll change our house into a hotel."

"What!" Nils bellowed. He tried to get up but Katherine grabbed the arms of the chair and holding on tight said, "If you get out of this chair I'll scream, and you know what they'll think downstairs!"

"Kate!" Nils exclaimed, falling back against the chair. "A fine thing for a schoolteacher to say."

"Nils, you know how many people are coming into the Valley now that the railroad runs out all the way. Drummers, especially. Nate Tarpee says he's seen twenty to thirty of them in a day. There are so many hunters and fishermen and tourists now. Ever since the railroad got to Gold Mountain, there have been more of them every month. There are many wealthy families in Seattle, people who take vacations. They would come out here if there were a nice enough hotel. A hotel such as this house would make would be a reason to come in itself. Don't you see? We'd be famous!

"Perhaps you could keep some of the hop ranch horses and a wagon or two. Or somehow we'd get money to buy a rig and hire a driver. He could meet the trains, take drummers and travelers wherever they wanted to go. They're hiring in Kirkland now. Wouldn't they rather go to the end of the line and get a rig there? That's two businesses already, a hotel and a livery stable." Katherine stopped.

Nils was frowning fearfully. "You've sure got a lot to say."

"I've been thinking."

"A *hotel*. I bought the best of everything for this house. Marble from Italy, hardwood from Minnesota, an organ that come all around Cape Horn . . ." He looked at her silently for a moment and then he shook his head. "This is your house, Kate. It's the biggest, finest house in the state of Washington. I lost the ranch but I won't give up the house, too."

"We wouldn't be giving it up. We'd be keeping it." Katherine looked at him earnestly. "Nils, whatever happens, I wouldn't want to leave the Valley, would you?"

"You said you'd been thinking," Nils said quietly. "For the past two weeks I've been thinking, too. Not very straight or clear, because I wouldn't admit anything." He looked toward the long windows, through which the dark stretch of the Valley and the great barren rock of Old Hi could be seen. "One thing I did decide for sure, and that was that I would not leave the Valley."

"That's what I decided, too." Katherine put her hand against his cheek and turned his head back so that he had to look at her. "We want to stay. This is our place. But the place itself is changing. Remember what you said about old Captain White? He's a failure, you said, because he couldn't move along with the times. We know it's the railroad that's changing things. Because of the railroad there will be a need for a hotel, a need for a livery stable. So here we are, with the changing times handing us opportunity on a platter. Why don't we take it and move along with them?"

Nils' blue eyes cleared. There was a look of expectancy about his weathered face. 'Gabby little thing, ain't you," he muttered. 'But what if I can't even raise the money for rigs and horses?"

"We'll mortgage the house."

His look was one of sheer amazement. "*Mortgage* the house I built for you," he murmured, but she could see it was beginning to strike him funny. No, she needn't have been afraid. Nils had never failed, even now. She said brightly, "I have never lived in a house that wasn't."

"Mortgages, hotels, livery stables. What all have you got in that red head of yours?" His arms went around her and he held her tightly. "I love you, Kate."

"The Gold Mountain Hotel . . ."

She saw his jaw tighten, and a mulish desperation darkened his eyes. He looked at her with such intensity that she stiffened, consciously bracing herself against the impact of the glance. Her heart pounded furiously as she waited for him to speak. Suddenly his face softened. He kissed her, whispering to her. "Kate, Kate, a few years ago if I'd lost the hop ranch I would have killed myself. Now all I want to do is get married."

She clung to him. "I was so afraid you wouldn't want me any more."

"I didn't," he said dryly, "until I found out you know so much about mortgages. Now I can't afford to give you up."

He kissed her again, on the mouth, on the throat and forehead. And then for a long time he held her close against him, her head resting in the crook of his arm. She saw his face gradually become thoughtful. When she moved he smiled absent-mindedly, one hand patting her arm.

"Nils!" she cried. "What are you thinking about now?"

"About that hotel," he said. "You know, we could make it the biggest, finest vacation hotel on the whole Pacific Coast. They'd hear of it all the way down to Frisco. What other hotel would have gold curtains and all that fancy crystal? Should we call it the Gold Mountain Hotel or would Bengstons' Hotel sound all right?"

Katherine slid gently off his lap, went to the dressing table and began to brush her hair. She was laughing so hard she was afraid he would notice. She'd have to hold it in for a moment. But only for a moment, for then, she knew, he would be laughing, too.

THE END

about the author

Charlotte Paul's formative years were spent in the Pacific Northwest where she was born in Seattle in 1916. After a year of musical studies in Germany and a tour throughout Europe, she returned to this country and entered Wellesley. During college she won first prize in the *Atlantic Monthly* collegiate short story contest of 1937. She made two further trips to Europe and after graduation from Wellesley held a variety of jobs. These included office work and ballroom dancing lessons. For two years she wrote news articles, first as assistant foreign news editor for the Chicago *Daily Times*, later as a roving correspondent for this paper in the Caribbean. Back in the United States she began a long and successful career of free-lance writing. She has sold her articles and stories to such magazines as *Esquire, Coronet, Good Housekeeping, McCall's* and many others. Her first novel, *Hear My Heart Speak*, was published in 1950.

Now married and living in Snoqualmie, Washington (the setting of this novel) Charlotte Paul with her husband owns a weekly newspaper and commercial printing plant. Their home stands in a meadow at the foot of a 4,100-foot mountain—*Gold Mountain?* At the rear of this property is a little cedar house with a big window, where the author does her writing. Intensely devoted to her valley region and its projects, she finds time to play golf, do some songwriting for a local show and cultivate her garden.